THE
A no

- Did Hitler's deputy, or was it a double?
- Was an imposter incarcerated in Spandau prison for more than forty years to perpetuate an official cover-up?
- Did the British secret services murder Rudolf Hess?

The debate surrounding the Hess Affair has always been a bitter one. The British Government has repeatedly denied that there is anything to discuss, but the controversy will not die. Fifty years after Hess's flight there are many questions still to be answered, yet the top-secret official files cannot be opened until 2017.

Frank Kippax's uncompromising new novel, which draws upon much hitherto unrevealed material, builds a thesis heavily at odds with the 'official' version. Ranging over fifty years of history, it confronts the unpalatable truth behind what has been called the last great mystery of World War II.

'Was Hess killed by Winston Churchill? Kippax's book is a story of duplicity and hypocrisy on a massive scale. If true, then the reputations of leading politicians past and present are permanently besmirched.'   *Glasgow Sunday Mail*

'If one day the official files on the case in the Public Records Office become freely available, it may in part be due to Kippax, whose novel, fifty years after the event, shows how ridiculous the official silence has become.'
Gloucestershire Echo

THE AUTHOR

FRANK KIPPAX was born near Southampton in 1945 and went to Tasmania when he was thirteen. He had returned to Europe, as a seaman, by the age of twenty-one, working thereafter on ocean tugs from Hull and Holland. Later he moved into road transport, driving lorries in Europe, Scandinavia and Ireland, where he lived for some years. From about the age of thirty he has written under a variety of pseudonyms. His last novel, *The Scar*, which is set against the background of the crisis-stricken British prison system, was made into a major BBC TV serial: *Underbelly*.

FRANK KIPPAX

THE
BUTCHER'S BILL

A novel about history

Fontana
An Imprint of HarperCollinsPublishers

Fontana
An Imprint of HarperCollins*Publishers*,
77–85 Fulham Palace Road,
Hammersmith, London W6 8JB

Published by Fontana 1992
9 8 7 6 5 4 3 2 1

First published in Great Britain by
HarperCollins*Publishers* 1991

ISBN 0 00 617905 3

Set in Meridien
Printed in Great Britain by
HarperCollinsManufacturing Glasgow

For Andrew R
The driving force

AUTHOR'S NOTE

Many people have helped me over several years in the gathering together and interpreting of the complex strands of truth and deception that make up this story, but unfortunately it would hardly be an act of gratitude to name them. My main informant, a friend and relative, is sadly now dead, but theoretically broke at least a code, if not a law, in telling me of certain things he observed or was involved in during World War II. More recent members of the undercover services have also responded with perhaps more generosity than discretion.

The book, of course, does not give all the answers on the Hess Affair, nor do I pretend to know them. Not only does it seem less and less likely as time goes on that the full truth will ever be allowed to see the light of day, but I ultimately found the deceptions and the machinations that are still rife, the half-truths and evasions, the cynicism and urbane brutality, as fascinating as the facts and demi-facts I was able painstakingly to uncover. Which led me to believe, in short, that the novel was the only form that could do justice to it all.

That there is, and always has been, a conspiracy of silence over Hess is hardly in dispute any longer, even among the driest of historians. While this book is an amalgam of fact, speculation and necessary invention, it would be hard to deny that the most extra-ordinary events and characters are the real ones – however secret they have hitherto been kept – not those of my imagination. This is not history – whatever that may be. But I hope it is not too distant from the truth.

F.K.
Galway City

Great armies and great empires have been overwhelmed in the sands of barren victories.

DAVID LLOYD GEORGE

BOOK ONE

Widowmakers

PROLOGUE

August 17, 1987

The Americans were in charge the day he died. That, at least, was something. It gave the British, on whose territory the prison lay, somebody to blame.

'What a cock-up,' said the young man in grey slacks and a light cashmere sweater, as he sipped his beer. 'Only the Yanks could do it, couldn't they? They couldn't organize a piss-up in a brewery.'

His companion, who was also dressed in civvies, nodded. He was examining the Praktica on the bar table in front of him. They were soldiers, anybody with a practised eye could tell. Their hair was short and neat, their shirt collars crisp.

'Aye,' he agreed. 'Tony got a box of paper hankies from the cell. Souvenir. Daft prat, who does he think'll be impressed by that?'

'The pictures should be good, though, if they come out. Have you got the hang of that thing yet?'

'I dunno. It's only Eastern crap. I was in a bloody hurry, too. Yanks or no Yanks, if I'd been caught it would've been the chop.'

The first soldier finished his beer. He looked at his watch, impatient.

'What d'you reckon, though? Can we flog it, if it comes out? Let's try and find a place, get it developed. We'd better shift, mate. I'm due in barracks, half an hour.'

The bar was filling, for the early evening rush. Outside, in Wilhelmstrasse, they saw another Land Rover go past, towards the prison. It was full of military police. It was not the first they'd seen, by any means. They eyed each other, nervously.

'Bleeding Redcaps everywhere,' said the soldier with the camera. 'Why don't we forget it? Have another beer? The place is swarming.'

'You're chicken.'

'OK. What is it, anyway? A picture of a garden hut. If it comes

13

out. Do you know how to flog things to a paper? Without being found out? Let's have another beer.'

The man in cashmere capitulated.

'We could take some pictures of the crowds outside, after,' he said. 'There's twats in Nazi tee-shirts there already, Tony said. They're mental, Krauts, there's no doubt in my mind, no doubt at all. They think he was a God, or something. Loony old bastard with dogsbreath. Get us a schnapps as well, tight-arse.'

His friend fished some notes from his back pocket.

'Yanks are mad as well, though. They'll probably let them in, for souvenirs. They'll probably sell off bits of brick and barbed wire.'

Both men became aware that people were listening to them, although they spoke in English. In West Berlin, of course, speaking English would hardly keep a conversation private. They decided to forget the drinks, move on. In any case, it was getting late. There was going to be a lot of shit flying about in the next few days, they guessed. They did not want too much of it to stick to them. As they walked along towards the prison gate-house they saw the crowds – not large yet, but growing – and they saw the queue of vehicles.

'Chaos,' said the soldier with the camera. 'Look at all those Redcaps. And the polizei. Look, there's a TV van. We've had it with the pictures, mate. We're miles too late. Hey, look – that prat's got a swastika!'

Indeed, there was a small knot of youths in jeans and black leather, strutting up and down and shouting 'Heil'. There were several women weeping, older women, and a man in his forties was screaming something at the marchers, grabbing at their flag. In other parts of Germany, slogans had already been daubed on walls and monuments, and former SS men, white-haired and benign of feature, had sought to air their views on local TV stations and to the press. The crumbling red-brick pile, they thought, should be a monument, with its meat-hooks from which the Gestapo chose to hang their victims still intact, its sloping concrete floors to drain the blood away. The Russians, for different reasons, would have agreed.

But inside Spandau Prison, on this summer evening, there had been little in the way of agreement for many hours. The senior officers from the controlling powers had shouted themselves hoarse, then allowed fresher throats and minds to carry on the infighting and the bitterness. Telephone messages, both scrambled and in-clear, had buzzed to and from their capitals, where high officials

14

had made decisions, then rescinded them, then begged for time to push the buck yet higher.

'We cannot call it suicide,' bellowed a KGB colonel, his face flushed dangerously with rage. 'If it is suicide, we have failed! Since 1946 we have guarded this animal to prevent that thing, and now at ninety-three he kills himself! No!'

The French representative, a tall, lugubrious man, was calmer. As if it were a help, he muttered: 'Ten francs a minute, it has cost. Eight millions a year. What is that in dollars? A ransom for a king.'

The senior American present said: 'At least the Germans paid the bill.' He was exhausted, his voice low and scratchy. 'In any case,' he added, 'maybe it wasn't suicide. He ordered—'

A thin-faced man three feet from him shot a glance that made him bite the sentence off. The prisoner had ordered things that morning: toilet rolls, notepaper, other items. But the thin-faced man was CIA. He had warned him to be circumspect.

The British representative, who had shortly before been as angry as the Russian, found himself, strangely, on his side.

'You are right,' he told him. 'Gentlemen, we must take account of what the colonel says. It is bad enough that he should have died so suddenly, although I fear it's typical of the bloody-mindedness he's always shown. But we can't let him be seen to have got one over on us. Martyrdom is possibly inevitable among certain sections of the German population, but they must not be allowed to couple it with preternatural cunning. It was not suicide. Not yet awhile.'

'Cunning indeed,' said the Frenchman, drily. 'To hang oneself with an electric flex and yet not be a suicide.'

'We'd better burn it,' said the grey-haired Englishman, ignoring the sarcasm. 'We'd better burn the hut, as well. We can't afford the souvenir-hunters to get their hands on anything.' He looked at the senior American, meaningfully. 'The flying boots and goggles disappeared some months ago. Unfortunate.'

'And British soldiers were in the grounds this afternoon,' came the tart reply. 'Taking happysnaps.'

The Briton paled. The younger officer next to him reddened.

'True I'm afraid, sir. There was a gap before the military police got here from HQ, it took them half an hour. There'll be a search, though. Locker by locker, bed by bed if need be. We'll find anything that's been taken. Including photographs.'

'Another thing,' said the Russian, still intensely irritated. 'The pathologist. I insist we have a joint autopsy. Physicians of all four nations.'

'Why? What do you expect to find? Poison? You begin to sound like the prisoner himself. He complained for forty-six years that people were trying to poison him, and lived to ninety-three. The procedure is agreed. We're on British territory, for the purpose of post mortem. Stop splitting hairs.'

The anger was surfacing once more. They had been through this several times, first in the hospital library, later in the prison, where the Soviets did not feel so threatened by the Western listening techniques. There had been too many of them, a shifting population of officers and officials, scuttling in and out of drably painted rooms. The underlying mood had slowly changed. Through excitement, to vague disquiet, to fury and frustration, to exhaustion. The British contingent, noticeably, had been bombarded with governmental signals. When the Special Investigation Branch had become involved, their role had become quickly decisive. Some things were unarguable. Procedure.

The Russian said: 'Your pathologist is not even here. Where is he? How long must we wait?'

'He has been located in Strasbourg. He will be flying shortly. Our top man.'

A gleam entered the Frenchman's eyes. The boredom lifted momentarily.

'A specialist.' He paused. 'In strange judgements, might one say?'

The senior British officer looked at him as if he had crawled from underneath a stone.

'You have the edge of me,' he lied. 'I don't know what you're talking about.'

But everybody else did. The younger Briton's colour heightened further. Dr Cameron, Professor of Forensic Medicine at London University and the Army's chief pathologist, had been involved in some bizarre cases, and had not always escaped with praise. A small smile lit the hangdog French face.

'The Dingo Baby, was it not? That *pauvre femme* convicted by a bloodstained scrap of cloth. And Mr Cameron.'

And the rest, thought the red-faced major. Michael Calvey, Maxwell Confait, he had looked them up. One had to wonder sometimes, at the decisions of the Great and Good. But the American flapped his hand, impatiently.

'What the hell? This time there's no mystery, is there? The old sonovabitch hanged himself, whichever way we cut it. It's not our job to get the details out, we just need consensus for a day or two. So far we've done not badly. The initial statement's issued. It can be worked over later – let the top brass make the top decisions, that's what they're paid to do. If a few thousand crazy Germans want to worship him, so be it. Who cares who signs the death certificate so long it's signed? Let's get out of here!'

'In a week, ten days, it will be rubble,' said the grey-haired English officer. 'We're going to build a Naafi supermarket, the plans are writ in concrete. Some sort of shrine that will be! No,' he said, raising a hand to the Russian colonel. 'No arguments. We can argue afterwards. Statements can change if need be. In a case like this, there will be confusion. There always is. First we'll act, then we'll sort it out. It is our ultimate responsibility, gentlemen, and that is the British way.'

'Confusion?' asked the laconic Frenchman.

'Decision,' snapped the English officer.

The Russian colonel muttered, in heavily accented French: '*Oui. L'Albion perfide.*'

'I'm pooped,' said the American.

The chaos had started, as far as it was ever established, at about 3.30 that afternoon. But the armies of four powers and their special services never achieved a thoroughly convincing timetable: it was not in the nature of things military, least of all in Spandau Prison. There were more than a hundred soldiers involved in the running of the crumbling structure – British, French, American and Russian – plus a staff of nationals of other nations. There were Italians, Egyptians, two Poles, two Indians, a Ghanaian, a Greek, Tunisians – and all to minister to the needs of one solitary, frail, half-blind old man.

It was a Tunisian, Abdallah Melaouhi, who had been closest to him for some months, and who had been looking after him that morning. Afterwards he was to claim that the prison log had been altered for that day, and that Prisoner Number Seven had been found dead or dying at 2.30 p.m., not an hour later. He would further claim that when he fought his way to the small garden hut – having been held back by a British guard for forty minutes –

there were two men in US Army coveralls already there, two men he did not recognize, as well as the American guard whose job it was to attend the old man constantly for fear of suicide attempts. The prisoner was on the floor, apparently lifeless, and the electric-light extension cable later said to have been used in the self-murder was plugged, as normal, into the wall. There were signs of a struggle, everything had been 'turned over', and he later discovered that the prison's emergency resuscitation unit had been destroyed. Shortly, the cable itself had disappeared, burnt by the British, and next day the garden hut was gone as well. So too was the US guard who had left the prisoner alone for a minute or two 'to take a telephone call' – flown back, on whose orders it was never disclosed, to the United States. Melaouhi, failing to evoke a serious response from the British, took his story to the West Berlin police, who immediately announced that they intended to investigate it as a possible murder case. The British response this time was prompt: the incident had taken place on their territory, and the West Berliners had no jurisdiction. The case was closed.

Whatever time it started, the chaos soon became overwhelming. The American director, once informed, immediately ordered that the man be taken to the British military hospital, with no time for a police escort to be mustered. Although his face was blue, no one was prepared to name him dead, and as the stretcher-bearers rattled clumsily up the spiral staircase into the main cell block, as they raced along the echoing, empty building towards the security door, the open air and the main gate, they pummelled inexpertly at his chest, breaking several ribs. In the ambulance, which had two miles to go and took seven minutes, a rubber tube was inserted down the patient's throat – it missed the windpipe – and oxygen was pumped into his stomach, which was later found to be inflated hard, grotesque. Whether it was ninety minutes after Melaouhi saw him on the ground or thirty, the prisoner reached the hospital at precisely four o'clock, where a team of doctors had been alerted. The rubber tube was re-inserted correctly, drips were attached to wrist and ankle, heart massage continued, even life-saving methods of last resort perfected in Vietnam were used. At 4.10 Major Carabot, the duty doctor, gave the thumbs-down. They were dealing with a corpse.

The chaos worsened. Even by the time the medics had given up, officials and soldiers of all four powers were cramming the hospital.

The British military governor, Lieutenant Colonel Anthony Le Tissier, bore the brunt, as his government was most intimately concerned. The furious rows erupted almost instantaneously, as the way to tell the world the news became the crucial issue. After two hours of wrangling the first release said the death had been in hospital, which enraged the Russians, who pointed out the man had been sent to jail to die, and *had* therefore to have done so. Further, they said, the slapdash methods of the Americans were to blame for the whole pathetic farce, and that fact should be noted. A second communiqué said the prisoner had died in the summer house, in the normal course of his captivity, and a third release, twenty-four hours later, said tersely that it was suicide with an electric cord. After another twenty-four hours — fortuitously — a suicide note was found in the dead man's jacket pocket, where it had been 'overlooked'. His family were not allowed to see it . . .

On procedure, the British were insistent. Whatever anybody else might think, or want, the matter was to be investigated solely by the British Army. An SIB investigation unit under Major J. P. Gallagher was under orders within an hour, with operatives on their way from Rheindalen and Dusseldorf. The autopsy was to be conducted by Dr J. M. Cameron and no one else, although doctors from the other powers could be present as observers. To prevent the possibility of souvenirs, treasures for the neo-Nazis, getting out, there were to be no still photographs of any sort during the examination. For the same reason, all the prisoner's effects were to be destroyed immediately, save a few which would go to his family. A few not of their choosing.

It was a long evening, a longer night, a fraught few days. But very soon — although details were sparse and contradictory — the simple words had flown around the world: Hess is dead. The same words, oddly, had been doodled on his scribbling pad by Winston Churchill.

That had been in 1941.

ONE

The morning of his son's eleventh birthday, Bill Wiley almost forgot to look underneath his car. He left the house at a run, fury fighting with despair in his stomach, his teeth gritted against the obscenities struggling to rise. A hot, dry wind was blowing, unusual here even in July, and the smell of grass, momentarily, was overwhelming. He would have to leave, he knew. It was no longer possible to stay, it was no longer tenable. He gripped the door handle of the new Q-car and stared back at the house. His son's face appeared at the bedroom window, white and stressed. Bill Wiley bent his head, pretending he had not seen, and fumbled with the keys, the new keys, unfamiliar. He dropped them, his fingers clumsy with the crushed emotions, and − bending − remembered. He had not checked the car. Oh Jesus, first time ever. It could not go on.

The check took half a minute, and the routine calmed him. When Bill Wiley straightened up, he had his fingers in control, his breathing. A group of women were close to, with buggies and a dog. Some toddlers, too. Three of the women knew him, and smiled tentatively. Among the Army wives he was not very popular, because they liked Liz too much. She had been a sensible woman, stable and attractive, who had been a help to many of them in a crisis. Had been. To the Army wives, the story was well known, happiness in marriage was not the norm. The younger ones remembered it, and some of them still practised it in secret, like a lost or dying art. If you had it, though, you did not flaunt it: that would have been unfair. As they passed Bill Wiley's car, the politenesses observed, their smiles diminished. They glanced at No 23, the lace curtains, the red-painted closed front door. Soon it would open and Liz would bring out Johnnie, and join the other mothers in the trek to school. Johnnie was eleven today, there was going to be a party.

'Poor little bastard!' Liz had been screaming, barely ten minutes earlier. 'What sort of a birthday is it, anyway! Ten to three this morning you got in, and you're like a dishcloth! He comes into the bedroom and you shout at him, you bastard, you *shout* at him!

21

"Happy birthday, Johnnie"? Oh not likely, not bloody likely! "Get out! Get Out! Don't come in here when I'm sleeping!" You pig. You utter pig. And you won't be here tonight, will you? You won't have remembered the party, will you? Or the present, or a bloody card! Go on, get out. Go to work. Go and be a hero. Go and drive your nice new car.'

Bill Wiley had just come downstairs, having pulled his trousers on and gone to the bathroom to try and make it up with John. But John had locked the bathroom door, and the taps were running noisily, and he'd flushed the cistern, no doubt to hide his crying.

'Look,' he said. 'Liz, for Christ's sake. Don't make it worse by shouting at me, he'll be listening.'

'He was listening when you bawled him out. He was listening when you yelled at me for telling you it was his birthday.'

'All right! I know! I didn't mean it, I'd forgotten! But don't make it worse, OK? Exercise some self-control!'

Liz's face was long, and white. Her pupils dilated, and she looked about her, wildly, as if for something to throw at him. He was dispassionate for a moment, felt a pang of pain and pity for her as a human being, not a wife. The pupils were probably dilated with the drugs, he thought. Jesus Christ, how had it come to this?

'Self-control!' She was almost spitting, her lips hardly able to cope with her rage. She picked up a fish slice, then dropped it. Her hand went for the frying pan, but did not arrive. She flapped it vaguely, then clutched her forehead. Her black hair, long and tangled from the night, flopped forward over her face. She began to cry, noisily.

Bill was aware of a movement at the door behind him, and half turned. The door was still. He heard feet rushing up the stairs again, softly. He turned back to his wife.

'Liz,' he said. 'Please. I got in late. I was exhausted. I know, I know! It's not an excuse, it's my job, OK! But I'll make it up to him. Johnnie understands. He'll let me off.'

'Well he shouldn't! You've got no right to be let off. You're a selfish, piggish, piggish . . .'

She ran out of steam and Wiley pulled the door open and shouted up the stairs: 'Come on John. I know you're up there! For God's sake come and tell your Mum you still love your selfish bastard of a father. It's upsetting her.'

'It's upsetting *everyone*,' hissed Liz. Her face, which he had once thought beautiful, was sharpened with the strain. The skin beneath

22

her eyes was crêpey and brown. The pupils were still large, but getting smaller.

'Don't shout,' Bill pleaded, as she began to fill her lungs. He smiled, or hoped he did. 'I'll be here for the party, I hadn't forgotten it. You do me wrong, sometimes. I'm not a nineteen-carat shit. Am I, mate?'

Johnnie was at the door, in his pyjamas. His face was pale, but then it always was, he got that from his mother. He smiled, but it was a pretty miserable affair.

'You're all right,' he said. 'Will you be? Honestly? Here tonight?'

'Don't bank on it,' said his mother.

'Shut up,' snapped Bill. Then: 'No, sorry Liz. Sorry, John, I didn't mean to shout. She has a lot to put up with, doesn't she? Poor old Mum. Yes, I'll be here, it's all arranged. Unless Paisley runs off with the Pope, I'm off tonight, OK? And I've got a birthday present lined up for you, to collect. I might be a bastard, but I'm not a total one. It's your birthday, for God's sake. Big school next term.'

Johnnie nodded, seriously. He was a quiet boy, small for his age, thin and wiry. Like his mother, he was not wild about the place they lived, although he did not actively hate it, as she did. He had his computer, and there were two or three other boys of his own age in the married quarters to play football with, and one especial friend living in another Army enclave at Holywood, whom he met as often as possible to play chess with. The thing he hated most was the lack of Bill. Until they had come to Ireland two years before they had spent an enormous amount of time together, they had been best friends. Sometimes, when they were alone now, John would think of those days, and Bill would know it. The quiet boy would become a silent one, and his lips would tighten. Bill, sometimes, would try to apologize, or at least explain, and Johnnie would forgive him, or so it seemed. Liz, perhaps, was beyond forgiveness. She thought he had destroyed them.

While John was upstairs getting his school clothes on, Bill returned to the kitchen. He was dressed for work – jeans, trainers and a sweatshirt – and he had trimmed his moustache in front of the dressing-table mirror. He hoped the fight was over, and he was holding a small pair of scissors as part of the truce. He waved them.

'There's a bit sticking up my nose. I can never get it without risk of bleeding to death. Give us a snip will you, love?'

Liz did not move. Her eyes were on him, bright with misery.

23

'You're trying to turn my son against me,' she said. 'You're trying to make me into the nagging, carping wife.'

'What?'

His surprise was genuine, but his wife did not believe that.

'You *had* forgotten, hadn't you, you liar? And you haven't got a bloody present, waiting to be collected.'

'I have! It's up in Belfast! I'm going up there!'

'Liar! What is it then? Tell me!'

'Don't be stupid, Liz. John'll hear you. It's a surprise.'

'It will be, when he doesn't get it, won't it! You don't even know what a boy of his age likes! You don't even know how bloody old he is!'

Her voice was rising, and Bill Wiley felt his hands, involuntarily, form into fists. In one of them, like a dagger, he held the scissors. He became aware of them as a shock. He lowered his own voice, a counterpart to hers, he was prepared for pleading.

'Liz, darling, please. It's all right. I've got the present, it's even paid for. For G— For John's sake, keep your voice down. Please.'

'No!' she screamed. 'I won't! I'll fucking shout my head off, if I want to! I won't keep quiet!'

'Liz! For Christ's sake!'

Johnnie was at the door once more, his white face whiter, like a sheet. Bill felt the small chrome scissors collapse within his fist. He hurled them to the floor.

'John,' he said. 'I'm going to work. Your mother . . . Look, son . . .'

'And he won't be back!' screeched Liz, big tears pouring from her eyes and down her face. 'Whatever he says, he won't be back.'

Bill moved towards her, forced himself to stop and turn, and went towards the door. He said to Johnnie: 'We'll talk. We'll see a doctor,' and Johnnie turned and ran, crashing into the newel post then lurching up the stairs. Liz was rushing at him, so Bill side-stepped and broke her forward moment, prevented her from hurting her body against the kitchen wall.

'I'll ring,' he said, opening the door.

She picked a beaker off the work-top – light, plastic, useless – and flung it at him. It bounced off the closing door.

'I hope you die,' she said.

Bill Wiley, on the other side of the kitchen door, tried to control himself. It was despair, not fury, despair in hot black waves. Then he heard Liz tear open the other door.

'Johnnie,' she called. 'Hurry up. You've got to go to school.'

Her voice was changed, almost completely. She sounded calm. Bill closed his eyes.

Then Liz said: 'We'll go and get you something extra. After school. Daddy won't be back, you know.'

Bill could either leave, or he could go back into the kitchen and kill her. So he left.

He did not make it to the birthday party, though.

TWO

The new Q-car, although it was a small and underpowered Renault 5, was prepared to go round corners as fast as Bill Wiley was prepared to make it, so he decided to try and burn off some of his frustration in the Northern Ireland way. He roared along the narrow country roads until he found another motorist, then jammed himself up underneath their back bumper and tried to frighten them into moving over. The first was an old woman who capitulated easily, giving him a glance of bored contempt as he screamed past. But the next two were the boys, all right, and he spent an enjoyable half hour dicing with death and generating armpit sweat. The enjoyment came from the attitude of his opponents: it was not done for the pleasure, it was done in deadly earnest, no surrender. When he found himself entering Belfast he knew the therapy had not worked, he still felt carved and raw inside. But at least it was good cover, behaving like a bastard from the Black North. It was only nine o'clock, and he was not expected anywhere until ten thirty. For a moment, he thought about Johnnie's present, and wondered about toyshops, what to get him. But he conjured up, instead, an image of the child's hurt face, and winced away from it. A man in front stepped off the kerb unthinkingly, so he blew his horn and cursed. A bastard from the Black North, indeed.

Bill knew he was going to see Veronica when he found the Renault 5 turning into Adelaide Park. For form's sake he did cruise past the big brick villa before turning round a little way along and driving back. The limo was away, just her little battered Polo in the drive, by the open double garage. Bill drove straight in and parked. No cloak and dagger stuff in Adelaide Park. It wasn't necessary.

She opened the door at the second ring, and she was in a long, velvet dressing gown. Her face, not yet made up, was clear and strong as ever, the ironic eyes apparently unsurprised at seeing him.

'Christ,' she said. 'You're very bold. What'll my high-caste neighbours say?'

Bill Wiley smiled.

'Am I welcome? I take it David is off hanging Micks as usual?'

'Ach, unfair! He's not prejudiced at all, even if their little eyes are too close together. He'll hang anyone, for a fee. You're a cheeky bastard though, aren't you Mister? This is all over between us, isn't it? What if I've got a man in? Turn up on my doorstep looking like a bloody plumber!'

She stepped backwards to let him pass. The door half closed, Bill tried to embrace her. Veronica laughed, pushed him aside, closed the door, then put her arms around him properly.

'You're a hopeless case, Bill, don't you know that? The grace of a gazelle with a broken hump. This is only friendly cuddles, mind. There'll be none of that filthy stuff.'

She led him along the elegant hallway through a door and into the dining room. It was sparsely furnished, all polished dark wood and gleaming floor. From the kitchen he could hear the radio, loud and popular.

'No filthy stuff. I'm not here for that, it was just a cool embrace, to show you how sophisticated I've become. You always thought I was a bit too rough, admit it.'

She glanced back, her humorous eyes wide.

'And you just remind me whenever I've turned down a bit of rough! I've even nothing against plumbers, *per se*. But you'll never be sophisticated, Bill. Your limbs are hitched up wrong. Clear a cat away, sit down. Coffee?'

He looked at the papers while she ground some coffee and found a new box of filter papers. He stroked one of the cats, listened to the mindless babbling of the radio. Irish DJs, he thought, were even worse than English ones – those that weren't from Ireland in the first place. He laughed, briefly.

'Well that's better,' said Veronica. 'Although it wasn't much of one. You've got a face like a second violin, what's got to you?'

'Oh, life's just full of shit, that's all. Nothing serious. I came in to get a birthday present for the lad. I was out late last night, three o'clock job. I forgot.'

'Bastard. Out what? Screwing?'

'No, working.'

'Screwing the Irish. My countrymen. Don't they recognize you yet, by the way? The MI6 man with the sneakers? God, I sometimes think we must be thick, like you lot say. As a race.'

She put an empty mug in front of him, and they both listened to the coffee-maker gurgling. As always, Bill made no comment on her speculations. Officially, he was an Army captain, despite the clothes. Veronica had always mocked and he'd stonewalled. She leaned inwards, touched his cheek.

'Seriously,' she said. 'You've been at it for a terrible long time. Isn't it getting dangerous by now? How's Liz shaping in the valium and sherry belt?'

Bill sighed.

'I can see your tits,' he said. 'Lean back a bit. Unless you've changed your mind.'

She straightened, but still touched his hair.

'Ach, to see you look so sad, I'm tempted. Bill, you're not meant to be a sad man. Come on. Is it Liz?'

Bill had met Veronica through Liz, when they had first come to Ireland. Liz and Veronica had been at college together, in Birmingham, and had vaguely kept in touch. They had had dinner together a few times, but Liz had felt the differences too keenly for it to last. For although Veronica was still an oddball and an extrovert, who kept a Catholic nanny and cleaner to drive her husband wild, she was at home in Protestant grand society, a lawyer's wife and stinking rich and revelling. Bill realized David was patronizing him quite early in the piece, but cared little about it; Liz sensed even sooner that she could not break the boundaries, that she was not free to mingle on anything approaching equal terms. By the time her husband and her friend had started their affair she saw Veronica only rarely, although they professed to like each other still, and probably did.

The coffee came, and was poured.

'Do you take sugar?' asked Veronica. An old joke of hers, one of her favourites. She flicked off the radio and sat herself across the table from him, her dressing gown falling open once again. She pulled it together.

'Come on, then. What's up with her? Is she having an affair?'

Despite himself, Bill laughed.

'Christ, I wish she was.' He drank. 'She's sinking, Verr, she's drowning. I thought she'd flipped this morning, I was horrified. I woke up and barked at Johnnie, I was blitzed. She accused me of rape and double murder. She's got nothing to do up there, nothing but drink while she's cooking and pop the odd happy tablet. They have parties, Tupperware and crap like that, and talk about their bloody babies' horoscopes and private education.'

'While you and all the other men do tricks with helicopters and guns. Are you still outside Lurgan? On that vile estate? It would drive me mad, I'm telling you. Get her to come round, Bill. Give me your number, I'll ring her up. I'll take her out on the town, find a real plumber for her. Catholics do it best, do you believe that? Belfast Catholic men don't give a shit for how a woman feels. That's liberating for a well-brought-up Proddie bitch like me. Or an English girl.'

Bill shook his head. No laughter there.

'Too late for jokes,' he said. 'I think some of the women have affairs occasionally, but even that's impossible on a closed estate, think about it. In any case, she's not capable of facing you any more. Not possible.'

Veronica raised her eyebrows.

'She doesn't know? About you and me?'

'No. She's lost, Socially. She doesn't understand Belfast. This country. Province. Call it what you will.'

'She's not alone in that, now is she? What Brit does? Can't you move her out of the estate? You've moved once, haven't you, can't you pull some strings?'

'We have to have the cover,' he said. 'There's John to think of. We get given horrible little houses on horrible little estates but they're relatively safe. I'm an Army officer. Target.'

'Then spakin' as a woize auld Oirish woman,' she said, unsmiling through the accent, 'Oi'd say you're banjaxed.' She returned to her real voice, light Belfast, with a lilt. 'Why did you come here, Bill? What do you expect me to do, or say?'

'I don't know.'

'You've been here too long. You should get out, go.'

He made a face.

'You mean just me, or all of us? The Brits.'

Veronica stood and poured herself more coffee. Bill's mug was still half full.

'You know what I think about all that,' she said. 'I'm never likely to alter your opinions, any more than you or your compatriots are ever likely to understand mine. I mean you. Go, get out, save your wife and baby.'

'He's hardly a baby. He's eleven today. My marriage, maybe.'

Veronica threw in milk angrily, and gulped coffee.

'I don't give a stuff about your marriage. I said your wife and baby. Save them.'

She sat, visibly steamed up. Bill Wiley slowly drained his cup.

'I wish it was so easy.'

'Balls,' snapped Veronica.

'I've been doing lots of thinking, lately. I've heard things, looked into things. I suppose that's why I came to see you. Talk.'

Veronica, however, was still furious.

'Ach, you're pathetic so you are. Look, it's getting late. Go and shoot a Catholic or two, why don't you? I want to get dressed.'

'Expecting your new lover, are you? What is he, Prod or Taig?'

It was meant to be a joke.

'He's not a fucking Brit, and he's not a fucking undercover gunman. Go away, Bill, I'm beginning to dislike you.'

He stood, feeling abysmal.

'Sorry, Verr. I wasn't trying to put it on you. Anything.'

She did not reply. She reached out to the radio and flicked it on.

Bill saw himself out. He knew the way. He checked under and around his car, and drove away.

THREE

He drove east into the city now, and he drove fast but carefully, his mind no longer prey to macho games. Veronica had unsettled him as he had guessed she would. He wondered if he had gone to try and revive something, to be led out of his troubles by his dick, but he doubted it. As she had told him many times before, he was not at home with promiscuity, it had always left him vaguely anxious. No, he wanted something else from Veronica, and he was not certain what. Reassurance? Guidance? Insight into Northern Ireland politics? He noticed a toy and hobby shop in a busy block, with models in the window. Johnnie's birthday present. But he was in a hurry, now.

He crossed the Lagan at a crawl, then took a left turn and a short cut to avoid the traffic. He wove in and out of the Protestant terraces, glancing with appreciation at the giant Harland and Wolff cranes. One of them was nicknamed Big Ian, after Ian Paisley. He noted wryly, not for the first time, that it was German-built, and wondered what the 'great patriot' thought of that. Twenty minutes later he entered the barrack gates at Holywood, hardly aware of the young squaddy's meaningful look as he compared the information on his plastic-coated checklist with the scruff sat brooding in the Renault 5. Bill Wiley parked discreetly and tried to gather his thoughts about his current operation. He had slight indigestion and he might have been hungry. There was a taste in his mouth, slightly sour, that struck him as significant of something.

Veronica Burnett. What a strange experience. She had seen him and Liz out to their car one evening after drinks, and put her arms about him. Bill, relaxed by whisky and knowing her a little, had enjoyed the sensation, although aware of Liz and David not four feet from him, making more formal goodbyes.

'You're very sweet,' Veronica had said. Her voice was low, her smile quite clearly lascivious. 'Why don't we have a drink alone sometime? A supplementary?'

That had been all, then – and their affair had been all like that.

Tangential, off-centre, worrying. Good screwing, but an edge of tension that was almost bitterness. She somehow knew exactly why he had come to Ireland, and was prone, ever more frequently, to talk about her own views of the situation. Her husband was high in the legal and professional establishment, and closely connected, therefore, with the British government. Bill never doubted for a moment that that was where she got her information from, but it took him longer to home in on her politics. She was a games player, he understood, but her protestations and pretensions, her Catholic friends and her Republican views, were a game that lost him in its subtlety. Sometimes, after fucking him, she would talk teasingly about *his* game, the filthy way he made his money, the great scandals run between the Protestant power-brokers and the British Government, like Kincora, and the rolling of John Stalker, and the murder of the showband boys in South Down. Bill, who knew a little about some of them and much more about others, would feel the sexual afterglow drain rapidly away, the untensed muscles start to reknot. He saw Veronica as beautiful and dangerous and mad, although not as a security risk, as his superiors might have done. Whatever way, he could not handle it.

Bill Wiley became aware, slowly, that somebody was staring at him. He brought the focus of his eyes back from infinity to a point in front of his car's short bonnet, and his mind back to the present. It was a thin-faced major whom he disliked, a mutual feeling. He was signalling with a clipboard, like a demented secretary, and his lips were pursed. Bill glanced at his watch. Shit. Late for Colonel A.

He climbed rapidly from the little Renault, and deliberately pulled at the crutch of his jeans to give his balls some swinging space. The thin lips tightened. The major disapproved of people who chose to dress like tramps, and had once informed Bill that he should behave more like a soldier. Bill, with not a little pleasure, had told him to piss off and whistle up his arse. He followed the immaculate trousers into the office block, mopping his brow. It was hot, he was sweaty, he was late.

Colonel A, though – so-called for so long that it had become his natural name – did not detain him long. He did not even proffer the expected seat. He stubbed out a cigarette when Bill entered, and waved the major out.

'Bill, good to see you. That job you're on. I've spoken to Kenneth

32

already, on the phone. He says it's not much, he can handle it alone, all right? You're late.'

'How d'you mean, alone, sir? Why? I've got nothing else on, and it's shaping up quite well. No one turned up last night, but—'

The colonel flapped his hand impatiently.

'Other fish to fry, Bill. Get back to Belfast, pronto. Boswell wants you. Urgent. Sounds like a lot of fun. More fun than crawling round in dirty little farmyards trying to catch the boyos by their smell. England.'

The indigestion shifted slightly. A trickle of sweat dropped from his armpit down his left side, surprisingly cold.

'What?'

'Don't gawp, Bill – go. He's been on twice already. What's up with you, man? Are you ill?'

Wiley snapped himself together.

'Sorry, sir,' he said. 'Things on my mind. I was just running through last night's little op to see if I had anything up here' – he tapped his temple – 'that Ken might need. No problem, he knows as much as I do. I'm on my way.'

'Oh, Bill—'

Bill Wiley grinned.

'Must rush,' he said. 'Urgent!'

Colonel A reached for a cigarette, laughing.

'That's better, chum.'

By the time he reached the office block in central Belfast, Bill had got complete control of his mood and mind. Although the venue for his meetings with Mr Boswell changed frequently, he approached with caution and did not enter until he was certain nobody was watching him. He rode the lift to the third floor, smiled at the receptionist – who knew him – and entered the outer room. Two minutes later the connecting door was opened, and Boswell took his arm.

This meeting was also brief. Boswell was a large fat man with a bald, shiny dome and a face not filled with humour. He watched Wiley like a hawk, as if he knew something detrimental to his character and standing. Bill, almost nervous, wondered if he did.

'Are you bored with it yet?' he asked. He had seated himself behind a big green desk, covered with papers. Considering his position, it was not very opulent.

Bill, perched on the arm of a fat leather chair, affected surprise. He was used to Boswell's gambits.

'I wouldn't say so, sir. It keeps me off the streets.'

'Two years nearly. I suppose that helps.'

'Sir?'

'The extra risk, the extra adrenalin. Jesus Christ Almighty, Bill, the boyos aren't as stupid as they're painted, are they? They must have at least an inkling by now of who you are. And what.'

Bill nodded, non-committal.

'They change, we change, I get around. It doesn't worry me yet. Not very often.'

'When did you last get to kill one? A bogwog?'

Boswell chose the word carefully, and noted Wiley's face. It was a word that neither of them would normally have used, so the man behind the desk was testing something. Wiley, face impassive, shrugged.

'I was involved in that shoot-out down near Omagh not so long ago. February, was it? Nothing face to face for ages, though.'

'Does that bother you?'

Bill let the pause develop, as if he was giving it deep thought. It did not bother him at all, in fact. Far from it.

'The boredom element, you mean, sir?' he said finally. 'That you already mentioned?'

Boswell sighed abruptly, and dropped the subject.

'We want you on a plane at one o'clock,' he said. 'That OK with you? Any commitments, loose ends, jobs need passing on?'

'I spoke to Colonel A.'

'I know. You're clear, then?'

Bill looked into the fat face. It was glistening with moisture. The window was open, but the heat was still oppressive.

'What is it?'

'A meeting. There's a job. I don't know any details.' He sniggered, sharply. 'Not that I'm telling, anyway. I think you'll like it.'

Bill said, unexpectedly: 'My son's eleven today. There's a birthday party.'

The voice was slightly puzzled: 'Congratulations. So?'

Bill stood, shrugging. He must get a sandwich, quickly. He was on the verge of sounding like a basket-case. A nut. He forced a smile.

'Nothing. The wife was keen on it, that's all. Me being there. She bawled me out this morning. The rules of fatherhood. You know.'

The face was crinkled like a big bag pudding. Humour.

'Oh I say, I'm sorry,' Boswell said, almost in a chortle. 'I'll ring Silversmith, shall I? Tell him you can't make it!'

'Christ,' said Wiley. 'Silversmith? Is it his?'

The smile, the chortle, humour, all were gone.

'It's Silversmith. I told you, it's a good one. Lots of fun. Something to blow away the cobwebs.'

'Yes,' said Bill Wiley.

Boswell levered himself upright and thrust his hand across the desk. Bill took it. It was clammy and immensely muscular.

'How is the wife, by the way?' asked Boswell, silkily. 'I heard she . . . well, no, let's put it this way. How is she coping with it all? The strain? Be honest with me.'

Oh Christ, thought Wiley. It's like living in a goldfish bowl. He dropped the hand, a fraction of a second too early.

'She's fine. We all have our little problems, don't we? But in general terms, she's fine.'

Boswell sat.

'Grand. One o'clock we want you on that aeroplane. See Anne outside. She'll organize tickets, parking, everything. You can use the telephone, can't you?'

'What for?'

'To phone the boy, of course. From England. It's his birthday party, isn't it?'

Of course.

FOUR

The flight, to Wiley's surprise and slight relief, was not the Belfast shuttle that 'bodies in swift transit' normally took, but from the Harbour Airport. It was a scheduled flight, in a De Havilland Twin Otter operated by a small private airline, to Blackpool via Ronaldsway on the Isle of Man. The fact that he was armed had been dealt with in advance, and the fact that he was scruffy was not as noticeable in the eighteen-seater as it would have been among the business suits and stewardesses. He gazed at the extraordinary beauty of Belfast Lough and the small, immensely troubled city as it wheeled beneath him, then settled back to enjoy the gin and tonic served by a fierce-eyed girl in jeans. He wondered what the hell was going on.

At Blackpool, the murk began to lift, but only slightly. As he checked out, he saw a man in clothes not dissimilar to his own, leaning casually against a partition. Takes one to know one: they wheeled into step together as naturally as breathing, although they'd never met. The man approached a silver-grey Sierra, and unlocked the passenger door.

'We're not formal are we, sir?' he said. Sir. So he was not an officer, probably a Finco in the Intelligence Corps, who knew Wiley's particulars. Bill – not formal – got into the passenger seat with a grunt.

On the journey, there was little talk. The sun was at its hottest, and the sea air blasting through the open windows was fresh and delightful. Bill was a southerner, and he studied the flat, lonely landscape with its scattered farms with interest. Lancashire, in his geography, meant cotton mills and mountains. When they pulled into a large ramshackle hotel/pub on the bank of the River Ribble he breathed the sharp warm smell of mudflats with deep pleasure. It was a sort of secret spot, beyond his expectation.

The driver nodded, and Bill Wiley followed him round to the front of the building. In the corner of a terrace, under umbrellas, sat seven men. Muscles in his neck and upper thorax tightened as he spotted a back he recognized. Silversmith. He had known he would be here, of course, but it made no difference, the air took on a different smell for a moment, the chemistry of his stomach altered. Several of the other men, facing him, smiled in expectation, although he did not know them. Silversmith turned. His face had not changed, in four years and three months. He raised a hand, swung heavily to his feet.

'Bill,' he said. 'Glad you could make it. Long time no see. Sergeant. A pint of bitter for our man. Yes, Bill?'

Bill Wiley nodded. So his driver was a Finco, and he was not of their party. Otherwise Silversmith would not have isolated him with a rank. He approached the table as the sergeant disappeared into the bar. All were facing him now. He knew none of them.

'Colonel,' he said, to Silversmith. 'I thought you'd given up on all this shit.' The 'colonel' was deliberate. As far as he or anybody else knew, Silversmith now ran an electrical goods shop in Bristol. Silversmith grinned, taking the hand.

'Prat,' he said. 'My name's Richard.'

Silversmith — whose real name, as far as Wiley knew, was Terry — was not a large man, although he moved like one. He had been in the SAS before attachment to the SIS, and he had smashed both legs up in a parachute refresher exercise. The SAS, in training, normally jumped from about eight hundred feet, and on this occasion the balloon had been at six. The rules were, if your parachute failed to open, that you did not look down, but upwards into the lines while you jerked in the direction of the twist to untangle them. Silversmith had followed the procedure until the chute was opening, then looked down to gauge his landing strategy. As he remembered it, he had seen the ground at the moment he had hit it. He had been in hospital eleven months, and 'jangled as he walked'. He was not a man to be rid of, though, and had rejoined the regiment.

The introductions were quite desultory, and were done by drinks, as an *aide memoire* perhaps. Tony drank halves of lager, Bryan pints of bitter, Les, Alan ditto, Piet (with an 'i', he was South African) gin and bitter lemon, Jerry tonic water straight. No other information was offered or sought. It was the kind of day, fortunately, to sit and contemplate the seabirds on the marshes, so while they waited for Bill's bitter to arrive and for Silversmith to move the thing along, no one was uncomfortable in silence. When his drink was in hand and the sergeant had removed to the far part of the terrace — casual but strategic, to make sure the private party was not invaded by members of the public who did not know the rules – Silversmith proposed a toast.

'Gentlemen. To a successful outcome to a pleasant meeting. We're not all here yet – we're one adrift – but he knows the ropes in any case. Now Bill's arrived from the far-flung bogs of Ireland, I'll get down to tacks. Cheers.'

They all drank, then moved slightly inwards on themselves, leaning over the hot white metal tables to concentrate on Silversmith. He had an open face, round and unthreatening, with a large bald patch fringed with silver-grey, and bushy eyebrows. A kindly face, humorous and bright. Bill Wiley had seen him kill three men, and had helped finish one of them himself. A heady, heavy whiff of mud came to his nostrils, but it pleased him rather than bolstering the thought: he was not a great one for the symbolic.

'I've got you here today because there's a job on. It's a difficult job, possibly the most difficult I've ever undertaken in some ways, and the men I need have got to be the best. Well, that goes without saying, doesn't it, and it also smacks of—'

'Bullshit.'

Silversmith left the briefest pause after Wiley's interjection, while he assessed the faces round him. Two of the men had moved back imperceptibly, as if slightly shocked. Two were openly amused. Piet, the South African, took a sip of gin.

'Bullshit,' said Silversmith. 'Quite. For those of you who haven't had the pleasure, Bill Wiley's a foul-mouthed bastard. Been mixing with the Army far too long. But he's right, isn't he? If I didn't think you could all do the job you wouldn't be here. To be quite frank, I only need a couple of you, two or three, so I'm looking for something specific, rather than special. You're all special, ho bleeding ho, aren't you? You can all spit further than any bugger else, pee higher up the wall. But this job's a strange sod. It's an attitude I need, that's what I'm looking for. An attitude.'

They could hear an outboard motor on the slight, warm wind. A white rowing boat, with two teenagers in it, moved slowly up the river, between the mud banks. Bill thought of home, the estate near Lisburn, empty and baking, the lonely Army wives sun-bathing in their bikinis on their dish-cloth garden squares. He thought of Johnnie's birthday, and refused to think of Liz.

'The trouble is,' Silversmith continued, 'I'm not exactly sure just

38

at the moment what that attitude is. I know I sound a prat, but I'm feeling my way. It's a foreign-country job, and it means treading on the feet and laws of a foreign power. Several foreign powers. And all of them, more or less, friendly. What do you think of perestroika? Anyone?'

'Dangerous,' said teetotal Jerry. 'Don't trust the bastards.'

'Alan?'

Alan was a tall, languid man in immaculate grey worsteds and a blazer. He had a killer's eyes and a top-drawer accent. Yet he drank pints of bitter? Wiley was amused.

'I'm with Jerry. The Russian bear's a wily creature. Untrustworthy. I can't see Thatcher swallowing it, can you? To sheathe the claws is not to blunt them.'

Silversmith's eyes were twinkling.

'Bill? Bear a wily creature? From another of the same?' There were a couple of blank faces among the chuckles. A couple of slow-boys. 'His name's Bill Wiley,' said Silversmith, noting them. 'Remember?'

'Too early to say,' said Bill. 'Gorbachev's a gambler, isn't he? If he can convince us he means business, he can cut his arms bill and give his punters what they want.'

'Bread and sausages,' said Bryan, cool in a sharkskin suit despite the heat.

'Drugs and discos,' put in Alan, quite severely. He looks like an Eton housemaster, thought Bill, who had never seen one. With killer's eyes. 'When I was last in Moscow, someone offered me his girlfriend for my jeans, practically.'

'You in jeans?' said Silversmith, gently. 'Good God.'

'Did you take him up on it?' asked Tony. He had an Ulster accent, probably Derry way. Bill wondered why he did not know of him.

'Whatever,' said Alan, primly. 'Bill's wrong. Ivan's playing games with us, as usual. Give him an inch and he'll swallow Europe.'

'Ivan?' said Piet. Was he pulling Alan's leg, or pig ignorant? Alan thought the latter.

'The Russian,' he said. 'The universal Russian. Call him Gorbachev if you want to, paint a smile on his face. He's still the waiting Russian.'

And you're a twat, thought Bill. He said, to Silversmith: 'It's not destabilization, is it? You don't want someone to take out Gorbachev?'

There was a definite frisson round the shining tables, a quickening of hearts. Eyes flicked from Wiley's to the boss and back. Silversmith responded as if to a sunray lamp. His pleasure was almost tangible.

'Daft prat,' he said, fondly. 'The attitudes are shaping up, though. Anybody here who wouldn't have a go at Gorby? Listen, we need more drinks. Sergeant!'

The sergeant took the order, docile as a three-star waiter, and Piet pulled out a clump of notes to pay for it. Silversmith waved them away.

'Save it, Piet. We're drinking on the firm today, this goes on the taxes. On your way, sarge. Get one for yourself.'

Tony said, when the coast was clear: 'Treading on foreign toes and laws. Friendly toes, or nearly friendly. So will we be pitching against their boys?'

His face was broad and square. He looked like a Protestant farmer – which he may well have been not long ago. Bill put him at twenty-eight or thereabouts.

'Yes and no,' Silversmith replied. 'Or to make mud even clearer, some will be against us and some will help. If anybody has strong anti-American sentiments they'd better tell me now. Before I've paid the tab!'

'CIA?' said Alan. Silversmith tapped his nose.

'Friends,' he said. 'We've had to rope them in for technical reasons. Personally, I don't like them very much, I don't like their methods, their efficiency level. But it's historical, logistical on this job. We can't get away without them.' He looked around the group, soberly. 'I was being serious,' he said. 'If anyone has trouble with the cousins. Bill's worked with them. For them. He's got no worries there, eh Bill? Anybody?'

Slow headshakes. Yanks were fine. Yanks were all right by them. They'd climb over a naked girl to give a Yank a cuddle. Bullshit, thought Bill, for a second time. They just wanted mayhem. No holds barred. Some action.

So did he. Action without pain or complications. A long, slow vista of his life in recent months unwound before his eyes. The drab reality of the war in Northern Ireland, more boring than a proper war and quite unwinnable, run by hypocrites for hypocrites against hypocrites. Days in the pouring rain, nights in ditches, endless, ball-aching, interminable meetings with the warring factions who were in control. The power struggle between MI5 and MI6 was over now to all intents and purposes, but the RUC and the British Army were still at each other's throats with silent, secret viciousness that mourned no casualties and gave no quarter. Oh Christ, he wanted action, something clean. A foreign-country job.

'I hate the bastards, actually,' he lied. 'You know that, Richard. But quite frankly, I'd nibble Nancy Reagan's tits if I thought it would get me in on this. You've done Ireland. You know the score. I need a rest. I want to stamp on foreign toes.'

Silversmith barked with laughter. He liked the 'Richard' in particular.

'Thank Christ some bastard's being honest,' he said. 'Even if he's lying in his teeth. Yeah, I've done Ireland, has anybody else? The biggest open mental hospital in the world. No offence meant, Tony, but it's a shit-hole. Check?'

Tony moved his lips. Non-committal.

'We've all got to be born somewhere. I wouldn't want my kids to be brought up there. Yet.'

The others were studying Bill and Silversmith anxiously, hoping for a lead. He was looking for an attitude, this man had said, and he was not helping them. To most of them, the surprise of Bill Wiley's little outburst was the greater because of the sudden animation it had wrought. They had seen him as a gloomy bastard, dull and introspective. He was reverting now, before their eyes, sitting almost slumped.

'There are good and bad everywhere,' put in Bryan, unaware apparently of what a fool it made him sound. He had a pleasant face and short blond hair. Coupled with the suit they made him look intelligent, efficient. Odd about clothes, Bill Wiley pondered. That man's got where he is because of clothes. He's thick.

'Go on,' said Alan, suddenly decisive. 'Don't keep us in suspense too long, old man. It's abroad, there are several powers in the frame, and it's illegal. If we're not culling Gorbachev, and I guess it's not the Pope, what is it? Is it Europe? Middle East? I suppose Berlin would fill the bill except there's nothing left there that anyone would want, that I can see.'

The sergeant pushed open the double door onto the terrace, emerging backside first. After him, with another tray, came a man in a brown leatherette coat and cheap greenish trousers. Medium height, rotund, with long wavy hair in silver-mouse, like a sepia picture of Wild Bill Hickok. His face was fattish, his moustache

41

luxuriant, and for a moment Bill Wiley did not recognize him. When he did, it was as if he had been punched. His shoulders straightened. He became watchful and alert.

Silversmith said: 'Late again, you prat. I've brought a friend to see you. Gentlemen, Peter-Joe.'

The newcomer ignored the 'gentlemen'. His eyes were on the 'friend'.

'Well hallo, Bill,' he said. 'What's this I hear you've lost your bottle?'

My my, thought Bill. News travels fast these days . . .

FIVE

That evening, while Silversmith saw off the other hopefuls, Bill Wiley had a drink with Peter-Joe in a double room that overlooked the river. It had clouded over and the wind was blowing harder from the west, although it was still quite pleasant. The tide had risen, and the wide expanse of water was grey and rippled. The outboard motor boat had not come back.

'What did you reckon to them?' said Peter-Joe, pouring whisky for the pair of them. 'Here, take your medicine like a man. Were you impressed?'

'Cheers.' Wiley raised his glass, but did not drink. 'Impressed? I was indifferent, to be quite frank. Like I am to anybody in the game. Does it matter what I think?'

The tubby man sipped. He had his coat off, but looked no smarter. His shirt was pale blue and dirty, with a hint of hairy belly two buttons up from the belt.

'You're right. Why should we give a shit? We're like the men who pick the tampaxes up off Blackpool beach before the kids get there in the morning. The dirty workers. Who asks for references? Nice to see you, anyway. How's things?'

'OK. I was surprised to see you, though. You'd dropped out of sight. And the new image. Jesus Christ.'

Peter-Joe was amused. He looked down at his clothes appreciatively.

'Not bad, eh? How would you describe?'

'Ageing alcoholic? A bankrupt with a dream of getting up again? You look as if you think you'll pull the birds, in face of all the contra-evidence. You look like a jailbird.'

'Holed in one. In actual fact, I got them off a man in a pub. He was pissed, and broke. Drinking a half of lager very, very slowly. His eyes were swimming, and he stank, I could smell him from six feet away. He thought he was it. In his fucking pretend-leather coat and a pair of breeks you could've gassed a dog in. Kept toying with

43

his hair and looking in the mirror behind the bar, trying to focus. I thought Peter-Joe — that's for you!'

'You took it off him?'

The hairy belly joggled up and down.

'Nah. I copied it. I hit a few Oxfams, grew my hair, got the grey tints in. Mind you' — the belly rumbled more — 'Mind you, since I went like this, I haven't had a sniff. Back to masturbation!'

Bill touched his tongue with drink. He had had too much today, he was thirsty and the whisky did not help. But his brain was still unfuddled.

'You said "holed in one". What did that refer to?'

Peter-Joe was sitting on the bed. He grinned. His brain was also clear.

'Jailbird. You said I looked like. I've been out eighteen months. US of A. Two years in the pen.'

'What for? Government or freelance?'

Peter-Joe stood up. He went to the window and stared across the water. His back was turned to Bill.

'Half and half,' he said. 'An early stage in this op. I think, anyway. It's a real bent one, this, even I'm confused. Only Silversmith knows the ins and outs, as far as I can see. The Widowmaker.'

Wiley smelled the Bells. He had not heard Silversmith called that for years. In his days in Ireland, in the seventies, Silversmith had made a lot of widows. It was also irony, a reference to the Provies' favourite rifle of the era, the Armalite. Silversmith had run assassination squads for the SAS, had helped dream up the 14th Intelligence Regiment, had tried to teach the politicians about reality.

'That's what it refers to,' said the man at the window, pointing out across the darkening Ribble. 'The sea. "To leave the farm and the neat home acre, and go with the old grey widowmaker". Did you know that?'

I could probably even quote it more correctly, thought Bill. He said laconically: 'Got poetry in jail, did you? Philosophy too, I shouldn't wonder. Did you hit someone? Why the sentence?'

'It was a failure. I'd gone over there to find a woman, get something from her apartment. They didn't tell me she had guards, but lots of them. I changed my hire car four times in four days but they still spotted me. Played it canny. Told the cops.'

'Two years for killing policemen's not so bad.'

'Very funny. No killing. I was arrested for having a faulty licence

44

plate. In court, the story was that a sweet old lady had noticed me cruising round the district and thought I looked suspicious. Two cops walked up to my car as nice as pie, guns in holsters, smiles on faces, I'm too kind-hearted that's my trouble. I regretted it, that's for sure. I had an Ingram on the seat beside me, and a three-five-seven Magnum, and a pair of snazzy night-to-day binoculars. I told them I was a bird watcher with a down on nightbirds and they didn't crack a smile. I made it big in the newspapers, because I wouldn't say a word except my name and some address in London and I didn't have a passport on me and I wouldn't tell them why I had the hardware. The Man With The Iron Mouth one paper called me. The cops were like kids with candy, they called in the FBI, the Secret Service, the Firearms Bureau, Scotland Yard, Interpol, the CIA . . .'

The room grew quiet. They could hear a fruit machine thudding tokens on a floor below.

'Ah,' said Wiley, quietly. 'The CIA.'

'Ah,' mimicked Peter-Joe. 'The CI fucking A. They couldn't help me. Believe me, mate, they said they did their best.' He snickered. 'They put a spanner in the others' works, I'll grant them. And they floated *lovely* stories to hide the scent. I was there to bump off Ian Paisley, according to one newspaper, I was there to waste some PIRA who'd brought the begging bowl out to a Noraid jamboree, I was there to knock off some Mafia bastard who'd got his fingers in the pasta jar, they even got me linked with two of their own men who'd gone bad and were running guns to Libya. All bollocks, but it worked like always, my own dear mother wouldn't have recognized me if our brave newspapers over here had ever run a single word of it, which they didn't. I was six feet tall, blond, red-haired, a dwarf, had a beard, a wooden leg, you name it. The man of a million disguises. It kept me quite amused for the first few days in Rikers Island. They even tried to get me legal aid.'

'What happened?'

'Oh, I had a stash of dollars in my passport back at Kennedy. I was staying at the Holiday Inn, usual thing. Do we have an account, or something? I've never been booked in anywhere else.'

'We probably own them.'

They laughed. Peter-Joe drank more Bells.

'Anyway, there was too much dollars. Fifteen K, no legal aid. I pleaded guilty on a promise of two years for illegal weaponry, the maximum was seven. I figured for a while I'd get quietly let out, nation speaking secret unto nation, but it was nix. Job too big and complicated, I suppose. No one ever told me. But then they wouldn't, would they?'

Two years inside. Wiley considered the chubby man with something akin to amusement. Funny old way to earn a crust.

'Who was the woman? The target? Is she still alive?'

'Far as I know. Her name – the name I got – was Catherine. Said to be well-born, an aristo. German. Lived in the US for donkey's years. Loaded. Maybe we got what we were after later, someone else did, maybe. I got two years.'

Rain began to spatter lightly on the window. Both turned their heads towards it.

'It's calling me back to Ireland. We don't like it over there, the sunshine. Unnatural. You said she was part of this current business, somehow. How?'

'I don't know, exactly,' Peter-Joe replied. He did not look as if he was lying. 'She used to knock off a German flier, apparently. A fighter ace, Adolf Galland or some such name. He was one of the good guys, they reckon, anti-Nazi and all that. He went to America after the war and did exhibition stuff, a flying circus. We didn't like him. Tried to get the CIA to kill him for us, is the story. They turned us down.'

'One of the good guys? Is that normal?'

'Ah. One man's good guy is another man's war criminal. He knew some things, I guess. About another flier, not so good. This Catherine had some diaries and stuff that Galland gave her for safekeeping, stuff about the war. According to Silversmith it was a long-term thing, he trusted her completely. She was twelve years old when she fell for him, she was up a lamp-post at a big parade for Hitler and she saw Galland in the entourage. She had a sexual climax, she came. Up a fucking lamp-post at the age of twelve! Not fair is it, why don't I meet birds like that? Even when she followed him to America she can't have been more than nineteen or so. Some bastards get all the luck.'

The two men stared at the faded pattern in the carpet, thinking different thoughts. Wiley wondered where Silversmith had got to, and what part was his in all this. He finished his whisky. His thirst was getting terrible.

'So if she was nineteen then, she'd have been in her sixties when you went to kill her. Bloody hell, Peter-Joe.'

'Bollocks. You've done worse. You will again, if you want your gold clock. You were on the Hilda Murrell scam, weren't you? That's what I heard.'

'I was not. I heard that wasn't us. I heard that was genuine.'

'A genuine mistake? There's too many twats running round with Uzis in their hands, that's for definite. Too many enthusiastic amateurs. That's why we wanted you in on this. Silversmith's sick of being given pillocks who've had three weeks training and done nothing on the ground. Trigger-happy pillocks who shoot and shit themselves. We want men who've done their killing. We want men who know how to stick a cast barrel in a Browning and blow someone away and not get traced. Fucking hell, he never forgave Nairac for going in that pub in Crossmaglen and getting wasted, it caused us endless problems. You wouldn't have used the same gun time after time, you're not playing cowboys and indians, you're mature. We want you on this job.'

'I'm flattered,' said Bill Wiley. He was not, nor did he sound like it. 'What is the job?'

'I wasn't meant to tell you. The Boss.'

'Yeah, fine. But come on, pal. German fighter aces, old ladies hanging upside down from lamp-posts, Silversmith getting all the funnies to a pub in Lancashire to pick a team. Give us a clue, for Chrissake.'

'It's Hess, you twat,' said Peter-Joe. 'I thought you could've guessed that, all the frigging clues I've dropped. It's Rudolf Hess.'

Wiley was bemused.

'The old guy? In the jail? So what about him? I mean . . . what?'

Peter-Joe gestured, emptily. He tried to joke.

'Well bloody hell, Bill, what do you think? I mean, he's been around, hasn't he? He's used his share of toilet rolls. We're going to move him on, that's all. Give him a little encouragement. We'd better get our skates on, too – he might not wait for us!'

'Oh,' said Bill Wiley.

He stood and picked the whisky bottle off the dressing table. He was still pouring when Silversmith came through the door. The Old Grey Widowmaker.

SIX

Despite all the odds, Bill Wiley almost made it home in time for Johnnie's birthday. Not for the party, but in time to kiss him on the day. He put his key in the front door lock at one minute to midnight, and it was one minute past when his son awoke. Bill was standing beside his bed in the pale darkness, watching the peaceful face, almost consumed by love and sorrow, when the eyelids fluttered and the boy awoke. There was a streetlight not far away, and the curtains were thin. They looked at each other for some moments, smiling, then Bill sat on the bed and they took each other in their arms. For a while they did not speak.

It was the boy, Bill knew, who was the cause of all his deepest problems, now. The boy was thin and small, and his hair smelled faintly sweaty, and Bill loved him. It was a love that had crept up on him over several years, and it was inexplicable. They did not spend much time together, because of how he worked, and they had no interests in common. Johnnie played computer games, sometimes with friends but often alone, and he fished alone, or walked the countryside. He was self-contained, self-sufficient, undemonstrative. When he saw his father, when they had time together, they did not talk a lot, or play. But they knew, they shared a secret which they did not put into words. They had love.

'I'm sorry I couldn't get back,' said Bill, finally. 'I had to go to England. You know how it is.'

The hair against his nostrils moved, as Johnnie nodded.

'I'd like to go to England. I'd like to go back to live there. Will we, Dad?'

Bill's eyes were on the bedroom furniture, the posters, the computer table. A boy's bedroom, on an Army housing unit in a foreign country. He was exhausted, overwhelmed with sorrow. Outside a car passed, the window lightened momentarily, the noise rose and faded.

'Yes. We will. I'm sick of this place too, old mate. We all are. Your mother's sick of Ireland, and my job, and the things I put you all through. She's right.'

The hair moved, as if Johnnie were going to sit up and face him. He changed his mind, kept his eyes buried.

'I wouldn't worry too much, Dad. I mean . . . Mum'll be all right. She loves you, doesn't she? She shouts, but . . .'

She doesn't love me at all, thought Bill. We neither of us loves the other. I've given everything to fight the bastard terrorists, I've thrown away my time, my life, my family, and she doesn't understand. She's right, maybe. Maybe she's right. I can't lose this boy. I can't.

'God, no,' he said. 'Of course she'll be all right. I'm never in, the job's appalling, the hours they make me work. But it'll get better soon. Soon we'll go back to England. Maybe I'll leave the Army.'

'But you'll still be a spy, won't you? At school they say you're not really in the Army, you're in the secret services. Will you give that up, too?'

Now John did look at his face. He rolled sideways, pulling the Superman duvet with him. His eyes were deep and troubled, the skin around them smudged with dark. Bill Wiley had to force himself not to look away. The absurdity of it came to him. He laughed quietly.

'I almost lied to you again. I almost said it was a load of rubbish, nonsense. The nonsense is, I'm not allowed to tell you things like that, you're not meant to have the faintest inkling of what I do, I'm just in the Army. God, my Dad was an engineer and I didn't really know what he did, not till after he was dead. He was a toolmaker. In fact, I don't really know even now exactly what he did. He didn't make hammers and things, not that sort of tool.'

He was changing the subject, while trying to be honest. He recognized the process without caring enough to try and stop it. This boy was eleven years old. He was too young.

Mum says you'll never give it up,' said Johnnie. 'Mum says you're incapable. She says you lie all the time, as well. She's drinking wine, Dad. As well as the pills. She smuggles bottles into the car and drives them into the country and throws them into fields. I was in a field two weeks ago, I nearly shouted, I thought she'd seen me. She chucked a plastic bag down into the ditch, a plastic binbag. When she'd gone I looked. It was full of bottles. I don't want her to get sick, Dad. I don't want her to have a breakdown. Wendy

Kerrigan's Mum's just had a breakdown. She's in a . . . she's in a hospital.'

John rolled forward, reburied his face in his father's lap. Bill gazed bleakly at the bedroom wall. He thought of the boy as someone else's, tried to picture it. How would it look from the outside, this life, if anybody knew? A smart semi on a reasonable estate. A variety of cars. A tired-looking wife, but not one whose problems had become exactly visible. A quiet, studious, well-behaved lad of eleven, older than his age. Not a bad picture. The reality was an unexploded bomb, or a bomb exploding in slow motion. And Johnnie called him a 'spy', a word that nobody, surely, used any more, a romantic word. A tired man but a young one, a killer for his country's good, a man who lived with danger, in sheep's clothing in a country full of wolves. Who had been asked that day to kill a man of ninety-three.

'Look, it's late. It's nearly half past twelve, we'd better knock this off, you need your sleep. I'm going to sort things out, John, I'm going to try. That's a promise. I don't always tell lies, you don't believe that, do you? Trust me and I'll make another promise. Anything I tell you will be true, OK, whatever anybody else says. First truth is this: I'm going to sort things out. Quickly. As quickly as I can. Believe it. I'll only tell the truth.'

An odd smile passed over Johnnie's features. He unburied his face, as if to show the look.

'Dad?'

'Yes?'

'Did you get my present?'

Bill had an urge to lie, to make up some story about time, and pressure, and orders. He grimaced.

'I'm sorry.'

'That's all right. You were going to pick it up, from Belfast. You weren't, were you? You hadn't bought me anything.'

'No. I'm sorry, love. It's not that I don't care.'

'I know. You didn't lie to me. That wasn't difficult, was it?'

Wiley's eyes widened.

'You're taking the Mickey out of me, you little sod! You cheeky little devil!'

They were laughing. After a few seconds, Johnnie said: 'Will you be here tomorrow? Tomorrow night? Maybe we . . .'

He made a face. The answer was in his father's eyes.

50

'I'll be here in the morning. Not the afternoon. I'll be away some days.'

'Yeah.'

Liz, in their broad double bed, was lying on her back, uncovered in the night's warmth. She wore a light nightdress which had ridden up to mid-thigh, and her mouth was slack and open, although she was not snoring. Bill watched her for a while, noting the signs of drugged sleep. Dispassionately, because he felt his love for John so keenly, he considered what he felt for her. Firstly – the one he never could get over – was the lack of the slightest spark of physical attraction. She lay there, a good-looking woman, well-made and slim, and she might as well have been a lump of meat. He could see one of her breasts, and the inside of her left thigh almost to the top, and he would not have wanted to if he had been alone with her on a desert island. Her hair was long and lustrous black, only slightly streaked with premature grey, and he remembered days of joy and passion when he had lost his face in it, had stroked it, washed and plaited it. Her white face, narrow, serious, now looked like an aunt's face, an ageing cousin's, without attraction. And when they made love, now, he ended feeling false and hollow. Bill Wiley undressed rapidly, down to his shirt, and got into the far side of the bed, nearest the window. He moved gently, although movement would not waken her when she had taken nitrazepam, and he lay on his back, not expecting sleep to come. He listened to the gentle wind outside.

His parting with Silversmith had been amicable, if nothing else. That had taken some achieving, because Silversmith had a shortish fuse and Bill, his mouth bruised and parched with spirit, had known that he was close indeed to doing something final, to spitting out the hatred and contempt that had been growing in him like a cancer. Silversmith had entered briskly and gone straight for the bottle, watching both the men as he poured and drank, assessing them.

'Well,' he said. 'I was going to propose we drink a toast to our little venture, but I guess I'm premature from the atmosphere. You've told him, Peter-Joe. And our man's not keen. Well well.'

Bill watched Silversmith, and Silversmith watched back. It was not a game, they were not trying to stare each other down, it was an assessment. Oddly, on Bill it had a calming effect. Silversmith was a solid man, a strange and classless man, who did not have the heartiness nor emptiness of most natural officers he knew. He had been in his forties when he had become the Widowmaker, and he had been grey even then. Now he was heavier, solider, but still with the quiet authority that had not come just from the military training process, at whatever level. He was smiling, approachable, and spoke like a normal man, neither too cultivated nor exactly of the people. But as Wiley knew, he had hidden sides, which could come explosively to the fore, he could unsheathe claws like a tiger. He might be approaching sixty now, it was hard to say. But there was iron there, still, and sabre teeth.

'Bullshit aside,' said Silversmith, at last, 'Peter-Joe rates you as highly as he rates himself, and that, as you are well aware, is pretty high. You were his suggestion, and I endorsed it a hundred per cent. Forget the others, Bill. That was a show, we'd already chosen. So what went wrong?'

Wiley considered. He did not want to go into the reasons in any detail, he could not, because he had not worked them out. But he had to say something.

'Look,' he said. 'Colonel. Terry. Richard. Look – that's part of my problem, can you believe? Looking-glass fatigue, secrecy blues, call it what you like. I don't know if I'm on my arse or my elbow, I don't even know what to call you any more, I don't even know who you're working for.'

Silversmith neither moved nor smiled.

'Peter-Joe calls me Boss. Terry was my real name when we worked together last. Let's make it Terry. Look, this Hess job. It'll take us a few weeks, no more. When it's over I'll get you leave, I promise you.'

Peter-Joe had shifted to the bed.

'He'll get you out of Ireland if you ask him,' he said. 'The effluvium of the bogs. Two years in pokey in the States was better than another spell in Ireland.'

Silversmith's grey eyes were on him. They were like lasers.

'You're tired of it, aren't you, son?' he said. 'You're tired of the way we knock them down and they spring up again. You're sick of the way the newspapers stand up for them, and the TV hammers us, and every time some bastard gets what's been coming to him, some twat in Parliament screams bloody murder. You're exhausted. You feel betrayed, and isolated, and alone.'

Bill Wiley found that he was panting. Not long ago, this assessment would have been complete, deadly accurate. But it had changed, he had changed, everything was back to front. He was panicking, his fingers round his glass were strained, the knuckles hurting. He licked his lips, the insides of his swollen lips.

'Peter-Joe said I'd lost my bottle.' He cleared his throat, his voice had been a croak. 'Maybe it's true. I must say I know damn all about this Hess guy, except his age. He's ninety, isn't he? Older?'

'Ninety-three. He was Hitler's deputy. A war criminal.'

'But Jesus Christ,' said Wiley. He stopped. He licked his lips once more, tried to squeeze some moisture from the insides of his cheeks. 'Jesus, Terry, you can't go killing people who are ninety-three. It's . . . it's fucking . . . it's obscene.'

The rotund figure on the bed stirred uneasily. Silversmith moved to a seat. He walked without a limp, but stiffly. Wiley had seen his legs once. They were lumpy and wrinkled, criss-crossed with livid scars, horrifying.

'He's a war criminal. He was Hitler's second dicky, didn't that sink in? I don't know much about it, it's not my war, it's history, but he was the one who made the laws against the Jews, or somesuch.'

'Final Solution,' said Peter-Joe, as if on *Mastermind*.

'But he flew a plane!' said Wiley. 'Surely? Didn't he fly to Scotland and give himself up? Wasn't he bananas, or something?'

'He was fit to plead at Nuremberg,' said Silversmith. 'In any case, what is this, Bill? We're talking job here. Why are you giving me this shit? We're talking job, I don't have to justify.'

The claws were close to slipping from the sheaths. And what the hell, thought Wiley. The man was right. They'd done worse things than killing geriatric criminals. If Peter-Joe was told to kill a babe in arms he'd do it. They all would, they were talking job.

'He was a monster,' said Peter-Joe. 'A murderer, a mass murderer. Bloody hell, Bill, you *are* going soft, aren't you? He's a fucking Nazi.'

'I'm not going soft. I'm trying to tell you. I'm . . .'

He tailed off. It had stopped raining, and the light outside was failing. He was getting in too deep, he knew it, he was in dangerous waters, he was with dangerous men.

'Terry,' he said. 'You were closest to it, you understand. I need a rest from Ireland, I need to clear my craw of the political stuff, the hypocrisy, the blundering in the dark. I need a change, you're quite damned right I do, but I don't think murdering old men is it. I don't think I'll be much good to you, I think there were better men here today, better for the job. Come on, it's bullshit, isn't it? "You'd chosen me already, Peter-Joe rates me as himself". It's moonshine. There are other guys. Who's number three, by the way? Come on, level with me.'

The Widowmaker's eyes were steady, bleak.

'Me,' he said. 'I'm leading from the front on this one. You were number three.'

Wiley was silenced.

'Big job,' said Peter-Joe. 'No messing. Silversmith leads, and we're his team. Privilege. And you want to turn it down. Gordon Bennett, Bill.'

'Can I turn it down?'

Silversmith drank whisky, his eyes levelled at Bill Wiley across the rim.

'It's a free country.'

'No thanks to Rudolf Hess,' said Peter-Joe.

'I need to think. Maybe I am finished. Maybe you're right. Maybe I have lost it.'

'But I don't really think so,' said Silversmith. 'Otherwise I'd chuck you through that sodding window, you awkward prat.'

'But I can turn it down?'

The glass was raised again, this time obscuring the eyes. Then the stocky man stood, heavily and awkwardly. He turned his back on Wiley, turned to the whisky on the table.

'The sergeant's in the bar,' he said. 'Get him to drive you to the airport.'

Peter-Joe's face was closed, all expression lost in hair and long moustache. Wiley began to speak, to explain, apologize, but thought better of it. He left.

They were waiting for him when he got back, which came as no surprise, whatever Silversmith had said. As he approached the Renault in the car park, two men detached themselves from an angled wall and came towards him. An MIO called Copthorne and his other-ranker buddy, Charlie Brink. Copthorne nodded coolly, and the Finco grinned. It was a lovely Irish night, clear and fresh and cooler, the air sweet from the early rain.

'Bill,' said Nigel Copthorne. 'Sorry about this, chum. Colonel's orders. What have you been up to?'

'What have you heard?' He bent to check the underside of the car, flashing around with a small pocket torch.

'It's clear,' said Brink. 'I checked it for you.'

Without replying, Wiley carried on his check. Fuck you, he thought.

'What have you heard?' he repeated, standing up. He put the torch away and sorted out the key.

Copthorne was uncomfortable.

'Nothing definite. Boswell's in on it, is the main buzz. He's hairless, apparently.'

Charlie Brink guffawed, although it was an old joke. Boswell — bald as an egg — was always said to be going hairless, even when he was not angry. In fact, he rarely lost his temper publicly.

'So what are you here for? Surely he doesn't want to see me now? He wouldn't interrupt his evening for the likes of us.'

He opened the car door and swung into the driver's seat. He was not making it any easier for them.

Copthorne said: 'We were told to make sure you arrived. Which presumably means they were afraid you wouldn't. We've got to take you home. Well, follow you.'

Instead of anger, Bill Wiley felt frustration. No adrenalin flooded his bloodstream, a dull ache, a vague depression, settled on him. To be watched by your own side was one thing, but to be guarded openly . . . It was intimidation.

'No chance of slipping somewhere for an illicit screw, then.' He tried to make his voice calm and casual. A laid-back joke.

The Finco said: 'Not unless we come, too.'

Nigel Copthorne could see the whiteness of Wiley's knuckles on the steering wheel.

'Listen,' he said. His voice was cultured, and circumspect. 'I'm sorry about this, Bill, but don't let it get to you. The buzz is that you're getting in a state, you're overwrought. Remember Holroyd, I'll say no more than that. Stay calm.'

Charlie Brink said nothing, but his lips thinned in unspoken contempt. The fate of Holroyd, an MIO who had been shunted into mental hospital when he started criticizing certain secret operations, could still open up a great divide. Brink was clearly of the side that thought he'd had it coming to him, mad or sane, honest or deluded. Copthorne said no more, but let the thought sink in.

'Right,' said Bill. He turned the ignition key, the engine fired. 'I'm going, if you want to get your car. I'll take it fairly slow, I've been on whisky. Are there any messages, or is the escort duty it?'

Brink turned away, jingling in his pocket for his keys. Copthorne banged the roof of Wiley's car, not hard, a salutation.

'You're to be in Boswell's office at nine o'clock. That's all.'

'Of course. Thanks, Nigel. You needn't follow if you don't want to. I'm not going anywhere.'

'Charlie's driving. Need I say more?'

'No.'

Liz had started to snore gently. Bill Wiley stared at her slack face, in a sort of horror. Once, he knew, he would have been moved by it, found it endearing. He glanced at his watch. Ten past three.

There had been another woman once, a serious one. He did not think of her, normally, he avoided it. But he would have to find her, he would have to get in touch. Because of what she knew.

He had made his mind up.

SEVEN

Bill Wiley managed to get out of the house next morning without crocks flying, before tears or blood began to flow, but it was a close-run thing. His wife had woken late, feeling terrible, and so had he. Johnnie normally would have woken them, but he had slept in, through the alarm watch he kept underneath his pillow but which bleeped politely and not for very long. It was the phone that woke all three of them, and Liz had got out of bed, snorting with vexation, when Bill's responses had made it clear it would be work. It had been Boswell's office, reminding him of the appointment, checking he was there.

Downstairs, John was at the table, bleary-eyed, waiting for his Shreddies. He smiled.

'Hi, Dad. You look terrible.'

'I feel it. Whisky, you're the devil. Stay off it, cock.'

Liz put a teapot on the table. Her skin was yellowish, she looked exhausted.

'Too drunk to buy the boy a present. Terrific.'

'Mum,' said Johnnie. His voice was instantaneously strained. A shadow, fear or misery, swept his face. Bill fought anger.

'We talked about it in the middle of the night,' he said. 'We understand each other, don't we, love? Anyway, I was drinking in the line of business. What's your—'

He bit the words off, gave a twisted grin to his anxious son, changed direction: 'More work today. That was HQ. I've got to be in Belfast by nine, I'd better go.'

Liz sat opposite. She looked defeated, old.

'It's always important, isn't it? More important than your wife and kid. More important than real life. And you won't be home tonight, I suppose?'

'Yes,' said Wiley. Then remembered. His eyes met Johnnie's and he winced. 'Hold on, I've just remembered. No. I'll be away.'

'How long?'

John's eyes held his. He sighed.

'The point is, this is awkward. Quite honestly, I don't know. No, I'll probably be back tonight, I'm not sure. But probably.'

He would not be, he could not be. But he had to do it this way, in case anybody checked. To him, it seemed as if his son's eyes were changing shape and colour. John thought that he was lying, but could not quite believe it.

'Well never mind,' said Liz. 'Who gives a stuff? We don't, do we Johnnie?'

Bill tried to get a minute with him on their own, before he got into the car. He tried to catch his eye, underneath the Renault, as they stooped to search for bombs, but Johnnie looked away. Liz stood deliberately on the pavement, a slight sneer on her lips.

'Goodbye, sunshine,' said Bill Wiley. 'Probably tonight. Goodbye, Liz.'

'Bye,' said Johnnie. His eyes were down. 'Try, won't you?'

'Yeah.'

Boswell, as always, was massively reasonable. He shook hands warmly, and put Bill in an easy chair half facing another, which he took. It was not so hot today, but the windows were still open to the noise of Belfast. Boswell, in a dark suit, did not sweat.

'Silversmith was on the phone before you reached the airport,' he said. 'I was in the bath. He said you didn't want to do the job.'

'And he thought I'd do a runner? Or was that your idea, to have me met? I suppose Silversmith could guarantee I got on the plane at Blackpool.'

Boswell was calm. He had already commented on Wiley's appearance, the haggard features, the strain around the eyes. It had probably been a warning. Bill breathed evenly. He would try to take it.

'I don't think either of us thought you'd be so silly. But it was worrying. Is worrying. You were chosen for the job, your work over here is excellent, your attitude exemplary. Then you sprang that. It was something of a bombshell.'

Attitude. That word again. He tried, and failed, to keep his mouth shut. It would have been better, at this stage, to have listened.

'It's a funny word,' he said. 'Maybe that's what threw me, sir. Peter-Joe. Have you met him recently? What do you make of his attitude?'

The fat man stirred. A smile crossed his hard moon face.

'I don't know the man that well. He's freelance, he always has been. I've been involved in ops where he's been used, and I've heard nothing but good of his abilities. Major Silversmith rates him highly.'

Major. Another cover for the colonel? Another little joke?

Wiley said: 'He's a killer. He'd kill your grannie for you. Anybody's grannie.'

What a roundabout way to get to Rudolf Hess. The smile was back on Boswell's face, a smile of appreciation.

'Yes. As I said, the major rates him highly. Good heavens, Bill, what do you suppose we employ people like him for? Because he's good with animals? He's been working on aspects of this problem for several years I understand. Made sacrifices.'

'Two years in jail in America. That's a hell of a sacrifice.'

'According to the major, he's a hell of a hard man. He was told to work in total secrecy, he was told if anything went wrong he was on his own, and he accepted it. In similar circumstances I would expect some people to operate the same, you for instance. I would have expected you to be intrigued by this proposition, but to have accepted that you could not know the whys and wherefores, and to have shut up. Frankly, Bill, I'm disappointed.'

Wiley crushed the urge to sound sarcastic, or too combative.

'Frankly, so was I.' He kept his voice quite flat. 'I actually didn't join the service to become a licensed murderer, at least, I don't remember that as one of my reasons. When I'm confronted with one, I'm capable of being thrown. I've worked with Peter-Joe before. I didn't like it. I didn't like him. This target's over ninety. A bag of bones. I could imagine Peter-Joe taking pleasure in his death. That's all.'

Boswell was scratching his nose, considering.

'A licensed murderer,' he said. 'That sounds quite odd to me. We kill people over here, you kill people. But it isn't murder, Bill, that's the direct line to insanity. If I thought we were murderers, I wouldn't do the job, it's as plain and simple as that. If I thought you were a murderer, I wouldn't talk to you. The enemy murder people, and we have to stop them, and sometimes it gets messy and unpleasant. There's a war on.'

'And Hess's ended in 1941. That was the flight, wasn't it?' A cod-German accent: 'For you, Rudy, ze var ist over. I'm sure you have a reason for saying he's got to be killed, and I know you're not telling me it, OK, that's the job.'

'I *will* tell you. Because it *is* the job. Do you think it's some damned whim? Do you think some politician-Johnnie woke up one day and thought it was a wheeze? Don't kid yourself, they haven't got that clout, there are more important people and considerations. I don't *know* the ins and outs, Bill, nor do I need to. Let us pity him by all means, Nazi and war criminal though he be. But our masters tell us he has to die, so die he must. Think it regrettable. Strange even, most bizarre. But don't imagine that anyone would undertake it lightly. It is neither whim nor pleasure.'

Bill thought of Peter-Joe. Not fucking much. It was a bit sudden though, wasn't it, for poor old Hess? He was hardly likely to escape and gas a Jew, was he? He toyed with the idea of putting this to Boswell, but Boswell's features had taken a different, less indulgent cast. Wiley had a twinge of apprehension, deep in his gut, that he had consciously to suppress.

'Another thing,' he said. 'I thought about it in the night. Isn't there some doubt? Some theory? That the man in Spandau isn't really Hess at all? That it's a ringer?'

There was a creak as Boswell heaved himself out of his armchair. He came up flushed and turned his back on Bill. He checked his wristwatch, then turned to lean against the mantel, his body filling the empty fireplace. Then silence, for a noticeable time.

He said: 'Why am I such a reasonable man? You are impertinent, Bill, and I'm beginning to think you're foolish. I know the rumours, and I can assure you that they're lies. As a man of honour, I can assure you that they are the maunderings of a few crackpots and cranks. Conspiracy theorists, Hess freaks, nuts, possibly malicious, there's a whole damn army of them. The prisoner is Hess, take my word for it. Look, I'm running out of time, I have work to do. What am I to say to Silversmith?'

Bill steeled himself. He was on quicksands, he did not believe for a moment that he had a choice, not any more. How could they trust him if he ducked out of this? What use would he ever be again? He swallowed.

'You put your finger on it yesterday,' he said. 'My boy's birthday party. It's not me who's got the psycho problems it's Liz, my wife. She's in a state, she's verging on a pretty awful mess. She's taking Valium, and I wouldn't be surprised if there wasn't drink involved.

You know how some of them can get, out there on the estates.'

Boswell said: 'The heart of Paddyland. Yes, it must be bloody lonely for them. Nobody sees it as a foreign posting, that's the problem.'

Wiley thought: You selfish bastard. It isn't real to you. Just the occasion for some romantic thoughts and pop philosophy. But he played the same hand, carefully.

'I mustn't lay it on too thick.' His voice was reasonable, concerned, had gravitas. 'Liz is a terrific woman, she won't break down or anything. It's just a bad patch, I expect. I'm sure it is. But the birthday brought it to a head. You know.'

Automatically, Boswell murmured: 'I do indeed, I do indeed.' He drew breath, deeply. 'So what are you suggesting, Bill? I wish you'd said before, you're a cantankerous old sod, aren't you?'

Devious would be a better word, thought Bill. It occurred to him that it wasn't real to him either, Liz's mental state. Just a useful ploy, a tool. He crushed the thought, and thoughts of Johnnie's face. He had made his mind up, in the night.

'The thing is, I need thinking time. I need time to be with her, to get it back to normal. I think it's a matter of tangents, there's nothing seriously wrong. I think she just needs me there for a day or two to sort her out.'

'Good man,' said Boswell. The automaton. The talking clock. 'What, take some leave? A couple of days or so? Three? Then back into the harness. The Silversmith job won't take long. Not really.'

'When would I need to go? To leave Ireland?'

Boswell gestured.

'Not certain. There'll be some training, briefing, you know the score. Work in England with Silversmith and Peter-Joe. Prelims. I could give you three days leave, I think.'

His manner was relaxed, avuncular, and Wiley did not trust it.

'Not leave,' he said. 'Thanks, but I really feel Liz would be better if I played it less unsubtly. I think she'd think she was bananas if I took time off, it isn't in my nature, it would scream "Serious!", she'd be terrified. There's a lead I want to follow up, a good one. It'll mean running round a bit, but home at nights. Nothing very taxing.'

'Running round?' said Boswell, sharply. 'I don't want you across the Border, mind. I don't want you taking any risks. D'you understand?'

61

Bill Wiley did. He left the office five minutes later a free-ish agent with a free-ish hand. He would be expected home at nights and to make a check-call in the mornings at a time that suited him. He was on a rein, but it was not a short one. Boswell, as he portrayed himself, was a very humane man.

His parting shot was this: 'About the Hess thing. Obviously, you've bought some time to think it over. I'm certain that when you have you'll come back raring. But Silversmith was right, and I must repeat it. In the last analysis, if you have real qualms, I won't force the job on you, God forbid. Think about that, won't you? The choice, finally, is yours.'

Wiley drove the Renault 5 to a spot near Adelaide Park and walked to Veronica Burnett's house. Half an hour later they left in her car, and she took him to Teaguy, a village about ten miles from Belfast. Dropped there, he went to a small transport yard, where he was well known, and spoke to the proprietor. Three hours afterwards he was in Larne, a lorry driver's mate, and by early evening he was in Stranraer. Dropped on the M6 where it meets the East Lancs Road, he hitched to Liverpool and found his way to West Derby and a Higsons pub he knew. The barmaid, a thin, bright woman called Chris who had been a friend for years, gave him a kiss and a pint of bitter, then the key to her house a mile away.

He had to make some phone calls, fast. He did not have much time, he thought.

Before they jumped.

EIGHT

Bill Wiley's life, it struck him with some surprise, was defined and circumscribed by women. He was in a woman's house, making phone calls – all but one – to women, trying to track a woman down. Even his way of leaving Ireland had been through Veronica – he had had to see her before he left because he'd thought that he would need her help, more serious help, quite soon. He worked with men, he played men's games, he was controlled by men. But he had none of them for friends, except his son.

'Am I allowed to ask?' Veronica had said – having expressed no surprise at all that he had turned up on her doorstep once again. 'It's very sudden and mysterious. Why me?'

They were in the kitchen, which was in the same state as the day before, untidy, noisy, lived in. Veronica also – the same dressing gown, the same insouciance. Later in the day, he knew, she would emerge like a butterfly from a chrysalis into clothes of gripping elegance, and the kitchen would be transformed by Maeve Maguire, her (Catholic) cleaner, before the kids got home from school. It was schizophrenia rampant, Veronica would laugh, if asked. She had a full red mouth, broad bones, red hair – not like a Protestant at all. She hinted darkly at some dreadful secret in the family past, some loose-legged ancestress, some filthy Taig footman or groom who had not known his proper place, contaminated blood.

Bill was nervous and a shade depressed, his mind still bruised by the rawness of some of what he'd said to Boswell. To talk of licensed murderers was to step right to the edge of the moral arena in which they lived and worked. The man's response – calm, reasonable, concerned – frightened him. Something bad was cooking.

'I'm expecting dirty tricks,' he answered Veronica. 'I've got to go to England for a while. I thought if I asked you face to face, apologized for yesterday, you might save my life.'

Veronica threw back her head and laughed.

'You're crazy, so you are! What dirty tricks? Answer me, or you get nothing, not even the forgiveness, you little chauvinist.'

63

She knew he could not answer all of it, but she sat expectantly to hear the parts he could tell. Bill said that he was involved in something complicated, that meant him bending rules, and he was afraid there might be retaliation from the top. Her eyes were serious, but full of animation.

'Surely, Bill,' she said, 'you've not been having doubts, have you? You've never started to come to some conclusions? Am I to be proud of you yet, one of these days?'

'You've got that house in Donegal still?'

'Surely.'

'When I said save my life, I almost meant it. I may need to hide. I haven't got the foggiest idea, really. What's going to happen. Would you . . . ? Can I . . . ?'

'Count on me? Bill, you sound like a country and western song, I love it! Tell me what you want and it's yours. Anything!'

She was laughing at him, but there was delight. First she gave him one of David's razors, and Bill shaved off his face hair in the bathroom off the master bedroom. As he shaved she dressed, he glimpsed her naked in the mirror. It was like old times.

In her slip, Veronica came into the bathroom.

'Should we fuck?' she said. 'Or would that lead to complications!'

And she screamed with laughter, and they did, sprawled across David's single bed, her face and neck smothering in shaving foam. As Bill came she whispered in his neck: 'That was for you, you poor bloody Englishman. Don't despair.'

The man Bill phoned to find the woman was a last resort, because he did not like him much, or want to speak to him. But the blanks he had monotonously drawn had a cumulative effect that depressed and deadened him. The information was withheld deliberately, not from lack of knowledge of the number. He was looking for a woman called Jane Heywood, and they were her friends.

After the fifth refusal, he sat back on Chris's old and grubby sofa, pondering. So far he had made it across the water, down the motorway and into darkest Liverpool. The house was in a terrace, on the rough edge of West Derby, and was probably perfect cover. But that was all. In an hour or less Chris would be home from work, and friend or no friend, she would be curious. There was no man in the question either, at the moment, and her kids were at her mother's being sat. Perhaps Chris would leave them there tonight, and come home alone. Bill did not want that, for the moment that was his only certainty. He picked up the bright red telephone and put it on his lap and dialled.

Liz's voice was thick and slow. She tried to give their number, but he interrupted her.

'Liz, it's me. What's going on?'

Fatuous. Her pause, punctuated by the sound of breathing, accentuated that.

'Nothing. What do you think?'

'Look, I'm in the Republic. I'm not meant to be. If the office ring, give them a message, OK?'

To a sober man, the pauses were almost endless.

'I might do. I might not.'

'Fine. Just tell them I'm undercover, and I'm all right, OK? I'm in bandit country but I'll get in contact when I can. I'm in the North, got that? I'm in the Republic really, but for them I'm in the North, OK? I'll be a day or two, tell them.'

Again the pause. The slow, uneven breathing.

'Liz? Have you got that? Liz, I . . . how's the boy?'

An unpleasant, throaty noise came down the telephone. He could not imagine how she made it.

'Fuck you,' she said.

He put the receiver down, and picked it up, and dialled another number, one of several he had jotted on an envelope. It was late but not that late. Colin would be in, please God. He was unlikely to be in bed, unless there was a woman, which was also unlikely. He could be down the pub.

Colin was a strange man, a strange man for a friend. His wife had been a nice woman, a friend of Jane's, quiet, intelligent, attractive. And full of cancer, it had tragically turned out. But Colin was the sort of man he would have run a mile from in normal circumstances, as would the wife who'd died, you might have reckoned, seeing them together. He was plump and plummy, given to cavalry twill trousers and pale shirts with assertive checks, and he wore cheese-cutter caps and hacking jackets. Cars were his life and passion, although he was also pretty keen on house prices. He and Sue had lived in antiseptic circumstances in a small, expensive flat in Old Windsor, almost overlooking the River Thames. What blocked their view was a medieval church, a tourist masterpiece, so that was fine with Colin – it put the prices up. When Susan died, the flat got even cleaner, sterile almost. Colin did bring women back, although they were not attracted to him much, nor he to them. With Sue it had been love; which had cut across several unlikelihoods.

Colin answered. The voice was just as plummy, with a faintly querulous edge. Bath, Bill guessed. Or sleep.

'Hi. Sorry to interrupt you, Col. Been slaving over a hot customer, have you?'

'Good Lord.' Colin's voice warmed instantly. 'Bill. Only you would introduce yourself so rudely after all this time. I was in the bath.'

'You'll wash it off one day. You should be careful. Look, business. Jane Heywood. I want her phone number.'

'I gave it to you! You're bloody rude. Where are you? London? Can't you say hello?'

'Hallo,' said Bill. 'Yes, you gave it to me, you fat twat, but it didn't work. I tried several times. I got a geriatrics' home.'

'Oh lord you didn't, did you? Sorry, I've done that to other people. I can never remember the last digit. Oh gosh. Hang on, I'll get my filo.'

Bill, left holding the red receiver, felt a smile forming on his lips. He could imagine Colin, dripping pinkly, wrapped up in a fluffy towel doubtless, scurrying amid the polished, gleaming furniture, leaving a damp trail in the carpet pile. Ivory, it had been. Still would be. He was relieved. He had assumed the number had been wrong deliberately. Jane Heywood had a tight-knit band of friends to protect her. A mafia. He heard the receiver rattle off the table at the other end.

'Bill? What have you got? I bet you've got six seven oh three. It's four! I always misremember because I do business at the old folks' home. I lay on cars on special days. You know.'

I do, thought Bill. At no cost. Colin, for all he was a jerk, was a nice man. Sucker.

'Well if you always forget, you idiot, why don't you remember? Tell people? I thought you were being cagey, like every bugger else. I wasted a small fortune trying to get through. I gave old ladies heart attacks!'

'That was months ago. If it was so important you should have rung back, tried again. You should have rung anyway. You're meant to be a friend.'

'Right. Apologies. That's why we have friends, Col. So we can shit on them. Listen – have you got her address, by any chance? It would be better if I dropped in on her. Surprise her.'

His mouth dried slightly as he said it. There was silence at the other end of the line, also. Which he took to be significant.

'How's Liz?' said Colin. 'How's the kids?'

'Kid,' said Bill, tersely. 'They're fine. Look, you suspicious sod, this is business. If you don't want to tell me, fine. But spare me the moral crusades, OK? I need to see her, to talk something through. Some history. I work in Ireland, remember? History's important, over there.'

'Sorry, old man. The sisterhood gets very serious sometimes. Protective.'

'I know. But I didn't do anything, did I? Not then, not now, not ever.'

Not strictly true, but not far off the truth. Other men had hurt her more, even at the time. Colin may not have known that.

'Bill. Where are you now? If you've got to go to Oxford to see her, you could call in. I'd love to see you, really, and it's practically on the way. Where are you?'

He looked round the tatty, tiny living room, festooned with uncleared toys. He needed a base, he did not need the complications that even Chris might bring. The television set next door was hammering canned laughter through the party wall. Colin had cars . . .

'I'm in Liverpool. A staging post. Trouble is, I've got to get a stage-coach. Train, at least. No wheels.'

Colin drew in his breath. The satisfaction travelled audibly through the wire two hundred miles.

'Well,' he said, 'surely that's logical? What do you fancy? Mercedes? BMW? Rover?'

He worked with a firm of car-hirers to the wealthy. He was a director. Sometimes the wealthy were too tired, or busy, to return the cars, sometimes they needed picking up. Colin quite often had a limousine or two parked on his patch of gravel, even a Bentley or Rolls Royce. The neighbours complained if it got epidemic, but in general terms it did give quite a good impression to casual visitors – and prospective buyers when a flat fell empty.

'Good God,' said Bill. 'What a daft idea! I can't afford your daily rates, you nutcase.'

'Don't play hard to get, old boy. You don't fool Uncle Colin. Usual terms. You buy me a pint.'

'Skinflint bastard. You drive a harder bargain than Scrooge. Do I get a bed thrown in?'

'Delighted. Hell, Bill, this is really nice. How soon can you make it?'

Bill checked his watch. Pointlessly, there wouldn't be a train tonight.

'I'll catch an early train, sixish, sevenish, there must be something. It's under three hours from the Pool, if I remember. Are you in all morning?'

'Come to the office. You know it, the Green Park branch. I'll be there. I'll take the rest of the day off, we can come back here, pub lunch. I'll sort you out a good'un, a BMW. Suit?'

Bill heard the front door key in the lock. He heard Chris's voice, talking to the children. Thank God for that, at least. To Colin he said: 'Sounds fantastic. But I'll be very busy, Col, I'll need to get to Oxford first, I'd guess. We may have to postpone the lunch till evening. That OK?'

'No probs. Easy. Is that company I hear? Children?'

'Yeah, my rest-home. A little family place. Listen, I'll see you in the morning. Take care, Col.'

'And you, old man. Looking forward to it. Cheers.'

Chris's face was narrow and vivacious, with long dark hair framing it. She was smiling quizzically, her eyes alight with humour. One of the children, the girl, was blinking woodenly in the light, a half-bottle of Scotch clenched tightly in her hands. Chris took it, and propelled both of them back out into the passage, towards the stairs, mocking their sleepy curiosity.

'Gerrout of it,' she said. Her accent was so strong it reminded Bill, as it always did, of a TV sitcom voice. 'He'll still be 'ere in the morning, if you're quick. Go'ead up that bloody wooden 'ill!'

They were still two-thirds asleep, they did not argue. Christine closed the door.

'What are you gawping at?' she asked Bill, as she pulled off her coat. She was thin and birdlike, dressed to kill, the demon barmaid.

'I think I've got a headache, dear,' he said.

'You better not have, la'!'

Ah well . . .

68

NINE

For a man who claimed he was not promiscuous, Bill Wiley thought, he had been doing rather well – or rather badly – in the last day or two. He caught a later train than he intended, not till after eight o'clock, and he had a hangover. Between them, he and Chris had finished the half-bottle, some of it before they went to bed but most of it in between times, and they had not slept much. Chris had been enthusiastic but Bill, dogged by whisky, weariness, anxiety, had not. He had played his part, though, browsed and wandered satisfactorily for both of them, and they had had a pleasant time. Chris's expectations of men were not exactly high, and she liked the kindliness she found in Bill, his willingness to lie still and hold, to cuddle and converse. Bill, although from time to time almost overwhelmed by a desire to fall asleep, was content enough to listen to her talking of her friends and family and relationships, although he knew none of them. He went into the spare bedroom before the children woke, and got an hour undisturbed.

The train was busy, so he did no more than doze as they rolled east along the river-line, then did the curve to head for London. His face was scratchy – Chris had had nothing in the house except a blunt ladyshaver for her legs – and his clothes were still the ones he had left Ireland in the day before. He had not dared to pack at home in case it led to comment and suspicion, nor had any of the clothes there been suitable. His wardrobe consisted of a suit or two, quite military and severe, a few summer casuals, and the 'uniform' of jeans, jerseys and bomber jackets that he wore for 'work'. He was dressed like that now, although *sans* jersey, and his cream shirt was crumpled and stale. Christ, he thought, I've fucked two women in it for starters – wouldn't you be jaded! If he was going to have a BMW, and live in Old Windsor, perhaps he'd go for cavalry twill, like Colin. He almost giggled, half asleep.

When he did drop off, Bill Wiley had a dream that horrified him. He was on one of Ireland's western strands, and a violent storm, a hurricane, was blowing from the west. Gigantic coamers, Atlantic greybeards, were rolling in, ten feet high and stunningly impressive. As they began to break, as the underwater contour of the strand shallowed rapidly, the screaming wind took off their tops, long unbroken lines of them, and blew them towards the shore like smoke, white smoke, or hair. The noise, unbroken and terrific, stopped his ears, as the wild wind stopped his mouth. And then he saw his son.

Bill, in the dream, began to run towards the coamers, through wet sand that deepened as he stumbled forwards, buried him to the ankles and dragged him almost to a standstill. He opened his mouth to shout, but it was filled with salty, biting spray that blocked all voice. And Johnnie, whom he had seen atop a breaker struggling to swim, had disappeared. Time dissolved, Bill was in jeans and singlet, his anorak and boots had gone, he was soaked with sea and tears. He was up to his waist in water, the Atlantic warm, the waves coming to him like faithful dogs, lapping round him, licking him. Then undertow. He saw his son, underwater, rushing out to sea, his mouth open and his hands clutching, and he was gone.

Bill woke up with a jump and a noise that frightened the girl opposite him at the plastic table. She became quite wild-eyed as he apologized, clearly terrified that talking was a social contact that preluded far worse. Bill stopped, knowing much of terror. She would have liked to have moved, gone to another seat, but that would have been an insult. He closed his eyes to reassure her, pretended to seek sleep. He checked, surreptitiously, to make sure his Browning was still concealed beneath the bomber jacket. Holy shit.

Through the flat Midlands, he tried for rationality, an assessment of the situation, but that was plain impossible. His wife was cracking up and hated him, his son was eleven and a day and could detect the strain. Did he hate his wife? He did not know. To her the problem was the job, the tension and the boredom, and the endless lack of him, the disappearances, the eighteen-hour days, the exhaustion and bad temper. His frustration, rationally, had always been her refusal to accept necessity, she had known the game when she had married him, he was wedded to the job. Not just a job, either, it was never just a job. In the old days, when the rows had been sufficiently new to embrace shreds of rationality, he had thrown words like patriotism at her, and service, and saving her and people like her from terror, saving democracy. Last week she had told him that she'd vote Sinn Fein next time. And here he was on the train from Liverpool to London, running from the job. Rationality? That was plain impossible.

When Wiley opened his eyes once more, the girl had seized her chance and sneaked away. He took the opportunity of a passing train to look at himself in the window – now a mirror for short, uneven seconds – and was actually startled. His face was sallow, his chin black with stubble, his eyes raw and cavernous. He straightened his shoulders, took the curve from out his spine, stretched his legs. The express – and his mirror – passed. He was a mess, entirely.

Jane Heywood. What would she look like nowadays? What would she say when she saw him? Just precisely what did he expect, or hope, to get from her? Was it he, perhaps, that was cracking up, not Liz? Perhaps she was married, although Colin would have mentioned that, he guessed. Perhaps she would not remember him.

Although he was not a promiscuous man – Bill smiled as the thought formed itself again – he had had an affair with Jane Heywood, a real affair. It had started as an accident, a sort of one-night stand, which had given it its gloss of haphazardness, its respectability. He had not entered into it, or into her, with thoughts of damaging his wife, or betraying her. It was one of those things that happens, once in a way, to certain types of male and female.

It had been at a conference, in a big hotel in Birmingham, the sort that had been built for such affairs, was universal. It had been an odd conference, more a historical gathering, held at the whim of an oil prince with a degree (from Cambridge) in enthusiasm, and a lot more cash than sense. He also had more enemies than oil wells, but was a valuable link in the Foreign Office chain of corrupt but friendly potentates they could more or less rely on when slush and contracts were in the question. Bill Wiley – on loan to the Office – had been there in a business suit as part of the British side in the security arrangements. One of their main jobs, and worries, being to keep the prince's own team from overstepping the bounds of diplomatic possibility, and strong-arming the police and public (to forget it) when they did.

Jane Heywood had been a speaker and a guest. She was a historian – and the niece of quite a famous one, an expert on the politics of Europe – who had taught in the Far and Middle East and had at one time caught the eye of the oil prince. She was indeed eye-catching. She wore a navy suit, square-shouldered but not padded, with a skirt that ended just below the knee, revealing calves that made Bill ache and small feet in blue kid mid-height shoes. Her face was open, make-up free and brown, and her shoulder-length hair was chestnut, gleaming as if polished. One of the Eastern security men, quite clearly, had marked her for his own and was taking No for Yes interminably. Bill had intervened politely, turned his back on Jane and showed the man their universal ident, and moved them far enough away to warn him, in low but brutal syllables, that the Prince was in the hunt and what, therefore, might happen to him. Affecting insouciance, and probably assuming she was Bill's, he had backed down and left.

They had gone to bed together, much to Bill Wiley's astonishment and delight, later the same evening. She had not been flustered by the incident with the strong-arm man, nor by Bill's intervention. She was flattered and amused, she said, but laughed out loud when he suggested she might have been in actual danger. He laughed as well, at his own pretensions and the ease with which her clear grey eyes had seen straight through them. Jane later told him that she had decided then to sleep with him, if he expressed an interest.

Why? Bill, a military man in all but rank at that time, had been slightly scandalized. Here was an educated woman, cool, calm and collected, behaving in a way he had been led to believe that her type did not, could not, should not. He was talking respectability. In the language of the barrack room, perhaps even the officers' mess, she was high-class crumpet. You looked and lusted, then maybe you wanked. After they had made love a few times, when it had become clear that it was no one-night stand, he had dared to tell her this, and Jane had laughed at him again. She laughed a lot, and found him funny when he least expected it. But she did not explain herself.

Jane lived in London then, because she was working at London University, near the Museum. Bill lived in Potters Bar, near Liz's parents, but as ever spent much time away from home, so was not missed much more than usual when he stayed the night in town. Johnnie had been eight, his life uncomplicated by fears that disappearances could lead to anything more permanent. Dad went away, but Dad came back again. No problem. Things were different now. The fear of dematerialization was mutual. Its reality as a touchstone of their lives affected both of them.

They screwed, and talked, and drank together, Bill and Jane

Heywood, and all the time he thought that it was wonderful. Her house was in a quiet street on the edge of Brixton, near the prison, and he got there twice a week for a short while, sometimes letting himself in at dead of night with the key she'd given him, and undressing on the landing outside her bedroom, and slipping into bed beside her, naked, the pair of them giggling in the dark, miscreants in a fantastic dormitory. He quickly got out from under the first big lie – that he was single – because he realised she would find out soon and anyway he hated to deceive her, and she had thanked him for having the guts to tell her. The second lie – that he was a businessman, at the hotel coincidentally – she had not believed from the word go. Her uncle had been an agent in the war, she told him, and she 'knew the signs'. Bill had been curious about the uncle, but relentlessly circumspect about his own job, and they had agreed a truce. He was in security, that was the 'business', but she would not pursue it. Of Uncle Edward, though, they talked a lot. It was why he had to see her.

Twelve weeks? Thirteen weeks? He could not remember in precise terms any more. He had found it wonderful, and easy, and relief, and Jane had looked into the future and seen the truth. They had parted without real bitterness, although his private anger had shocked him when it dawned on him at last that she meant every farewell word and that she'd keep to it with grim determination. It was her fate, she had decided. Attractive, intelligent, house-trained – and doomed to end up in affairs that could not last. It was her fate, but she would buck it and go on bucking it, she would not go under. She had made Bill promise not to contact her again, and he had kept the promise, for an eternity. Once, eighteen months ago, he had rung and a man had answered and he had put the phone down. Then later, hearing she had moved, he had got the number from Colin Smart and tried again, not even certain why, or what he'd say if she picked up the receiver. But an old dear did, who said that Jane was out, which whetted his curiosity and his appetite to know her circumstances. It was only after he had spoken to a succession of old dears, male and female, that he got one who was sufficiently unbatty to tell him his mistake. It was a twilight home; pre-cemetery. He had not rechecked with Colin. Let fate be the decider . . .

* * *

When the train pulled into Euston – four minutes early – Bill Wiley was fully asleep. In true British fashion nobody woke him, probably because he looked so disreputable, and he opened his eyes to those of a startled black woman with a plastic bag and duster, who hoped he was not drunk. Bill smiled at her and dragged himself upright, but she pursed her lips at him, making a hmphing noise. Apart from a crush at the exit barrier, the platform was almost empty.

First, clothes. He emerged from Euston Station into a muggy London day, and turned back on himself to the King's Cross hinterland. On a whim, to wash the whisky staleness from his mouth, he went into a big Victorian pub and took a half of Guinness. The barman and all the customers he could hear were Irish, which amused Bill. The warm weight of the nine-millimetre Browning was intrusive and significant, although he doubted if many of the people in this pub would have recognized it. They looked like south and western men, across the water for an age, labourers perhaps, or dossers. In an English pub, a London Irish house, he was invisible.

The drink done, Bill wandered further into King's Cross and found a good, cheap clothes shop. He bought a pair of dark trousers, lightweight and anonymous, some socks and pants, two quiet shirts. Two doors away he got a pair of leather shoes, and further on a light wool jumper. The bomber jacket, assessed in a shop mirror, looked all right. Standard and respectable for the time of year, for summer '87. And it had the special stitching, fabric reinforced, for the automatic. He bought a small, light nylon bag to put the clothes in, a pack of razors and some shaving foam, a toothbrush, toothpaste, underarm deodorant, soap and flannel. Then he returned to Euston Station, washed and shaved and cleaned his teeth, and went into a cubicle to change. He tried a shit, but the whisky had bound his bowels, so he gave that up after five minutes. His old clothes he left neatly on the floor. London, he noted, was full of dossers these days, it reeked of poverty. Someone might find them and consider it a stroke of luck, you never knew. He took the Victoria Line to Green Park, ten minutes and another world. No dossers visible among the tourists and the wealthy. The few cars in the plate-glass showroom window behind which Colin worked were worth a million.

Colin spotted him as he came through the open glass doors, and made his pleasure clear. He bustled across, much older than his

74

years, beaming. Bill's response was more ambivalent. He was the same age as Colin, but he was much younger, the same background and education, but of a different planet, there was no way in the world he would have been there on business. It came to him that he was beginning to be an oddity, outside normal life. The gun beside his chest, which for years had been a part of him, had started to intrude, like the roots of a carbuncle growing in. He was *aware* of it.

They went for a quick drink and a sandwich, up New Bond Street, a surprisingly noisy and insalubrious pub. Colin was effusive, Bill guarded, and the racket from the juke box and the lunchtime office crush made a useful barrier to conversation. Colin was not the sort to ask too many questions, preferring to tell Bill the technical details of the BMW he had got for him, so the time passed painlessly. He was given Jane Heywood's address, a street map of Oxford – you think of everything, Col, you're a mate – and a hand-drawn map of Old Windsor and Colin's flat, in case he had forgotten how to get there. The BMW was parked in a narrow sidestreet behind the showroom 'where most of the damage gets done, collecting and delivering, it's crazy'. He got another briefing, an exhortation to make it back early enough that evening for a pint or two of Courage in Colin's new, terrific 'local', and a rundown on how to reach the M40 from where they were. Bill smiled, nodded, agreed, waited.

Finally, Colin Smart said: 'I'm not doing wrong, am I, Bill? I'm not making a mistake, putting you in touch with Jane after all this time?'

Bill shook his head.

'Business, like I told you. There's nothing between us, Col, there couldn't be. For God's sake man, d'you think I'm crazy? I'll see you tonight. I'll tell you all about it.'

The traffic was appalling. It got worse visibly, ridiculously, every time he came to London. For nearly an hour, he never got the sporty little BMW out of third. The M40 was a disaster, too. Not so much a motorway, more a three-lane crawl. This country's grinding to a halt, he thought. In Oxford he stopped and had a cup of coffee, studying the map. He was nervous, physically uncomfortable. He went to the lavatory, again without success, and drank more coffee, read a paper. He wondered if Jane worked at one of the colleges, or if she worked at all, except at home. It was late afternoon. Even if she went into an office she might be back. She was not married,

Colin had said, but as to a boyfriend, who knew? Bill ran his forefinger along the route he had pencilled in, then paid his bill. The unease in his stomach did not go away.

It was a terrace in a long one-way street. He had to park a hundred yards away and walk. The house was narrow, with lace curtains, neat and unexpected. The front door was bright yellow. Bill pressed the doorbell and heard it buzz. After a few moments he heard footsteps. He heard the Yale lock turn.

Jane Heywood stood in front of him in jeans and a lemon-coloured shirt. Her hair was shorter, her face older, her eyes wide and startled. Bill Wiley felt as if he was going to drop.

'Christ,' she said. 'Bill. What do you want?'

'What do you know about Rudolf Hess?' he said.

TEN

As an introduction line, after all that time and all that had passed between them, it was absurd. It had not been calculated, but it worked. Jane Heywood, instantly, was laughing. Bill felt that keenly, not as relief but pain. She had always laughed, he had always made her laugh. It hurt.

'Rudolf Hess?' she said. 'Not a lot. Not enough to detain you, Mr Wiley. You'd best come in.'

She had changed, and Bill wanted to pin it down, isolate the elements of the change. Her hair was shorter, and in a style he thought of as 'old-fashioned'. It was dark and clingy, close to her skull and sticking to the sides of her neck, just behind her square jawbone, in small, assertive strands. Her eyes, still, were startling, frank and very grey and widely set, unflinching, but the new hair made her even more bold, somehow. She was alive with intelligence, snub-nosed, strong-chinned, and massively unafraid. Bill pictured her in a flapper dress, taking on the world, and simultaneously pictured his wife, pale and drooping, drugged and miserable. He thought: I ought to go. I ought to turn and run. Jane turned, and he followed her into the house.

It was very tiny, and furnished in the style he remembered from Brixton. He remembered some of the furnishings as well, and some of the ornaments. The sofa they had made love on sometimes, once during breakfast. The toaster – faulty – had failed to pop the slices out, and they had finished amid clouds of smoke gushing from the kitchen, and gales of laughter. Jane had been at the square table working when he had rung the bell, and she returned to it, sitting on a hard dining chair with a loose floral cushion, surrounded by her notes and books. She indicated an easy chair for Bill, who took it, sinking into the upholstery, looking upwards into her face darkened by the window light behind it, feeling he might sink forever. Fuck, he thought. Wiley, pull yourself together, man. Think of someone else. Veronica, Chris, anybody. Fuck.

Jane said: 'I'll get you a coffee in a minute. I felt really queer,

77

seeing you standing there. I was halfway through a sentence. The best thing is to try and finish it, does that sound ridiculous? Deathless prose. Anyway, I've got to make a living.'

Whyever she'd done it, he accepted. Better not to talk. Jane bent her head, picked up a ballpoint, wrote. When she concentrated, she moved her mouth slightly, as if chewing on a secret. Sometimes the tip of her tongue appeared between her lips, then slipped out of sight. She rested her weight on her left elbow, wrote quickly, determinedly, hunched over the paper. Bill looked round the room, fought the hollowness inside, breathed more evenly. There was a clock on the mantelpiece, a thirties or a fifties clock, like a polished humpback bridge. It ticked softly. He was soothed.

'*Voilà*,' said Jane, after five minutes. 'Sorry about that. Was that sense? Thoughts don't come often enough to let them get away, in any case, not good ones. Look, my hand's trembling. You bastard. What do you want?'

She looked straight at him, and her eyes, maybe, were not quite so unafraid as he had thought. She jumped up, turned towards the kitchen at her back. As she did so, the sun shone through her lemon shirt and Bill, for the fraction of a second, saw her breast outlined, pictured as if naked, the nipple, everything. Then it was gone and Jane was in the kitchen doorway, her back to him.

'Coffee,' she said. 'Instant. No sugar, splash of milk. I'm going to close the door. Sorry. Read the paper.'

Bill Wiley could smell sweat, sharp, from his own armpits. He stood, looking round the room, thinking of her outlined breast. The room, even though knocked through from front to back of the terrace, was very small. It was pale, oatmeal and green, with a sofa-bed in the front window, a TV set, a stereo, three armchairs and a lot of fat beanbag cushions that one could sit or sink on. Or make love. He studied the pictures, too modern for his taste, gaudy daubs that no doubt cost the earth. He picked up the paper and dropped it. The *Guardian*. He did not trust himself to read the *Guardian*.

Jane's face was serious when she returned. She put the coffee mugs on a corner of the table, and quickly swept her notes into a pile. She put them to one side, collected up the books, and piled them on the notes, leaving most of the table clear. She put her mug on one side, nearest the kitchen door, and slid Bill's to the place opposite. She sat and took a sip. Wiley, hesitating briefly, sat opposite. They both drank.

'You said you wouldn't get in touch,' she said at last. 'It's years, it's over two, it's getting on for three. What went wrong?'

She was not smiling. The clear grey eyes avoided his.

'I thought you wouldn't mind. Not after so long. I thought you'd be married or something. Have another bloke. I didn't think it would matter that much.'

'It doesn't. It shouldn't, anyway. I mean, it shouldn't mean a thing, should it? A few months a long time ago. Oh, I don't know. It's still a shock. Don't you feel that?'

'Yeah. Worse than I expected. Although I was expecting something.'

She glanced at him. Then away.

'What? As the injured party? The one who got the bum's rush?'

'No, no. No, Christ Jane. I'm not that stupid. No, I meant . . . I had anticipation to contend with. I knew I was coming. Ringing the doorbell. Waiting. At least you had no idea who was out there. It could've been the milkman.'

'Mm.'

They drank their coffee. Bill studied her, in detail, surreptitiously, ready to withdraw his gaze. She was recovering, relaxing. So was he. She was just a woman. Someone he had liked or loved. Nothing ultra special. She glanced up, caught him at it. They both smiled, their eyes level.

'You've deteriorated,' she said. 'You look older. Your back's not straight. Did you get made redundant, or something? You look battered.'

Wiley laughed aloud.

'You cheeky bitch. It's probably old age. You don't look so hot yourself. Anyway, you always said I was a secret service man. They don't get made redundant, do they?'

'You tell me. And come on, Wiley! If you're not a secret service man, why are you asking about Rudolf Hess? I wasn't born exactly yesterday, you know. Or have you become a historian as well? That would explain the drab dull look, at least!'

He had thought this out. His cover story. He was still in business but on his own these days, he was in consultancy, research. He had been approached by a man who was thinking of putting money into a new book on the Hess affair, who had been convinced that there was in fact a conspiracy afoot but wanted independent views before he parted with the cash. There was, he told her disingenuously – taking his information and his cue from Mr Boswell – a whole group of people, in several countries, who were sure that something fishy was being covered up. It sounded cracked to him, but it was money, so why not?

The wide grey eyes were unreadable.

'Two things,' said Jane. 'Why me, why you? I'm not an expert on the era, which I'm sure you know quite well, and if this supposed backer wants an opinion on the Hess affair and you know nothing about it, why go to you? I've heard of the Hess freaks, what historian hasn't? Why doesn't your mystery backer ask a Hess freak?'

'Because it's one of them that wants his money. He needs an independent voice. A bit of background. A cool-hand Luke. Me.'

'I don't believe you.'

So that was that. Impasse. Bill Wiley thought again. He thought of options. He could not see any.

'Your Uncle Edward,' he said.

'Ah.'

Jane Heywood was angry, although she tried to hide it. His ploy had been pathetic, and it was blown. Should she have been flattered that he had come to see her, or have slammed the door in his face? Academic. He had not come to see her after all. Bill, gleaning all this from her face, wondered what he should have said. 'Look, I need your help, I've been told to murder Hess?' Maybe not . . .

'Perhaps you'd better go,' said Jane. 'I'm not an expert but Edward is, your memory does you credit. But he's hardly going to talk to you about it, is he? Bill, you're bullshitting, you're lying, I don't know what you're up to. Let's change back to realities, shall we? How's your wife? How's your life? What have you been doing these last few years?'

He had hurt her, she was fighting back. Bill said: 'Jane. I am an agent. Don't boot me out, please. Listen.'

It sounded ridiculous. There wasn't any way of saying it that did not sound ridiculous. To think he'd once been proud of it, felt special. How Liz must have hated him, despised him. An agent. A secret agent. A spy. An eternal adolescent, with a gun.

Robert Nairac always used the same gun. An obscure automatic. A Star. You could trace his history by it. Ridiculous.

'An agent,' repeated Jane. She added, melodramatically. 'At last the truth is out! What, MI5, MI6? Should I be thrilled?'

'Piss off,' said Bill, gently. The whole thing seemed hopeless, impossible. 'I shouldn't have told you,' he said. 'We were talking about my wife.'

Something in his face slowed her down. She dropped the mockery.

'Go on.'

'There's not a lot to tell. She's in a bad way. We live in Ireland now, the North. I'm attached to a brigade. The Army. We live in married quarters and I roam the countryside running sources, as we call it. Handling a variety of crooks, and traitors, and idealists. They tell me things about the terrorists for money or for other reasons, and I feed the information into the melting pot. We all try to stay alive.'

'And Liz is in a bad way. Why, exactly?'

Exactly, Bill Wiley did not think he knew. Perhaps he did. Perhaps he was beginning to.

'Perhaps it's not much fun,' he said. 'They sit there in their little boxes while the men live lives. At the top of the estate, at the gateway in the wire, there's a sentry post, men with machine guns, you know. Inside, well in, there's the brigadier's house, out of RPG range, armed guards all round it, searchlights, maximum security. How many brigadiers have died in Ireland in twenty years? How many have seen a terrorist, face to face? The wives drink and talk about nappy rash and going home to England, and watch blue films sometimes and have hen parties, and wonder why there's no guards or searchlights on their houses, and risk the occasional quick fuck with their friend's husband while she's shopping or inside for a scrape. Only occasionally, though, because estates have eyes and ears, especially married quarters. And the wages of this particular sin is death, give or take being still alive at the end of it. Black eyes and ostracism. Beatings behind walls that the stone deaf could hear through. "And where's your man?" In Liz's case, at work. Morning noon and night, day after day, day after day.'

He was looking into the bottom of his mug. It was empty. Jane said nothing. Bill Wiley sighed.

'I should have left her and run away with you,' he said. 'I think I was in love with you, probably. Do you remember I had a son? Johnnie? He's eleven now. It was his birthday yesterday. No, day before. He watches me and Liz and it tears my guts to pieces.' He raised his eyes to hers, ruefully. 'Excuses in advance. The coward's way out. I can't leave her now because of him.'

There was a long silence. Jane stood, and took both mugs through to the kitchen. This time she left the door open. The kettle clicked, and soon began to sing and buzz. He heard the coffee jar lid snap off, a spoon tinkle. The kettle clicked and the boiling water splashed into the mugs. She returned.

'Not,' said Bill Wiley, as she sat, 'that I'm expecting you to want me back. I'm not insane, I just express myself badly. I'm sorry if that was how it sounded.'

She moved her head. A small negative.

'I'm sorry, Bill. It sounds terrible. And is there nothing you can do? I mean, can't you leave, or anything? Don't they give you time off? Compassionate? And what's this Hess stuff? I mean, what's that got to do with it? Why *did* you come to me?'

'Oh, it's all too complicated. I can't bear to think about it. Tell me about you. How have *you* been? You're not married. Is there . . . ? I suppose I'm not entitled to ask, really.'

He was looking lost, feeling exhausted. Jane decided something.

'Uncle Edward's still here, of course,' she said, 'he still has his rooms in college. I'm having dinner with him tomorrow night, do you want to come? He knows much more than I do about the Hess thing, but then you know that, don't you, it's why you're here, you bastard.'

'Would he have me, though? I mean, I don't know him from Adam. It would be terrific.'

She said, drily: 'He likes a foursome. He'll probably call you Arthur, it amuses him.'

'Oh. Is Arthur . . . ?'

'Arthur went twice. Other men have been more frequently, but Edward disliked the name more particularly than most, so he tends to call everybody Arthur. He's a typical academic historian in many ways. He lives a pose, he's quite Establishment. He's highly unlikely to tell you anything you don't already know.'

'You don't like him?'

'Of course I like him! I adore him. And he's not like all the others really, not underneath. He poses, but he's not got their pomposity. He's not jealous of what he knows, he doesn't insist that everything he says is Holy Writ. If he likes you he might surprise both of us, it's possible, there's even a chance your job might swing it, all spies together and all that, although I severely doubt it. Listen, tell me. Why do you want to know?'

Bill Wiley, fatuously, looked at his wristwatch.

'Christ,' mocked Jane. 'Is that the time! Must rush!'

Bill, caught, reddened faintly.

'No,' he lied. 'I was thinking of my belly. How about dinner tonight? *A deux*?'

'I have a date already, thank you. And intimate dinners are not on the agenda, OK? Be here for sevenish tomorrow and we'll have a drink before we go. And Bill. I'll want some answers. So will Edward. He won't like it if you waste his time. You'll be an Arthur to the end.'

'I'll see what I can do. I have stopped lying. Started stopping.'

'You're a bloody marvel.'

Back at Colin's, before they raced out to the pub, Bill rang home. Liz answered, and her voice was brisker than it had been the night before. She sounded vexed.

'Bill, where are you? They've sent men round. Colonel A's been on. Furious.'

'What did you tell him?'

'What you said. In the North somewhere, undercover, you'd be in touch.'

His heart lifted. Affection, unexpected, for her.

'Good work.'

'Oh yes? That's what you think. He put the phone down. An hour later the men arrived. Bill, what are you up to?'

'Nothing to worry about. It'll only take a day or two more. How's my boy? Can I speak to him?'

'He's at Tim Foster's. Chess. Bill, they asked about him, too. They said they might come back.'

'What!'

The lift in his heart turned to a plummet. No reason for it, he told himself. That was stupid, insane. His breath had become jerky.

His wife repeated it. The men had asked about Johnnie. What school he went to, the times he finished. Wiley swallowed. He said nothing.

'Bill?'

He cleared his brain. They were probably men who knew him. Being pleasant. Softening the blow of turning up because he'd disappeared. He licked his lips.

'OK,' he said. 'Nothing to worry about. Look, I'll see you in a day or two. They won't come back, they know it's not to do with you. How are you feeling, you sound better?'

'Not so bad. I only took one pill today. I've run out, I almost panicked. But I'll last out till morning. You're not here upsetting me, are you? I'll see the MO in the morning.'

The MO, the Army doctor, who smoothed the pathways with his pills. Smoothed the pathways for the Army, not his patients. His first duty was to the Army, it was in his oath, the Army was his moral arbiter, not Hippocrates. Bill felt the old arguments, the old pleas, rising in his mind, but he held back on them. Time later to sort her out, to save her, when he was out of it, the mess was finished.

'OK. You do what you think's best. Give a kiss to Johnnie for me, right? And don't worry. They won't come back.' ·

After that, with Colin hopping impatiently in the plush cream passageway, he rang Veronica's number. He might get David, but so be it.

There was no reply.

ELEVEN

In the morning, he drove into London with Colin. They were both hung over, so conversation was no problem. Which was a blessing, because in the pub the night before they'd talked each other out on beer and had had to go on whisky. Nice fellow that he was, Colin Smart held little interest and few mysteries for Wiley. He wondered, as he had done often in the past, what Susan had seen in him. After breakfast he had asked for a lift, as he had business in London and did not fancy taking the BMW. He would find his own way back, probably take a kip before his date with Jane.

He rang headquarters more in hope than expectation, but was put straight through. The pause was only long enough for the switchboard to announce his name.

'Well,' said Silversmith. 'Well, well. Where are you, Bill? We've got to talk. This is getting serious.'

'I'm in London. I'll meet you, but you'll have to come alone. No messing.'

He was standing in a phone cowl in Euston Station, where he had waited for ten minutes to get a phone. It was noisy and specific.

'Sounds like a station,' said Silversmith. 'Euston's nearest. Shall I send a car for you?'

'I said no messing. No games. I've been hearing things from home. Things I don't like.'

'Fair enough. You can trust me, Bill. No silly stuff. Can I bring Peter-Joe? He's in the office.'

'On your own. You know the Museum? The pub? Meet me there in half an hour.'

'It's very crowded, Bill.'

Wiley hung up.

'Precisely,' he said.

The pub, indeed, was heaving, a mixture of passing trade, and office workers, and tourists. Wiley perched himself at the corner of a table full of Japanese, not asking them, because he figured they would soon be leaving. Their glasses were well down, and they

85

would be too busy taking pictures to bother with more Western drinks. His timing was lucky. As the table cleared and he slipped along the side facing the door, Silversmith limped in. Not limped, exactly, Bill Wiley thought: more hove himself along. It was effortful, but his face betrayed no effort. He saw Bill, smiled widely, noted his full glass, bought himself a pint of bitter. In the meantime, Wiley fended off takers. Their side of the table was kept clear.

'Now then,' said Silversmith, craning himself into his seat. He glanced at the couple opposite. Students or the like, young, chattering, self-absorbed. 'What's it all about, Bill? What's been going on? You're beginning to get up people's noses.'

The steely eyes were calm, the grey-fringed face quite friendly. Wiley wondered where this man was in the hierarchy of the outfit, and guessed at very high. There was not, nor ever would be, any way of confirming that.

'It gets up my nose,' he replied. 'I spoke to Liz last night. My wife. She says the lads came round. Asked questions. Put on the frighteners. Asked about my little boy. It's got to stop, Terry. That sort of thing's not on. We're not in fucking Russia.'

Silversmith smiled.

'You're sounding paranoid,' he said. 'If you don't mind me saying so. What would you expect us to do in the circumstances? I asked you to do a job with me and you disappear. Of course we sent men round. For all we know you might have been up a lamp-post. Under the bed gibbering, hiding in the airing cupboard. Stranger things have happened, haven't they?'

'I left a message. I can read your sub-text, Silversmith. I'm warning you.'

'You left a pack of lies. You're hardly in a position, I'd have thought, to issue warnings. And as for sub-text, you're sounding like a proper prat. This is a business, not a drama school. You're paid to do a job.'

The couple opposite paused for a second, as if the words 'sub-text' and 'drama' had flicked a trigger in their heads. Their lips came together and parted, they re-entered their private world. Both men were aware that they had roused attention.

Wiley said quietly: 'I'm sorting something out. I told you, and I told Boswell. Both of you said go ahead, both of you said the final choice was mine. Fucking hell, what is this deal? I'll probably come back and do it, I just need time to get my thoughts together. You know what the sub-text is, don't try to kid me that you don't. We're talking Holroyd. We're talking little threats, psychology. "Stranger things have happened", my arse! "Under the bed gibbering". Who do you think you're kidding?'

Silversmith wiped his lips.

'I'm surprised you believe that Holroyd claptrap,' he said mildly. 'As far as I'm concerned, he was put away because he needed it. Stress. It had got to him. But true or false, I'll tell you this. We won't pull any stunt like that on you. Honest injun. The trouble is, you've put us on the spot. It was all voluntary, I told you and I don't lie. Boswell, too. But it's getting less so by the minute, son. You must know why?'

'Tell me.'

'You're getting away from us. People feel it. People don't like that. This op is big, important, gigantic. Decided by the highest in the realm. It's not pleasant, but it's necessary, and it's delicate. You're a subtle man, a foil to our Peter-Joe, God bless him. You're one of us, as they see it. Not top-drawer, not a chinless wonder, but good solid grammar school stock, intelligent, a brick. No one's going to do a Holroyd on you, but you've got to mend your ways.'

Wiley had finished his drink. He needed a piss, quite badly. The supreme irrelevance of bodily functions. The need attacked his concentration, blunted it.

'So it's no longer voluntary, but if I refuse you pull no stunts on me? No trips to the funny farm with my arms tied round my back?'

'Absolutely not. See sense. You're a good operator, a star. We want you in. We don't want to lose contact again. Time's getting short.'

'Hm. Will I be followed? Out of here?'

'Nah. Don't disappear, Bill. Please. Your wife and kid, too, remember? They need you. We'll be leaving soon. For Germany.'

'I said I spoke to Liz. She sounded fine.'

The Widowmaker drank his last two mouthfuls. He placed the glass on the wet and dirty table-top.

'I'm very glad to hear it. If she wasn't, for instance, think of the boy. What would happen to him? Are you coming? To the office?'

A pause. What would happen to the boy?

'No. Things to do. Later maybe. I'll be in touch.'

87

The lean, strong face remained impassive. Silversmith ground to his feet, holding the table-top and his chair-back for support. The students glanced at him, curious for a moment.

'I'm going for a pee,' said Bill.

When he returned, two Americans sat at the table with the students. Silversmith had gone.

Edward Carrington — the oldest fellow in his college if not the most distinguished — enjoyed the trappings of a feudal lord. His rooms were extensive, the furnishings of another era, and his reputation distinctly odd. He answered the door to Jane and Bill Wiley in person, and to Bill it had an air of theatricality, an 'entrance' in reverse. He did not look at Bill, but ravished his niece with his eyes, through half-glasses, holding both her hands in both of his. When he had gazed, he moved in to kiss, soundly, on both cheeks. Then he smiled up at Bill, and nodded.

'You must be Arthur. No! That's bad of me. Jane?'

'This is Bill, Uncle. An old friend. You must be especially nice to him because he's come a long way just to see you. He's in the secret services.'

It was nicely timed, Bill thought, but fielded consummately. A small smile flickered on the strong, thin face. The academic, sprucely dressed, adjusted the blue wool scarf that dangled incongruously at his lapels.

'But surely not?' he said. 'If he was, after all, you would not know? Isn't that the rule, young man?'

The eyes above the halfmoon lenses were only slightly paler than the scarf, and despite a certain ageing, very keen. There was speculation in them, knowledge. Bill had no doubts: this man had been in the business at some time. Before he could reply, however, Edward's wife appeared.

'Hallo,' she said. 'Jane. How nice to see you!'

Had Wiley not been warned, he would have been thrown, perhaps. Mrs Carrington — Erica — was very old and frail, much frailer than her husband. She was stooped, tiny, and walked with a stick. She spoke indistinctly, slowly, her accent impossible to place by class or region. Jane had told him it was arthritic, a condition of the jaw. Following them into the sitting room, matching his pace to theirs, he was laughing inwardly. Jane had been right, he'd learn

88

nothing here, it was a social situation as crazy as a regimental dinner. He'd be an Arthur all his life.

Maybe he would have been. For, like the men Bill had suffered at those awful dinners, Edward seemed at first prepared to play the games he could not stand, or understand. The patrician and the pleb, the master and the man, the Oxford fellow and the boy from grammar school. Bill challenged him not from courage but from a sudden gloom. If it was to be a waste of time, entirely, he would blow it fast, and leave disgracefully. The game was no longer worth the candle.

It started with the sherry, which was poured, to Bill's astonishment, by servants. It was a very rare pale fino – Edward told him so – and he circumspectly agreed that it was excellent. So far so good. Jane was watching him, and grinned encouragement. Was it her joke? A small revenge? Erica, despite the difficulty she had in articulating certain words, was kind and charming. He tried to look relaxed, not to search too hard for small talk. He caught Edward watching him, and there was something behind his eyes.

The servants – as if it were the most natural thing imaginable – reappeared when they were seated round the oval table, to produce tiny mounds of hot poached salmon. Edward, however, served the wine, which he had on a double-decker trolley parked next to him, his 'mobile cellar'. They started with a Mâcon, that he spoke of almost as an old and valued friend. He held his nose above the glass, he tasted, savoured, and watched Bill taste. He raised his eyebrows in enquiry.

'Any comments? I have this from a man I've known for more than twenty years, he bottles it for himself and half a dozen intimates. The bouquet alone is worth a hundred pounds. *Nicht wahr?*'

Bill put his glass down.

'I'm sorry, sir, I'll have to risk offending you. To me it's just a wine. Very pleasant, but just a glass of wine. We're not necessarily gentlemen these days, in the service, you know. Times have changed.'

Erica Carrington made a noise that could have been a laugh. She had a severe face, somehow sad, with dusty, failing eyes. Now she smiled.

'Bravo,' she said. 'But please don't call him "sir", Bill, we can't have that. Edward's not a gentleman, he just has lots of money that I like to spend. In college, certain things are expected of us.'

Jane said: 'Aunt Erica likes to keep him in his place, Bill. He's an awful old sod, aren't you, love?'

In an officers' mess, at a regimental dinner, this would have been disaster. But Edward Carrington only smiled. The challenge, apparently, had paid off.

'At least I'm not a philistine,' he said quietly, to Bill. 'And it's a damn good glass of wine whichever way you drink it.' He paused, almost imperceptibly. 'Why did you talk of "the service" like that, you seemed to be including me. What damned nonsense has my lovely niece been feeding you? I'm an historian. And a wine bore. That's all.'

Bill had relaxed. He took a large mouthful of the wine. It was indeed delightful.

'I just thought you were in the business. In fact I'd put money on it. A hunch.'

'Tosh. Jane rang. She said you wanted something. Something to do with Rudolf Hess. She said you were a consultant. What are you? MI6?'

Bill checked the women, although he was not sure why. They were talking, heads together. Erica held a napkin close beneath her chin.

'It's hard to say who I'm with,' he said. He wasn't going to tell the truth, either, but he would skate around it. 'I started in the Army, like most of us. Volunteered for Intelligence, got taken up by the Regiment, SAS, then got run by SIS. Ireland changed a lot of things, some politicians got angry, tried smacking wrists, a lot of distinctions began to blur for one reason and another. I've been hired out, loaned to the cousins, done freelance stuff, you name it. I imagine it was all much simpler in your time? More straight-forward?'

Edward filled his mouth with food. He chewed it, swallowed, replaced the food with wine. He appeared to be enjoying himself, the games were over, but he was still considering.

'That's a pretty obvious come-on line,' he said at last. 'But I'll rise to it, what the hell? The temptation to say nothing's very ingrained, one gets so used to sitting on the past, especially as an historian in a place like this. There are a number of us you know, ex-spooks, although more in Cambridge than this place, and none of us ever mentions it, or talks about those times. Gentlemen, you see, you were quite right, it was the tradition. Although God knows, the things we did were hardly fitting, were they? Erica's right, I was never fully of the breed, I just had the wherewithal. And no, it wasn't that much simpler, the confusion level sounds quite familiar. I was recruited privately to start with, someone liked the cut of my jib as they said in those days. It was Churchill's crew who grabbed me, before the war, but they didn't have much clout, it was fairly ludicrous. Being a linguist saved my bacon. Still dabble.'

The salmon was finished and the servants, two quiet men with black suits and stone faces, cleared away. Edward busied himself with a bottle, a red Bordeaux that was already open. The women had keyed back into the conversation, interested.

Aunt Erica said: 'In those days, Bill, it was very amateurish. Not just the spies. The government as well. There was hardly a mister among them, you know. In the Cabinet. They were all sirs, or lords, or scions of mighty families. All incompetents and fools. They had sex problems, too. The public schools in this country have got a lot to answer for.'

'My wife was something of an expert in her younger days,' said Edward. 'I went to public school as well, but I was lucky. Very minor and most unfashionable. By the time I left I knew damn well which way up I liked *my* partners.'

'Quantity was Edward's only trouble,' responded Erica. 'Sometimes I think he's never going to stop.'

Bill stared at Jane, and Jane was laughing. Jesus Christ, a madhouse! But now, he was beginning to enjoy. Jane winked at him. It had been worth the candle, after all.

Later, they got onto Rudolf Hess and Edward Carrington became more foxy, although Bill did not at first detect it. The subject was approached quite openly, he thought.

'The whole thing is a myth, you know,' said Edward. 'A modern one. Haushofer described Hess as a motorised Parsifal, and he wasn't meaning it to be insulting. The truth of the whole affair hardly matters in a way, it's not important.'

'Except to Hess,' Jane put in. 'The poor old prisoner of Spandau. I doubt if being Parsifal means much to him these days, motorised or not.'

Edward fixed Bill across the spectacles.

91

'But is it Hess in Spandau?' he asked. 'What do you think? Just exactly which part of the myth do you suppose I can illuminate?'

Jane could see through Bill, the profundity of his ignorance. Her eyes were dancing. He avoided them, took a sip of port.

'I think he is confused,' she said, quite gently. 'Maybe agents are more literal these days, Edward. Enough of myths, forget them for the moment.'

'All right,' said Edward Carrington. 'I'll un-confuse you, first. Hess flew on May the tenth, 1941, from Augsburg, all agreed? He parachuted in at Floors Farm, near Eaglesham, south of Glasgow five or six hours later, at just after eleven in the evening. A Saturday. A farmhand called Davie Maclean found him hobbling about, and took him into his kitchen. The Home Guard came. The police. The Army. They took the man away to Maryhill and kept him overnight. He said his name was Alfred Horn. He also said he'd "popped across" to see "his friend" the Duke of Hamilton, to make peace between Germany and Britain. Any voices of dissent?'

Bill, although he'd known almost none of this, shook his head. Aunt Erica was peeling grapes.

'Next day the Duke of Hamilton, who was Wing Commander the Duke of Hamilton, RAF Turnhouse, near Edinburgh, went to see the man, who told him he was Hitler's deputy, and that they'd met in Germany, some years before. Hamilton was prepared to agree, although he didn't recognize him, and he flew a Hurricane to Northolt airport, near London. Then he drove to Ditchley Park, in Oxfordshire, where Churchill was weekending with some friends. Hamilton was a friend of his as well, and also of the King, which was lucky for our Rudolf, wasn't it, such good connections! Not so. For Churchill said words to the effect that he didn't care who had just dropped in from the sky – Hess or Parsifal or God himself – he was going to watch a Marx Brothers film. A strange reaction, possibly, but then the tale is full of little oddities, isn't it? The film the Great Man watched, for instance, was called *Go West*. And Frau Hess, back in Germany, was reading a book by Hamilton the night her husband flew, it's no wonder people worry at it, I'm afraid. Whatever, next morning – Monday – Hamilton and a Foreign Office German expert were sent north again to interview our man. The Foreign Office type was called Ivone Kirkpatrick, I knew him well.' He inclined his head at Bill. 'He was MI6. Don't let any historian tell you otherwise.'

A mouth noise came from Erica. She was trying to speak, wincing with the effort.

'They're very competitive, historians. Like little boys.'

Her husband smiled.

'Liars, all of us,' he said. 'But some are worse than others. Anyway, on this there's no dispute. Hamilton and IAK interviewed him exhaustively, and reported back. It was Hess, they said, no doubt of it at all. He did a few days in a Scottish military hospital at Drymen, to recover from a minor back injury and twisted ankle, then came to London on the night sleeper. Then five days in the Tower until his new quarters were ready – which meant wired up for sound, of course, in direct contravention of the international rules of warfare. We listened to him for about a year at Mytchett Place – it was a gloomy hole by all accounts, a nasty, damp house near Aldershot. He didn't say much, not much useful, that is – just generalized nonsense about how we and the Germans were natural friends, not enemies, and should join up to crush the Reds. He still wanted to see Hamilton – which was ruled out – and the King, which was ridiculous, and high-ups in the government, although not Churchill, whom he did not trust, and he claimed we were trying to poison him or drive him mad, or both. He got to see a couple of high-ups in the end, Lord Simon, then Beaverbrook, to show the Cabinet took him seriously, but it was all a blind. After a year or so he was quietly shipped off to Maindiff Court, South Wales. An ex-mental hospital, another little irony. Officially Hess was always sane.'

'Of course.' Erica's face was working. Indignation. 'If he'd been mad, we would have had to send him back. Geneva Convention. Bah!'

Edward made a gesture with his glass.

'Erica thinks such things important. We didn't bother then, except in rhetoric, of course. Enemies break the rules, one's own side never. Lord Simon actually shouted at Hess for daring to suggest his quarters might be bugged, although he naturally knew they were. He called it a Nazi slur on British honour. That's the way it went.'

'Bah!'

Carrington got up and went to stand beside his wife. She began to rise, with him helping her.

'Come on, old girl. Let's go and have some coffee in the sitting room. Bill, Jane?'

Aunt Erica, settled, soon regained composure. She had paled

slightly, was visibly tired. The clock on the wall, a handsome, round-faced clock, showed 9.20. The alcohol was warm in Bill, and Edward poured more port. They took deep armchairs, stretched out their legs. The silent men brought coffee, which Jane elected to dispense so that they might leave.

'So there you have it,' said Edward, when he was comfortable. 'The facts, the basic myth. Our Parsifal, a weird, misguided man, a hypochondriac, a believer in astrology and destiny, takes it into his head to fly to England one early summer day and sue for peace. Unfortunately, the story goes, he omits to clear this with his Führer, who really is insane, and seems to think that Churchill, our hero, our one and only legend in his time, is not the man to talk to on the subject because he's in reality a warmonger! Instead of getting to see the King, though, he gets to see the inside of the Tower, is adjudged a wittering idiot, and drops out of sight. We're so confused by the whole affair that we don't even announce he's come, until the Germans say on their radio that the Deputy Führer's had some sort of mental breakdown and disappeared by plane, they know not where. We make some ham-fisted, and belated, propaganda points which leave Goebbels gasping with delight at our ineptitude, and get our heads down. Ever after, the tale goes on, the man's a war criminal, useless but quite sane, whom we are keeping in safe custody until he can come to trial. When he's incarcerated at Spandau we make noises of compassion from time to time, along with France and America, but the Russians insist that Number Seven remains a prisoner for life, even after his six companion criminals have either died or been let out. Miserable swine these Russkis, don't you know? Inhuman.'

He stopped. He removed his spectacles and touched his eyes with a white handkerchief. Bill cleared his throat.

'And is that tale the true one, do you think? I mean . . . well, it's nothing, is it? Sad, but meaningless. You call it myth. But is it true, in fact?'

The spectacles remained in Edward's hand. The eyes turned inwards on themselves. In the pause there was the ticking of the handsome clock, a sucking noise from Aunt Erica's crippled mouth.

'What a question to ask an historian,' he said, at last. 'Of course it's true, as far as it goes. But how far does it go? Yes, Hess flew on Saturday, tenth of May. It was the night of the heaviest German air raid of the war. Coincidence? And after it, the raids virtually ceased, there was not another massive one, not ever. Coincidence? Hamilton and Hess did not know each other, we're told, but they shared certain odd interests and achievements, not least the fact that Hamilton was the first man to fly over Everest, and Hess the winner of mountain air races in Germany. Coincidence? Also, Hess flew to Scotland in an unarmed aeroplane, its cannons packed with factory grease. Scotland, as you can imagine, was swarming with fighter planes, but none of them was scrambled to pursue him, although that was to be denied and records changed. By whom? Hamilton. Why Hamilton? Because he was in command of fighter cover for Scotland that night. The very man that Hess set out to see. Coincidence? Good God, I should say so! Or would I?'

He put his glasses back on with a rapid movement, grinning like a schoolboy. He still had all his hair, although it was severely short and almost silver. His face was alive, attractive, amused.

'D'you know,' he said, 'the thing I love most about history is that it's all baloney. Lies, myths, romance. The arrogance of the human being, to think we can reconstruct what's gone before! Henry Ford said history is bunk. Or was it junk, or bunkum, or the bunkum or the bunk? You read letters in the *Guardian* from time to time arguing it out, with everybody claiming that their version is right. They miss the point, the only point. Henry Ford made a pronouncement about history, and *even that* has gone astray. The arguments themselves are actually the history, the actual *thing* is lost, the point is nobody can ever know for sure again. There had to be a counter-myth around poor Hess. It was inevitable.'

Jane, now that she knew how little Bill knew, helped him out.

'But some elements in the counter-myth are pretty powerful, aren't they, Edward? The fact that Hess was Hitler's deputy but the man who landed knew nothing about German policy? The fact that Hess was a non-smoker and the man who landed had a cigarette? The fact that Hess was more or less teetotal and the man who landed slurped whisky whenever he was given half a chance? Which' – she smiled at Bill – 'was far more often than you would have expected for a prisoner of war. The fact he ate his food like a peasant, and was a boor, and a fool and an oaf, according to his captors? I know what you'll say, you'll say circumstantial evidence. But what about the bullet wounds?' She turned back to Wiley. 'Rudolf Hess was shot through the lung in 1917. He was an infantry-man. He was in hospital for nearly four months, at a time when if you could stand, you were fit to fight, you had to be. He never fought again, in fact. He got fit enough, finally, to train to fly a plane, but the war ended before he saw action. The man in Spandau has no bullet wounds. No scars, in or out. That's a fact.'

Edward Carrington snickered.

'Not according to the government it isn't. The best and highest in the land say the scars are there. Not that anybody's allowed to look, of course. We must believe our government.'

'And who briefs the government? Who tells the ministers what to say?'

'Ask Bill,' said Edward. 'You know the answer to that one, don't you, Bill? The secret services. The old firm. Your firm.' To Jane, down his nose: 'You're not suggesting they'd tell lies! Good gracious!'

'Hang about,' said Bill. He was conscious that his level of urbanity had slipped, so tried again. 'I mean, sorry Edward, but what are you suggesting? That it's not a myth? I mean — you think it really isn't Hess in there? It's a ringer? A double?'

'Not at all,' said Edward. 'If it was a double, he would indeed be mad. He's been in prison since 1941, one way and another. That's forty-six years. If it wasn't Rudolf Hess, don't you think he might have mentioned it by now? Or do you imagine a life of contemplation was what Alfred Horn was seeking, when he flew his Bf110 across the sea to Scotland? It's completely ludicrous. Doctors make mistakes. Medical records get falsified, or confused. Maybe young Infantryman Hess was just a coward, bribed the medicos or something. Good lord, if there was a cover-up, it would be a monumental blot on Churchill's name for a start-off, but even Irving says it's Hess, no doubt in the world, have you seen his new book, Jane? Very, very fine. And David Irving's the most anti-Churchill of us all. He refuses to recognize the sainthood of the Blessed Winston! Whippersnapper!'

The eyes were gleaming, he was delighted with himself. A peculiar snorting emanated from Aunt Erica. Her hand was raised, she was struggling to speak.

'Churchill. Churchill. Churchill.' Her jaw worked, she had to catch a run of spittle in her handkerchief. Her eyes, blazing in her crumpled face, sought Bill's. 'He knows,' she said. 'Don't let him fool you, Bill, he knows. There are three people left alive who know the truth, possibly, and he's one of them. Don't let him fool you.'

Jane moved quickly to the old woman's side. Her hands were

trembling violently, her coffee cup had slewed sideways in its saucer. Jane put an arm about the thin shoulders, held her gently. Bill turned away, embarrassed. Edward was watching him.

'She doesn't like Winston,' he said, conversationally. 'She never did. She was an Attlee man, Red Erica we used to call her. Attlee, with a bit of time for Uncle Joe. To be fair, that was before we knew the facts, exactly. She went off Stalin, in the end.'

'And do you know? The true story?'

Edward tapped his nose.

'You're doing it again, Bill. "The true story." Do you know the Goering quote, you must do, everybody does. Goering is supposed to have said "When I hear the word culture I reach for my revolver" – and this from a man who loved fine art and artefacts, who cared for them so much that he looted them shamelessly in fact, from everywhere he could. What he actually said – I believe! – was "When I hear the word culture I reach for my Browning", which is, characteristically, a complex and rather brilliant joke, a paradox. It doesn't suit the British view of him, however, does it? So it was changed. Yes, maybe I do know what happened to Rudolf Hess, as well as anybody left alive. But am I right, and if I told you, would I tell the truth? I might have axes to grind, reputations to destroy, my own myths to foster or engender. Why should you believe me? The official myth is right, it's good enough for me, it's stood the test of time. Hess flew in 1941 and he'll die in Spandau, soon. How old is he? Ninety-three? It can't be very long now, can it?'

Bill said: 'If it is the real Hess, can you think of any reason why anyone should want to murder him?'

'What?'

Erica and Jane turned to him, too. Erica's jaw was in one thin hand.

'That's what I've heard,' he said. 'In fact, they wanted me to go along.'

It was Bill's last throw. It had occurred to him at last that for all his apparent frankness, Edward Carrington had given him very little. Jane had warned him that he might learn nothing that he did not already know, but his ignorance had blinded him into imagining he'd heard great revelations. Jane could have told him all these things, he realized, but there was more, much more. Unfortunately, Edward did not seem shaken.

'You're serious, aren't you?' he said. 'How very interesting. How fascinating.'

'Uncle!' Jane was shocked. 'It's appalling. Bill? It's not true, is it?'

He smiled a slightly crooked smile at her.

'I knew I never should have told the truth. We have to do some very nasty things.'

'All for your country,' said Aunt Erica. She made the funny noise, the laugh.

'But I refused,' said Bill. At least, he thought, I was revolted. I didn't say I would. That's the closest to the truth available. 'I wanted to find out why it was dreamed up, if possible. It seemed weird to me. Demented.'

Edward was nodding to himself, his glasses in his hand.

'Extraordinary,' he said. 'Most extraordinary. So many, many mysteries.'

But he would not talk of them. Not any more. History, he repeated infuriatingly, was merely junk. The truth was otherwhere.

TWELVE

Veronica Burnett tracked Bill down at last well after three o'clock next morning. He was in bed, but not asleep. The news she gave to him was frightening, and her voice was hoarse with tiredness, and fighting with her husband, and persuading a most reluctant Colin Smart to give the number. Within fifteen minutes, Bill was in the BMW, heading out of Oxford, heading for Whitehaven on the coast of Cumbria. He had been in bed with Jane.

The dinner party at Edward's rooms had broken up not long after Bill had said his piece, not precisely in confusion but less smoothly than everybody might have wished. Aunt Erica had become quite animated, and had spoken volubly despite her clicking, painful jaw. She had apparently been taunting Edward, challenging him to tell them things, and Bill had heard a word he took to be 'honours' or 'honoured' several times. Her husband had snapped at her, genuinely peeved, and flapped his hands and told her she should go to bed. Jane had calmed things down, warned Bill off further speech, and manoeuvred them into the lobby. Then kisses all round, and handshakes, and they had gone into the warm night, down ancient creaking stairs and across a quiet quadrangle lit mainly by the spill from students' windows. They had walked for some moments in silence.

'So,' said Jane. 'A murderer. An assassin. I feel like Macbeth. "Let it come down!"'

Bill felt obscurely hurt, although he had expected something. He had half expected Jane to refuse to walk with him.

'I have killed men,' he said. 'But I've never killed anyone I wasn't convinced deserved it.' He heard her sharp intake of breath. 'Men who blow up little kids,' he said. 'And women and old people and each other and anyone who might walk by. I'm not ashamed of that, Jane, whether they're monsters or misguided. Someone has to kill the cowards, or they make cowards of us all.'

She walked for many steps without replying. Oxford was quiet, although it was not very late. Their way was through peaceful roads.

'OK,' she said. 'I can handle that. Even the way Shakespeare's muscled in. I was going to ask if you believed they had a cause, a justification, but it doesn't really matter, here and now. I suppose no one has a right to blow up little children. Not even by mistake.'

Bill Wiley had killed people by mistake, although he did not think little children. The State, he now believed, claimed the right to kill anybody. He said neither of these things.

'It's easier not to talk about it,' he said. 'It's safer. In any case, it's against the law. For me to tell, or for you to listen. Can you believe that? What about your uncle? How d'you feel about him? He'll have killed more men than me. That was a proper war.'

Silence descended again. 'Let it come down!' Only that was rain, he remembered. When Banquo mentioned to one of his assassins that it looked like rain. 'Let it come down!' And drove the knife into the King.

'Perhaps you're right,' said Jane. 'Perhaps it's safer not to talk. It had never occurred to me that he might have killed. He's a historian. A bit of an old poser, a lovely old lad. He's broken hearts, that I do know. He still has students going ga-ga for him, students who are young enough to know better! I can't imagine it, can you?'

'What, Edward in the sack? God, I'd rather not. What about Erica? Don't tell me she's still at it? I nearly collapsed when Edward said she was an expert. Please tell me it's not true! That sweet old lady!'

They had reached Jane's front gate. She unlatched it and they walked up the pathway. Bill sniffed the sweet scent of the garden while she opened the front door.

'He probably meant on problems, not just sex,' said Jane. 'She's a lesbian, or was. It was a funny marriage. My father was always scandalized, although Mum didn't mind. He hated her. Politics as well as sex.'

Bill had been rocked.

'It's enough to make you say By Gum,' he said. 'That's a quote from Arthur Ransome, if we're into academic games. Why in hell's name did they marry?'

Jane pulled off her short wool jacket. She was in a dress, blue with white spots. She favoured blue. It favoured her. She pushed fronds of hair out of her eyes.

'Why does anyone? Marriages are a complete mystery to me. It wasn't just the sex with Edward and Red Erica, either, they've fought a war on every front for as long as I can remember. A friendly war usually, maybe that's the secret. Did you pick up on any of that about honours, at the end? That's a rich vein for her.'

She walked into the living room, flicking on the light. She drew the curtains, threw cushions around a bit. Bill, in his bomber jacket, stood in the doorway. She hadn't told him to go, she hadn't said anything. Let it develop. He'd been drinking, but he'd presumably have to drive. He didn't want to.

'I half heard. What did it mean?'

'Oh, Erica takes the piss unmercifully. She thinks he knows all sorts of dreadfully scurrilous things that any historian really worthy of the name would give his eye teeth to bring to light, and sits on them because he hasn't had his knighthood yet, and wants it. It's true all the other boring old farts are sir-something this or lord-something the other, and lots of them worked with him, apparently. In the same line.'

'It doesn't sound exactly logical. What does he say?'

'Well spotted. He says they've all had honours because they've agreed to keep their mouths shut and he won't, on principle. He's been approached, but he's refused. That's the system, actually, it's crafty, isn't it? If you're approached and you say no, it all remains dead secret, you can't make capital out of it.'

'Except if you're Aunt Erica.'

'Oh yes. Aunt Erica can and does. That's not a principle, she says, it's a bloody good excuse. The odd thing is that she's right in one way. As historians go, he's very much Establishment, he's never tried to rock the boat, whatever things he does know. He says the honours system is iniquitous, moral blackmail, buying off treacherous old dogs by throwing baubles, playing on their vanity, he'd rather die than take one. But he keeps his mouth shut. *Viz* Hess. Trust, he'll talk about if pushed. And real honour, as opposed to honours.'

'And Erica the Red just laughs. Poor sod!'

'She cackles. You should hear her with her teeth out!' Jane's mood seemed to change. The humour left her face. 'I don't think she's long for this world, really. She slips into senility from time to time. Forgetfulness. Falling over things. It's very sad.'

She went into the kitchen, and returned with a bottle of red wine and two glasses. She took the corkscrew from a sideboard drawer and handed it to Bill.

'Aren't you going to sit down? I suppose you're staying for a drink? Or are my family secrets boring you? Not shocking!? Edward's still quite right-wing really, isn't he? Although not like he used to be. He used to be really gung-ho British Empire when he was young, according to my mother. He only started backsliding when he met Erica, and that took years and years. She still calls him a blimp. God knows who's right about the honours thing. Or who's telling the truth.'

Bill pulled the cork. He poured two glasses. Jane took one and held it in salute.

'What is truth?' said Bill, ironically. 'Your uncle doesn't know! Here's to it.'

Jane sipped, and made a face.

'Christ. That's the difference, isn't it? How can a man who buys wine like Edward's ever be a socialist? Sorry about this — it tastes quite good till you have it after his.'

They talked some more, and Bill sat in front of the sofa, his back resting against it, his legs stretched out in front of him. Jane switched on the electric fire and perched her bottom on the arm of an easy chair. She did not look easy, though. There was a growing tension faintly in the air. Bill could see the inside of one of her thighs.

'Sit down with me,' he said. 'You look uncomfortable up there.'

'No, I'd better not.'

'Better? What do you mean?'

Jane stood, shaking her hair impatiently. She put her glass on the table.

'I need a pee. Look, Bill, you'd better go in a minute. Are you all right to drive? Are you going back to Colin's?'

'But you've just given me a drink! How much do you academics earn, for God's sake, to be so profligate? Look, go and have your pee. We ought to talk. I'll sleep on the floor, the sofa bed, anywhere. I won't bother you, I promise.'

Jane said no more, but went upstairs. Bill half sat, half lay among the cushions, staring at the wall, not seeing much. He had taken off his bomber jacket, it lay crumpled on a chair. The Browning was locked in the car boot. He was hollow, hungry, desperate.

Jane returned and perched back on the chair arm. For half a minute they looked at each other. She was breathing deeply.

'Can I turn a somersault?' she said.

'What? What do you mean?'

102

She moved quickly, and came to his side among the beanbags. She glanced at him, then away.

'I meant this. Changing my mind. Sorry, I'm in a state.'

She was on her side, propped on one elbow, and the top of her dress was not tight to her chest. Her breasts were not very large.

Bill said: 'Sorry. Jane, I can see your . . . it's killing me.'

She moved, pulling the back of the dress-top. She rolled back slightly.

'I like my tits,' she said. 'But they never were that well behaved.'

Bill lifted her a little, put his arm around behind her back.

'I want to see you with no clothes on,' he said. 'I don't want to make love, well I do, but I can live without it. But I want to see you naked. Christ, Jane.'

'I can't sleep with you, I can't. I can't go through all that again.'

'No.'

He put his right hand to her neck, then lowered it to the top button of her dress. His fingers were clumsy, they would not work. She did not try to stop him, nor did she help, or speak.

Bill gave up. He touched her breast, on the outside of the cloth, then slid his hand between her chest and arm, around her back to meet his other hand. His face moved close to hers, and hers to his. Their lips remained apart, two inches, three. They breathed each other's breath, sweet, winey. Jane moved her mouth forward and caught his, her lips only slightly parted. They kissed very gently.

She said: 'Why do you want to see me naked, Bill? Why should I find that so erotic? Christ, what are you doing to me?'

'Nothing!' he said. 'Honestly, nothing!' It sounded like the truth to him, although that made him think of Edward. He put his mouth to Jane's, repeating the word. Their teeth clashed, then their lips softened, their mouths matched, clung.

'I'll go then,' said Bill, when they drew apart. 'I'll bugger off to Colin's if you want me to, I'll never see you again, I'll go back to the promise. Jane, Jane, I've dreamed of seeing you, I've dreamed of it.'

'Oh,' said Jane. She breathed it, rather, almost moaned it. 'Oh Christ, that's terrible, oh Bill.'

Suddenly she wriggled, extricated herself from his enfolding arms, moved sideways among the yielding beanbags. She was on her knees, then standing up in front of him, she was panting. So was Bill, still on his side, still on the floor, his mouth slightly open, breath hissing. Jane undid her top button, then caught the dress in both hands at the hips, and jerked it upwards, and wriggled once, convulsively. The dress rose over her hips, over her trunk, then, as she bent forward towards him, in a bundle over her shoulders, arms and head. She threw it sideways, missing the electric fire by an inch, and stood in front of him, wearing a pair of briefs in soft maroon, cotton, with a white lace edging at the top. Then she bent forward, went onto her knees, and leaned into his mouth. This time their mouths were wide, although still soft, and their tongues lay against each other, moving gently. Jane moved her legs and body sideways, lay down, and Bill disengaged, and slipped her pants off. She lay there, rolled onto her back, her legs slightly apart.

'Oh Christ,' said Bill. His voice was barely audible. 'I remembered, but I'd forgotten. Oh Christ.'

Jane's body was brown – not tanned, but brown – and lean and strong. It was not that of an athlete, not muscular or skinny, but lithe and soft at once. Her pubic hair was dark and massy, and – Bill remembered before even touching it – coarse in fibre, surprising, thick and rough. It spread widely on her rounded stomach, and, he knew but could not see, continued down and outward, onto the tops of her thighs, to make small, secret tufts. From her navel, a line of loose hair led down her belly to join the rest, a line he had loved to follow with his finger or his tongue. He was on his knees now, staring, while Jane had her eyes closed, luxuriating in the knowledge she was being watched.

Bill put his hand out until he touched the line of stomach hairs, which made her jump as if in shock. She neither spoke nor opened her eyes, however, so he moved the finger slowly on to touch the dark luxury of the tangled curls, which parted as he continued downward. The texture amazed him, not soft, not wiry, full bodied, each fibre making itself felt. He remembered what he would find next, the memories shaking him as they were reawakened. He felt the top of her clitoris, wet, glossy, large, the largest he had ever known, like a tiny finger, a baby's finger he had once said. Bill used both hands to part the hair, his tongue between his lips, as hers had been the day before, sitting at her notes. He spread her vagina wider, using the sides of both hands to stroke, and watched a small pool of fluid form, a crystal pool, which overflowed, trickled downwards, sideways into the darker hair. As Bill stared and touched, Jane made a noise and arched her back and began to come. He held his breath in awe, touched her as she drew her knees apart, watched her stomach muscles clench, her head roll on one side, touched her gently until she made a muffled groan, of orgasm and instruction, that he should stop. As his hand moved off, she closed her thighs, put one across the other, trapping his hand, stopping it from touching her again, too delicate, too delicate. He was kneeling between her legs, one hand trapped, still fully clothed. She opened her eyes, lifted her head, there was sweat in her brows and on her nose.

'Oh fuck,' she said. 'I want you now, what's the use? You made me come by hardly touching me. I want you now, I want to come again, oh what's the use?'

Bill, not clumsy any more, but almost bursting, withdrew his hand as she relaxed her thighs, and unbelted, unzipped, yanked his trousers and his pants down towards his knees. Jane spread her thighs and he dropped forward, lay on her, his penis probing blindly until her hand slipped down to guide him in. It was hot, and lustrous, indescribably hot and smooth. It was too late for much control, he had hardly time to feel his penis fuse into her flesh, melt. But as he began to come, Jane did as well; her wide-open mouth caught the corner of his jawbone and she yelled into his face. Her body arched and kept the arch, and they both felt his orgasm as a pump, as he emptied into her, pulsing, neither of them moving any other muscle. Then she sank down into the cushions and he sank onto her and they lay there, warmed down one side by the electric fire, bathed in facial sweat, and from him some tears, strangely. Neither of them spoke, but Bill Wiley thought: it is like coming home. Jane Heywood, had he asked her, could only have agreed.

After that they talked, wrapped round each other for a long while, Bill Wiley still only half undressed. They moved occasionally, to drink wine, and when the bottle was finished Bill got up and fetched another from the kitchen and they went to bed. They went under the duvet, nuzzling each other, occasionally emerging for a slurp, sometimes pulling back the quilt to look at one another, smiling quite a lot. Bill was on his back when the phone rang, his prick slowly unfolding as Jane's breath played on it, warm, her head resting sideways on his lower stomach. They both jumped, as if stung. It was twenty-two minutes past three.

Jane picked it up and said tentatively: 'Hallo.' Bill saw her eyebrows lift, and heard, distorted, a woman's voice. Jane said: 'Yes,' and handed him the phone. Her face was not angry, or resentful, it took on a look that he remembered even through his own shock — a strangely hurt look, unable to understand why things should fail so frequently, that fate should play her such bad hands. To recognize Veronica's voice, for Bill, was a terrific relief. But not for long.

'Bill. I think you should come back. They're doing something over here and I don't know what it is. I've been trying to run you down for hours, I've lost you all your friends and mine. David's flipped, there's blood on every wall. I think you should come back.'

'But they *want* me back,' he said. 'Verr, that's what they want. What have they done, what's happening?'

You lying twat, he thought viciously, of Silversmith. You lying, lying twat.

'I don't know.' Her voice was weary, her throat sounded raw. 'I went to see Liz this afternoon. It seemed a good idea, to keep an eye on her, to make things up. She was blitzed. She was practically a zombie. A woman two doors away said a doctor had been round, an Army doctor. She said before he came Liz seemed all right, quite normal. When I called she couldn't really stand, she held on to the banister to open the front door. It was pitiful.'

Bill's face had changed, and so had Jane's. She watched him, concerned, and covered up his lower half and sat up straight, beside him. Bill closed his eyes, thinking furiously.

'John,' he started. Veronica cut him off.

'Yes. The neighbour was going to meet him from school, warn him. She rang me later, it all worked out. I put Liz to bed and Sally — Kimber, is it? — she got hold of Johnnie and told him she was ill but it would be all right. He took it very well, she said, he's used to . . . well, he's used to Liz's illnesses. She popped in and out, gave him his tea, gave Liz a wash and things. He'll be all right.'

'Until tomorrow,' Bill said, bitterly. 'And when I come back, they'll grab me. Bastards.'

'And if you don't, what will they do to Liz? To Johnnie? They might put him into care. You know what's going on, don't you?'

Too well he did. Only too well. Bait and trap. If he went within five miles of them he was caught, and they knew he would not stay away.

106

'Tomorrow,' he said. 'I mean today. Will Johnnie go to school? How bad will Liz be?'

'Sally Kimber rang at ten o'clock. She's much better. My guess is John will go to school, and the doctor will call again and check the situation. My guess is they think you'll soon hear, they know you'll keep in touch. My guess is they'll be expecting you. What do you think?'

Bill reached for his glass of wine, and Jane picked it off the bedside table and moved it to his hand. He moved his lips, a token smile. She nodded, grey eyes unhappy.

'I think the same. I think we can screw them. You said you'd help, I know you'll help, Christ, you're helping! The key is Donegal, you know what I mean. Why am I being cagey, if your line's not safe we're done already, they'll take him in the morning, now, in half an hour. Pray your line is safe. Meet him for me, please, Veronica. Pick him up from school, I'd say at lunchtime, catch them unawares. Tell him Liz has gone to hospital, I'm on my way. Remind him what I told him on his birthday, no more lies, so that he knows the message really comes from me. I'll ring you at your house. In Donegal. I'll be somewhere close, where you can pick me up.'

'But they'll be watching for you, surely? They're not stupid, Bill. The planes and ferries will be under microscopes.'

He nodded, made a gesture.

'Yeah, sure, leave that to me. Veronica, I'll get there. You'll do it for me, won't you?'

'Surely,' said Veronica. 'But the dear knows how you'll bring it off. Bill? Who's the lady?'

'You know already, Verr. You tracked me down.'

'I don't. Your man was cagey. Colin Smart. It was like getting blood out of a stone.'

'Good man,' said Bill. He smiled across the receiver at Jane's still, solemn face. Some of the weight had lifted from his heart. 'Her name is Jane. She's giving me a hand.'

Jane plainly heard the snort of laughter down the wires.

'You always were a wanker, so you were! Tell her from me she's crazy!'

Bill put the phone down.

'She's right, of course,' said Jane. 'And who is this Veronica?'

He told her, some of it, while he dressed.

THIRTEEN

The BMW ate the miles, and as he drove, Bill Wiley thought. He knew where he was headed for – Whitehaven – and he tried to clear his mind of everything except the job in hand. He took the A43 out of Oxford, as being the fastest route towards a motorway that he knew, and joined the M1 a few miles north of Towcester. He had the Browning safely in its nest once more and felt better for it, which worried him. In any case, if he were stopped by traffic cops he was in trouble. He'd have blown a breath-test meter six feet in the air. He figured to make Whitehaven in about four hours, going fast.

The parting had been a very painful one, for both of them. It was somehow as if they had found something, discovered something new, and decided, independently and tacitly, that it was important and would need to be examined, thought about, considered. As they had walked down the stairs, Jane had stopped, turned back to face him, looked up into his face.

'I never meant anything like this to happen, ever,' she said. 'I felt so lonely, so mind-blastingly lonely, even with other men about the place. And now you're fucking off. Oh Jesus, Bill.'

He had sat down on a tread, taken her face in his hands, then put his arms around her neck. They had held each other silently for half a minute.

'I'll ring you up,' he said. 'I promise you. I don't know how long this will take, I don't know what's going to happen, but I'll ring you when I can. They're not going to beat me, Jane.'

'And then? And then? Your wife and child. I wish you'd never thought of me. I wish.'

Earlier, before Veronica, they had avoided the subject, keeping the shadow of real life from darkening the edges of their night, although it had been there in both their minds. They had paid each other compliments, ridiculous but true, about how uniquely wonderful the sex had been, and was, and had both suffered thoughts, like flickers of black lightning, about the days ahead. But they had talked, when they had talked at all, of other things. She had mocked him for pretending that he knew anything of Rudolf Hess when he so patently did not, and he had almost replied that one's mind was concentrated excellently when one was asked to murder somebody. He had not, though, he had drawn back from that, because of the other caverns in his mind it might unlock, the dragons that were doubting there, breathing fire to be free.

'It's a lovely mystery,' she had said. 'One ought to think about the poor old victim, I suppose, but it's a terrific story. It's not even true, you know, that he never claimed he wasn't Rudolf Hess, he did, several times. When somebody at Nuremberg came into his cell and asked for Rudolf Hess, he said "there's no one in this cell who has that name", or somesuch. He also failed to recognize all Hess's former friends and colleagues, said he had no memory of them, and if he was bluffing he was bloody brilliant. Hermann Goering asked him in the dock one day when he was going to tell the court his "great secret", and he wouldn't agree to see his wife and child – and Hess was crazy about the kid, wild about him – for well over twenty years.'

'But he looked the same, presumably? I mean, even after twenty years, his wife and son would know?'

'The boy was four when Hess flew off from Augsburg. Maybe three, I can't recall. As for his wife . . . well, he was certainly very changed. Hess was a big, beefy man, but Prisoner Number Seven was skeletal. The Germans went in a lot for doubles, you know, even more than we did, in the war. One of Hess's went to Hollywood and became a minor star. Victor Varconi. He played Hess in *The Hitler Gang*, you could hardly tell them apart. Churchill had them, and Montgomery. Come to think of it, Tommy Steele's father was a Churchill stand-in, there's a thought to conjure with! That would have kept the enemy guessing, if he'd spoken, wouldn't it?'

They had been in bed, drinking, communing, half making love. Wiley, grinding up the M6 at eighty-five, could see her body now, and groaned. Fuck Hess, fuck Ireland, fuck Tommy Steele, fuck everything.

He had asked her why the cover-up, even if it had been a stand-in Hess, a *doppelgänger*, and Jane had outlined, with a certain glee, the Royalty connection. Most people in the know, she said, especially left-wing lunatics like Aunt Erica had been, favoured this one over all the other theories. It involved the so-called Peace Party, the aristos who thought war with Germany was a waste of time and money and that basically the Nazis weren't far wrong, in aims if not in methods.

'Lord Londonderry, for instance,' she said. 'He had secret contacts with SS officers in Ireland just before the flight. And the Duke of Buccleuch, who was put under house arrest just after it, for the rest of the war. The Duke of Westminster apparently held strange meetings in his London house, and Lord Halifax got kicked off to Washington as Ambassador, a strange fate for a Foreign Secretary, eh? Stranger still with Halifax, because he was Churchill's rival to be PM when Chamberlain stepped down. *And* he was very thick with Montagu Norman, so the Hess freaks say. President of the Bank of England – and Barry Norman's grandad, if I'm . . . anyway, the pair of them were reckoned to be plotting to call in Winston's debts and bring him down, so Montagu was hated, too. Churchill was in tears when he thought they'd bankrupted him in the New York markets, so the story goes, but he got his revenge. He was a terrible spendthrift, Churchill, almost a wastrel. A South African millionaire financed him during the war, he "lent" him a small fortune. Deathly secret, totally irregular, he was a canny old lad.'

'But is it true?'

'What?'

'All of it. Any of it? I don't know.'

She'd grinned. She'd taken wine.

'Me neither. Some of it, maybe. Churchill certainly hated them, he'd spent a long time being crushed and patronised in the Party. Maybe it suited him to call them fellow-travellers with Adolf and his thugs, it gave him power to humiliate. He called them in, and rapped their knuckles, and issued dire warnings. Toe the line or go to prison was what it boiled down to.'

'And Royalty? You said the Royalty connection. This is aristos.'

'Well yes, it's all inter-connected, this was Britain before the Fall. Hess worked through the Duke of Hamilton, and Hamilton was pally with the King. The fact that he was friends with Winston too may have been unfortunate, an end they couldn't tidy up. Hess didn't want to speak to Churchill though, if you remember, and one theory is that these dirty dukes and earls were going to band together and give the lad an ultimatum. He would step down, probably be replaced by Halifax, and the Peace Party would take charge in the Cabinet. Hitler would cease hostilities in Europe, and probably withdraw from France and the Low Countries. The Duke of Windsor – Edward the Eighth as was, until he abdicated – would be brought back from the Bahamas where we'd made him governor to keep him out of the way, and put back on the throne. With Mrs Simpson, the Yankee divorcee, as his queen!'

Jane, naked and squeaking with laughter, rolled round the bed with Bill chasing her, demanding sense and explanations. It sounded mad to him, fantastic. Jane drank wine, large mouthfuls, and he licked the spillage off her chin and breast.

'Fantastic, yes,' she said. 'But not half as crazy as it sounds. In fact, it may be true. Queen Wallis, though! Can you imagine it! She and Windsor were as thick as thieves with Hitler's lot, that's on record. They'd had dinner with the Hesses at least once, and Edward was quite prepared to give the Nazi salute in public. Wallis probably spied for Germany from the Bahamas throughout the war, and she'd apparently once been made pregnant by Mussolini's right-hand man, Count Ciano. As well as screwing Ribbentrop! She was an awful old tart, by all accounts.'

'Bloody hell,' said Bill. 'This wasn't in the history books I read! I'd've got straight A's!'

'Precisely. It isn't in the history books at all, you've got to ferret for it. I told you, this isn't my era, I can't vouch for it, it's crumbs from Uncle Edward's table. But a lot of it makes sense. Let's face it, there was nobody in Britain who stood to gain financially from the war, and that's a powerful argument for a peace plot. By 1941 it was bankrupting us. It was bankrupting Hitler, too, and he had Russia looming over him. What better idea than for the English robber barons to link up with the industrial princes of Germany, and turn our joint attentions east? Russia was the real enemy, everybody always knew it. Together we could smash them into pieces. Capitalism versus the Reds! No contest. Churchill wouldn't play. The British Bulldog stands alone. We'll fight them on the beaches, and so on.'

She lay back, as if exhausted, Bill's fingers tangled in damp fronds of pubic hair. Neither spoke for several seconds.

'It's a point of view,' she said. 'It's possible. The Royal archives on the subject are locked solid, no one's saying anything. The Foreign Office files on Hess are closed until 2017, and most of them have been got at anyway, we know that for a fact. Hess might know, but if he does he's never said so, or it's never come to light. A few

111

old men might, ditto, Uncle Edward to name but one of them. But honours or no honours, they're keeping schtum, lips sealed. Soon they'll all be dead.'

Bill stirred. For the old man in the prison it would be very soon. Someone had decided. And someone had to do it. Why?

The fish dock at Whitehaven was busy when he walked down from the town. He had parked the BMW in a side street, a street of dark and sleeping houses, as close as possible to three or four other expensive-looking cars. There was nothing that could link his name with it, and he would ring Colin later to tell him what was going on. Colin's cars often went missing for days, abandoned by the feckless rich ruled by the Iron Whim, so Bill did not think he would mind much. He'd probably be more upset by the night of mystery phone calls, and the thought that Bill and Jane had presumably been screwing once again. Never mind.

The quayside was a mass of fishermen, dealers, lorries. Bill stood in the background for a while, until he had isolated his targets. There were five boats from Ireland in, two of them from Portavogie. They often made the trip across if conditions suited them, to get a better price in England than in Ulster. Bill knew Portavogie well, he had had dealings there. It was a stronghold of black Protestantism, clinging to the bitter coast. He climbed on board a boat and found the skipper, showing him the Browning automatic and mentioning some names. Fifty pounds on top of that, and he had his trip. Even patriotism had its price.

By midday, Wiley was on the quay at Portavogie. He moved fast, up into the tiny town, and out at an angle along a track. From there he cut across some fields to approach a farmhouse, a low, modern bungalow in the Ulster style. Twenty minutes after that, having drunk a cup of tea and eaten bread and cheese, he was on his way, heading west. Outside Derry, at another farm, he would drop the borrowed car and disappear. An uncle, or a cousin, or 'your man' would bring it back to Portavogie, silence guaranteed.

The weather, as he had driven up the coast of Cumbria in the rising sun, had been wonderful. Even given his exhaustion, the wine he'd drunk, the constant round of thoughts and worries chasing round his head, the Lakeland fells and estuaries, the sparkling, wakening sea, had soothed him. The sea trip had been quiet and unruffled, and he had dozed alongside the black-haired, silent skipper at the wheel. Now, in Northern Ireland, the sky was darkening, with a threat of rain in the west, as there so often was. Bill Wiley, with the philosophical tendency of the exhausted, wondered why anybody fought for it. It was a blasted country, full of pain and bigotry. Even the green beauty of the land beside his road was spoiled. He passed big houses, shrouded in the trees, with stone eagles on the gate-posts and flagpoles at their corners, flying the Union Flag, defiant, medieval, pathological. On the smaller, meaner farms he imagined young bitter men, their minds twisted in the opposite direction, stowing Semtex in milk churns for burial, oiling AK47s and RPGs, their hearts wedded to eight hundred years of tragedy, their brains prepared to face eight hundred more. He had had enough of Ireland, he had had a stomachful. He would take his son away.

And his wife . . . ?

He used a public telephone quite near the border, and crossed into Donegal on foot. That was easy, although he knew that people on the mainland imagined miles of barbed wire with machine-gun towers and checkpoints, as in films of central Europe. Veronica had answered on the first ring, and they had made their rendezvous for half an hour, outside a ruined roadhouse they both knew, a mile inside. His new leather shoes were pinching him, possibly not designed for actual walking, but his spirits were high. He wanted to see John again, and he was going to.

What did he expect? Johnnie to spring out of the Polo, a glad cry in his throat, a smile splitting his face? Probably he did, but sanity returned as the small yellow car drew into the overgrown parking area in front of the ruin. Bill saw his son through the windscreen, and he was crying. Veronica's face was pale, also, pale and strained, with dark patches underneath her eyes. She pulled round in an arc beside him, so that the passenger door was next to him, but she did not get out or stop the engine. John, in the back seat, twisted his body away, hunched himself into the seat-back. Bill Wiley, the smile dead on his lips, opened the door.

'Verr,' he said. 'I don't know what to say. Thanks.'

She did not answer, but shoved the gear-stick into bottom, and moved off. There was a broken bottle on the ground and she had to stop, reverse, to avoid it. Her face was dark.

'Johnnie,' said Bill. He tried to reach his son but the boy squirmed away from him, his face hidden. The car bumped back onto the road, with Wiley half across the seat, almost grabbing.

Veronica said testily: 'I'm trying to drive this car. What about your seat-belt? For Christ's sake, Bill. How did you suppose he'd be?'

'John,' said Bill. 'Johnnie. Everything'll be all right, I promise you. John. Look at me.'

The knotted body grew tighter, and Bill forced himself to sit back properly. He put his belt on, glanced at Veronica.

'Sorry,' he said. 'It must have been appalling. For you as well. How's Liz?'

She hissed at him, furious.

'Shut your mouth, why don't you? Have you no sense? No sense at all?'

They drove fast along the main road, then down twisting lanes that finally turned to tracks. The sky was darkening when they saw the sea, not from evening, but from cloud. The sea looked forbidding, but still sun-dappled, beautiful, with Atlantic rollers crashing onto the strand. Bill remembered his nightmare on the train, and shivered. He had his hand on Johnnie now, and Johnnie no longer twisted himself away, although his face was hidden still. When they reached Veronica's house, a tiny limewash cottage beside a copse of trees, she switched off the engine and they sat, not talking. From over a grassy hummock they could hear the breakers, crashing on the sand. She got out and hauled her seat forward. John, after a moment, crawled after her, his eyes averted from his father's. Bill climbed out, too. The wind was strong, with a raw edge to it.

'John,' he said. 'Johnnie. Look at me, old lad. Please. Things will be all right.'

For an instant, John raised his face. His eyes were black with hurt and misery.

'We've left my mum,' he said. 'Why have we left my mum?'

Next day, there were phone calls to be made, things to ascertain, bridges to be built. Veronica had told him, before driving back to Belfast, that she would check on Liz, see what the situation was around the house, ring him up. Bill had vetoed it, because of the security aspect. They might have already checked her car, the married quarters were under observation, however inefficient, and once they knew she was connected they would find out about her 'secret' seaside cottage, tap the phones, flush him out. He knew about these things, it was his bread and butter.

'But what will you do, then? Without me, you're completely isolated. What if they do something terrible to her?'

They were in the kitchen, drinking tea, at eight o'clock at night. Johnnie, uncharacteristically, was sleeping on the sofa in front of the TV. Outside it was blowing hard, and raining.

'Now we've spirited him away they'll probably let her alone. They know enough about me to know they've lost their bait. If nothing else, she'll have told them that.'

Veronica lit a cigarette. She had been smoking almost constantly, he noticed. Bill did not smoke.

'If nothing else,' Veronica responded, 'she'll be on Valium for real, now. Morphine, anything. You don't know what you've done, do you? You really are a selfish, heartless, shit.'

'I do. You don't know what's going on, Verr, why all this has happened. I promise you I had to do it. For Liz's good as well, in the long run.'

She flicked ash, morosely.

'I should lose my temper, maybe. Ach, Bill, it's an awful messy one. That poor wee boy has been excoriated. Can't you tell me why?'

'Not yet. Can you hang around tomorrow morning? I'll ring you before twelve. I'll use a public phone, I'll go long walks with Johnnie, try to sort him out, poor little sod. Shit. These shoes.'

She smiled, wanly.

'Rubber boots of all sizes in the outhouse. David is the perfect host, and this is Ireland, where you go on holiday to get rusty. I'll be in. Who's this Jane?'

'Like you told me on the phone. A crazy. Verr, go. It's a long drive back.'

They kissed, chastely, like old friends, and Veronica went. Bill covered his son up with a blanket, and got a sleeping bag out of a bedroom for himself. He lay down on the rug beside the boy and thought for many hours. Around midnight, Johnnie awoke, and cried in Bill's arms. Then they went upstairs into a big, saggy double bed and slept until gone nine o'clock, like babies.

Boswell, on the phone next morning, tried to keep him talking, to get the call traced. He said Liz was very ill, was in hospital, and would be going into a psychiatric ward. She had had a mental breakdown, and he should return immediately to her side. Bill said he was in England with his son, and that he must place his trust for Liz with doctors, and with honour. Boswell said unless the boy was given up, legal moves might have to be put in train, wardships of court and so on. Bill disbelieved him. Bill said he would not do the German job, under any circumstances, he had decided. Once Boswell had accepted that, he would resign.

'And starve?' snapped Boswell. 'No job, wife in a lunatic asylum, on the run?'

'Fuck off,' said Bill, and put the phone down.

There was no reply from his own home, and Veronica could tell him little. She had spoken to Sally Kimber, who said an ambulance had arrived at Liz's front door late the previous afternoon. Earlier, when John should have come home from his school, Liz had been in the street, still in her dressing gown, looking for him, worried but not frantic. No one knew what had happened in the interim, and Sally had not thought to ring the bell, not knowing anything terrible was up. Where was John, she had asked Veronica. Did anybody know? The whole thing, she said, was getting circular, insane.

On the strand, Bill tried to explain some of it to Johnnie. He said that Liz was ill, and had had to go into a hospital near Belfast. It was not her body that was ill, it was her mind. At just eleven, John had seen enough of mental breakdown among the Army wives to know what that meant, and enough of his own mother's troubles to believe it had happened to her. What he could not understand was why they had come away, why a woman he hardly knew and did not like had lifted him, why they could not go and visit her. He feared – although it took Bill more than an hour to prise it out of him – that it meant marriage breakdown, which to him seemed much more shameful and hard to bear than anything his mum might go through. Divorce.

Bill held him, with the waves crashing almost to their feet, the sun shining, the wind and seabirds whistling. And – with a picture of Jane Heywood clear in his mind – denied it.

'No more lies,' he said. 'I promised you, no more lies. Everything will be all right.'

* * *

He knew they had to go, to get out of Ireland, but he was not sure how to do it, and where to head for. On the second day, while Johnnie dammed a small stream near the phone box, he rang Jane. For both of them, it was a wrecking experience, although they managed to hide it from each other.

'Jane. Bill.'

'Oh. Oh hello. Oh, how you doing?'

'Fine. It all went fine. We're . . . the boy and me. We're taking a holiday. We'll be in . . . we'll be on your side, soon. I'll get in touch, when we're fixed up.'

'Yes. How's . . . how's your wife?'

'Look, I can't really talk. I'm in some God-forsaken phone box, it's ridiculous. Jane. I want to see you.'

'Yes.'

It was as if they were in a room full of strangers, listening. It was pain.

Then Jane said: 'Bill, I think you ought to come. It's Uncle Edward.'

Her voice had changed. It was more animated.

'Go on.'

'I told him about . . . about John and everything. About what happened. What they've done to you.'

'And? Did it amuse him?'

'Bill, he wants to see you. He wants to talk to you. He wants to tell.'

Johnnie was splashing in the stream. He saw his father, through the glass, and waved. Bill waved back, abstractedly.

'Bill?'

'I'm speechless. I'm amazed.'

'I spoke to Erica. She said Edward had been overwhelmed. He'd thought the Hess affair was over, wrong or right, true or false, it would soon just fade away. She said he couldn't bear the thought that people were still prepared to do awful things like that. To kill a man of that age. Whatever needed covering, whoever's reputations were at stake. He wants to stop you doing it. Or anybody. He wants to tell you why.'

Bill thought. Of Boswell, Peter-Joe. The old grey Widowmaker.

'Darling. I'm going to have to hide. In England. They'll be searching for me. Hunting.'

'It's all right. He's got another house. Naturally. It's the long

117

vacation, he doesn't have to be at college, it's all arranged. We'll all go.'

'But I've got the kid.'

'Of course. Edward joked about it, he can't bear to be too serious, I think. He said he couldn't guarantee it would be true. Inevitably. "What is truth", et cetera. But it will be. I know it will. Bill. Come. Please, please come.'

A smile had broken out, across his face. His son looked beautiful, splashing in the stream.

'You couldn't stop me if you tried,' he said. 'Just tell me where and how. Jane Heywood. I love you!'

'I know,' she said.

BOOK TWO

The King
Over The Water

PROLOGUE

May 10, 1941

The Chief, thought Karlheinz Pintsch, was suffering from nerves. Dragging him away from the house at Harlaching had been like drawing teeth, and on the drive to the airfield he had stopped the car to pick wild flowers, in the name of God! Now he was bitching about all matters technical. A possible fault on one of the aero-engines, the camera playing up. To Pintsch it seemed unfortunate. God help us all, he thought, there's pain and suffering enough ahead: let's not worry about the details.

The problem with the port engine was soon sorted. The aircraft had been flown already that day, before refuelling for Herr Hess's trip, and the motor was still warm. D-type 110s were fitted with 601A units, which did not like warm starts, the Chief had been told that often enough, he was behaving like a *Mädchen*. Within minutes, both were throbbing comfortably, almost purring. A deafening purr, quite ear-splitting!

As Hess approached the plane, Karlheinz trained the movie camera on him and turned the little switch. Thank God for that, it worked. He raised a hand, thumb upward, smiling. The Chief twitched his famous eyebrows, that stuck out of the flying helmet like two ledges, showed his famous teeth. Nervousness disappearing, Pintsch could see. The sound of aero-engines. The thought of action. Like all the big bosses of the regime, he would have it on film, this great historic moment. Not for posterity, however: for his own collection, assuming he returned. For the Gestapo, thought Karlheinz, if anything went wrong. He switched off almost sadly as Hess disappeared into the cockpit clumsily, too big in the leg for such acrobatics.

There were checks to be done, now that Hess had replaced the mechanic, so Karlheinz backed off a few paces with the camera. It was not a professional affair, only a home-movie job, but it worked well enough when it was working. Pintsch had become an addict of the hobby early in the thirties, as had most of his friends. Most of the other bosses had official cameramen, who photographed their every step, practically their every cough and spit, but he was glad Hess was not like that. For a boss, in fact, he was a very human man, who had hardly tried to hide the tears behind his eyes as he had stepped into the Mercedes earlier. Frau Hess had not come to say goodbye – ill in bed – and little Buz had been in the nursery. On the pot, in fact, the Chief had said. What a way to remember your only son. The Chief had been quiet for a kilometre or two. Wondering, beyond a doubt, if he would ever see the little boy again.

In any case. Karlheinz Pintsch jerked his mind back to the present. The ground crew were making ready. The engines were being revved, full, throaty, reliable. In any case, the first leg wasn't very far. Only to Aalborg, up in Denmark, for refuelling. Maybe something would happen, then. Maybe the flight would be aborted, as it had been back in January. Although the weather today looked ideal, the forecasts perfect all the way to Scotland. Ah well, something else might happen. He clicked the lever, and the clockwork motor whirred. Pictures.

Out of the cockpit, Rudolf Hess waved, his face obscured now by mask and goggles. It was his own mask, although the flying suit was Kaden's, borrowed because his own had disappeared, peculiarly, from its hook. Karlheinz caught the wave, then turned the camera on the group of figures standing by. Messerschmitt himself was there, the Prof, which was a surprise. Surely he did not know precisely what was going on? Kaden, too, and a couple of other senior staff at Haunstetten. The engine noise rose, the chocks were pulled. Smoothly, Karlheinz Pintsch panned round as the aircraft passed him, sweeping down the runway. The sky was dull, and the last few seconds were almost certainly wasted film, but he did not switch the camera off until the fighter had disappeared. He returned to the Mercedes then, his heart becoming heavier as he walked. The time scale had been altered slightly, there was much to do. The letter for Herr Hitler, most importantly, to be delivered personally. His train was booked, *hin und zurück*. He doubted, to be perfectly frank, if he would ever get to use the return half.

But other things. He checked his wristwatch. Vital calls to make. The timing had to be exact.

In the cockpit of the Bf110, Rudolf Hess, Deputy Führer of the

German Reich, stabilized the motors and concentrated. Udet had listed the permitted zones and heights for the day, and his path was relatively simple. He was heading for the North Sea coast, which he would cross near Terschelling then follow for a while before turning in for the approach to Aalborg. The fluttering in his stomach had ceased, and he worked to clear his mind of images and worries. Little Buz sitting on his potty was the hardest, the lovely, curly-headed boy. But now he was the pilot. The flier. He had started on the mission . . .

Reinhard Heydrich – the President, as he liked to call himself – drove alone to Gatow that afternoon. His car was instantly recognizable, as was his profile, so by the time he drew to a halt there were three men waiting to do his bidding. He gave one the keys to the SSK, and told the other two to have an aircraft ready in twelve minutes. Heydrich did not need to file a flight plan – had no intention of so doing – but he strolled to the control tower to tell them he was going for a spin. It was normal.

Heydrich, a man of many talents, considered fighter flying one of the most useful and relaxing of them all. He had come to it relatively late in his short life, having dulled the joys of promiscuity, music and organization early on, and like everything else he took an interest in, he did it with terrifying brilliance. Having mastered aerobatics in his little Deaky before the war, he had gained Hitler's permission to go on bombing runs, although – boringly – only as a gunner. While others had sweated and trained, whored and drunk like madmen to control their fear, he had practised for his fighter pilot examination – in time stolen from all his other jobs – passing, inevitably, *summa cum laude*. He flew Willi Messerschmitt's master-piece, the 109, in the Norwegian campaign, and over France, Belgium and Holland, while fitting in some high-level photo re-connaissance over England in a modified 110. Both Himmler and Hitler disapproved of all this dangerous activity – they needed him – and Heydrich often had to sneak back to Berlin on late-night transport planes to cover the fact that he had been battling with the RAF instead of with the enemies of the State at RHSA headquarters. If Heydrich had a regret about life on earth – and he had never been heard to express one – it was that a day held merely twenty-four hours. *Lächerlich!*

The Bf110, he thought, as he flew sedately north towards Denmark, was not half the plane the 109 was. It was a pity, one of the small mysteries of flight and aerodynamics. It had twice the power of its single-engined sister, but far less of practically everything else. Its top speed was lower, and at anything near that speed, its range was laughable. It was a pig to fly, a dog to fight with, an animal. Hess planned to get to Scotland in one, and rather him than me. Heydrich was grinning to himself. Hess would never get to Scotland in a 110. Oh no, no, no!

He gazed around him at the late afternoon sky. It was leaden, but clear. No other aircraft, Germany laid out around him like a pale map, yellow and green. He sang aloud, in what he amused himself by imagining was a passable accent, 'Oh you tak the high road and I'll tak the low.

'And I'll be in Aalborg afore ye!'

Poor old Hess.

The man they called The Fat One — Reichsmarschall Hermann Goering — was enjoying himself when Karlheinz Pintsch rang him with the news. He was in Carinhall, his country home near Berlin, and he was naked. He had, in fact, just stepped from his bath and, on a whim, had called upon the services of a maid called Ella. He was in front of a mirror, and the sight had brought forth gusts of laughter. Emmy was away, in case the Royal Air Force came with bombs again, and *Der Dicke* was feeling frisky. Plotting was afoot, deep plotting.

'Ah,' he said, when Ella appeared at the bedroom door. 'Come in, my sweet. Don't be shy. I need a second opinion, that's all.'

The girl, who was new but a Berliner, was even so a little shocked. Her eyes rounded at the sight of so much flesh, although she stepped quite boldly into the room. She was dressed — nicely, he considered — in a black uniform in the French style, trimmed in white English lace. Doubtless the other girls had told her what she might expect. Hermann loved Emmy, no one doubted it. But he was a playful man, and generous.

'Two whelks,' he said, smiling at her. He opened his arms as she joined him at the mirror. Their eyes met in the glass. 'A whale, two whelks, and a winkle!'

124

'Very nice,' said Ella, and she meant it. Goering had noted many times before that the fatter and more powerful he got, the more attractive women found him. What a pity he was so old! He read her expression – enquiring – and touched her on both shoulders. As she sank to her knees, the Reichsmarschall felt the winkle underneath the whale begin to rise. From above, he saw only his belly, though, and Ella's fine brown hair. Changing his mind, and watching in the mirror, he slipped his hands underneath her jaw and pulled her gently up again.

'On your back, I think,' he said, propelling her towards the bed. 'I'm going to pull your skirt up, Ella, and if you've got no knickers on you will get a bonus, you saucy little minx. I'm going to envelope you in flesh, I'm going to cover you like an Austrian feather quilt, like an enormous dumpling, you'll like that, won't you? And when you've lain there, and thought of Adolf or whatever good girls do these days, you can watch me dress in my fine underwear, all pristine silk and nicely sticky balls. You won't have read your Henry James, of course?'

So Hermann Goering was a little on the miffy side when Karlheinz Pintsch rang up before he'd finished. His man had been warned that Pintsch was not to be put off, whatever the occasion, so The Fat One – without irony – shouted 'Come' when the bedroom door was knocked. If the NCO saw Ella's limbs protruding from beneath the supine lard he did not comment.

'Telephone, sir. Karlheinz Pintsch.'

'Ja, damn it.'

Withdrawn from silent Ella, still naked in an office off the bedroom, Goering shouted down the receiver: 'You're early, damn you! What's going on?'

Karlheinz Pintsch replied: 'The bird has flown, Herr Reichsmarschall. He left a little early. I have the letter for the Führer. Everything except the time is normal.'

Goering scratched his balls, felt his drooping penis. That bloody Hess, that *Piesl*. He always cocked things up.

'Right,' he said. 'You've done well, Pintsch. Get your train, as planned. Get to Berchtesgaden. Are you scared?'

'Naturally, sir.'

'Don't worry too much. You've got protection. Herr Hess showed you the letter he's written Himmler, didn't he? When the Chicken-farmer reads it, you'll be in the clear. Exonerated.'

Like hell, he thought. Pintsch did, too. But both of them were prepared to live with it, for slightly different reasons.

'Train,' he said. 'Move. I've got calls to make. And Pintsch?'

'Sir?'

'Good man.'

Before he made his next call, *Der Dicke* put on his underwear. Ella he had dismissed, as pleasure could be recalled at any time, while the business in hand was urgent. Somehow, he had never thought that Hess had had this in him, he'd never thought the flight would ever – to coin a phrase – get off the ground. Grudgingly, he was impressed. The old windbag still had some spunk left, despite all the shit his dear old Führer made him eat. He had set off early, too. A crafty touch, a crafty touch indeed. Still, Adolf Galland would not be thrown by minor details such as that. Still like a whale, now a silken one, he returned to the small office and put the call through to Galland's unit in the Netherlands. It took four minutes to connect.

'Dolfo? Hermann. Look, I'm furious, I can barely contain my rage, every gram of flesh I have is quivering with anger. Do I make myself clear?'

He could imagine Galland, a small man who looked as if he had permanent indigestion. Galland would not be smiling at this jollity.

'I have to tell you,' he went on, 'that the Deputy Führer has gone insane. He has obtained a fighter, Bf110, and he's flying it to Britain. Augsburg to Aalborg, then to Scotland, all right? Naturally, he must not succeed.'

'I'll get an intercept worked out immediately,' said Galland. 'I'll scramble shortly.'

'Oh Dolfo. This is unprecedented, you understand, totally unprecedented. I have every confidence in you. Let's have some wizardry, all right?'

'The orders will be given as soon as possible, Reichsmarschall.'

Which means, thought Goering, get off the line. He dismissed Galland. The humourless little shit. A good man, though, a genius in the air, and Stahl was also in on it. Nothing would go wrong.

Hermann Goering put the receiver in its cradle slightly downcast. He glanced at the carriage clock on the polished rosewood desk. It had come from a chateau outside Paris, as had some of the other beauties. And the desk! He was taking care of everything for the owners. Oh, what a good man! He cheered up a little.

A few minutes, a few checks, some calculations and Galland would be airborne. That would be all right, then. Fine. Perhaps he should phone the Führer, perhaps a little later. He thought of the evening's scheduled raid on London. They'd be fuelled up by now, bombs loaded. Six hundred of them. The biggest one he'd ever mounted.

It was going to be some sort of a night for Mr Churchill and his friends, he mused. He hoped – just hoped – it might prove to be conclusive.

Heydrich, who was never late for anything, was too late to stop the flight to Scotland. As he taxied to a halt at Aalborg, he saw a small contingent of SD approach, keen and hungry, and his lips curved. I'll feed you soon, my dogs, he thought. As he pulled back the perspex canopy he permitted himself a small smile at Stallen, whom he knew. The engines grumbled into silence.

'Good evening.' He pulled himself athletically from the cockpit. 'Where is he?'

Stallen looked slightly perplexed. Heydrich jumped down from the wing, face set. Something!

'Speak.'

His voice had quietened, his nostrils flared. The SD men were watchful.

Stallen said stiffly: 'We arrived on time, of course. The Deputy Führer had made other arrangements, it seems. Another plane, in fact. I could have arrested the manager of the field, but I thought it might be better to wait to see which way the cat jumped. News of arrests might . . .' He left the thought to hang.

They were standing by the aircraft. It was whistling slightly, as some part hidden in the cowlings cooled down. A rhythmic ticking from the starboard engine. Reinhard Heydrich swore, richly and obscenely. Nobody responded. The wind blew, ruffling Stallen's hair.

'What plane? Did they provide it here?'

'Naturally. It was ordered. It was a new one, Mark E2 or some such jargon. Half-painted, only, guns still packed with grease.'

'I'll kill the bastards.'

'The Deputy Führer. They could hardly have said no.'

Reinhard Heydrich wiped the portion of his face that had been covered by his mask. It was sweaty. He was beginning to overheat in his flying suit. He spat onto the concrete.

'You're quite right, Burli. A telephone. I have some words to say.'

Goering laughed at him, like a drainpipe full of shit.

'I know already, Reinhard! I've scrambled Dolfo Galland to shoot him down. Imagine! Old Rudolf being smart enough to pull a trick like that! Imagine! To outwit Reinhard Heydrich!'

I'll get you one day, you fat sow, Heydrich told himself. I'll boil you down for soap. He said, mildly: 'You also were outsmarted, Hermann. Or are you in on this aspect as well?'

'Oh no, no plotting, no I'm clean, my dear. No, it's you he doesn't trust, Reinhard. Does anybody?'

'Does the Führer know yet? Has anybody bothered to pass the news on?'

Goering's gurglings were even richer.

'Well you can't, can you? If you knew there was a plot afoot, shouldn't you have mentioned it before, you know how paranoid our glorious leader gets! It's terribly suspicious, Reinhard, you being up in Denmark when the old fox flies away. Even if you do claim you went up there to do him in! I'd keep your head down, *nein*?'

For the moment, there was very little that the President could say.

The navigation for the second leg should have been extremely easy. From Aalborg it was largely a matter of following the setting sun, which had broken from its cloud cover even before the flier had reached his chosen height. The earlier start had complicated matters slightly, but that had been remedied by flying a simple box pattern, by compass and clock, to lose time in the middle of the North Sea, as far as possible from either British or Luftwaffe fighters. As he approached the coast the Bf110 was in a shallow dive, the new, high-power DB6O1N motors driving her very fast. Course and landmarks were clear in his mind's eye, Holy Island in clear reality below him. At Dungavel House, where the Duke of Hamilton had his residence, there was a private landing strip. If his luck held, nothing could prevent him using it.

Almost as the thought formed, two aircraft appeared in front of him. The shock was terrific, he gasped into his oxygen mask, his hands clenching involuntarily. They were Spitfires, dead ahead and so close it was impossible, coming directly at him. Then they were gone, and he craned back to see behind him, to see if they were following. But he saw nothing, nothing but dark sky. The oxygen mask was filled with sweat.

I am Rudolf Hess he told himself, again and again. I am Rudolf Hess, and I have come to see the Duke of Hamilton. He commands 602 Fighter Squadron and he is on duty tonight, at RAF Turnhouse, near Edinburgh. He controls all hunters, so they will not hunt me down. I am Rudolf Hess, and I come in peace, for peace, to end the war.

The repeated incantation calmed him, as it had throughout the flight from Aalborg. The news from Gatow that Heydrich had flown north had been the great shock, the confirmation of all their fears, but Heydrich for once had missed the boat. Here, in twilight's faded blue, was Rudolf Hess, flying over Scotland, still. Fast and low and nervous. There ahead, a flash of silver. The sea. He looked down in a sudden panic. That should not be! He had gone astray! He checked his flight map, controlled his racing thoughts. He had gone too far, but all was not yet lost. He concentrated.

At nine minutes past eleven, confused but still not hopeless, he baled out. He had flown over the sea for a short time – the western sea, the wrong sea – then swung back on a reciprocal. He had other information in his mind and on his lap, information that would guide him to Dungavel House. But it was late, the light had almost gone, he was unsure. He was certain only of one thing. *Ich bin* Rudolf Hess. *Ich bin* Rudolf Hess.

He hurt his back and ankle baling out. It was an operation he had never done before, and it was *schrecklich* difficult. He hurt his back as the tailplane hit him glancingly, and his ankle when he hit the ground. He was in a field, and after the awful smashing of the grounding 110, it was very, very quiet. He forced himself from the parachute, offered thanks to God for his deliverance, and hobbled off to find someone. The Duke of Hamilton. Too much to hope for, but he *was* expecting him. *Ich bin* Rudolf Hess . . .

He was confronted, in fact, by a farm labourer, who helped him into his small cottage and offered him a cup of tea. The flier, smiling reassuringly at an old lady, roused by the excitement from her bed, said he would prefer a glass of water.

When asked, he told the labourer: 'I am *Hauptmann* Alfred Horn.'

*　　*　　*

A couple of hours earlier, on a hunch, Hermann Goering rang down to his main office in Carinhall and gave them a Stockholm number to obtain. He had a fair idea of what Heydrich had been up to in Aalborg, and he hoped he might get confirmation this way. The man was a serpent, and – who knew – he might have been more successful than he claimed, in the matter of Rudolf Hess.

While he waited, another call came through, from Adolf Galland. Everything, he said, had gone perfectly. Dolfo was very circumspect about trusting telephone lines, even lines to Hermann Goering, whose *Forschungsamt* controlled which ones were tapped. That was all he said, and he was not asked to embellish. Two minutes later, the set jangled once more. Goering's secretary.

'The call to Stockholm, sir. Impossible, I'm afraid.'

'Why?'

'The lines are down. Some time ago. We've no idea when they'll be restored.'

Reichsmarschall Goering – fully clad now in an opulent lounging suit of pearl grey with wide lapels and double vent 'to give my arse some room to breathe' – thought long and hard about this information.

Surely not coincidence?

ONE

Edward Carrington was not always a historian. In fact, he was recruited to the discipline by what some insisted was the arsy-versy way. Instead of starting off in Oxbridge and becoming a spy, he started as a spy and ended up in Oxbridge. It happened by accident, or at least with no intent at all on his part. It was haphazard, and surprising, and even rather funny, it was the nature of the times. A week or so afterwards, the Second World War began.

The approach came after a reception in a large private house in Belgravia. Edward's father had worked in the diplomatic service in India and had amassed a fortune also, by irregular and secret membership of a Burmese rubber syndicate. His only son — well provided in those days with cash — had come back to Europe in the early 'thirties with little in his mind except escape. Like many other boys with India in his blood he had been forced into rootlessness by education. At the age of seven he had been put on a ship to Britain, kissed by his mother and sisters, shaken hands with by his Pop, and banished from their sight for the next eleven years, save two brief holidays. When he had left, he had loved them desperately, and had hidden in the stifling furnace of his cabin for days, weeping himself dry. By the time he was reunited with them — for good, if he so chose — he viewed his parents with an indifference that probably masked hatred. They were proud of him, they said, so pale, so educated, so English, and paraded him in the clubs and messes for a while. For Edward, India had lost the only element he had liked in it — the easy affection of the Indians that he had taken for granted as a child — and gained nothing in compensation. There were three rows with his father, behind closed doors, then they reached agreement. Edward left.

His father, fortunately, had certain eccentricities. Although it struck him as being perfectly right and natural to tear a seven-year-old boy away from his parents and send him 'home' to be educated, it also struck him that the English public school system was iniquitous, a hotbed of beatings and buggery. So Edward, almost alone among his fellow unfortunates who sailed that particular August, did not go to one of the great English educational establishments, but to a small academy near Dumfries. Beating was on the agenda, certainly, but buggery very definitely was not. In fact, about the only contact Edward ever had with other people's flesh was when the school maids, and then their friends from round about, began to share their sexual favours with him. It started when he was only fourteen, and he was more or less alone among the boys in being smiled upon. Even when he could not do it properly he loved it, and very soon he pleased as much as he was pleased. He never told, either, a lesson he learned very young, which made him everlastingly popular with the girls. Formal education he hardly bothered with. He had a flair for languages that was extraordinary, and that was quite enough. When asked by the masters where it came from, he put it down to being 'good with my tongue', and they nodded sagely, wondering why he smiled. When he left, he had added German, Danish, Swedish and Norwegian to his Hindi and Urdu. All, it was pointed out acidly by the headmaster, fairly useless languages (except *perhaps* the German), but that was his lookout. Edward, who was depressed already, homesick for the bodies he was being forced to leave, agreed without agreeing and shook hands listlessly. He had been offered university, naturally, but went 'home', this time to India. That lasted four months.

Despite the violence of the schism with his father, the eccentric streak prevailed to the extent that he was offered funds until he found his feet back West. In northern England there were branches of the family with interests in ships and trading, and eventually Edward ended up with them, on a roving brief. The next few years he spent in travel and (dread words) in commerce, drinking in the wonderful perplexities that Europe, after India and Scotland, threw at him. As early as 1933, when he was nineteen, he watched in joy and fascination as Germany burst into a new era, and Russia fed her revolution on the flesh of her own children. Everywhere he went he smelled fresh blood, and was exhilarated.

Not in England, though. As the decade rushed on, as he saw or read about slaughter in Abyssinia, beatings and murder in Hungary, Romania, Albania, racial violence in the Memel, Carpatho-Ukraine, Slovakia, fascist killing in Italy, Germany and Spain, communist in the east, Edward Carrington grew more and more amazed, then horrified, by the country that he supposed his own. To him and to most of his European friends, it was as clear as daylight in the sky that a war was coming. Central Europe, and some of its fringes, was not an unexploded bomb, it was in a state of constant, barely controlled explosion. It was burning, fraying at the edges, riddled with violent cancers of nationalism, spite and greed that could not go on without a climax for much longer. The First World War had destroyed an empire and left a vacuum at the heart of Europe. Hitler – a blind man could see – was going to fill it.

So was his country blind? Certainly his father said so, in letters. According to him – and Edward, separated by thousands of miles and great relief, was now prepared to listen – the Empire was retreating into cowardice and insanity. They were all, save Winston Spencer Churchill, trying to give India to the fuzzy-wuzzies, and the cuts in arms spending would leave us quite defenceless. The National Government was a disaster under Macdonald, worse under Stanley Baldwin, and unspeakable under Chamberlain. On his returns to England, Edward more and more frequently mixed with people of like opinion, many of them friends or associates of politicians. He was at the garden party on Guy Fawkes Night in 1938 when the honourable member for Stockton, Harold Macmillan, burnt Chamberlain in effigy, and he earned the thanks of Bob Boothby later the same evening when he happened upon him making love to Macmillan's wife against a turkey-oak tree – and went deaf and blind. He drank with Brendan Bracken, the red-haired Irishman who many thought was Churchill's bastard, and slept more than once on a settee in the great man's flat in Morpeth Mansions when they had all drunk too much whisky – although never while Churchill was in town. Edward had met him only twice, but what he saw he liked. The man was not a grey-suit, not a whey-face, not a pusillanimous, coughing politician. He was a buccaneer, and Edward admired that. By god, it was what his country needed.

Not everybody agreed, inevitably. To many Churchill was not so much a buccaneer as a straightforward pirate, a political outcast who skated on thin ice deliberately to keep himself in the public eye, a man who polished brilliant and wounding phrases that tacitly suggested himself as the alternative should his jeremiads turn out true. Edward, in bed one day with a clever country girl rebelling deliciously against the perceived repressions of her class, learned between kisses that Sir Joseph Ball – a former MI5 man who now led the Conservative Party's organizational machine – had used his old position to tap Churchill's phone for Chamberlain and monitor his associates. Edward had passed it on and – although it had already been known about – was confirmed in the eyes of Winston's men as somebody to trust. He particularly enjoyed the fact that his vaguely cosmopolitan, vaguely raffish air not only made him attractive to certain high-born English gels, but led to such useful pillow-talk. Their menfolk – educated, constipated, correct – tended to despise or (perhaps) fear him for his manners. It was on the cards that he should be drawn into the circle of dissent.

The suggestion that he might do something positive, however, came completely from the blue. It was August 17, 1939, and Carrington had spent most of the reception swallowing champagne. He did not recognize the man approaching him in a quiet corner of the drawing room, but feared he might be a drunken bore. He had a large gin in his hand, and at least a few inside him. He introduced himself as Major Desmond Morton.

Edward, who was hopeful that he had made a conquest some minutes earlier, found it hard to gather his concentration. The reception had been a glittering affair, and an odd one. After months of fits and starts, scares and rumours, the outbreak of a war in Europe was unavoidable. Since Munich, the mood of the British people had changed almost tangibly, with only Chamberlain's grey men in Parliament, backed by their poodles at the *Daily Mail* and the *Express*, not positively, atavistically, desiring the first shot. Poland was on the brink, it was only a matter of time before the heel of the jackboot smashed down. In Berlin and in London, in Paris, Warsaw, Rome, only the diplomats and power-brokers were hanging on, making desperate efforts, in the open and in secret, to avoid the blow-up. The people, it appeared, had clean forgotten what war meant. Some of the grey men, apparently, had not.

At this reception in the heart of London, the atmosphere was schizophrenic. There were civil servants there, diplomats from Germany and Russia, with their ladies old and young. On one level the social niceties ground on, the minutiae of dress and behaviour observed and chattered over. A string quintet played in the largest of the reception rooms, and guests spilled out into the garden in between light showers. But beneath it all, beneath the strange rituals that passed in this milieu for normality, there was an undercurrent of fear, of latent panic. And for some of the young, a dizzyingly exciting feeling, deep in stomach-pit, that something terrible was about to come about, something wonderful and dreadful.

There was a young woman there, an attractive girl he guessed at twenty-two, who had been introduced to him as Suzanne Simonis. She was imprisoned in a long silk gown, her face pale and rather beautiful, with dark circles around deep, exhausted eyes. She seemed on the verge of tears, somehow, which Edward found both strange and quite exciting.

'Simonis,' he said. 'May I say what an unusual name? You are German, I presume?'

She was a German. She was the cousin, she said, of Herr Theo Kordt, the Counsellor at the German Embassy in London. She had travelled overnight from Germany, by boat and train, and had had little sleep.

'How strange,' said Edward, slipping into German. 'You must have had a reason. A very important one? As I hear it, you may not have many days in which to get back home!'

It was couched in the form of a joke, or at least of banter, but it had the directness that he knew many women responded to. Edward was dressed impeccably, but he retained his raffish air. He could see himself in the garden with Fräulein Simonis, investigating those dark eyes at closer quarters. But she did not respond. The eyes slid sideways, looked over his shoulder. A small smile lit her lips.

Turning his head, Edward saw another young woman. She was shorter than Suzanne, with dark hair and eyes, a sultry, sulky mouth. She said, in Swedish: 'Are you all right, Suzanne? You look like death. Shall I tread on his toes for you?'

'No,' Suzanne replied. 'But take him over, will you? He's asking awkward questions, he's probably a spy. I might burst into tears.'

'Poor thing. Do you want to lie down? Shall we go and find a place for you?'

Suzanne Simonis smiled wanly.

'I'll go and get coffee. Find Theo. I must sleep soon.'

To Edward, in German, she said: 'I'm sorry for that rudeness. This is my friend, Hannele Malling. Would you like to talk to her? She speaks German, of course, and English. I'm rather tired, I'm going to find my cousin. Excuse me.'

When she had gone, Edward said: 'Hannele. Short for Johanne? Is that German or Swedish?'

He spoke in Swedish, looking directly into her eyes. They did not flinch.

'So you speak Swedish, also. Very good. Yes, I am half-half. Suzanne is German, but she is my friend. You are an unusual Englishman, to speak languages. MI6, I suppose?'

The eyes were deep, fearless and unreadable. Edward Carrington much preferred his new companion, taken though he had been with Suzanne's tired, tired eyes. This one was like a dynamo.

He said: 'I've never heard of MI6. No, I am just a simple man of business. Hence the languages. I almost live in Europe. Have done so, I should say. I'm afraid it won't be so easy, very soon. Would you like a drink?'

A waiter was approaching, with champagne on a tray. Edward took two glasses, handing one to Hannele. They moved slowly towards the garden.

'I have a choice,' she said. 'It is not easy. I have not made up my mind yet. To live in Sweden or in Germany. What do you think? When the war comes?'

'Self-evident. Sweden is a beautiful country that will probably stay neutral. Germany is full of misery and danger, bestiality, violence. She will fight bravely for a while, then be bombed and strafed and ruined. There will be blood in the sewers, pestilence and death. She will probably be destroyed completely.'

'Germany, then,' said Hannele. 'Yes, I think you're right. Sweden is so very, very boring.'

Later in the evening, standing beside a huge rhododendron that dominated one whole corner of the garden, Edward asked Hannele if she would sleep with him. She had short, bobbed hair, and she swept a lock from out of her eyes before she answered.

'No,' she said. 'Tonight I must go with my friend. She is here on business, you understand? She is a courier from von Weizsäcker. You know? Ernst von Weizsäcker, State Secretary. He still thinks there can be peace, he is determined. Many people think Herr Hitler mad, you know. Suzanne has brought a message to her cousin, to tell him the date the war will start. August 25, or within three days after that.'

'Good God. Are you sure?'

'Of course. That is Hitler's plan. By revealing it von Weizsäcker hopes to shake the dunderheaded British out of their lethargy. To make you be decisive, tell Hitler that you will march immediately, crush him. Suzanne worries over it, she would not approve that I have told you. She slept not at all, throughout our journey. Do you think that it will work?'

Edward Carrington almost said something indiscreet, about Chamberlain and his Cabinet of sheep. In his opinion, they would make peace on almost any terms, they were shot through with cowardice, they lived in a perpetual funk. But who knew, perhaps this extraordinary girl was in fact the spy, not he, was trying to provoke an opinion that the Germans might find useful, was probing him.

'I'm a businessman,' he said. 'I really can't imagine how they will respond. I notice, however, that your reasons for not sleeping with me are purely practical. That surprises me.'

She cocked her head, cheekily, tilting backwards to look into his eyes.

'As an Englishman? Or as a businessman? Or as a spy?'

'Let's say — as an Englishman.'

'There is a war coming. I am twenty years old. Who knows, in six months I may be dead. Most Englishmen I know, no one would sleep with, they presumably sleep with each other. You do not look like that to me. I would like to have a try.'

'Tomorrow, then? That's a very pessimistic view. About the war.'

'Is it? I have lived in Germany for a year now, all the time. I am at university in Dresden. You are slim, and rather beautiful. Ring me at the Embassy tomorrow, ask for Suzanne. If it is possible, we will sleep together. Ja?'

She had smiled and dipped her head, and slipped away from him, amusement visible in every curve and angle of her body. Edward Carrington had wondered if he was drunk, or if she was just a dreadful tease, mocking the Englishman of European myth. He longed for the opportunity to destroy it.

Back inside the house, he found himself confronted by the gin-filled man.

'I saw your encounter earlier,' he was saying. His face was slightly blotchy. 'With Miss Simonis. Then the pretty little one, bright-looking filly, in the garden. Did they tell you anything? Interesting?'

'I beg your pardon? Major . . . Morton, did you say? Should I know you?'

'You might have noticed me around. Smart young man like

137

yourself. I'm with the IIC. Industrial Intelligence Committee. Mean anything to you?'

'I'm sorry. Not a thing.'

'No harm done. I'm eyes and ears. Intelligence. The committee's just the cover, I only work for one man. I think he'd be interested if you heard anything tonight. I think he'd be interested in you working on his behalf. I've checked you up, if you don't mind me saying so. Done my homework.'

Edward Carrington stared. As he raised his glass, Major Morton raised his also, as if to make a toast.

'You know the man I'm talking of, don't you? Friend of Bracken, Boothby, scourge of Halifax and the dreaded Hun.'

He touched his glass to Edward's, inclining his head.

'Happy days,' he said. 'To Winston Churchill. Our Man of Destiny.'

TWO

After she had gone to bed with him, Hannele Malling began to call Edward Carrington 'Carruthers'. When he had rung the German Embassy, after a thoroughly unsatisfactory morning, neither Suzanne Simonis nor Hannele had recognized the name, although both had known immediately who it was. Hannele was calm and collected when she took the telephone. She spoke in Swedish.

'So. Edward Carrington. Some gentleman you turned out to be! You did not give a name.'

Edward, tired of the rules, encouraged by something in her voice, replied: 'If I were a gentleman, I should not be telephoning. Do we have a date?'

'I leave for Germany on the evening train, I'm afraid. It all depends on what you have in mind, and how long it would take. I have little experience in these matters. Nor, incidentally, a premises. I'm afraid you could not come here.'

A noise of stifled laughter charmed him. Two finishing-school hussies! They were outrageous!

'Of course not, Fröken Malling. I have a flat. Could you walk out from the Embassy? In twenty minutes, say? Turn left from the entrance and wait on the first corner. I won't leave you standing.'

'How will I know you? Will you wear a red carnation! It was very dark!'

The phone went down in laughter, and Edward replaced his receiver with a pleasantly hollow stomach. It was ten minutes brisk walk to the Embassy, and he was waiting on the corner as Hannele approached. She was wearing a thin silk dress, sheer stockings, a small fur jacket. He found her entirely ravishing.

They took a taxi to the flat, which was in a quiet, imposing block overlooking Bedford Square. Edward rented it from a woman who lived abroad, a woman he had never met, and it suited him perfectly. It was far too big for one, but it was regularly cleaned by the leaseholders of the building, who maintained all services and looked out for security. The lifts, however, were unmanned, a feature he had also found convenient.

Not that Hannele would have minded being seen. The boldness of her eyes when she had greeted him had spoken of no social fear. It was Carrington who was at the disadvantage and the realisation came to him as yet another pleasant shock. As he opened the front door to his rooms, his shirt collar was slightly damp.

There were no preliminaries. Hannele glanced around the large, light, high-ceilinged rooms approvingly, then chose a room with a double bed. It was not the one that Edward used, but that was no concern of hers. She plonked herself firmly down on it, flicked off her shoes, and hitched her dress up delicately, first across one thigh, then the other, as she unpopped her stockings, rolled them swiftly down, and plucked them from her feet.

'Silk,' she said. 'And there's a war about to start. Forgive me for not inviting you to remove them with your teeth!'

Her face was blazing with amusement, she was making fun of him. Edward did not mind at all. The soft whiteness of her inner thigh was blinding him.

'Well? You either undress yourself, or you help me. Don't just stand there like a dummy. I don't like that.'

'I thought you said you weren't experienced in these matters. You have strong preferences.'

'I said I was not experienced with Englishmen. I'm wary of you, as a breed. We hear terrible things of your schooling system in my country, and I've met a lot of you. If it was dark, I would make you turn the light out!'

While she spoke, Hannele undressed herself, unhurriedly. Edward undid his tie, but for the life of him he could not take his eyes off her. She stood to slip the dress down over her hips, and pouted at him in her petticoat. Her underwear was white, all of it, and she was surprisingly pale herself when she stood naked in his view. Her vaginal hair was a tiny bush, high on her pubic bone, sparse at the sides, pointing downwards like an untidy arrow. Her nipples were a surprising red, as if they had been rouged, which they had not. Across, they measured probably an inch, and the nipple in the centre was also small.

'Now you. You bother me, standing like that. Don't move.'

She came towards him softly, like a cat, and stood on tiptoe to ease off his tie. Her eyes were on a level with his nose and they were brown and full of life. Edward had never been treated like this before, and he felt dazed, swoonlike. He was probably wrong, he acknowledged, but he felt like a woman must feel, when an attentive man undressed her. Hannele's fingers, as they ran down his shirt buttons, were like electric probes, even through his cotton vest. She had unbuttoned him to his waist, and pulled his shirt and vest out of his trousers, before she spoke.

'Come on,' she said. 'You must help with the boring bits. Take your jacket off, at least!'

He was surprised to discover it still on. He shrugged his shoulders and it fell down his arms. Hannele pushed it to the floor. As she leaned foward her breasts hung, brushed his vest. Convulsively, Edward jerked the garments over his head and discarded them. He put his arms around her and pressed her naked breasts to him. His chest was hairy, especially towards the stomach, and she sighed. She moved her body slightly, brushing her nipples with the hair.

'More like an ape,' she said. 'Than an Englishman.'

Edward moved forward, moved her back towards the bed, but Hannele sidestepped, turning him around instead.

'No. Me.'

Edward, in the modern style, wore no braces. Hannele unbuckled his belt, then reached her slender fingers into the tight, well-tailored fly to the waist-hook. He thought he would have to help, but she was strong and sure. The sensations that he had were extraordinary. His penis was pressing hard against the inside of the fly, bent, desperate to escape and straighten. Hannele, sensing this, whipped down the buttons very quickly and, before pulling down his trousers, put her fingers into the flap of his white cotton underdrawers and freed it. As she touched his skin a noise escaped from Edward, an exact match for what he felt. It was incoherent, inchoate, indescribably excited.

'No,' he said. 'Don't touch. Not for a moment.'

Hannele pulled back, and both of them looked downwards. His penis was standing through the cotton slit, throbbing. If it was touched again it would explode, they knew. They watched it, silently, until the crisis passed its peak. Then Hannele eased his trousers down his legs to his ankles. She lifted the underdrawers carefully, sliding his penis through the slit without touching it, sliding the drawers down to meet the trousers.

'You still have shoes and socks on, silly man.' Her voice was thick and husky. She sat him on the bed, and knelt to untie his laces, slip off the shoes. Then she unbuttoned his suspenders and pulled his socks off. Her hair was too short to fall far across her face, so Edward could see her expression, tender and deliberate. Her small shoulders were frail, her back bent over him, her little breasts made fuller by their angle. Edward closed his eyes.

'Back.' He opened them to find her pressing him, by the shoulders. 'Shift onto the bed. There.' And she squirmed quickly on beside him, turning so that her breasts touched him. Her hand ran up inside his thigh and touched. He closed his eyes again.

'Oh God,' he said. 'You're making love to me.'

'Of course. That's why we're here. Now keep your eyes closed. I am really ready.'

He did, and Hannele's weight left the bed for a moment. He did not peek, but was strangely reassured when he felt her knees press the mattress down again. Then a sensation on the end of his penis, and fingers down its sides. Hannele said 'Ah' softly, as she unrolled the contraceptive to his root among the hair.

'In me now,' she said. 'Oh Carruthers, I want it in me now.'

He opened his eyes and rolled — still almost blindly — onto the girl. His blind penis found its home immediately and he slipped gently inwards, slowly, trying desperately not to come. Hannele's mouth was open and her arms were flung outwards, bent, her palms half-closed. Almost instantly, Edward began to come, in slow, tearing waves. He came for ages, so it seemed. They breathed in unison as he moved. They felt as one.

'You didn't . . . reach orgasm,' said Edward. They were fully on the mattress now, a tangle of hair and arms and legs. He was delighted, delighted and regretful, both at once.

'Oh Carruthers. I did not expect to. That was what I wanted. Next time is for me, perhaps. That was what I wanted.'

He moved sideways, to bring her fully into view. She lay contented, sprawled, one heel on the bed-edge, one knee up.

'Carrington,' he said. 'Not Carruthers. But Edward's my name, Hannele.'

'No. Carruthers. Surely you have read the book? In Germany, in my set, everyone is reading it. We are looking for the key to your character. And for hints about the way you spy. You don't know what I'm talking of?'

'Not an idea. I'm not a very bookish chap, you know. *Vive la commerce!*'

'And *vive la différence*. Carruthers is the spy in *Riddle of the Sands*. He becomes involved in a wicked German plot to invade England across the North Sea, from the Frisian Islands. He is not very much like you.'

'Not?'

'Not.' She scratched the inside of her thigh. She moved closer in, and put her cheek on his shoulder. 'But then, I am not like Clara. She was a prim and proper little Fräulein, although her father was the villain, and Carruthers loved her, but dared not speak to her without a chaperone. Were people ever really like that? I'm sure they weren't. But that is how we see you British, still. Poor Carruthers. He probably went to his death without once seeing Clara in this state!'

'If she had behaved like you, he would have run a mile. We're certainly not used to it.'

'Oh thank you. Now I am a tart?'

'No! No, I didn't mean that. It's just . . . in our society. No, really, I was criticizing us, not you.'

'Your morals are too tight and ours too loose? Well, never mind, Carruthers. I expect you will not see me again, eh? And although you are very beautiful, there are always other men. You are a spy, aren't you?'

He eased his shoulder, as an excuse to break her gaze. He had met Desmond Morton that morning and, briefly, Sir Robert Vansittart, the chief diplomatic adviser to the Cabinet. Morton, in the cold gleam of sober day, had tended to make light of Edward's 'chatter with the fillies', and appeared to have nothing concrete to offer although exhorting him to 'keep his eyes and ears open', and harping on his private means. Van was the man to cultivate, said Morton — he had a finger in every secret service pie — and Van indeed had offered him a certain irascible encouragement. But so far Edward, very definitely, was not a spy. It seemed terribly important to him that Hannele should not find out.

'Why do you find me beautiful?' he said. 'You are beautiful. I'm a man.'

'Hah! Carruthers! You have such a lovely slim build. Your body is long, and your legs are shorter, like a monkey's. Your belly is very furry and quite sweet. You have lots of hair, here, and here, and here. Your penis is quite excellent.'

143

She had it in her hand, and it began to stir. She let it grow to about half, then left it and took his testicles in her cupped hand.

'And you are a spy. I like that. You are not like Carruthers, you are not one of these truly awful Englishmen. You do not even disapprove, very much, of the way I came to bed with you. I bet I know your rationale. I bet you're thinking what odd times we're living through, how behaviour can be different for a while, how I'm a little brash, and very ill-advised, but possibly forgivable.'

Edward stayed silent. She had been very accurate. On the other hand, she had not taken into account the effect her presence had on him. Brief encounters he had had before, not just with Swedish/German girls. But Hannele Malling, body and brain, had filled his spirit.

'Are you a spy?' he said. 'You are, in a certain way. You've brought messages that the German High Command would shoot you for. If I'm a spy, can we work together? Could you get messages to me from Germany? Have you come to work for us?'

Her hand was unmoving on his balls. His penis had gone small. Hannele breathed evenly, slowly.

'No. I am not a spy. For me to spy would be a betrayal of my friends. We brought messages to save the peace, not to be traitoresses. That is why we have all been doing it, von Weizsäcker, Theo Kordt in London, his brother Erich in Berlin, Canaris, Carl Burckhardt, Dahlerus, Wenner-Gren. You do not think the war is worth averting, do you? But you will be on the winning side.'

Edward said, rather piously: 'There is no winning side in war.'

For a moment, something like contempt glowed in her eyes.

'If only you believed that. You English. You know nothing of war, it has never touched you. You are an island, you have not known the wolves. Europe is a cockpit, a chessboard stained with blood. I am Swedish. Have you heard of the Thirty Years War? You are an island. Suffering, for you, is just a story, an old man's tale.'

Sunlight was streaming through the high window. Amid the rumble of the traffic, birds were singing in the trees of Bedford Square. Two people lying naked on a double bed. Edward did not want that spell to end. For a long while he said nothing.

'So you are Swedish, Johanne Malling? Or German? Yesterday, you were half and half. And Sweden was so very, very boring, you wanted blood. This is me speaking as Carruthers, by the way. The dedicated agent.'

'I am Swedish, but my family are a mixture. We have interests in Germany, technology, metallurgy, industry. I am studying at Dresden, and I probably will stay. The blood and boredom . . . well, perhaps I was a little drunk. I can't see even Hitler causing trouble for the Swedish, he needs our iron ore too much. I can always leave.'

'Hitler is a mad dog. If anything – if I agree with you at all – that is surely why a war is necessary? Many of us in Britain see it as our duty, now. Killing Hitler. As much as anything, it's a matter of honour, and some of us are afraid that that's in danger of slipping away from us. The Munich Disease. I'm a Churchill man myself. He thinks Chamberlain has wrecked this country. I'm awfully afraid he's right. He must come to power, soon.'

Hannele wriggled. She moved from off his shoulder, swung her legs round, then crossed them under her. She faced him, earnestly, sitting like that, her hands inside her thighs, her vagina exposed to him amid soft hair, smooth skin. Edward Carrington had never talked to a woman like this before. It shocked him, thrilled him, filled him with a kind of ache, a hunger. This woman of twenty spoke to him like a mentor, like a sage. But he could not shift his gaze from off her sex.

'Churchill has read history,' she said. 'Churchill should know better. Mr Chamberlain has tried everything, and he has lost. But he knows what will happen if war comes. He remembers carnage, the blood and misery. Mr Churchill caused Gallipoli, and would do it all again. He is a playboy, a gangster with a rich uncle. Between them he and Hitler would lay everything to waste, and the uncle would have to save your side again. America.'

Still Edward felt no irritation. He concentrated on her breasts, small and soft, tipped so brightly in their red, moving in her agitation. He put a hand out, touching her knee, tenderly. Her head was haloed in the sunlight pouring through the casement. He wanted her at peace.

'Many of your countrymen – no, many of the Germans we have talked about – think Hitler would have stepped back if Churchill had been in power. He would have been afraid. But let me be Carruthers, Hannele. History means nothing to the English. At school I was no great shakes at it, or anything. I'm ignorant.'

It was a lifeline he was offering, a last throw to save the mood, enjoy the bed and sunlight. Hannele, making a small face, decided to accept it. There was on her lips the slightly sulky look he had first noticed in her the night before, but she was fighting. A smile broke through.

'Ignorant and arrogant. You are right, Carruthers. How did you gain your empire, I wonder. Were those your weapons? What did you learn at school?'

Laughing, Edward moved sideways, sweeping her with him, untangling her legs, straightening her until they were facing each other, side by side. Joyfully, they made love again, this time at his pace, not hers, even with a contraceptive he produced, both of them delighted by their mutual daring. Still, she did not come, which almost dampened Edward's happiness. It was nothing, she protested, it was something she could not control today, it did not mean she thought the less of him, or their sex together.

'But we may never meet again! Hannele, I couldn't bear that!'

She tapped his nose with her index finger end.

'You're being quite ridiculous. Should I ask Hitler to postpone the war because of your dreadful vanity? You were excellent. I am a woman, not a machine. Everything was excellent.'

As she spoke she stood. The sun was lowering, painting her pale skin gold. She began to dress.

'Don't go, Hannele. Another hour.'

'Third time lucky. But I have a train to catch. No! Don't stand. Stay there, naked. I'd like to take that image. A photograph inside my head.'

They kissed lightly when it was time to say goodbye. Edward Carrington had a heavy certainty that the lightness was more genuine on her part than on his. How ridiculous that the world would guarantee to keep them apart. How ridiculous that he should care. Hannele did not, she did not care to even hide it.

'Don't look so sad, Carruthers. Have no regrets.'

'I doubt if we'll . . . You have no plans to return to England?'

'Oh no. But Edward, you can come to Germany. On a parachute! I promise I'll be waiting, if you tell me in advance!'

She laughed, deliciously, and he laughed with her. He watched her from the window, half hidden, naked, behind the curtain. She walked across the corner of the square, and did not look back. He resigned himself to the single thought, that he would not see her again.

But two days later, Hannele Malling returned to London, and sought him out. She brought amazing news.

THREE

That Friday evening, after Hannele had gone, began the drabbest weekend of Edward's life. Outside in London, if he cared to leave the flat, he would have found an atmosphere, an edge, that any man of twenty-five with money in his pocket and an afternoon like that behind him should have delighted in. In the last few weeks, in the last few days especially, a suppressed excitement had been growing. Chamberlain may have shrunk visibly as the clouds across the face of Europe had grown darker, but the British people had taken a different path. Sandbags in the streets, gas-masks issued, ration books and evacuation procedures explained – all had induced a kind of mild hysteria, a desire to 'get up and at 'im'. Like Hannele, nobody who was nobody had any doubts that Britain and her Empire would be victorious: only the grey men in their boiled shirts and wing collars, who strode the streets of Westminster in rain or shine with black hat and rolled umbrella, were afraid. And lately, they had disappeared, gone to Scotland, Yorkshire, Cumberland to fish for trout and salmon, or shoot grouse. What did they know of real life?

After Hannele had gone from view, Edward turned from the window and surveyed the bed. It was rumpled, with the impression of their bodies clear on one side and across the middle. His clothes were in a heap, sadly formal clothes compared with hers, one sock suspender hanging from a chair-rail, a jacket sleeve turned inside out. Amid the jumble was a contraceptive, leaking onto the mat. He should have tied it. One of his mentor-girls in Scotland had told him once, in all seriousness, that it was against the law to use a rubber johnny then throw it away without knotting in the dangerous effusions. It probably was, in Scotland . . .

Perturbed by the keenness of his loss, afraid that it made him, in truth, a stuffed-shirt Englishman as Hannele had assumed, Edward Carrington went to the bathroom and began to fill the mighty iron tub. While the taps were thundering, he poured himself a large whisky and soda, and gulped it. He tested the water with his hand, adjusted it, and climbed in. His penis floated, moved in the swirling surface water when he lay down, and he fingered it, remembering. He let it come erect, then looked at it, with Hannele in his mind's eye simultaneously. He stroked it with the side of the whisky glass, smiled, drank. Ah Christ, he thought. What a thing to happen.

Dressed once more, in lighter, more informal clothes, he went to the telephone table in the lobby. He fished out the number Major Morton had given him and dialled. A girl's voice answered. A secretary's voice. No, Major Morton was not in, she had no idea. There was more implied than said: it was Friday afternoon, it was getting on, the watering holes were filling up. He wondered if he dared ring Brendan Bracken, perhaps drift round to Morpeth Mansions, who knew, Winston might be up, himself. But damn them. He felt like a hanger-on, a toady. Damn everything, being born in a far colony, being cursed to cruise round Europe, to be on the edge of everything. He would not chase, that was demeaning. They could come to him.

He thought, briefly, of going to a night-club later, picking up a girl. The febrile atmosphere of pre-disaster London had already wrought a gear-change in the night scene, the numbers of men away at training barracks having produced a seemingly equal and opposite number of women on the spree. Edward had no uniform, which was the biggest draw, but he had cash, and what the girls called style. He also had a picture behind his eyes, of Johanne Malling, naked. He did not want another woman, not even as emetic.

So. Get drunk in London, or get out? Edward dialled the operator and put in a call to Portsmouth. He had two friends there, two male friends, who had a little boat they could take fishing. They were always asking him to come and join them, although he did not like the sea and did not fish. They were homosexuals, although their little house at Cosham was very respectable, with separate bedrooms visible to anybody who cared to look. John and Simon always left the doors open upstairs, as if casually, so that anyone who suspected, but did not know, would think they'd been wrong. Edward knew. He had met them on business once, in Denmark, and found them quite congenial – save for the sea-obsession. When the operator put him through they were pleased to invite him. If he motored fast, he would be in time for dinner. They would hold it.

Seventy miles to Portsmouth, but the A3 was congested. There were motor lorries in their dozens, most of them in Royal Navy blue, and convoys of staff cars and vans. South of Guildford he got stuck behind a road-train of three steam traction engines hauling a low bogey. The load was covered in tarpaulins, but was recognizable as a gigantic naval gun. The lead engine had a canvas dodger along its canopy, that was stencilled in crude letters: Look Out, Fritz! As Edward motored down Portsdown Hill, from the George, the harbour stretched out before him in the dying light. Extensive though its waters were, it was jammed with warships.

John and Simon, although they had sounded cheerful on the telephone, were fractious, upset, and ultimately a crashing bore. At first, after the normal welcomes and politenesses, the pre-dinner drink, their bitch had been about their little boat. They were unsure as to whether they would be allowed to use her any more. Although they had not seen the Harbour Master's orders themselves, there seemed a distinct possibility that all 'normal' use of the water was about to end.

'Why?' demanded Simon, a stocky, angry man. 'We're not at war yet. It's an infringement of our liberty.'

Behind the bluster, there was a deeper fear. John had received preliminary notice that his services would be required by the Navy, as he had extensive knowledge of commercial diving technology. Simon was expected to be called up by the Army, and sent off God knew where. Edward, disaffected, could only try to hide his lack of sympathy, or interest. Why, he wondered, did they expect to be treated differently from anybody else? Even any other married couple . . . Pleading tiredness, he went to bed early, and masturbated.

Saturday was worse. They drove to the little creek where they kept their fishing boat, and moaned extensively to other men with blue-knit jumpers and glowing pipes. There were assessments of Herr Hitler's chances (poor), Chamberlain's ability (poorer), and the courage of the Italian fighting soldier (poorest, by a long shot). On balance, Chamberlain would win although he did not deserve to, because Hitler had the Eyeties on his side, and the Eyeties had sent six hundred thousand men to crush Albania and almost been repulsed. Hitler was fit only for the loony bin, his generals would kill him within five minutes if he ever declared war, and he only had one ball. Ivan was the real threat, and if only Adolf had the sense he'd do a deal with Churchill, they'd kick Neville into touch, and the pair of them would whip the Reds from here to Kingdom Come, or from arsehole to breakfast-time, whichever was the shorter route. Carrington said little.

He stayed till Sunday morning, but the tensions only grew. Simon and John hinted that he was preoccupied, but in fact he was downright bloody rude, and everybody knew it. When they set off for church he set off for London, driving fast. He had never believed that anything like this could happen to him – this being, he supposed, love at first sight – but he acknowledged that it had. With the proviso that it was probably only lust, because he was already feeling slightly better. He stopped for an early beer at a roadside pub in Surrey, then dropped the car off in its lock-up garage and strolled to a café for lunch. There were still visions of Hannele, intermittently, but they were growing less. Distance and impossibility were a help. He had no address, no way of contacting her. She lived in Dresden, possibly. Or in Sweden . . . At ten past eight that evening, when he ran downstairs to answer his outer doorbell and found her on the doorstep, it was as if he had been kicked in the stomach.

Hannele was all in. Her hair was greasy, her face white, her eyes smudgy. She wore a light travelling raincoat, and was carrying only a small leather bag. Edward was dressed to go out, immaculate. They stared at each other, however, in equal disarray.

'Hannele. Good God alive.'

'Edward. I'm sorry. Can I come in?'

'But you're in Germany! What happened? Didn't you go back?'

He touched her sleeve, guiding her through the doorway. He took her bag, then put his free arm around her, involuntarily, hugged her. Hannele, when they got there, pressed the button for the lift.

'I've been there and come back,' she said. 'I have some information that your government needs to know. Suzanne Simonis could not return, she has problems in Berlin. It is not official information, it is better that it goes directly to a department that can deal with it. It is about Hermann Goering.'

The lift arrived as she said the name, and the two people inside looked at her curiously through the metal lattice. Edward jerked

151

open the door, interposing himself so that they should not stare. He put a finger to his lips.

Inside the flat, he was at a loss. He closed the door, and faced her in the lobby. He opened his arms, then his palms, desperate to hug her again, to hold her. Hannele's arms stayed at her sides, although she tried to smile. Edward turned away.

'I'll put the kettle on. Take off your coat and come into the drawing room. Hannele, you must be exhausted. It's only two days since you left! London to Germany and back again! Hannele!'

Unbuttoning her raincoat, she followed him, watched him light the gas.

'I could not get a flight to Croydon. That would have been easier. Edward, you do have contacts, don't you? This information is of the first importance. Goering wants to fly here. To avert the war. He wants to come and talk to your Cabinet.'

'Goering?' Edward's brow was furrowed. He was holding the lighted match. He blew it out. 'Hannele, Goering is a painted fairy. He is an evil, preening thing. He baits Jews, he founded the Gestapo. He is a Nancy-boy.'

Hannele's eyes, black holes in the pale, smudged face, held his.

'I hoped we had buried Carruthers,' she said quietly. 'Are all your countrymen as prejudiced as you?'

'I'm sorry,' Edward snapped. 'Some of my closest friends are homosexuals. But Hermann Goering is revolting. He is a beast.'

The kettle had begun to sing. Hannele rubbed a hand across her forehead.

'He is a strange man,' she said. 'He is eccentric, should that not appeal to your race? Much of what he says and does is just to shock. The clothes, the make-up sometimes, the jokes. He is not a homosexual, he is married to a Swedish woman, the sister of a count, and his first wife was also devoted to him, she died. He is prepared to risk everything to avoid this war.'

'Jokes,' said Carrington, with disgust. 'A Jewish friend of mine, in Germany, said that after *Kristallnacht*, last November, Goering suggested that the Jews should be charged for all the damage that was done. The shop windows, the synagogues, the cleaning of the streets. Was that a joke?'

'Probably. You would not understand. Men like Goering have to live with Hitler. Under Hitler. Some compromise is necessary, some protective stances. Even Hitler cannot control the *Sturmabteilung*, the Brownshirt animals. Self-preservation, Edward.'

He did not reply. He rattled in a cupboard, fetching cups and saucers. He banged a teapot onto the table, pulled the lid from off the caddy.

'Is this the fight we almost had on Friday?' asked Hannele. 'I will not have it, Edward, because I think you are being stupid, or obtuse. You know nothing of Herr Goering, only what you are fed by propaganda. You know nothing of me, only that we went to bed together for a while. You must stop treating me like a naughty girlfriend, for I am neither the one nor the other. Goering has been negotiating secretly for months. One of his deputies, Helmut Wohltat, has been working on behalf of your Sir Robert Vansittart for years, even, feeding information. Three weeks ago Goering met some Englishmen on Sylt, you know it? One of the German islands. They also failed to take him seriously, and made him angry, but he has carried on the struggle. There is a Swede called Birger Dahlerus who has been aiding him. Now things are very black. So Goering is going to fly to England. Place himself in your trust. If you will not listen, Edward, take me to somebody who will!'

The kettle was boiling. Edward lifted it and splashed a little water into the teapot, swirling it.around. He made the tea, conscious that Hannele was close to him, unmoving, unanswered.

'You take a European view,' he said, finally. 'You think we want this war, we welcome it. That's not true. But Hermann Goering . . . Forgive me, Hannele. Of all the German leaders . . . Look — have some tea. Go and sit in the drawing room, I'll bring it through. I'll ring some people. Of course. I did not know he was married. Not that that matters, naturally.'

'Naturally,' she said, bitterly. 'Nor that his wife is Swedish, either. No. Only Germans are prejudiced, *naturally*. That sounds like a Goering joke, in fact.'

She left the kitchen, and Edward watched the teapot for a minute, a small trail of vapour escaping from its spout. In the drawing room, Hannele had removed her raincoat and was sitting on the edge of a hard armchair. She had a white blouse on, and a severe grey skirt that reached halfway down her calves. Her fist was bunched under her chin, she was staring into space. Edward poured the tea.

'Sugar?'

'Thank you. Sorry, I mean no. I'm in England, aren't I, a different language. I'm very hungry, Edward. Is there any food?'

'We'll go out. Hannele, you're whacked. Would you like to take a bath? Drink your tea and take a bath? I'll make some phone calls, then we'll go out.'

She nodded.

'I would like that, but I expect they'll want to see me. Make your phone calls. We will see.'

Ten minutes later, as he rang number after number, Edward Carrington was aware of her behind him. He turned, to find her chewing on a loaf of bread, watching him. Then he heard her prowling, then the rush of water. Five minutes after that, he had exhausted all the numbers that he knew, and drawn a blank. He felt a fool, an utter fool. He tried to get back to the drawing room unheard, but she was waiting. As he tiptoed past the open bathroom door she called.

'Edward? What is happening?'

'Nothing much. I'll tell you in a minute. You have a soak.'

'Carruthers! Come here! I won't eat you!'

He did not want to go. If he saw her naked, he knew he would be lost. He would fall into a pit, he would descend to hell.

She was lying in the bath, all underwater save her face, chewing the last crust of the loaf. The water was clear, unblurred by soap, and she was visible, naked and distorted, lovely. Her hair was wet, in dripping ringlets beside her ears, and steam rose to the lightbulb. Her face was no longer white, but pink, although her eyes were sunk deep still, deep and dark. She moved when he came in, her shoulders sliding up the curved enamel, her breasts breaking the surface.

'Well?'

He was wretched.

'It's Sunday. Most of the government are still on holiday.'

'What? With a war about to start! Even spies!'

'I'm very junior, Hannele. I may have deceived you. I'm hardly in the game at all.'

She was on the last mouthful. She grinned at him.

'If I tell Goering this, he might change his mind. He might decide Hitler's is the winning side after all. Is there nobody we can raise? What if we went there?'

'To the House? 10 Downing Street? It's not like that, in England.

Could one go and knock on Hitler's door, in Germany? Perhaps you should go to your Embassy. See Theo Kordt.'

'No. It would not do, this time. Will you be able to get them in the morning?'

'Oh yes.'

He hoped he was speaking the truth. Good God, he was! To tell them Goering was coming – well Halifax, or Cadogan, or Vansittart, anyone would want to hear that news.

'Edward?' She raised herself, amid a slosh of water. Her breasts came clear, the nipples flattened with the heat, but still that lovely red. Edward answered in his throat.

'I have eaten all your bread. I am very tired, and I am all wet. Can we forget the restaurant? Can we go to bed? It's not too early for you?'

To be honest, Edward told himself, I do not know. It was painful to be looking at her, her face open, a tired and unfrightened girl. He was frightened, and there was no component of desire in his response. He was beyond desire.

But he capitulated without a fight. Without a semblance of a fight.

'Third time lucky?' he said. His voice was not his own.

'I'm probably too tired. For anything like that. Shall we just wait and see?'

Ten minutes later, still damp and pink, she was asleep, her black hair dripping into his pillow. Edward lay beside her, fully clothed, with one arm crooked across her back.

He lay like that for ages, until cramp forced him to change position. Hannele slept on.

FOUR

Admiral Sir Hugh Sinclair – Quex – looked like a dying man to Edward Carrington. His skin was pale and crêpe-like, his eyes too bright inside loose, unpleasant-coloured lids. His office was heated, despite the warmth outside, it was overheated. When Sinclair spoke, his teeth – presumably dentures – clicked. At first he said very little, only listened.

Carrington, still naïve though learning, had thought it logical that Hannele should tell her story to the proper authority in person. They had woken at eight, and he had made tea and toast for both of them. She had been like a lazy cat, refusing to wake up properly, a phenomenon that he had known in young girls before. Twenty, she had said, and in some ways she seemed younger. Edward, at twenty-five, felt staid and mature, and also privileged. Also urgent, as he served her tea and she sat up in the bed, exposing her small breasts without a thought. She caught the look.

'You're terrible, Carruthers, you think of nothing else. I'm here on urgent business, I've come to save the world from self-destruction. Let me eat some toast first. Where did you get the bread?'

'They leave it outside my door, with the milk. The porter fetches it every morning.'

'How very civilized.'

Afterwards, they made love, but Hannele had very little interest in it as a process. She did not actually check her watch, but the effect was there, and Edward felt it keenly. As soon as he had come she pushed at him to move, all efficiency.

'That was very nice. Now, let's get up, shall we? Edward! Are you sulking?'

He was. Sulking and hurt. She tutted.

'Please. Don't be a foolish boy. I'm here to do things. I'm refreshed, I've had a lovely sleep. *Um Gottes willen*, Edward! There are better times for this! There are other times!'

She jumped from the bed and harried him, like a terrier, towards the door. The look of fierce determination on her face soon made him laugh. He was nude except for a drooping condom. She seized it, flicked it off his penis, waved it round her head.

'Go!' she cried. 'Let us save the world!'

It was not easy, though. Morton, even at ten past nine, was nowhere to be found. The Whitehall switchboard was a model of inefficiency as usual, and it took twelve minutes to try the various rooms and people who might know. Hannele, perched on a chair in the lobby like a greyhound, grew more and more impatient.

'It's Monday morning! Hitler is due to march on Poland this weekend! Is this some English joke!'

It wasn't. From what he knew of government, it was normal. He considered going to the House, or Whitehall, looking for Morton or someone else he knew. But he did not have an appointment. Nobody would see him.

'Are you sure we can't do it through Kordt? The Embassy? There are official channels. It's very, very difficult.'

'Absolutely not. Under no circumstances at all must the Germans know about it. Edward – act!'

He rang Vansittart. He felt that he was making a mistake, but that was that. Please God he would remember him.

'Who was that man?' he asked Hannele, after asking for his offices. 'The Goering man you said worked with Vansittart?'

'Wohltat. Doctor Helmut Wohltat. Say you're him.'

That wasn't necessary. Edward gave his own name, mentioned the meeting with Morton, mentioned Wohltat. Within thirty seconds Van came on the line.

'Yes? Don't waste my time, young man.'

'I won't, sir. Those girls we talked about, the couriers. I think I'd better see you face to face. One of them has come back. May we come and talk to you?'

'I have a meeting. Can't Morton deal with it? I've got to see the PM.'

'I'd rather not say on the telephone.'

'Poppycock! Well damn you, then.'

'Sir! It's about . . . it's about Doctor Wohltat's superior. It really is important.'

There was a pause. Edward lifted a hand, the fingers crossed.

'Quex Sinclair's on this number. Take it down, memorize it, destroy it. Ring him now and tell him it's from me. If you waste his time he'll roast you, if you don't you might just get that job. Don't take the woman.'

'Sir?'

'Are you stupid, boy? Do you know who Quex is? Do you know who *she* is, more to the point? By the end of the week we'll probably lock her up. Don't let her know a thing.'

Quex Sinclair – also known as 'C' – was head of MI6, one of the great non-secret secrets of the intelligence machine. He did not tell Hannele that, but he told her he had to go alone, and she took it calmly. She had expected no other outcome, even if he had. She stayed in the flat, while he took a taxi. She was prepared to meet an intermediary, anybody, any time. But she suspected it would not be necessary. There are other channels, she told him gravely. Edward, again, felt foolish.

Sinclair made him tell the story twice. He drew doodles on the pad in front of him, occasionally dabbing at his loose, wet lips with a handkerchief. Carrington was uncomfortably hot, but did not like to use his own in case it was insulting.

'That's all, is it? Goering means to come, and he wants us to give him clearance. Does he think we'd shoot him down? Going a bit far, eh?'

Hannele had given Edward a sheet of paper with names and numbers on it, which now lay on the desk. He indicated it.

'My contact says—'

'Yes, yes. And who is she? Johanne Malling, Swedish national, resident in Germany. Hhm. Do you know what the German girl brought? Last week. Simonis?'

'As I understand, some dates. When Hitler intends to invade Poland.'

'Good. Not good enough to bring Chamberlain back from his holiday until today, but good. Something else. A message from Count Ciano. Mussolini won't necessarily support them. What d'you make of that?'

'Oh. Well.'

'Nothing? Very wise. Can't trust any of them. This latest nonsense. Goering flying from Germany to keep the peace. Damn man's too fat to fly a plane, I'd say. To damn fat by far. Which university did you say?'

'I beg pardon, sir? Oh, oh I see. Neither. I'm a colonial, actually. Father helps run India. I got my schooling on the hoof.'

'Good, damned good! I don't like Oxbridge men, don't trust 'em, they don't always play the game these days. Cambridge in particular. Nest of perverts, so they tell me, I won't have 'em in my service if I can help it. Clubs?'

'None, I'm afraid. I'm not in England much you know, sir. I've quartered Europe in the last few years. Had to make a living, actually.'

'Good again. Novel. If you make a living, you're not an intellectual. Not bad rule of thumb, that. Not, are you?'

Edward gave a deprecating smile.

'I don't believe so, sir.'

'Want to join the service? Of course you do! If I don't snap you up someone else will, won't they? We'll fix you up with something, avoid conscription, eh? Cover, or a regiment, no need to decide just yet. Welcome to the team.'

The old man stood with difficulty. As his face came close to Edward's, his breath hit him in a shocking wave. His hand was gnarled and bony. Edward Carrington was on his feet as well. They regarded each other.

'Sir? Major Morton—'

'Hah. He's been at you, has he? He won't mind, he can't pay you, anyway. I'll sort him out.'

'And . . . and the Goering information?'

'Leave it with me. Give your details to the girl outside, we'll fix everything. That German girl?'

'Swedish. Yes?'

'Get rid of her. Quick. Whatever the wops say about not dying for Danzig, those dates that came were genuine. The engine driver says so too. Send her home.'

The engine driver? He did not ask.

'If you want someone to talk to her—'

'I don't. Be nice to her, mind you. Thank her prettily, see if we can keep in touch somehow. The Swedish connection could be very useful when the war comes. Very useful.'

Outside in the corridor, his mind still easing itself in to the thought that he was now an agent, an MI6 man, Carrington met Desmond Morton. The major's puffy face took on a look of deep suspicion.

'So Quex has got you, has he? Damned nuisance, all this poaching. What did she want, the girl? Nothing new, I suppose? Just confirmation, or denial? Of the dates?'

'That's it. Confirmation, actually. But Sir Hugh—'

'Quex.'

'Quex knew already.'

Desmond Morton was pleased.

'Of course he did. At least you're on the payroll, though, remember who put you up for that, eh? Listen, just because you work for Quex, you understand, doesn't mean we can't liaise. It's very much a team affair, intelligence. Don't put this round, but when Ramsay Macdonald was PM, Quex used to keep a lot of stuff back from him, thought he was unsound. He passed it on to Winston. So bear that in mind, won't you? You are on the payroll?'

Edward, reluctantly, nodded confirmation.

'I knew it. So bear it in mind, there's a good chap. Won't you?'

'I will,' said Edward, truthfully. But the major struck him as an odd fish, rather. Strangely inferior, somehow, for Churchill to have placed so much trust in. He mused about it, as he hurried to the flat.

The Goering flight did not happen, but even as an agent, Edward Carrington was never able to find out why. Over the next days, he was taken round the various offices used by the SIS in London, and introduced to many men, and a few women, with whom he was to work. Most of the women were secretaries, models of deferential, under-educated Englishwomen who filed and typed and processed the enormous piles of bumph that came from many quarters. Some of them worked in the field, he understood, but these were the younger, smarter ones who had been trained as cipher clerks and radio operators, usually to serve a male agent. He quickly learned that he was to be used in Scandinavia, because of his languages, but at present – with no expertise of any sort in clandestine communication – he had to train.

His parting with Hannele had been low-key, and saddening. He had told her, as frankly as he could, that the person he had spoken to – 'a person high in British Intelligence' –, had wanted her to return to Germany (or at least, to leave England) and would not allow her to meet anybody else. He passed on the thanks, and the remarks about the possibility of keeping in touch in the event of war. Hannele eyed him coldly.

'I suppose you've not reconsidered, have you?' he said, trying to ignore her expression. 'We don't want you to spy, exactly, but . . .'

He made a face, exonerating himself from such indelicacy.

'You frighten me,' said Hannele. 'You are such amateurs, you English, such awful amateurs. It seems to me that I am exactly the sort of person that you need, that you should cultivate me, prime me, pay me, even. You could interrogate me, at least, and if you thought I was a double agent you could put a bullet in my head. But you pat me on the bottom and send me home, and hope I'll "keep in touch"! Pfui!'

'Rather more than that, I think,' Edward replied. But he was uncomfortably aware that she was precisely accurate. 'In any case, you did say you wouldn't do it.'

He had hoped for better things than this. He had had visions, striding back to Bedford Square, of proper love-making, of tenderness, perhaps some tears. Then, obscurely, he had thought they'd work it through, he would recruit her, sort out a way in which they could communicate, even meet. His very own private source in Germany. Instead, contempt.

They were in the kitchen, where Hannele had been drinking milk when he returned. She drained her glass and stood.

'No,' she said. 'I haven't changed my mind, if that's what you're angling for. And if your Intelligence wants me out, I'd better go. I've checked the aeroplanes from Croydon, I used your telephone, this time I shall fly. I shall take a taxi to the aerodrome.'

'But I'll drive you! Hannele . . .'

He had a lot he wanted to say, but her face forbade it. She refused to let him drive, and she had no time – no inclination? – for making love with him. She moved round the flat like a whirlwind, and in minutes she was in her light raincoat.

He said miserably: 'Let me at least come with you and hail a cab.'

'And kiss me goodbye in the street? No, here.'

She moved towards him, smiling. Edward, utterly wretched, put his arms about her and she raised her mouth to his. Hers was open, but his lips stayed closed. She held him, stroked his back, laid her head, after a few seconds, on his chest.

'Carruthers,' she murmured. 'Sometimes Edward, you really are Carruthers. Don't grieve. I am immensely fond of you. Don't grieve.'

Edward Carrington was grieving.

*   *   *

161

Goering did not fly, and Hitler's first attempt at starting World War II was a failure. The orders were indeed issued, and the attack should have begun at 4.30 a.m. on August 26. Concentration camp prisoners dressed in German uniforms had been collected near the Polish border and were waiting, drugged, to be shot by their fellow German soldiers, real ones, and used as evidence of provocative atrocities that would justify invading Poland. Reinhard Heydrich had dreamed up this idea, and also the name for the unlucky decoys – *Konserven*, or, let's say, tinned meat. When the plan fell through, he put them back into the larder till the next time.

Case White, as the invasion was codenamed, was aborted by a signal issued at about 7.30 p.m. on August 25, because Mussolini and Ciano, when it came to it, summoned up the courage to tell Hitler the truth at last. Pact of Steel or not, they could not support him physically without large injections of armaments and raw materials: if he went into Poland, and France and Britain sprang to her defence, Italy would collapse. Forced by Mussolini's courage to be unusually clear-sighted in his turn, Joachim von Ribbentrop, the champagne salesman, advised his Führer to call it off, an undertaking that would take about eight hours. A few units, inevitably, were not warned in time, the radio messages and despatch riders did not get through, but nothing serious happened, a few more border incidents at dawn, adding to a list already long, was all. Later that day – the 26th – Hitler was still in command of his mental state sufficiently to send a telegram to Mussolini demanding a precise list of what he needed, but after that he almost snapped. The German people, too. On August 27 they awoke to find that food had gone on ration, as had petrol and many other necessities. In several towns rioting broke out, rioting for peace, and Nazis found themselves the victims of the kind of abuse and maltreatment they normally handed out to others. Party flags and posters were destroyed.

Carrington, on initial training in London, gleaned snippets from his colleagues, and from Desmond Morton, who remained clubbable and generous as long as there was gin in evidence. It emerged that Ribbentrop had accused Birger Dahlerus the Swede of being a British agent – which in a way he was – but that the Führer luckily had ignored it. There was hope of an Army rebellion to unseat Hitler, but firmer news that he had ringed himself with his most loyal SS units, doubling his personal security. There was an even stronger rumour that Herr Hitler had finally become unhinged, had gone bleating, weeping mad and would end his days – soon – dribbling and counting posies. Sadly, this turned out to be the standard stuff of innumerable intelligence reports, as Carrington got to know them better. A little fact, a lot of wishful thinking.

However, the scramble to keep the peace went on. The Swedish connection, working mainly through Hermann Goering still, set up meeting after meeting, held session after session, made proposals by the score. Diplomats like Sir Nevile Henderson in Berlin – already dying of cancer – wore themselves grey and corpselike in the struggle, while in London every avenue was open. The news of the Nazi-Soviet Pact, which broke mid-week, confused the issue, but the conviction that the war would never come appeared to grow in Whitehall, whatever evidence emerged to the contrary. Goering, via Dahlerus, insisted that Hitler was dead set on it, and even transmitted a new invasion date, the night of August 30/31. The Reichsmarschall also showed his Swedish intermediary maps of the whole German battleline, disposed to enter Poland. But when no war came on August 31, Vansittart – not noted for his pacifism – told Carrington over lunch with Desmond Morton that Herr Hitler had undoubtedly lost his nerve. At an adjacent table in the Carlton Club, the skeletal Lord Halifax, a hunting man, was telling his own entourage loudly that he 'smelled a beaten fox'.

Optimistic or not, though, the government had taken their precautions. Outside the club, the busy streets of London would next day be awash with evacuees and their parents, and third class carriages on special trains awash with tears and urine. Similar scenes were scheduled to take place in other major cities, while country areas were bracing themselves for the influx of tragic refugees or louse-infested slave labour, depending on the children's luck. Complete mobilization of the forces was scheduled for the same day – one of those strokes of government that real people marvel at. Quietly, too, Morton confided to Edward, the stiff and priggish Chamberlain had been pulling chestnuts from the fire. He had been in touch with Winston to sound him out. At any moment, an announcement of a job would surely be made – a Cabinet position.

It was Saturday before the balloon really went up, despite the fact that the invasion came at last on Friday morning. The news was first disseminated by DNB – the *Deutsche Nachtrichten Büro* – at 5.40 a.m. when the Führer's proclamation revealed to an incredulous world that the action had been forced on Germany by the insane campaign of terror waged against her by Poland. Reuters flashed the news to London shortly afterwards, and Sir Howard Kennard, the British Ambassador in Warsaw, sent a coded phone call at 8.30 reporting the attack. It emerged much later that the first casualties had been on Thursday night – *Konserven*, one at Gleiwitz, six at Hohnlinden – who had been dressed as Polish soldiers and shot. They had, these dastardly 'Poles', been caught committing terror acts and killed by brave SS units in the ensuing battle. Their faces had been beaten off to make sure nobody could later link them to a concentration camp, or even their homes, in Germany. Tinned meat had been served, and served its purpose.

In London, though, life went on that Friday almost as if the invasion had not happened. True, evacuees milled and wept and choked the stations, mobilization added to the confusion, the Cabinet dithered – but all that was preordained. Food-rationing details were announced, surprising nobody, and radio censorship made no difference that anyone could discern. Sandbags appeared in Whitehall and the blackout officially started, and at six o'clock Parliament assembled to hear Mr Chamberlain speak. Balloons did go up, literally, as the first of the silver monsters climbed slowly into the sky to cripple or destroy the bombers, if they came. But when the country went to bed that night, precisely nothing different, or exciting, or decisive had been said or done. Edward Carrington, weary of the chattering and intrigue at Westminster, was home in bed by midnight. His thoughts were not of Britain's fate, nor Poland's, but of Hannele's. He ached for her.

On Saturday, the edges frayed. Carrington spent most of the day in the House, in the company of Churchill's men and, briefly, Churchill himself. They followed the saga of France's panic and Mussolini's attempts to backslide from dribs and snippets, and hung around the bars and tea-rooms as Chamberlain's new statement was announced and postponed twice. By 7.45, as he crammed himself into the visitors' gallery, Edward could see that not only Desmond Morton had been drinking. In fact, the only men in the Chamber who seemed entirely sober were the Prime Minister and Halifax, his Foreign Secretary. They looked as if they needed alcohol, or perhaps a blood transfusion: they were cadaverous.

Chamberlain's speech was worse than his appearance. The House, prepared to sympathize, listened in growing anger as he doddered on. It was as if – or so it seemed, to that excited, tired throng – it was as if no one had invaded anyone, no one had been bombed or slaughtered, no treaty obligations were being fudged. He talked of an Italian plan to stop the war and have a conference instead, he said he was in touch with France to agree a time limit for Germany to withdraw and be forgiven, it came across as craven. Morton, crushed in next to Edward, spluttered: 'Winston must speak! Winston! Winston!'

It was Arthur Greenwood who did speak, however, the Labour leader. When Chamberlain subsided, Greenwood rose.

'Speaking for the Labour Party—'

Speak for England!' someone roared, and the House erupted. Later that evening, as the Churchill faction talked and drank and lived it out again, Bob Boothby claimed the honour, although Edward thought he had seen Leo Amery mouth the words. No matter, it was said. And when the noise died down, Greenwood continued.

'I am greatly disturbed.' His features were working, he clearly showed it. 'An act of aggression took place thirty-eight hours ago. The moment that act of aggression took place, one of the most important treaties of modern times automatically came into operation.' The roars and shouts grew louder. 'I wonder how long we are prepared to vacillate at a time when Britain, and all that Britain stands for, and human civilization, are in peril?'

Poor Chamberlain tried to save himself, but his reply was yet more pathetic than his first attempt. The Tory Chief Whip, David Margesson, ended his agony by moving the adjournment, and the corridors were filled with yelling, scurrying, frantic men, taking up their cliques and groupings, pooling their opinions, consolidating. Edward allowed himself to be swept by his particular tide, and spent the next few hours in a blur of short motor trips, a meal, many drinks, shouted insults, conversations. Half the Cabinet or more, the rumour went, had rebelled and demanded Chamberlain give an ultimatum to the Germans, whether or not the French joined in. The seriousness of the revolt was evidenced by the fact that Soapy Simon, an arch-appeaser who wanted above everything to be liked, had become their spokesman and had let them cram into his room and sit it out (with a break for dinner at the Savoy, of course) until the PM gave his answer.

All evening, great men came and went at Downing Street and at the Palace of Westminster. Phone lines buzzed between Rome and

Paris, Paris and Warsaw, Berlin and London, London and Rome. The Poles reported Warsaw under bomb attack and wanted help, immediately, from whoever would honour their commitments. The French Cabinet, split and demoralized, wriggled and trimmed, while their Embassy in London was besieged by people and by telephone. The assembled friends were told by Brendan Bracken in tones of wonderment that Churchill – that great Francophile – had rung to bellow that he would watch them die without a qualm if they 'ratted on Poland as they had ratted on Czechoslovakia,' while Bob Boothby told them repeatedly how he had exhorted Winston to 'break Chamberlain and take his place'. Churchill, while being 'too much a man' to kick the PM on the ground, had agreed to send a letter to Downing Street demanding to know by midday on Sunday the exact position he could expect to hold in the government.

There was an emergency Cabinet meeting shortly after 11 p.m., and as it progressed the storm clouds that had been gathering all Saturday evening came to a head. Like characters in a Thomas Hardy novel, the Cabinet left Number Ten to wild lightning and torrential rain – nor were they unaware of the almost vulgar symbolism. An ultimatum had at last been agreed, which gave Hitler until eleven o'clock next morning to withdraw from Poland lock, stock and barrel. No one believed for a moment that he would, but it was backed unanimously. The largest thunderclap of the storm had followed the Prime Minister's words 'Right, gentlemen, this means war', and the subsequent flash of lightning, it was remembered later, had lit up the entire room, despite the blackout curtains. Edward believed it when he heard the tale. By midnight, he and everybody else would have believed almost anything. Without a miracle happening, Hitler had achieved his war, and Chamberlain had lost his peace.

There was no miracle, although across Western Europe Sunday morning saw the last throws of the diplomats and the last prayers of the people who believed. When the moment of the ultimatum came and went, Neville Chamberlain sat before a microphone at 10 Downing Street and read the speech that was to become his monument. Before the National Anthem had finished playing, the first air-raid siren of World War II had sounded, a false alarm that sent the British nervously into the shelters, some – like Winston Churchill – defiantly clutching bottles of strong drink. That afternoon a U-boat sank SS *Athenia*, carrying eleven hundred passengers and three hundred crew from Liverpool to America. Of the three hundred Americans on board, anxious to get back across the Atlantic to safety, twenty-eight were among more than a hundred people drowned. A Swedish yacht helped pick up the survivors.

Edward Carrington returned to his flat in Bedford Square at just after seven o'clock that evening. It had been a melancholic day, although Winston Churchill had at last been called into the War Cabinet, gracing its inaugural meeting as First Lord of the Admiralty. Not only his men were cockahoop, either. Even the worst dummies, according to Bracken and Bob Boothby, were quietly confident that Britain would win a brief, efficient war. Carrington, however, was drained, and worried, and prematurely hung over.

Then his own small miracle took place. The phone rang, and the operator connected him to Stockholm. It was Hannele.

The call was brief, the line appalling. She said Suzanne had telephoned her from Germany. Berlin was stunned, the population cowed, rebellious, sullen. Dahlerus had spent the morning in one last effort to save the situation, and Goering had, in fact, ordered a plane to be prepared and standing by to fly him to London if the British would accept. They had turned him down. Goering's second flight had also not come off.

Carrington said: 'But Hannele—'

'No. I'll talk. Carruthers, I don't know what will happen now, but I have changed my mind. I do not know why, or whether it will work. If this war goes on, there will be networks. People will organize, and I will be among them. Tell your people who I am, that I will be in touch, I will be waiting. Carruthers?'

'Yes?'

'Carruthers, fourth time lucky!'

She put the phone down. Through his window, Carrington could see a silver barrage balloon, rising slowly on its cable into the clear blue sky.

It was very beautiful.

FIVE

The beauty of that late summer came to seem, finally, quite bizarre. Although most people were relieved that the waiting game was over, the first days and nights were nerve-racking. All the preparations, all the propaganda, had led them to expect Herr Hitler to start it with a bang, an airborne cataclysm, probably with fire and with deadly gas. Although few people still retained the Great War view that German soldiers wore dead babies on their helmet spikes and lived on human flesh, there was little doubt in many minds that the Führer was related to the devil. It was a schizophrenic view, as he was depicted by cartoonists as a buffoon, a cringing halfwit with cap constantly in hand, but the balloons, the sandbags, the innumerable air-raid shelters attested to the underlying fear. And nothing came. The war in Poland raged tragically, but even the French had pulled themselves together sufficiently to coin triumphalist slogans about their might and will. It continued warm and pleasant, no bombers terrified or destroyed, and euphoria returned and grew. Not until October 14, when a U-boat penetrated the defences of Britain's 'safest harbour' at Scapa Flow and killed the *Royal Oak* and more than eight hundred of her sailors, did the chill of autumn begin to bite. Churchill, the First Sea Lord and England's hero, could only describe it in the House on October 17 as 'a remarkable exploit of skill and daring'. There were many more to follow.

For Edward Carrington, the early weeks brought little but frustration and disappointment. He had learned from Desmond Morton that there was a plan afoot involving iron ore and the Swedish port of Oxelösund, which – had he not 'joined the wrong eleven' – he might have had a hand in. Edward knew Oxelösund, and guessed that the idea might be to cripple it, to cut down ore shipments to German industry, although Morton would not confirm his hunch. The major, grander now but no less approachable, had been promoted to a joint directorship of the Ministry of Economic Warfare.

'Try for a transfer, my lad,' he said. 'It might sound damned stuffy but it's not. Winston calls it the Ministry of Ungentlemanly Warfare, you know — although we have no riffraff, naturally. We get up to all sorts, I can tell you, and we're not fully in our stride yet. God knows what'll happen now that poor old Quex is going home. Perhaps I'll put in a word for you sometime.'

Quex was dying, fast, of cancer. By October his days in the saddle were over, and his deputy, Lieutenant Colonel Stewart Menzies, was preparing to clear his desk for one last time and transfer to Sir Hugh's enormous office overlooking Whitehall, an office so secret that it had a private door and staircase that could not be overlooked. There were some who hoped and half expected that he would never get there, and indeed, fought viciously to prevent it. Not because of his background — among Menzies' credentials was the widely held belief that he was the illegitimate offspring of Edward VII — but because, as Carrington was to slowly learn, the secret services, like most other scions of government and the Establishment, were run by envy, fear and favouritism. One of the most heinous of Menzies' sins was the fact that he was not a Navy man in the tradition of the one-legged Smith-Cumming — who had coined the title 'C' for holders of the post — or Admiral Sinclair. He also spent too much time a'hunting (which endeared him to Lord Halifax) and too much time drinking fine brandy at White's (which had the same effect with Churchill). Many members of the Admiralty were furious with their First Lord when the temporary appointment was ratified on November 28, but Churchill did not give a fig. He knew, as they did not, of Enigma and of Ultra. Stewart Menzies was master of the key that might one day win the war.

Long before Quex died, however, Edward Carrington had discovered better reasons than inter-service rivalry and backstabbing to make him doubt the quality of the organization he had been so proud to join. He was interviewed by Menzies — still as the deputy — in the second week of September, and taken out of a class in pistol shooting for the occasion. He found the lieutenant colonel, although only touching fifty, almost impossibly grand. He had been educated during Eton's greatest days, been President of Pop, then had straightway graced the Grenadiers, transferring later to the Life Guards. The only human thing that anybody whispered of him was that his wife, the daughter of the Eighth Earl de la Warr, had had to be divorced for granting bedroom favours to another. Given his carriage, his square face with downturned mouth, his iron self-regard, Carrington could see her point.

The interview was short, and devastating. Edward, invited to give an account of himself and be frank about it, did so. He emphasized his knowledge of parts of Europe, in particular the North, and his grasp of Nordic languages. He could pass for a native of Sweden certainly, and probably of Norway and of Denmark. He already had a contact in a Swedish woman who had expressed a desire to work with the British, who was studying at Dresden. His greatest use, he felt, would be in forging this connection, with the help of the agents he imagined were already in place in these countries, and developing it. Fröken Malling, his contact, had very high and useful connections of her own. He named Suzanne Simonis, her cousins the Kordt brothers, Erich von Weizsäcker, Birger Dahlerus. And added, tentatively, that members of the German High Command might be linked.

Colonel Menzies listened with apparent interest. He raised his eyebrows at the list of names. He consulted a dun-coloured file in front of him. He cleared his throat.

'Well.' His voice was deep, cultured, sonorous. 'Self-confidence is of the greatest importance in an agent. Self-knowledge comes with time. We have assessed your capabilities, and we find your potential interesting. There is a proposal to send you – when you have completed basic training, naturally – to the Netherlands. We have great need of people like you there. You'll fit in perfectly.'

Edward Carrington gasped.

'I don't speak Dutch.'

It was all he could get out. The face across the table hardened.

'Then learn. You will be groomed as a Dutch businessman, based in Rotterdam, who has returned from the East Indies. You are in rubber, which the Germans desperately lack. We note your father is a Burma expert, that is good. You will be able to cross into Germany, with a view to doing deals. It is a most important posting. Any questions?'

Plenty sprang to Edward's mind, but he prevented any of them from passing his lips, which he momentarily pursed. He thanked the colonel for the interview and returned doggedly to his pistol lessons in the basement range two doors away. After that he went back to the offices to receive details of his next step. He neither complained nor commented to anyone.

At the flat that evening, lying thinking in the bath, he was aroused by the telephone. In case it should be Hannele, he had to answer it. It was not.

It was a woman's voice, though, one he did not recognize. It had an American tinge, and it was light and pleasant.

'Hallo. This is Erica Lucas. I'm just nearby. Can I come up?'

His mind was blank.

'Erica Lucas?'

'Your landlady. I own your apartment. I have a key, of course, but . . .'

'Good God. I'm in the bath.'

'Ten minutes, then? Is that OK? I've just got into England from the States.'

Fifteen minutes afterwards, the doorbell rang.

Edward Carrington took quiet pride in his modernity. The British, he felt, for all their supposed superiority, were marked by insularity, and were by European terms quite backward, culturally. Their class system was hidebound, their rulers unjustifiably smug, their attitude to rising talent blinkered. He recognized these things and hoped he was above them. But Erica Lucas took his breath away.

The view he had of her through his spyhole was distorted. She looked undefined, the sides of her face slipping to infinity, her body woolly, soft. Feeling foolish, he jerked the door open to the reality. It was completely different.

Erica Lucas was five feet six, with a thin, strong, intelligent face. Her hair was black, but streaked dramatically with silver grey. It was not her age – she told Edward within minutes that she was twenty-seven – and it was not the effect of cares or worry, the lines around her eyes were laughter lines. It was nature that had turned her grey, she said, and she did not give a damn. Her clothes proclaimed the message. Her skirt was short, above slim, silk-stockinged legs, and her peach-coloured rayon blouse was open almost indecently low upon her well-formed bosom. She was carrying a lightweight jacket and a travelling bag of solid leather. She behaved as if she owned the place.

'Come in,' said Edward. 'I hope it's not too much of a pigsty. It lacks a woman's touch, you know. I'm sorry.'

'Bullshit,' said Erica, and Edward jumped as if he had been stung. 'Why should a woman keep it any different? Anyway, it's yours, it's no business of mine at all, I shouldn't really be here. You don't

171

have to let me in, you know, Mr Carrington. May I call you Edward? Or is it Ted? Call me Erica.'

She had walked in as she talked, so he assumed the offer to be turned away was her form of politeness. She dropped the heavy bag, the jacket on top of it, and looked around. She opened doors, walked up and down, inspected rooms. Edward's dirty clothes were in a pile beside his bed but his embarrassment did not interest her. He was sweating slightly, overheated from the bath, his shirt open at the neck.

'Very nice,' was Erica's verdict. 'No complaints here about the way you've kept it. It's an enormous place for one, however, I always thought so. Would you consider a sub-let?'

She moved past him to the kitchen, where she put the kettle on the gas. She rooted through the cupboards, turned her nose up at the dishes in the sink, selected tea cups and located the caddy. Edward took up a position at the door-post. A defensive one.

'It's against the rules of the lease. The agents have always been most strict with me. More to the point, it suits me.'

'I'd be a model lodger. I'm quiet, I have few dirty habits that would trouble you. Economically, it makes perfect sense.'

'Oh. You.'

'Of course me. Naturally. I wasn't expecting to come back to England, not for years, maybe never. But since I've had to, and since the old place is so empty, how about it? You weren't thinking of anybody else? I see only one bed is used.'

'But . . . well, if it doesn't sound ridiculous – what would the neighbours think?'

Erica Lucas laughed expressively.

'Screw the neighbours. I used to live here in the old days, before my mother left, then my father died. They know me well enough. They never said a thing, they never dared.' She moved to the stove, poured water in to warm the pot. 'It's not that sort of place, Teddy. They're not that sort of neighbours. Do you talk to them? There, then. Besides. Times have changed.'

The pot was ready. She put it on a tray with the cups and saucers, sugar, milk. Edward still watched from the doorway.

'Still, if you're adamant. There's the gutter if I can't find a cheap hotel. Why should you care? You heartless bastard!'

Over tea in the front sitting room, overlooking Bedford Square, she filled him in on her background. She had lived in America for more than two years this time, and had grown up there, basically. Her father had been an economist, who had come back to Europe with Woodrow Wilson to try to hammer something workable out of the ruins of the Great War, and after that the family had divided themselves between the USA and Britain. She had been born in this apartment — in the bedroom that he slept in, maybe the very bed, she grinned — and she loved the place. Not as much, perhaps, as New York or Washington.

'Why did you come back? It seems a strange time to choose. Most people are rushing off the other way. There's been a mass exodus of Americans in the last few weeks.'

'Am I American?' She sighed. 'Oh, I don't know. I'm here for the reasons that they've gone back there, I guess. It's a pull. Not rational. I worked out for myself that there's going to be a blow-up. London's going to be bombed, invaded, over-run, who knows? So I booked my passage. Also . . . well, there's an awful fascination. I worked with journalists in New York, I worked in radio. They're pouring over here, the last contingents, to see the fun. War as a spectator sport, you know? There were eighteen of them on the boat with me. I guess I got infected.'

They drank tea. Erica lit a cigarette, and Edward refused one. He had been trying a pipe recently, but was not making much progress. Smoking, he had found, gave him a headache.

'Are you a journalist?'

'Hell, no. I studied politics, economics, like my Pop. But I thought I might be able to earn a crust by it, you know? Offer my services to some of the magazines, a "gal's eye view" of Little England's struggle. That's the angle over there, believe me. The gallant fight against the last barbarians. They're pushing it like crazy. I guess I'll find a better job. Something I can believe in.'

She blew smoke in a pale blue stream through rounded lips. She smiled easily. She was not attempting to be provocative.

Edward, provoked, said: 'Don't you think Hitler's a barbarian?'

She was surprised.

'They're all barbarians. Good God, Teddy, the US arms industry has been praying for this war for years. The British too, surely to God? Woodrow Wilson nearly tore his liver out trying to get a reasonable settlement at Versailles, a settlement that would last, and look what Europe did to him. A blind man with his head tied in a sack could see this one coming, couldn't he? The Germans aren't insane. They were screwed. Twenty million of them dispossessed, twenty million told they now lived in a foreign country and they could never be Germans again, for ever more. You would have fought, if you'd been them. If somebody had told you Wales was part of Poland. Come on, Teddy!'

He was beginning to feel uncomfortable. This was heresy, or at least beyond his comprehension. Erica could see the effect her words were having. But it only made her smile.

'I'm sorry,' she said. 'Have I become too much? We see things differently over there, you understand. There's a pretty powerful body of opinion that thinks Germany and Britain will link up one day soon and turn on the States. You don't believe that? I'm telling you, it's true. You heard of William Bullitt? Sumner Welles? Nah, you're English. You have heard of America, I suppose? Have you heard of Nancy Astor? Cliveden? Of course you have. Well, Stateside lots of people think they lead a group of aristos and bankers and industrial giants who see Mr Hitler as the future. You know Joe Kennedy? US Ambassador here in London? A Boston-Irish gangster. He swills champagne with Lord and Lady Astor, so they say. He's one of the set.'

'They can't believe it's true, though? You don't believe it? It's insane.'

'Why insane? A different perspective. Europe is Nemesis for America. The devouring myth. Americans sprang from her and she always calls them back. Europe's always dying and Americans can't leave her alone to die. They go back, they interfere, they try to save her from herself. And they get slaughtered in the process. Without thanks or understanding.'

Edward had a sudden, uncomfortable memory of Hannele. 'Your Rich Uncle,' she had called the States. This woman apparently saw Americans as wandering children, unable to break with a bloodstained, hopeless parent.

'You won't need to help this time,' he said, lamely. 'Against France and Britain, Hitler hasn't got a chance. Poland might fight him to a standstill on her own. The Poles beat Russia in the 1920s.'

She crushed her cigarette out in an ashtray. The butt still smouldered.

'I wouldn't bet on it,' she answered. 'But I hope you're right. There's a lot of Americans this time round who'd rather die than

die for Europe. Like I said, it's a spectator sport. The good ol' boys'll
sell you tanks and planes aplenty. But if you hit the canvas, Uncle
Sam won't pick you up and dust you off. Roosevelt might want to.
Rumour has it Roosevelt's already making secret moves, although
he's too damn fly to let anybody in on it. It's against the US law,
Teddy. The Neutrality Act has got a lot of watchdogs. There's a man
called Borah. There's senators whose families came from Germany
and Italy and Ireland. And there's cash. Industry invests in Germany
as much as it invests in England, maybe more. If they fought for
one side or the other, Standard Oil would be fighting Standard Oil.
And the loser? Standard Oil. Forget it!'

Carrington was silenced. Erica took another cigarette and lighted
it. The ignition of the match made a significant roar in the quiet
room. She inhaled deeply.

'Am I too much of an American for you, or can I stay?' she said.
'And if I can, here's another question. What do we do about sex?'

Smoke was rising from her nostrils as from a pantomimic devil's
mask. Her smile was growing. She moved her head from side to
side.

'Teddy,' she said. 'You are just priceless.'

SIX

Edward Carrington, with heavy heart but great determination, threw himself into his training as an agent. Like any bureaucracy given a green light, the Secret Intelligence Service grew like mushrooms in a wet field overnight. It was riddled, in his opinion, with old and stupid men, most of whom had been recruited by word of mouth or by membership of a certain club or school society, but to give Menzies his due, he did bring in new blood of a different order. Carrington learned Dutch under a young lecturer from Manchester who was brilliant, and his radio and cipher training was handled by men whose accents were extremely low, while their skill levels were precisely the opposite. He was taught unarmed combat by a former plumber, and was later told that the famous novelist Gerald Kersh gave lessons in how to kill a man in total silence using only a handkerchief or a bunch of keys. In other classes learned men told him about the economic infrastructure of the Low Countries and Germany, and the Burmese rubber nexus. He often found his thoughts, unfortunately, turning to Hannele's face and body, and to the economies and peoples of Scandinavia, both of which he knew quite intimately.

The other intelligence services also proliferated, and there were dark tales in the clubs and messes of rivalry and hatred. Many MI6 officers made no pretence at co-operation as a desirable aim, instilling in some of the newer men a conviction that MI5 saw its main purpose to encroach on MI6 domains, and suggesting that all such moves should be pre-empted. Vernon Kell, Carrington was told, was not only an incompetent head of MI5, but possibly a traitor and almost certainly a homosexual. He recruited from the ancient universities, and many of his agents were believed to be Russian sympathizers. Carrington knew only one of them by name, Lord Victor Rothschild, with whom he had played cards occasionally. His views were certainly of the left, but one of his houses, in Bentinck Street, was always full of pretty girls, which redressed the balance. Kell, his back exposed to many knives, was bizarrely blamed by

Churchill for the 'skill and daring' of the submarine that destroyed the *Royal Oak*, and after a couple more botched jobs was summarily dismissed. But in MI6 itself the rivalries flared and smouldered. Colonels Valentine Vivian and Claude Dansey, theoretically the right and left hand men of 'C', fought each other bitterly, and their colleague Felix Cowgill, head of Section Five, with even greater vigour. There was MI(R) in the question, first one then two 'D' departments added to SIS, plus military intelligences attached to each armed service, PWE and the EH group. The Ministry of Economic Warfare hung on the periphery and stirred the witches' brew.

Carrington, a colonial, possibly in love, detached, watched all this with a definite slight unease and hoped the battle in the field was conducted with more competence and panache, not to say goodwill. His target, when he should be considered fit and ready, was the European centre of SIS operations, a house in The Hague disguised as the 'Continental Trading Corporation', where he was to join the staff of agents run by Major H. R. Stevens and his deputy, Captain S. Payne Best. From there he was to work up his cover as a rubber man and make the contacts that would get him into Germany. In theory it sounded plausible enough. In practice, luckily for him, it never happened. On November 9, Britain's two top agents were lured to the border town of Venlo by some Germans and simply kidnapped. A Dutch intelligence officer, Lieutenant Daniel Klop, tried to save them but was shot and later died. Stevens and Payne Best spent the war in prison and in camps, and almost every SIS man in place in Germany, the Low Countries and France had to return to England. Carrington's adventure in Holland was over before it had begun, by two short days. Unlike Sir Vernon Kell, Menzies had a talisman. He carried on.

That night, Edward took Erica to dinner at the Savoy Grill in the Strand and explained that he would not be leaving after all. The dinner had been arranged as a farewell, but never mind. The food was still good, he could afford it, the table was booked. Erica, who had been dressed to kill when he got to the flat, had agreed. She would relish it the more, she said, knowing that it was not a wake, and who knew how much longer such restaurants would still be open, such food and drink available?

'Except for the rich, of course.' She ironically raised a glass of whisky and water, her aperitif. 'To the Black Market.'

When they were shown to their table, Erica asked the sixty-four dollar question. Why? Carrington was prepared.

'The project's been delayed. As far as I know, the boffin in control has had second thoughts about some calculation. I doubt if I'll be off the hook for long. But it'll be an excuse for another farewell binge.'

To Erica, Edward was a metallurgist, a researcher into alloys at the leading edge of science. It had occurred to him that simply to refuse to discuss his movements would have led Erica inevitably to his real job. And science, she had revealed the day after they had met, was a total mystery to her.

'Good,' she said. 'I'm glad you'll be around. But I may be working soon myself. I've come out of the woodwork. I've declared myself. I'm going for a job.'

'Well congratulations! You've saved me the embarrassment of having to turn you in! What are you hoping for?'

Erica, in all the chaos of her arrival back in Britain, appeared to be on no one's files. She had turned up, been noted as arriving, then forgotten. Had she been a foreign agent, she could not have done it better.

'Ministry of Information. I know a man there, so I thought I'd see if they could use my services writing leaflets, or propaganda or something, I don't know. I used to do scripts in the States. I know radio. They're seeing me tomorrow.'

He tried to hide it, but Carrington was surprised. She caught the rogue expression, and grinned.

'I'm not a fifth columnist, you know! Just because we disagree on everything! I thought you'd be amused, me telling lies to bolster up morale. I'll be very good at it, as good as Churchill. You can tell me what to think!'

He made a rueful face. Their views on everything, from what to have for breakfast to the course and conduct of the war, had remained diametrically opposed. Churchill had been the latest bone of contention, as he had begun to make public speeches which Chamberlain clearly found embarrassing. They were violently anti-Nazi, patriotic, jingoistic some would say. Erica, for instance. She called him rabble-rouser, windbag, fraud. Everything he said or wrote was calculated for posterity, in her view, he sounded like a sheaf of notes looking for a history book.

'Well, the very best of luck,' he said. 'But for God's sake don't tell them what you really think, will you? About anything. Otherwise you'll end up in the Tower, not writing leaflets.'

When the meal was over, they went for a late drink, then for a dance. Although they were not lovers they stayed together, sought no other partners. When they reached home, happy and a little tipsy, they drank cocoa in the kitchen, then went to separate rooms. The 'sex arrangement' she had joked about had been about other people, and their attitude to strange bodies cluttering up the place. They had agreed that each of them should have *carte blanche*, no questions asked nor opinions given, unsolicited. But Edward had lost interest in easy conquests for the present, and Erica hinted at the ending of an affair when she had left the States. They liked each other, they rubbed along quite well. It was enough for both of them.

It was several months before anything significant happened in Edward's life – by which time he was so sick of the stagnant war that he would have been prepared to be parachuted into the heart of Germany wearing a kilt. His training had benefited from the extra time, he was assured by any superior who could spare the energy to talk to him, and indeed he was an expert radio operator and cipherist, who could also – in theory – kill, survive, and use a parachute. He knew the details of ident laws and rationing for every country in Europe, he had mastered Dutch and French, and he still could not get a pipe to burn for more than three minutes at a stretch.

There were things in the air, he knew, everybody knew. The centre of activity, of the universe, was Bletchley Park, north of London, where signals intelligence had something big. But Carrington did not get to go there, and secrecy was high, with many rumours but few facts. For him, after the Venlo fiasco, being a British agent meant reading newspapers in Swedish, Danish and Norwegian, studying reports, poring over decodes, analysing situations. In February he was told that Britain would probably be invading Norway soon, but his pleas to be in place beforehand fell on deaf ears. His spot was London, his usefulness all of the intellect. As spring progressed he wrote briefing documents on the life, the people and terrain of Scandinavia, and gave assessments of how a British 'intervention' (the word invasion was never used) would be received. He knew beforehand that on April 8 the Royal Navy were to mine the fjords off Narvik, in neutral Norway's territorial waters, and he was one of the first to learn of Germany's devastating response, a full-scale invasion the next day. He monitored the course of the campaign to retake the country, exchanging messages with an MI6 man called Frank Foley, who organized the evacuation in an Irish Sea ferryboat of the Royal Family and much of the government. After both Norway and Denmark had fallen, Neville Chamberlain also fell, on May 10. It was the day Hitler tore into Belgium and the Netherlands, and the day that Winston Churchill became Prime Minister.

Edward Carrington was in the flat with Erica when Chamberlain broadcast his farewell. Any tendency he might have had to crow, or scoff at his achievements, was modified by the dreadful news from the continent. The Twilight War, as Chamberlain had dubbed it, was over with a vengeance. The Norway disaster had been just an appetizer, it would seem.

'Well, your man's won,' said Erica, when the broadcast was over. 'Al Capone has got his finger on the trigger at long last.'

'What can you possibly mean?' flared Edward. 'What possible alternative is there? At least we'll fight now. At least there'll be a fight.'

'Yes,' said Erica. 'To the death, and probably beyond. Churchill didn't do too well at Norway, though. Why should he do better now he's ousted Chamberlain? How was Norway Chamberlain's fault and not the First Sea Lord's? I only ask.'

The telephone rang in the lobby, and Carrington went, gladly, to answer it. It was Desmond Morton.

'My boy,' he said. 'I might have need of you. Terrific news about dear Winston, we're all delirious. But there are moves afoot. Treachery. Menzies can spare you, I've spoken to him. See me tomorrow morning, at my office.'

'It would be an honour, sir. Ten thirty?'

'Fine. Carrington, you'll not believe this, but I'll tell you. Utterly shocking. After Chamberlain had quit, there was a meeting in his chambers. Him not present, but others, utterly disgraceful. This must not get out, of course.'

Of course, said Edward. Morton, he realized, spoke with the confidence of the man who tapped the phones. His breath wheezed faintly, down the line.

'They drank a toast. To the man who gave us Munich, the guilty

180

man. ''The King Over The Water.'' In champagne. Rank treachery.'

It did not sound that serious to Edward, given the circumstances of Neville Chamberlain's fall from grace. It sounded more like a courtesy than a threat, a valediction. Morton had been celebrating, hard.

Then Morton said: 'There is a king, you know. Over the water. I don't mean Chamberlain. He lives in Portugal, he deals with Nazis. Married to that dreadful Yankee woman, Wallis Simpson. Our information is that Hitler's offered him the throne. Our throne. Edward becomes king again, d'you understand?'

'But how can he? How can Hitler offer anything? He'd have to win the war!'

'Or end it. There are people in this country who would do anything to end it. Powerful people, people in the highest echelons, people in the deepest sympathy with Hitler. And they would have a king again in sympathy with them. Edward the Eighth.'

'But Churchill. He is PM now. He would never . . .'

'Precisely. That's the devil of it, isn't it? The import of the toast. The King Over The Water will forever remain so, while Winston lives.'

His voice had grown thick, with anger or emotion. Edward waited.

'So Winston Churchill,' said Desmond Morton. 'Would have to die.'

SEVEN

Drunk, or mad, or stupid? Or maybe utterly sane, perhaps it was he who could not come to grips with the topsy-turvy world they all now lived in, Edward thought. When he had come off the phone the night before and Erica had asked who it had been, he had replied, with a certain confidence and an audible distaste, 'Someone talking nonsense'. But after meeting Morton, the verities had slipped once more. The major – still puffy-eyed from the night of celebration – had backtracked rapidly from wild tales involving Winston Churchill's death, but had offered calmer possibilities to replace them. More powerfully, he had offered Edward action, linked with Scandinavia.

At first, Carrington had listened with unease as Morton had blandly slid around his assassination claims. There were dark schemes afoot, he said – some with their roots going back for years – and if Hitler could achieve it, the replacement of King George by his brother could only occur at the cost of Winston's life. But Morton's job was to prevent such things, which was why he wanted Edward's help. He had, after all, been originally his protégé, and 'C' had confirmed his excellence in all things Nordic. Edward had smiled modestly and, of course, agreed to do his best, if it were so ordained. While wondering, with well-concealed impatience, at the details.

But with details Major Morton was less forthcoming, and Edward's unease turned into something deeper when he named the 'traitors' who had drunk the shameful toast. They were the young Lord Dunglass, who had gone to Munich with Chamberlain as his parliamentary private secretary in 1938, Chips Channon, an amiable but half-witted American who was Rab Butler's PPS, Butler himself – a friend and admirer of Chamberlain who worked in the Foreign Office under Halifax – and a fourth as yet unnamed. Morton caught Edward's involuntary eye-movements, but instead of pouncing, instead of switching on the bluster, he changed gear. He pondered for some seconds before speaking.

Then he said: 'I can see you're dubious. But don't dismiss it out of hand, that would be foolish. It is not as unlikely as it appears, you know. You are young, and you are a colonial. You perhaps do not realize how long and desperately people have fought to keep Winston Spencer Churchill in the wilderness, and how furiously angry many of them are that he is back where he belongs. Between these walls, Carrington, I will pledge to you that there are plotters in high places, and as an indicator of just how high, I will add that Lord Halifax himself is possibly among them. Halifax, note. A friend and confidant of R. A. Butler. Halifax was called in privately to Chamberlain's room at the same time as Winston, and he assumed he would get the PM's job. There were just the three of them, with Chamberlain holding one man's future or the other's in the palm of his hand. Churchill did not speak, but he won by force of personality. He told me that he projected, by sheer will, the scenes in Parliament after Norway into the atmosphere of the room, and Halifax finally quailed. The job went to Winston, but Halifax will not forget it, or forgive. Believe me.'

Carrington felt strained. Lord Halifax was a cold fish, a man of steely rectitude, a religious man. But a *traitor*?

'Lord Halifax is the Foreign Secretary,' he said. 'He hates Hitler. He has worked with Chamberlain against him tirelessly.'

'Yes. To what end? Appease, appease, appease. They lost their fight to prevent the war, but never their desire for peace. You have seen the way the war has been conducted. Now it's getting more violent by the minute. If Chamberlain had not fallen, he would have caved in. Halifax as well.'

There was something in that, and there was something plausible in Morton's attitude. Despite the paleness of the eyes, the aura of post-alcoholic suffering, his exposition now was grave and measured. The misplaced bonhomie, the unchecked schoolboy enthusiasm that Edward distrusted in him, was tightly reined. Wild phone calls were of the night: this, perhaps, was serious. He tapped a light tattoo on his desk-top with his fingernails, and sighed.

'No one's suggesting, do you see, a full-scale plot to undermine Winston on the spot. Not at the moment, anyway. But there's an undercurrent you may not be aware of. This war is costing money. It is costing Britain millions every month. It is costing our industrialists dear, and our exporters. War is a moral luxury to some of these people. However just our cause is, they see only their cash balances dwindling. Germany's in the same boat. War is financed by industry, and the power in any land, behind any throne, behind Hitler or behind our own democracy, is a body of immensely wealthy men whose allegiance is ultimately to their wealth, and perhaps to each other. They talk to each other, they commune with each other, and there is a pressure for peace among them. It's international, my boy, and that's the danger. It's international in that they see themselves above nationhood, beyond patriotism, and they want the war to end. It's only a short step from desiring peace to seeking it, of course. It's only a short step from thinking Neville Chamberlain hard done by to blaming Churchill for his ills. Winston's going to win this war for us, as I'm sure you understand. *Only* Winston can win this war for us. But believe me, Hitler is not the only enemy.'

For the moment, they were on the same wavelength. Morton, eyes narrowed, hands clasped before him on the desk, seemed decisive, intelligent. Edward Carrington, relaxed but keen, had excitement in his guts.

'And my part, sir? The English aristocracy, I'm afraid, is a bit of a closed book to me. But on the German side . . .' An idea fell into his mind, so obvious. 'The Scandinavians. War industry. That's how they'd communicate. Am I to go there?'

Desmond Morton was chuckling.

'Hold up, hold up! Not yet awhile! I admire your perspicacity, and yes, that's the ultimate goal. But softly-softly. You're not the only Nordic expert in the service, you know. We have a man, a man called Foley. Your first job will be to work with him. In fact, your job will be to work *on* him, to watch him, to check him over for me. He's good, he's brilliant, and he's probably as sound as a bell. But there are certain indicators, little worries, and we need to know. What do you say to that?'

For many moments, Edward said nothing. He had heard of Foley, had worked with him – tangentially, and through the medium of crackling morse – during the Norway campaign. In as far as anyone could hope to be in the bitterly envious soil of the SIS, Foley was unblemished. Morton, watching carefully, was nodding.

'You've heard of him. So be it. You think I'm raving. But it's not what it seems. Nobody's suggesting he *is* a traitor, he's one of our very best men. He was an agent in the Great War, he's done wonderful work, wonderful. But there are indications, hints, which we must check out. He's close to some of the Germans, he married one, for heaven's sake. What's more, he spent ten years and more living in Berlin, speaks the lingo literally like a native, and after Berlin – he came out when the show blew up – he went to Oslo. Now, as you've already guessed, if there is a link-up between our high-born plotters and their equivalents in Germany, that's the way it's going to come. So is it coincidence, or is it not? Wherever you look, there's Francis Foley and there are Scandinavians. Birger Dahlerus, Wenner-Gren, you know the names. Quite frankly, young man, we would be insane not to be vigilant. We want him watching, and you're the man to do it.'

They both paused for thought. It was a fine morning. Perhaps the summer would be as marvellous as had the last. The traffic noise in Whitehall was muted by the heavy curtains, despite the open window.

'It would be inappropriate in me to say it felt un-British,' Carrington said, at last. 'It's just—'

'Foolish, too,' Morton interrupted. 'We all have sacrifices that must be made. And for the moment you are not watching on a colleague, because you are not working for MI6 but directly for Winston. And the good of Britain. You are a very lucky young man. We want you in France in three days time. Try to get to Paris before the blessed Boche.'

'France?'

'That's where Foley is. There's some gunk called heavy water that the Frogs want to off-load onto us. Our man in Paris is Lord Suffolk – a rum'un and no mistake. Working with a chap called Allier, French but very sound. They're expecting you. You've not done this before, have you? Active service?'

'No, sir.'

Desmond Morton grinned like the Cheshire cat.

'Enjoy yourself, then. But remember – Foley is your target. Be vigilant, and don't be taken in. He's come straight from the heart of it. Norway.'

They shook hands.

Inevitably, perhaps, Frank Foley was not in Paris. But Edward, delighted to be carrying a gun at last, hardly cared. When he met Lord Suffolk – officially the science attaché at the British Embassy – the delight increased. Suffolk loved the war as he had loved nothing else in life, and had turned his part in it into romantic fiction. As France slipped into chaos he let his dress and demeanour slip to match. He greeted Edward half drunk, at eleven in the morning, and offered him champagne. He was in stained black trousers and an open shirt, and his chin was rapidly disappearing beneath a growth of soft, curly hair. Their job, he explained, was to quarter Paris and the surrounding towns collecting scientific and industrial hardware from factories and labs, arranging their dismantling and packaging, then sending them to Bordeaux to be transhipped to Britain. To this end he had selected two Embassy secretaries as helpers, with brains to equal beauty, who matched him drink for drink late into the night, then killed their hangovers in work. It was something of a relief to mind and liver when Edward was assigned to help Jacques Allier, a less flamboyant man than Suffolk, who did not like champagne. He had tracked the heavy water to a hiding place in an Auvergne jail, he said, and needed muscle and another gun. Edward, feeling neither strong nor very brave, shook hands with Suffolk and kissed both girls goodbye. The plan was that they would meet again in Bordeaux, where Suffolk was soon to go to commandeer a freighter for his scientific booty and machine tools.

Jacques Allier was a sombre man, although prepared to talk. Before the Germans overran Norway, Edward learned, he had mounted an operation to smuggle out all the heavy water stocked at the Norsk Hydro, which was the only producer in the world. The twenty-six canisters had reached Paris via a flight to Edinburgh – organized by one Frank Foley – a train journey down the length of Britain, and a ship across the Channel. Now, after a month of nervously transferring it from place to place as the situation worsened, the French government were giving it to the British. When they reached the prison, at Riom, and an official tried to argue that they had no authority to remove the canisters, Jacques Allier took out a pistol and levelled it wordlessly at the bureaucratic face. If the man had held out for five seconds he would have been dead. He collapsed in three.

The roads to Bordeaux were heavily congested. As the British had retreated to the beaches of Dunkirk, the government of France had run for the southern port in case the worst should happen. Allier's Simca, freighted with nearly four hundredweight of heavy water, groaned and squeaked its way through the lorries, cars and refugees on foot. Petrol could have been a problem, but once more Allier's ruthlessness paid off. He explained, tersely, to Edward Carrington what their cargo was and what it would mean if German scientists got hold of it. Quite simply, that was worth dying to prevent. For Edward, the stainless steel containers, and the job, took on a deeper significance.

It was in Bordeaux, when they crawled through the traffic to the docks, that he at last met Foley. They saw Suffolk first, on the cluttered deck of a filthy coalship called the *Broompark*, looking more piratical than ever. His shirt – once white – was open to the waist, and his beard was long and straggly. One of his girls was next to him, incongruous in a floral summer dress, and with them was another girl, more soberly turned out, and a small man in a brown suit. Allier, at the steering wheel of the overheated Simca, gave a grunt.

'Ah. *Bon*. Foley.'

Carrington was fascinated. Foley looked like anything in the world except a secret agent. A shipping agent, more likely, standing on the *Broompark*'s deck checking bills of lading. His face was round and turnip-like, a soft felt hat crammed on it, and his boots were brown and polished. The collar-points of his white shirt had rolled up in the heat. Edward approached cautiously, following Allier. There were handshakes all round, and congratulations. Suffolk placed a dirty paw on Edward's shoulder and pushed him forward.

'Frank. A new young man. He's done sterling work.'

'Let me guess.' Foley's voice was soft and mild, but not particularly friendly. 'Edward Carrington. I have been warned.'

Over the next few days, as the rush to load the *Broompark* became more frantic, there was little time for anything except work. Lord Suffolk served his purpose as a liaison between the French scientists and government officials who were going to Britain to carry on the war, and he was good at smoothing difficulties with pantechnicons of furniture and the occasional arrival of a weeping mistress, or in one case two. In some way he appeared to hearten the French, many of whom were disoriented and depressed by the appalling events, by his insouciance. He took to drinking almost constantly from a champagne bottle in his hand, while his two girls – one fair, one dark – gave the proceedings a weirdly festive air. Foley, on the other hand, laboured with officialdom, consigning space to microscopes and industrial diamonds, helped tirelessly by his cipher clerk, Margaret Reid. Edward was delegated to meeting new arrivals, screening them for importance to prevent the *Broompark* sinking under her weight of refugees, and commandeering essential supplies.

At 11 p.m. on the night of June 18, when Edward was sitting bog-eyed with weariness in the small metal box that served him as a cabin, Foley sought him out. His round face was grey with tiredness.

'I know why you're here,' he said. 'You probably imagine that I don't. You young men are all the same, at heart. Gullible. Take my advice, Edward. Don't trust anybody too far. Do what you're told, but think about it. They're usually using you.'

Edward had no reply. The possibilities were endless. He was being pumped, or he was being warned. Those were just two of them.

Foley said: 'Well done. Don't trust me, either. Don't be drawn. You're interested in the Swedish angle, aren't you? The Scandinavian connection. Good. I think you could be useful. We'll talk about it later.'

Still Carrington could think of nothing sensible to say. He was aware of the clattering of shipboard work, the chatter and clang of steam cranes. They had been working night and day since his arrival in Bordeaux.

'The *Broompark* sails tomorrow morning,' said Frank Foley. 'France will go under in the next few days. I'd ask you to stay with me but we might not survive together. I'll talk to you in London.'

Carrington was shaken.

'You're not coming? Why?'

'It's what I'm paid for. Curiosity. To see what's what. There's no one left in France, you know. Not at present. We'll have to build from scratch. A network.'

Carrington picked his words.

'And is there one in Scandinavia? Is there actually a Swedish connection?'

Foley said nothing for a good few seconds. Then, suddenly, he yawned. He covered his mouth with his hand, and seemed to swell with the oxygen he drew in.

When he had finished, he said: 'Edward, does the name Carruthers mean anything to you? I have another one: Hannele.'

Edward flinched, then reddened. Even after eight months the

nerve was there. Foley turned, and dragged the white steel door open.

'Yes,' he said. 'We have something growing there. We'll talk again in London. Edward?'

'Yes, sir?'

'We have hope.'

EIGHT

From Desmond Morton's point of view, Edward struck gold the first time he had a proper conversation with Frank Foley. It happened a month after the *Broompark* had rolled and wheezed her way out of Bordeaux to face the U-boats and the bombers, and it happened in a Soho pub. Edward's trouble was that the tell-tales he was looking for, the subtle marks of treachery, were the main – and open – subject of the conversation. If Foley were a traitor, he did not care who knew it, it would seem. He also had a rank contempt for Desmond Morton.

Edward turned up late for their rendezvous, and found Foley standing at the bar with a much younger man who had a long, intelligent face and a quiet manner, whom he introduced as Harold Philby, known as Kim.

'He's with the opposition,' he said, jocularly. 'Section D. I'm afraid "C" wouldn't touch him with a bargepole. Cambridge. He's just off, though.'

Indeed, Philby was at the bottom of a pint of mild. He shook hands with Edward, tapped his pipe out at the bar, nodded, and left. When the door had closed behind him, Foley said: 'Funny lad. He doesn't speak a lot because he stutters. Useful. You can understand "C"'s point in a way. There's a group of them, all intellectuals, all educated to infinity and beyond in poetry and stuff. Look at Harold. Kim, I ask you, because he always wanted to be a spy! It's a dream. I doubt if any of them's ever seen real blood, except maybe in the Carlton Club. What will you take?'

'Pale ale, please. They certainly look a different breed, the ones I've met. I can't imagine him being taken for anything other than an Englishman abroad. Why the Carlton Club? Blood? Is that some sort of joke?'

Foley's eyes darkened, momentarily.

'No. There's a cellar there, I'm afraid. Some of these young men ask questions. They don't actually get abroad a lot, in theory, although they don't always stick too closely to their brief. Which of us does?'

'Questions? Do you mean—'

Foley interrupted him.

'I mean they have a job. Results to get, like everybody else. I'm involved in some of their work, now. Hence the meeting. They've pitched me into Section Five.'

'Am I allowed to ask? Or should I congratulate?'

'Margaret thinks it's demotion. You remember Margaret? Of course you do. She thinks we should be abroad, where the real work is. Katherine's delighted. Wife.' He paused, drank beer, sighed. 'On balance, I agree with Margaret, although Section Five's important. We're looking for the foreign boys wherever they turn up. Counter-espionage. My feeling is the job should be strengthened in the field, especially Norway and Sweden, which is why I want to talk to you. If there is anything in this Duke of Windsor nonsense, the peace at any price brigade, that's where it'll come from, you can count on it.'

Edward almost coughed into his beer. It sounded like an echo of words he had heard before. Foley had a light of humour in his eyes.

'I thought I'd strike a chord,' he said. 'Just what do you know about all this?'

Edward thought fast, achieving little. He swallowed a mouthful of pale ale.

'Nothing, I suppose. Not really. They never let the right hand know what the left one's doing, do they? I was asked to keep an eye on some people, is all. People they suspect of being . . . over-zealous in the search for peace.'

'Including me,' said Foley. 'Which means, in one guess, Desmond Morton. The trouble with this service in a nutshell. Anyone can stick an oar in. It's a mare's nest. Anyway, the man's a fool.'

Despite the calmness of his voice, Carrington realized he was angry. The avuncular face was set. So bang went any chance he might have had of hearing things he did not know. In that, though, he was wrong.

'What infuriates me,' said Foley, 'is the cynicism of these people. The assumptions that they make. I'm certain there are people in Germany who want peace. Powerful people. I'm certain that there are people here who feel the same. The question is, is it treachery, or is it sense? The nub of the matter, the *heart* of it, is what the

191

terms are. Good God, Edward, if you had the power to end this war, wouldn't you seize it with both hands? Wouldn't you?'

Impossible question. He did not know. But it did not take him long to sort out what was wrong with it. It was not a question for the likes of him, or even Foley. It was a question for the top, for the Cabinet, for Winston Churchill. Realizing that Foley was studying his face, he flushed. He sipped more beer.

'I'm sorry, son,' said Foley. 'I must sound soft. I'm not. When Hitler offered peace after Norway I agreed with Churchill, it was meaningless. But Hitler is a hated man in Germany, I know that first-hand. There are movements afoot at every hour of every day, there are men and women risking their lives. Every time something stirs, every time someone makes a contact, we should cherish it, examine it, and hope. Not crush it underfoot and talk of treachery. I'm sorry, I've put you in an invidious position. If you're being run by Morton, he'll want to hear all this. It won't do any harm, but I'd rather not give him food for thought, because I consider him an idiot and I don't think he's capable of interpreting it correctly. The service is in ferment at the moment, the knives are out. I'd rather carry on in my own sweet way, and I'd rather be in Stockholm. Failing that, I'd like to see you there.'

The directness of the man, the quiet honesty of his face and manner, confused Edward more by the moment. He thought the unthinkable, it seemed, and spoke the unspeakable.

'But why? What have I done that . . . No, first, aren't you worried by what Morton might do? That I might report all this to him?'

'No. There are still wiser men. And more powerful, thank God. Morton's an irritant, he has many of his master's vices without the virtues, but I can deal with that. I have friends, too. I was tipped off about you when you came to France, remember? I'll fare all right. As to the other, I heard about you from the other side as well, didn't I? Carruthers, a name to conjure with! I heard enough to make me think it worth my while to talk it over. There is an organization, the Norwegians laid the bones of it even before Oslo fell. It's well-advanced now, based in Stockholm, working into Germany. Hannele, the other name, one of the brave. I'd like to see you there.'

There was a long silence between them. The pub was noisy, but neither of them noticed.

Edward said: 'I'd better not mention it to Morton, then, had I? I'd like to get to Stockholm. But will they let me?'

Foley was lighting a new pipe. He indicated the tobacco pouch on the table with a finger. Edward shook his head. The short man blew the match out.

'I think they will,' he said. 'I think you ought to tell Morton I've taken you into my confidence. Tell him I've hinted that there are high Germans trying to make contact, and we need a conduit. If he wants anybody to lead him to the so-called English plotters, it's the very best possible way to go about it. In the meantime, I'll talk to "C" and set you up from my end. I won't mention Morton because he hates his guts, of course. They all hate each other's guts. It's a peculiar way to carry on a war, isn't it? If I didn't know the Germans were exactly as bad, I'd say it was a very British thing. We're remarkably similar to the Germans in some ways.'

'And have you taken me into your confidence? Are there high Germans trying to get through? Am I working for you, or am I working for Desmond Morton? Will you trust me when I tell you anything?'

Foley's turnip head was wreathed in smoke and smiles.

'I like you, son,' he said. 'But don't get silly, will you? I'll trust everything you tell me on the evidence and on my instinct. You'll have to do the same with me. You can trust me in this, though. I'm not a traitor, whatever any fool might tell you. We are fighting a barbarian, and we must beat him. Personally, I will refuse to be barbaric in the process.'

The smile had faded.

'Otherwise, I really can't see the point, can you?'

Having rolled up Western Europe like a carpet, Hitler sued for peace. To everyone's surprise his requirements were not punitive, not even the return of territories Germany had lost after Versailles. As Erica remarked to Edward, he seemed, underneath the rhetoric, to 'want to be friends'. The rhetoric, however, was inevitably warlike. The hour of Britain's total defeat was at hand, and Winston Churchill would soon abandon England to preside over the ruins from the safety of his Canadian dominion. Although gossip was that Churchill had been tempted, given the mighty scale of Germany's achievements in so short a time, the iron returned to his soul and he steamrollered furiously through his doubting Cabinet. It had been left to Halifax — surely not by accident — to broadcast a rejection on the radio. Hitler had talked of an offer 'in the name of reason', and Halifax threw it back at him as a 'summons to capitulate to his will'. Erica and Edward had their usual disagreement, and Edward announced that he was leaving next day on more unspecified scientific business. To his surprise, Erica offered to sleep with him, to prove that they could argue without falling out. To her surprise, he declined – and they laughed about it. He had Hannele in mind and, he hoped, almost in his grasp. The 'scientific business' was his flight to Sweden.

Getting there, despite his expectations, was extraordinarily easy, and by leaving Britain, Carrington missed the Day of the Long Knives. One of Churchill's reactions to the fall of France was to put into effect his long-brewed plan to vent his anger and frustration on his secret services. The day Halifax spurned Hitler, the War Cabinet approved a memorandum setting up the Special Operations Executive. Large chunks of MI6 fell to it, and the infighting between departments grew distinctly worse. The idea was classically Churchillian, to 'set Europe ablaze', to send saboteurs and subversives to create a reign of terror and make the lives of the occupiers 'an intense torment'. The torment, to begin with, was all at home. Somebody had to run the show, and everybody wanted to. The War Office and the Foreign Office lost, and the Ministry of Economic Warfare – run by Dr Hugh Dalton, a non-military man and a socialist – triumphed. Carrington was well out of it.

He flew from Leuchars on a fast, unarmed courier flight, and he flew as a Swedish businessman called Lansen. The sensation of sharing airspace with a murderous enemy – although in fact he saw no other aircraft – was disconcerting, as was the coming to terms with the idea that not all the world was locked in war, but only parts of it. In Stockholm he was met by two men, and driven to a quiet house in the suburbs. His companions took extreme precautions against being followed: the place, they said, was alive with Abwehr and Gestapo men. To get four miles they covered twenty, and they took nearly two hours. Edward was sweating lightly when they walked into the house.

Perhaps he had hoped that Hannele would be there, miraculously. She was not. For the first five days she was not mentioned, and Edward was treated with polite caution. First, they wanted to see if he could pass himself off as Swedish, or if there was anybody working for the enemy who might have an inkling of his presence or identity. When they were sure of him they eased up, and the introductions became more frequent and less formal. One man he had assumed was Swedish revealed himself as Jim Taylor, despite his name a Welshman, and he was taken to meet the SIS chief of station Cyril Cheshire at the passport offices in Birger Jarlsgatan. His most important contact was Brynulf Ottar, the head of the Norwegian secret operation in Stockholm, whose HQ was at Skeppargatan.

Although Stockholm was the base for spies of every warring nation, the Scandinavian connection that Foley had talked about was run by Norway, whose government-in-exile had set up in the neutral city. Brynulf Ottar told him the organization, known as XU, involved a secret network based in Oslo, a courier line to Stockholm, and Swedes, Germans and Norwegians in Germany to provide the information from source. Johanne Malling was a student at the Technische Hochschule in Dresden, near where her family had engineering interests. The Norwegian military attaché, Alfred Roscher Lund, had graduated there in '37, and considered it the perfect cover and a fine recruiting ground. Fröken Malling worked with a new entrant, a Norwegian who had taken advantage of the Germans' relatively relaxed attitude to the Scandinavian students there. He was only twenty, although, Ottar said drily, he was a Nordic giant, more than six feet tall, blonde and handsome. His bent was technical, while Malling concentrated on the politics.

Edward Carrington, hating himself for it, acknowledged the expected stab of pain. There was no doubt in his mind what collaboration would mean to Hannele. He acknowledged, too, that it was crazy. It had been eleven months since they had parted. There had, of course, been no letters. He pulled his attention back to Brynulf Ottar, who was explaining the way information was telephoned from Dresden, via Berlin, to Stockholm through newspaper and business intermediaries. It was done in code, naturally, and sometimes people had to meet, for handovers or to relay difficult intelligence. Johanne Malling would be coming soon, he said, with something enormous, dangerous, and vital. Would he, Edward Carrington, be prepared to meet her?

The bland Norwegian dropped it in so casually that Carrington made something of an idiot of himself. He jumped, then had to cough to cover the noise that rasped unbidden from his throat. Ottar waited patiently, enjoying the reaction he had caused.

'If you agree,' he said, 'the meeting will take place in Stettin, on a ship. I know Frank Foley wished you to help us extend our network here, but this is a task I think potentially more important. You will not need to go into Germany, it is largely a question of detailed talk with Fröken Malling. She has information which must go back to England urgently, to be considered in depth. There is a question of a leader having second thoughts about the war. A very important man indeed. The Deputy Führer, in fact. Rudolf Hess. Well?'

'What can I say? Beyond good God? This is extraordinary.'

'I meant,' smiled Brynulf Ottar, 'do you agree? To go?'

'Of course! Of course! I'm sorry.'

'Good. On Tuesday, then. In two days time. Good.'

'I'd like a drink,' said Edward Carrington.

NINE

The freighter was Swedish, and the Baltic Sea, to all intents and purposes, was Germany's. Carrington had been advised to keep himself as private as was possible, as one never knew who might be paid by the Abwehr, and neutrality as a concept was very fraught. He was a Swede, in iron ore, and he kept himself firmly to himself. The captain, who had done this sort of thing before, did not discuss it and discouraged any of his officers and men from doing so. Carrington watched the sea for the first two hours, enchanted by the Scandinavian night, then went to sleep. When he awoke, he would be in a German harbour.

When they did arrive in Stettin, they were immediately boarded by port officials, carrying guns and deep suspicions of supernumeraries. Lansen's papers were in order, however, and his story watertight. Neutrality again. Germany needed high-grade iron ore to feed the Ruhr, and Lansen was an important link in the chain providing it. He was left alone to think and wait.

Hannele arrived two hours later. Carrington was lying on his bunk, fully clothed, and he told himself afterwards that he had known she was outside his cabin before she touched the handle. Certainly he heard the knob turn, which considering the battering of cranes and donkey-engines as the ship was emptied of her cargo was phenomenon enough. As the door opened he swung his feet from off the bunk and stood. Hannele closed the door behind her and pressed her back against it. Her eyes were large and bright, her breath uneven.

'Edward. I am so pleased to see you.'

They moved forward slowly, as if both terrified. Edward was hollow with love and fear, shaking at how fierce and fresh all the sensations were. Before they even touched he knew it had been wrong to come, he knew he had reopened a wound that would never heal and could never be soothed by consummation, unless the war should end soon and they should both survive. Hopeless even then. He watched her eyes fire with the old, familiar irony, and it hurt him like a blade.

'Carruthers. Won't you hold me? I've thought of you so often.'

Silently they hugged each other, with Edward trembling for both of them. Hannele was thin beneath her sober business dress, thinner than he remembered her. He looked into her eyes and they were different now. The mockery was gone, and the skin around them was lined. Her face had lost its flesh, she had aged. Her hair was scraped back in a bun.

'Don't mind,' she said. 'I will recover, when the war ends. This is not a happy country, Edward. I prefer to look like a hungry governess, it keeps me safe from questioners. Today I am a shipping secretary, a clerk. Tomorrow I will be a student again, but no better fed. How's the food in England holding out? How is England?'

'Pretty much the same. We're fighting in the air but we don't see it in the cities. They bomb the airfields and we shoot down their bombers, lots of young men die but we expect to win. You know England. No one's too hungry and we think we're charmed, the holocaust won't come.'

'England is charmed,' said Hannele, 'but the holocaust will come. Germany is dying, but she will take the rest of the world with her when she goes.'

'Dying? What, starving?'

She shook her head.

'Not starving, yet. Although the food is deteriorating, and only the powerful eat well. No, dying morally, dying inside. The land is just as beautiful, and their heroes strut across the world, but only the stupid still feel proud. Too many people know what is happening to the Polish and the Slavs and to the Jews and the dissenters. It is only that I live in Dresden and that I fight like this that keeps me sane. I have an apartment that overlooks the Elbe. It is a lovely city, the war seems very far away, as if it can never reach me there.'

They had unwound their arms from round each other, and they sat on either side of the small table, held by brackets to the bulkhead. Each thought of home.

Edward said: 'My flat's still just as peaceful. It's hard to imagine war coming there, either. Still no gas, still no bombs, we were so panic-stricken in those early days. Oh, there is one thing less peaceful. I have a sharer now. In fact, my landlady, she owns the place. She's loud, like an American. I think she sees herself as American, actually. She acts like one.'

'And do you sleep with her?'

There was a faint light of amusement in her eyes, but faint, as if she already regretted asking him.

'I'm stupid,' she said, quickly. 'We should not talk of things like that. We both have to do things that are necessary. I would like to sleep with you, Edward. I am a changed woman, I'm afraid. I'm very staid. I would like to sleep with you, however. Also, to make love.'

He moved his lips.

'Fourth time lucky. It will be sad if we never make it. Why not here? Now?'

'No. Perhaps one day in Sweden, students have holidays, you know! Perhaps I'll break, go back for good. No. I will not break. Edward, enough of us, we are being irresponsible. I must get to the station, go south again. I must tell you about Hess. There is a chance that he will dare to leave. To break with Hitler, defect. It would be the greatest thing.'

'But why?' said Edward Carrington. He was aware that it was trite, but the alternative was to express the scepticism that had grown inside him in the intervening days. 'Hannele, I must be frank. It sounds incredible.'

For the first time, her eyes sparkled. She nodded vigorously.

'Yes, doesn't it? The unlikeliest of men! He's been with Hitler since the street-fighting days, he was in the famous putsch in 'twenty-three. But we believe him, Edward. We believe the worm has turned.' She sobered. 'We believe there are others with him, too, shadows, but we don't know who they are. If he does it, Edward, it could mean collapse. It seemed beyond belief to start with, we approached it as a trick, a lure, but now we're confident. It would be an appalling blow to Hitler, a crippling blow.'

'OK,' said Edward. It was a stand-off, he was picking up the Yankee jargon. 'Hannele, I don't know much about these men, I must admit. What I do know's probably distorted, as you told me once in London. But there are people at my end who will take a great deal of persuading, you understand that? Rudolf Hess, to me and most of us, is a strutting Nazi, the one with the eyebrows. Wasn't he behind the crackdown on the Jews?'

She nodded.

'In a way. He helped to frame the Nuremberg Laws. But in Germany, everything is complicated. His mentor, the man who taught him at university, is married to a woman who is half-Jewish, and their son has worked for Hess for years as his adviser. Hess has protected them, although in theory they are people he should not even know. In fact the father, Karl Haushofer, is godfather to his little boy. The other godfather is Hitler. Everything is complicated.'

Hannele reached across the table and touched his hand.

'They are funny men these people, listen. Hess did not have a normal christening for Wolf Rüdiger, the Führer does not think them good enough for Nazis. Instead the leaders of every *Gau* in Germany sent a sample of the soil from their district to go underneath the cradle at the naming ceremony. Joseph Goebbels is *Gauleiter* of Berlin. He sent a piece of dogshit. A touching gesture, don't you think? He said it was the soil of his city. The Nazi sense of humour.'

'Did anybody laugh?'

'It is not on record, but I doubt it. Joseph Goebbels is the most hated man they have, other than their most beloved leader. But they all hate each other, this is not understood in England. Goering and Ribbentrop keep bodyguards to protect them from each other. Goering almost destroyed Goebbels in a scandal over his mistress, who was a film star. Himmler is a nonentity who thinks he should be Führer in Hitler's place and Himmler's deputy is Reinhard Heydrich who is brilliant and daring and handsome and will kill Himmler first and then the Führer, if they don't pre-empt him. Compared with most of them, Hess is a decent man, a sane man. We have seen documents, secret orders under his signature trying to protect the Jews from Stormtroop lunatics. After *Kristallnacht* he forbade further attacks on Jews and tried to have the worst ringleaders punished by the courts. Since then, of course, things have got much worse. As I said, we think that even some of the less sane of the lunatics would like to leave the madhouse if they could. Or at least have the superintendent put into a straitjacket.'

She sighed. Her face was sad.

'You look dubious. You are right to be so. It would not be easy, nothing any more is easy. But it is worth a try, believe me. We do truly believe that Hess wants to go to Britain. If he could get there, surely there would be a hope?'

A shaft of sunlight blazed through the cabin scuttle, then as quickly faded.

Edward said: 'Is there a plan, or do we have to work one up? Assuming that our government agrees, how would Hess hope to get to us? How big is your group? Dresden is a long way from Stettin. You were not chosen for this trip just to see an old flame, were you?'

'No. I was chosen because it was safest for me. I'm a neutral student and I'm allowed to travel without too much explanation. Also, my uncle owns this ship! You know some of the network, the names have not changed. My contact in Berlin is Suzanne, and her family connections cross with mine in Sweden. There is a plan, the start of one, but of course we need co-operation, guidance. That is also why I was chosen. You know and trust me. The core of it, in Germany, is Rudolf Hess's adviser, Albrecht Haushofer. He has friends in Britain, important people, aristocrats.'

There were alarm bells ringing in Edward's skull. Aristocrats. He had been conditioned.

'Who? Which aristocrats?'

'Well, one in particular. A young man, an aviator, called the Duke of Hamilton. Hess met him in 1936, at the Olympics in Berlin, but he was called Lord Clydesdale then, your system is confusing. Albrecht Haushofer became a friend, a very close friend, they corresponded up until the war, Haushofer visited him in Scotland.'

'So what is the hope? To renew the connection?'

Precisely, Hannele agreed. Haushofer wished to contact Hamilton and have him prepare the ground among the company he kept. Hess would probably fly as well – there seemed no other way so well-known a figure could leave the country, and he was a skilled aviator – and Albrecht Haushofer understood that the Duke was now a high-ranking officer in the RAF, which would surely aid the details of the flight and landing? When she had finished, they sat in silence. Outside the cranes clattered on.

'There is a fear,' Edward said, 'that some so-called noble people wish to sell Britain's interests out. There is a fear of treachery. Why this duke? Why not approach us through the proper services, through an agent, me for instance? Would Hess not fly under our aegis? I only ask, it is a confusion. Why this duke?'

'In the first instance, Haushofer and Hess raised the idea. Logical, surely? Now I am approaching you, Edward. It will not be done behind anybody's back, if you should veto it it falls, quite clearly – I mean your masters, naturally. But we have fear, also. There is a fear here that some of your people don't want peace, at any price. And how do we know whom the secret channels would enlist? Herr Hess might be arrested out of hand and shot. Or blown out of the sky. We have our fears to match yours.'

Carrington did not believe that such a thing could happen, or would. But Hannele lived in Germany. He did not contradict.

'In any case,' she said, 'this Hamilton is no traitor. He is a friend of Winston Churchill, that is another reason. He is a friend of Winston Churchill and also of your royal family.'

'The Duke of Windsor?' asked Edward, sharply.

'No, the King.' Hannele was surprised. 'What is wrong, Edward? Surely the King is not a traitor? Nor Mr Churchill?'

Slowly, something was igniting in Edward. Excitement. He stared at Hannele's pale, drawn, serious face and he knew that she was genuine and convinced. She was offering him the deputy to Hitler, through an intermediary who was a friend of George VI and Winston Churchill. Slowly, a grin spread across his face. She responded, her facial muscles relaxing, the furrows in her brow fading visibly.

'Oh, Carruthers! Do you understand at last? Do you understand what we might have here? This could mean *peace*.'

They kissed each other then, leaning across the cold steel table, but only gently. They were very chaste, their lives felt very fragile at the moment. Not long afterwards she left the cabin, and Edward returned to his bunk to wait for the ship to sail, to take him back to Sweden.

After that, London, as quickly as was possible. Hitler's deputy was willing to defect . . .

TEN

If Edward Carrington had assumed the process would be quick or easy, he was quickly disabused. He returned to London to find the chaos in the secret services growing, with talk among the younger and more foolish elements of resignation, betrayal, even suicide. His instinct was to take the news to Foley, but Foley, for the moment, had disappeared. As Menzies, Vivian and Dansey were locked in bitter combat with one another and the SOE, he inevitably fell prey to the predatory curiosity of Desmond Morton. But even Morton, installed now in luxury at the Ministry of Economic Warfare, refused to show much interest. Great things were afoot, he hinted, and the secret services had bigger fish to fry than propaganda nonsenses dreamed up by Joseph Goebbels. In view of the weight he had given to the idea of an aristocratic plot, Edward found his flat reaction to the name of Hamilton quite puzzling. A week later, of his own volition, he provided him with proof that Albrecht Haushofer had written to Douglas, Duke of Hamilton, before the war – and that Hamilton had shown the letter to Winston Churchill at his Morpeth Mansions flat. Morton had become immediately more thoughtful, and had ordered him to keep the matter firmly underneath his hat. Fearing that he might end up excluded, whatever steps were taken next, Edward managed next morning to get a memo through to 'C''s personal assistant, with a promise that it would end up on his desk.

It was a long game, and despite his dogged determination not to be shuffled to the sidelines Edward, naturally, was not privy to all the machinations. There were months of planning, false trails were laid, tests and traps set up and sprung. Albrecht Haushofer was contacted, certainly, and communication lines were established in Portugal and Switzerland. In November, Edward was given sight of a letter from Haushofer – he signed it 'A' – written to the duke. 'My dear Douglo,' it began, and referred, significantly in Morton's view, to 'your friends in high places'. Hamilton, presumably to fool the Abwehr if they had wind of it, was told not to reply to the suggestion of a meeting outside England until the day after Hess had flown.

The endgame started suddenly, with final confirmation of the flight coming from a source that Carrington, at least, found totally unexpected. The Minister of Labour, Ernest Bevin, received a message which he had decoded for him in a Leeds hotel by Albert Heal, a trade union leader who had run a pre-war escape route for German socialists that still had watertight communications. Bevin rang London from the hotel room, and Edward was rung at home half an hour later. It was late on Friday evening – Friday, May 9, 1941 – and he was ordered to present himself at the office at ten past seven in the morning. An hour after that, provided with rail tickets and a reservation, money, petrol coupons and instructions, he was at Euston. When he arrived at Glasgow, there would be a car to pick him up, with a driver who knew the Scottish lowlands 'like the inside of his sporran'. The train pulled out to the minute.

During the interminable journey Edward turned what he knew of the affair over and over in his mind, and wondered if it could possibly, really, happen. Throughout the months since he had brought the word from Hannele, he had sometimes had the impression that the British viewed the escapade with distaste, embarrassment, that sat ill with its potential. On the very narrowest level, it seemed to him, Rudolf Hess must be a gold mine of strategic information, although the experts at SIS had said his position in the Nazi hierarchy was not perhaps all it had been or appeared to be. He was Number Two in name, they said, but Number Three in power, and possibly fading. Hermann Goering was the man behind the throne, and Hess had become increasingly of the margins. On the other hand, the selfsame experts named Hess as one of Hitler's very few close friends, a loyal sidekick from the early days. That struck Edward as suspect, as if they wanted to have their cake and eat it too. If they got their hands on Hess he was important – if they failed, he was a nobody.

It was the attitude to peace which nagged him most, however. The last few weeks, indeed the last year, had been appalling for Britain, and as Churchill said – ad nauseam, in Erica's view – Britain stood alone. West Europe had gone, North Africa and the Balkans. London and other cities were slowly dying underneath the Blitz, and intelligence on U-boat building (top secret) was terrifying to those who knew. But despite the Hess initiative, despite feelers via

Switzerland and Spain as well as Scandinavia, even to talk of seeking peace was treated in secret service circles as defeatism, almost treachery. MI5 had reported the possibility of peace demonstrations in several major cities – and censored any hint of them by press and broadcasting – and almost all the Cabinet's home and office numbers were being tapped on Churchill's orders. Erica, although knowing none of this, had grown more scathing, with her outsider's eye, not less. She had been appalled by Churchill's decision to shoot down German aircraft – marked with the red cross – picking up ditched fliers in the Channel, and she argued passionately that the saturation bombing of Britain's cities – bombing that Hitler had promised would never happen – had been forced on him by Churchill's repeated refusal to stop the air-raids on Berlin that had set the whole thing off.

'But they were small,' yelled Edward. 'Germany's too far away, we've got to fly across the occupied territories. Hitler killed fourteen thousand Londoners in fifty-seven days!'

'Precisely! Are you stupid? Churchill knows he'll never win this war, but he can't give it up! Resistance makes him great! He's a V-sign and a fat cigar! I truly don't believe if Hitler offered peace on *any* terms he would accept, he couldn't! So he needs America, doesn't he? He's had their arms, he's got their sympathy, but he needs more. One day, God and FDR willing, America will join in with him. And the more poor little Britain takes a battering, the more bombs that are called down on the wreck of London, the sooner it will be. *Truth!*'

They had had many rows like this, and it was a measure of how far their relationship had come that Edward, while sometimes scorched by the depth of Erica's cynicism, fought his corner without descending into rage and came back for more. They were lovers now, and he preferred today to dwell on that than on the knottier problems. Even in peacetime the London–Scotland journey had been a long one, but in wartime it was dreadful. This train, like every other one, was packed to the doors, and when it was left in sidings periodically to allow trains of troops, and ammunition and essential war materials to plod by, the hum of conversation hung about the carriages almost tangibly. There was no chance to stretch one's legs, as even the first-class corridors were packed, while getting to the reeking lavatories was an assault course and using them much worse. As often as he could, Edward dozed in and out of sleep and thought of sex. It was not perfect with Erica but they were honest with each other – as honest as two lovers can be – and Erica was forgiving. Sometimes they made love brilliantly, and for the rest they acknowledged a pleasure in each other, and a deep need for the comfort that each brought, in bed or out of it. And they argued.

It was late afternoon when the train pulled into Glasgow, and Carrington was grubby and exhausted. The station concourse was a seething mass of people, civilian and uniformed, with a fair spattering of the drunks that had always been part of the city's landscape when he had ridden up from Galloway on weekends free from school. Mussolini, he reflected, was reputed to have made the trains run on time if nothing else, and he wondered if it might not be a good idea to offer him a job controlling Britain's network. He was just over three hours late to meet his guide, locating him at last on the edge of a ruck of Army drivers, forlorn in Air Force blue. When Carrington spoke he jumped, and a powerful aura of beer hung round him. But he was not drunk, he insisted, no sir! He had stayed away from the whisky.

As long as he could drive, Edward did not really care about his condition, and the man, Corporal Miller from Dundee, was perfectly capable behind the wheel of the Austin Ten. He did not try to talk, indeed he was a morose type even half-cut, and he manoeuvred out of Glasgow's traffic and onto the Edinburgh road with only the occasional muttered swearword. The first stop was RAF Turnhouse, where Carrington would dine with Hamilton, he hoped, or at least have a good wash and sandwiches before their briefing session and the antics of the night began. Miller dropped him at the main administration then drove on to the vehicle pool and, he said, some food and shut-eye. He opened pale, hurt eyes when Carrington told him not to take more drink excepting tea, and swore it had not entered his head.

Hamilton was a tall man, who treated Edward briskly, and clearly as a social inferior. Luckily he was engaged on operational matters when his 'guest' arrived, and turned him over temporarily to his intelligence officer, a flight lieutenant called Benson, who recognized the symptoms instantly and prescribed a double whisky. When Edward suggested ablutions first he grinned engagingly and led him to the bar.

'A whisky'll take thirty seconds, man. Then come to my quarters and leap into a bath. Then more whisky, then we'll eat.' It sounded, put like that, like a damned fine plan.

Later – several whiskies later – Hamilton did emerge, and they went into a private office to talk. He still treated Edward coolly, stating with conviction that he had his orders direct from London and saw no need to go over them in detail, and no possibility that he would modify them on the say-so of a junior officer he did not know. He was expecting the 'target' to enter his 'field of jurisdiction' sometime late that evening, and his instructions had gone out. The plane would certainly not be shot down, and as he had not alerted the Observer Corps, there was a good chance that it would get close to its destination – Dungavel, his family home – before being spotted. After that, assuming Hess survived whatever form his landing took, he would no doubt be apprehended on the ground in the normal manner of crashed enemy aircrew: there were plenty of Army units in the area.

Feeling slightly at a loss, Edward said: 'But how do you see your part after that?' And noting the widening of the haughty eyes, amended: 'I mean of course, sir, what are your orders?'

Benson was smirking slightly. Edward felt like a colonial or a schoolboy, and it irked.

Wing Commander the Duke of Hamilton replied: 'My instructions are to let it run its course as if I know nothing at all about it. That is rather obvious, I should have thought. Either Hess will name me – which God forbid he should be stupid enough to do – or I will be contacted in the normal run of things. I do, after all, control this sector. Either way, he will be locked up and guarded, and in the fullness of time I will be conveyed to speak to him. Your instructions, as I understand them, are to sweep up all the pieces, tie the loose ends, make sure nobody goes dancing about the countryside shouting that Rudolf Hess has landed. Correct me if I'm wrong.'

In the officers' mess afterwards, Benson laughed at what he said had been Edward's expression in the last moments of the interview – 'pained, old boy, quite pained. It's clear that you've never been in the services.'

'Or gone to a public school,' Edward rejoined. 'God, Benson, how do you put up with it?'

'Oh, he's a good man underneath it,' said Benson. 'In fact I think it's you that's got on top of him. Or this Hess lark in general. He's being ruled from London, and he's not used to that. He moves with

Royalty, you know, his ma-in-law's chief lady of the chamber or what-have-you to the Queen. To be quite frank, this cloak and dagger stuff is beneath him, and he feels it keenly. You're just the whipping boy. Listen, don't mind the Wingco anyway, have another drink. I'll watch your back at this end, you can count on me.'

It was getting towards ten o'clock, and they had switched to beer some time ago, to keep their brains clear. According to Benson it would be getting dark soon after ten, so Hess would have to show up soon. He had keyed up all the radar stations and they would be alerted the moment anything significant was plotted. Then they could follow Hess by phone, and Carrington could head off immediately to the spot where he'd 'kissed the deck' to make sure some Home Guard maniac didn't put a bullet in him. Carrington remembered Miller.

'Talking of maniacs, my driver,' he said. 'He was tiddly when he picked me up. I'd better check him.'

'I'll send a man. You're worrying too much. I chose Miller for you, he could drink a distillery dry and chase it with a brewhouse. This is Scotland. Have another drink. It's Saturday night.'

The first news came shortly after ten o'clock, and it was followed up, annoyingly, by a report from a Royal Observer Corps post on the coast near Berwick. Carrington and Benson had joined the Wingco in the control room when they'd received the radar tip-off, and heard him cursing under his breath. The ROC had identified the interloper as an ME110, which was more or less unheard of this far north because of its range. Indeed, Hamilton suggested crisply that they had got it wrong and left it at that. When he came off the line he smiled his first genuine smile in Edward's presence.

'If anybody dares to wonder why I'm not scrambling, there's my answer,' he said. 'Carrington, I must admit I never much believed in any of this malarkey, but it looks as if I've been proved wrong. We've got a bloody German in our air space and we're meant to welcome him. I think the show's about to start.'

For Edward Carrington, over the next hour, 'the show' degenerated rapidly into farce. The next reported sighting was from RAF Ayr, then the ME110 was tracked intermittently until overshooting Scotland altogether and flying out to sea. It returned, 'wove about like a drunken hoorie' in Benson's words, and disappeared from radar south of Glasgow. A couple of judicious phone calls, and they had a more or less exact location: Eaglesham. At twelve miles from Dungavel, the pilot had not done too well.

Edward was kitted up and ready to go, and Benson went with him to the car, which was ticking over outside the control tower. Miller jerked himself into some sort of alert state as they approached, smiling glassily.

'Miller,' said Benson, warningly. 'If you're pissed, man, I'll have your balls for breakfast.'

'Never in this world, sir,' slurred Miller. 'Just tell me where the gennleman wants to go.'

The reek off him was now of whisky.

The night, when Edward relaxed into it, was really quite amusing. Miller had two uncanny knacks — one of missing other vehicles, or walls, or signposts, by inches, and the second of missing their destinations and the action by a mile. By the time they reached the Mearns Road near Eaglesham and trudged to the wreckage of the Messerschmitt, it had acquired a small crowd of sightseers, who were bantering with the Home Guards trying to keep it safe from looting. Carrington was directed to a nearby farmhouse where 'a tall, dark German airman had been arrested at the sharp end of a pitchfork' to find only another crowd of excited neighbours and a labourer called Davie Maclean who was getting fed up with the whole affair. Carrington managed to get him to one side long enough to ask him what the airman had said.

'Not a lot,' replied the Scot. 'He'd hurt his back a bit, and couldnae walk so well. He took a glass of water till the Home Guard barged in and waved a muckle pistol in his face. He said he was called Horn and he'd popped across to see the Duke of Hamilton or somesuch. His English wasnae good, I'm thinking, he didnae seem to understand a word I said.'

As Edward could hardly understand a word the man said either, that did not surprise him. Nor did the false name Hess had given. With Home Guard revolvers in the question, it would be a foolish man indeed who claimed to be a Nazi warlord.

'Look,' he said. 'Well done with the pitchfork, but don't talk to the neighbours too much about this, will you? And especially not the newspapers if they start nosing. From what I've seen of it, this is a perfectly normal thing, the pilot probably got lost.'

'I didnae use a pitchfork, that's just nonsense. And he mentioned the Duke of Hamilton, he said he was a friend of his.'

The crush of people in the kitchen were beginning to take notice. It was amazing, Edward thought. Did they not have beds to go to? He looked at his watch. Well gone midnight. And the plane had crashed at 11.10, or thereabouts. Ah, what the hell? The gabblings of a Scots farm labourer would hardly matter.

'Unlikely, isn't it?' he said. 'He must have read his name in the German papers, unless he's crackers. Well, I must go, no rest for the wicked. And remember — not too much talking.'

'Walls have ears,' piped up a white-haired old lady. 'Careless talk costs lives!'

Fuck off, thought Carrington, sourly. He stumbled into the blackness and made his way to the wreckage, where Miller was meant to have found out the location of the Home Guard HQ. He found him chatting with two soldiers, and sharing their bottle of whisky. For a moment, he was furious.

'Miller! You're on duty! For God's sake, man!'

The two soldiers looked at him, uncrushed. As one of them turned away Carrington heard him mutter something, undoubtedly obscene. Miller winked.

'Ach, sir,' he said. 'Unwind, why don't you? Have a dram.'

He offered the bottle, and Carrington took it. He was in a foreign country, and he was lost. Miller looked surprised, the other two astonished.

'Hey!' said one. 'You wouldnae drop it?'

Carrington raised the bottle, swallowed, and sneezed hard as the fumes went up his nose. He drank again.

'I bloody wouldnae,' he said, in a perfect Dumfries accent. 'Thanks. Now — where the hell's the next stop?'

The next stop was a scout hut in a Glasgow suburb called Giffnock. By now Miller had dropped all pretence at knowing where he was, and the night was exceedingly dark. The headlights, in their blackout cowls, threw about as much light as a candle, and finally they went off the road. They missed the ditch-lip by a foot, but Miller, required to reverse with delicacy and skill, got a fit of giggling. So it was that Edward Carrington became the driver, and so it was they turned up at Florence Drive to learn that Major Barrie of the Home Guard had gone with a lieutenant and two soldiers of the Eleventh Cameronians to escort the prisoner to Maryhill Barracks, on the other side of the city.

'Have we identified him formally?' asked Carrington, of the senior NCO left in charge. The man looked strangely shifty. He fiddled with some notes.

'Well, sir, he says he's Hauptmann Alfred Horn. But there's some here have their doubts.'

'Ah,' said Edward, casually. 'Hauptmann Horn. No mystery there, surely? Who's the doubter?'

It was an ROC officer, who had already left. The rumour was that he thought Horn resembled Rudolf Hess, and had rung Turnhouse to tell the Duke of Hamilton so. No one else was sure if they agreed, but they did know it had taken him nearly half an hour to get through, and the conversation had been brief. The phone exchanges were manned by civilians, and they were being more recalcitrant in responding as the night wore on. Edward, given a private room, discovered the problem first hand: it took twenty minutes before he raised the operator, and another ten before he was talking to Flight Lieutenant Benson. They shared notes.

'No trouble on the ident here,' said Benson. 'The ROC man was Graham Donald and the Wingco sorted him out, he'll keep his mouth shut. The Army HQ have also been on, trying to get us excited, but our Duty Pilot turned them off pretty effectively. He told them we knew all about it, and said we'd be over in the morning. He had their duty wallah fair squeaking, about this mystery man being the Duke's best pal or some stuff, but he got nowhere. Just check that no one's taken anything away from him, will you? Oh, and if anyone has made inventories of his possessions, the Wingco says to pick them up. The less that gets out the better, whatever happens.'

Miller was fast asleep in the passenger seat when Carrington got to the car, but he did not try to wake him. The Home Guard had drawn him a map of how to get to Maryhill, and he was quite happy now. The whole thing had a total air of unreality, it was so different from anything he had expected. There was a war on, the military were in control, and all was chaos and confusion. Probably Germany was in a similar state. It was a pity one could not invade without giving advance warnings and following the rules: it would be a pushover.

At Maryhill Barracks, he met his first instance of bad temper of the night. The Home Guard officer, Major Barrie, was beside himself with pompous fury at the way he and his prisoner had been treated. The gates had been shut and unguarded, he said, and he had been forced to blow his horn to attract attention. Carrington made the mistake of allowing a small smile to show.

'You may not realize it, young man,' said Barrie, witheringly, 'but in so doing I was breaking the law. It is not permitted to sound a car horn after a certain hour. I could be prosecuted.'

Lieutenant Whitby of the Cameronians confirmed that laxness had been rife, although he was more worried at the lack of respect meted to the prisoner than the damage done to his self-esteem. The night duty officer, he said bluntly, had been drunk, and so had most of the NCOs detailed to the job.

'Lieutenant Fulton was in bed!' said Barrie. 'I was not saluted, I was not given my proper form of address. He conducted the matter in his pyjamas, and wanted to shove Hauptmann Horn in the guardhouse for the night. There will be complaints about the matter, and my language will be most stiff.'

Carrington asked Whitby: 'Where is he now? Who is in charge of his possessions?'

'I've got them, sir, they're in a bag. I also have an inventory.'

He pulled a piece of paper from his tunic, and Carrington took it. He glanced through it. A Leica, letters, photographs, headache pills. He would take care of all that later, when he'd got the bag.

'And Hauptmann Horn?'

'He's been driven to the hospital. Major Greenhill's given him a draught. He's not badly injured, just a few aches and abrasions.'

Major Barrie put in acidly: 'He was driven over there by a second lieutenant called Bailey, if you have any jurisdiction in this matter. Another disgrace. He was wearing tartan trews and a glengarry. The German was appalled.'

'Oh?'

'Aye,' said Whitby, rather sheepishly. 'He did complain at one point, actual fact. He said a British officer wouldn't be treated like that in Germany. Bit rich from what I've heard, but unfortunate. That was when we first got here. They'd locked him in a dirty little hole with a bed you wouldn't put a dog under. Would you need to speak to him, sir? In the hospital?'

But Carrington did not. Herr Hess was safe, and sedated. He collected the bag of possessions from Major Barrie's car and returned to his own. Judging that Miller had been snoring long enough, he shook him till he woke, and made him drive to Turnhouse. As Miller related it to his mates later, they were both asleep when they drove through the gates. It was nearly 5 a.m.

While the Duke and Lieutenant Benson went to Maryhill later in the morning to talk to Hess, Carrington sorted out a few more ends. He spoke to intelligence officers at several airbases and made sure that certain records were amended. If the censor ever allowed any of the story to appear in the newspapers, there would be tales of hot pursuit and near interception – the hot pursuit line giving the I.O.s particular pleasure as the fighters mentioned were Defiants, which everybody knew could not have caught a cold. He discovered that two Spitfires from 602 Squadron had actually met the ME110 head on – quite fortuitously – but it had been going so fast they had lost it by the time they'd turned around. This had been good fortune, as they had not been aware that it was a 'protected' aircraft, but Carrington arranged in any case for the record of their flight to be blotted from the squadron's sortie book. One of the pilots had been the ace Al Deere. It would not look too good if a 110 flown by a man well over forty had outpaced and outmanoeuvred two Spitfires piloted by 'the cream'. He also followed up a rumour that another ME110 had crash-landed north of Glasgow the same night, although he did not get to the bottom of it, and assumed it was more evidence of the Scottish Saturday Night. A trip to Eaglesham followed, where he met the Duke and Benson. The field was swarming with sightseers from Glasgow, and the sweating guards from RAF Abbotsinch were having little luck preventing the looting of souvenir items from the scattered wreckage. Carrington had already arranged to have it carted away as soon as possible by a salvage unit, and dumped at the old railway sidings at Carluke.

Back at Turnhouse, after a light lunch, Carrington and Benson sipped beer. Both were pale and tired, although Edward was conscious of an almost manic elation. Benson was quieter. He had been excluded from the interviews with Hess on the German's insistence, but said Hamilton had confirmed that the Horn nonsense had been immediately dropped. There had been something in the Wingco's demeanour that Benson did not like much, however, a quietness, an air of brooding.

213

'You're MI6, aren't you?' he challenged Edward. 'Perhaps you could ask him?'

As it happened, Hamilton called Carrington into his office shortly after half past five that afternoon, again excluding Benson. He had been on the telephone for more than half an hour, he said, and had got precious little sense out of them. He had been trying to talk to Sir Alexander Cadogan, the Cabinet's linkman with the secret services, but had been told that he was busy. Too busy, Hamilton added drily, to be informed the Deputy Führer of Germany had just dropped in. He'd had a blazing row with a 'Foreign Office Johnnie', and was on the point of bursting when a third voice had come onto the line. It had identified itself as Churchill's private secretary, Jock Colville, and said they realized he had some news to tell them.

'Which means,' said Hamilton, looking hard at Carrington, 'that the line was tapped. The Foreign Office line. Is that possible?'

Carrington made a neutral gesture. Which also means, he thought, that Churchill was expecting something. Who knew about all this, who knew?

'It would surprise me,' he said. 'But ... And what did he suggest?'

'Mr Churchill was not in London last night,' said Hamilton. 'There was an enormous raid, some thousands of people killed. Mr Churchill was luckily in Ditchley Park, in Oxfordshire, and I am to fly there now. I shall take a Hurricane.'

'Well at least you got through at last,' said Carrington. 'Is there a problem?'

The Duke tapped his desktop nervously.

'Everybody thinks I knew Hess well,' he said. 'I told them several times I had met him only briefly. The problem is this, perhaps you can advise me? I'm not absolutely certain, you see, as to whether I should say it. Whether it is what they want to hear. Your masters.'

There was a short silence.

'I'm sorry,' said Edward Carrington, 'but I'm rather at a loss.'

Hamilton picked up a pencil, and deliberately snapped it in two.

'I'm horribly afraid,' he said, 'that the man in Maryhill Barracks, the man who flew from Germany last night, is not Rudolf Hess.'

'Good God!'

'Yes,' replied the Duke. 'Well I'm sorry to burden you with it, I thought you might know more than ... It was foolish of me. I'll think about it as I fly.'

He stood.

'In the meantime, you'd better keep your mouth shut, hadn't you?'

He left Carrington standing in the office, dumbfounded.

ELEVEN

The fact that Winston Churchill knew that Rudolf Hess was coming was finally confirmed beyond doubt for Edward Carrington when he heard how Hamilton had been received. Until then he had suspected that the whole bizarre affair might have been kept under wraps by Morton and his cronies in the secret services, to see how it turned out. But when the duke – still in his flying gear – was ushered into the presence at Ditchley Park, he found Churchill in a playful mood. Hamilton showed him the photographs he had taken from the German flier, and told the Prime Minister that they were of Rudolf Hess, who had crashed a fighter plane into a field in Scotland the night before. Churchill, who liked to watch a film at night whenever possible, merely chuckled.

'Hess or no Hess,' he said, 'I'm going to see the Marx Brothers.'

It was Frank Foley who told him this, in his small office in Broadway. Edward had arrived by the overnight train and felt like death. Since Hamilton had flown south two days before he had been mainly involved in fighting pressmen, and briefing intelligence officers on how to counter the rumours and counter-rumours that were sweeping Scotland. The news was general now, although the chief censor, Admiral Thomson, was keeping all comment and speculation very firmly out of the newspapers. German radio had announced on Monday night that Hess had disappeared by plane, and had either 'jumped out or met with an accident'. There had been, the broadcast added unexpectedly, a history of mental instability. Only then had the BBC followed up the statement, saying baldly that the Deputy Führer had parachuted into Scotland.

'But is it Hess?' asked Edward. 'And if it is, what do we do now?'

Foley regarded him through clouds of aromatic smoke.

'If it isn't Hess,' he said. 'Where is he? If we try to make something of it, will he pop up like a maggot from an apple? Do you remember, about three weeks ago, German radio announced that Hess *wasn't* going to go to Spain, when no one in the world had said he was? Could we have been hoodwinked all the way? Whatever, there's something awful fishy going on. I'd say offhand, they've dropped a monstrous spanner in our works.'

Edward nodded. He was smoking some of Foley's black tobacco and it tasted terrible. He wanted bed, sleep.

'But who are they? And what exactly *were* our works? What was the plan? Do you know?'

'I have a rough idea. It was to do with propaganda, obviously. Suggesting that life under Hitler was so bloody that even his deputy wanted to get out. But there was more. There was a hope that we could persuade him to go back, "turn" him, if you like. That was to be my job, I'm on the Double X, you know. And when we'd turned him, if I managed it, we were going to send him back.'

'What, as a spy? That's ridiculous!'

'No, not as a spy, you idiot.' Foley laughed. 'Look, why don't you put that out? You're making me feel sick. You'll never be a pipe smoker. No, not as a spy, it was more complicated than that. Imagine if, for instance, we could get him standing up in public, get him photographed, on newsreel, all around the world, saying that we were fighting a just war, that Hitler was insane, that we had to win. Imagine him appealing to America to come in quickly, fight the good fight with us, shoulder to shoulder. Imagine if he told the Russians that Hitler was going to turn against them, soon. Imagine that.'

'Christ,' breathed Carrington. 'Is it true?'

Foley gave him a certain look.

'It could hardly harm us if it was, could it? But imagine, if after we'd persuaded him to say all that, we announced that he'd decided to go back. Into Germany, by parachute if necessary, of his own free will, to plead with Hitler to give in, or to rally the German Volk against him. What could Hitler do?'

Carrington's pipe was out. He laid it on the desk.

'Shoot him? What else could he do?'

'What, the man who sued for peace? The man who risked his life and flew to Britain? The eyes of the world would be on him, wouldn't they? Difficult.'

'Jesus.'

'You swear too much, son. But you can see why Churchill was devastated, can't you? It was very brave of Hamilton to show his doubts, collossally. In Ancient Rome they'd have chucked him to the lions. Blame the bearer of bad tidings. You can also understand why everybody identified the photos Hamilton brought down as being Hess. It *had* to be Hess, or everything collapsed.'

'But the photos were of Hess,' said Carrington. 'The man who landed brought them with him. Didn't they look at the real man?'

'Just the opposite. Churchill banned all photographs. None are to be taken of the flier, under any circumstances. At first they lived in hope, I think, they were willing Hamilton to be wrong, they needed it to be their man. Then *Deutschlandsender* made their announcement yesterday that Hess had flown the coop and I think that clinched it for them. It was Hess, it had to be, but even if it wasn't, they were safe. The Nazis had lost him, and we had someone who would do. They sent Hamilton back to Scotland with Ivone Kirkpatrick, one of our men working for the BBC who'd met Hess a couple of times in Berlin, when he was with the FO. Unless this chap's got two heads they'll confirm it's Hess, I'll put my shirt on it. Otherwise it's months of planning up the wall, and Mr Churchill crying in his brandy. Strange animal, the human being.'

'But what if the Nazis haven't lost him? What if it's a trick? Haven't they considered that as being possible?'

Foley lit a supplementary match. He drew in smoke.

'Hard to know,' he said. 'That would be the devil, wouldn't it? Maybe they just can't bear to contemplate it, or perhaps they'll just be forced to wait. You see, if they wanted to know the truth beyond all doubt, they'd have sent me up to Scotland, wouldn't they? I knew the man, I know the questions that we've got to ask. It might come to it. In the meantime, I've cabled for an X-ray report on the fellow's chest. That'll sort it out. Hess was shot in the Great War, through the lung. That'll sort it out.'

There was a question. Edward marshalled it, through the fog of tiredness.

'Peace,' he said. 'You didn't mention peace. As part of the plan. If it is the wrong man, what about the peace proposals?'

Foley's eyes held his, for seconds.

'Yes,' he said. 'Or even if it is the right. Very astute of you to notice that. They didn't mention peace.'

Over the next five days, events behind the scenes moved at breakneck speed, although with Admiral Thomson keeping the lid screwed down tight on the newspapers, radio and newsreels, the

British public had little to feed on except rumours, and snippets – not to be trusted but disturbingly suggestive – gleaned from German broadcasts. Berlin's line was now that Hess had flown to England to suggest peace, an idea, they said, that the British government was terrified might catch on. What neither German radio nor the public knew was that the Duke of Buccleuch was placed under house arrest on his estates in Scotland, several aristocrats were personally warned by Churchill that if they talked of peace they would be jailed, and Lord Londonderry was questioned inconclusively about a meeting that was alleged to have taken place on his Mountstewart estate in Northern Ireland with four German agents who had travelled up through the Free State.

In America the scare was possibly even greater. Industry was geared up, under Lend Lease, to produce the armaments that would defeat Hitler, and also pull the country finally and forever out of the stagnation that had crippled it for a decade. The thought that it might all come to nothing through a peace-outbreak had bankers, politicians and industrialists shaking in their shoes. The OSS – forerunner of the CIA – held joint meetings with MI6 to hammer out a viable response, and Roosevelt was advised to cook up some scheme with his 'Former Naval Person' friend across the water suggesting that Hitler's real hope was to bring about a peace in Europe so that he could attack and destroy the US and her interests. Even the expressions of support and sympathy that flooded in for Rudolf Hess from all around the world were ruthlessly destroyed by the British censors. Kim Philby, who had got a job at last with SOE and was working to get into SIS, fed rumours to the Russians that Hitler was behind the flight, and wanted Churchill to join him on an eastward march, or at least stay neutral while he did the job himself. No one ever knew who had fed this line to Kim.

Quickly and inexorably, however, the evidence built up that the man in military hospital at Buchanan Castle, Drymen, was not Rudolf Hess. He failed to recognize Ivone Kirkpatrick, and he spoke only in the most general terms about why he had flown to Scotland. While the reports that IAK sent for the official files expressed no doubt at all, by Thursday he was complaining that he could hardly get the prisoner to mention politics, let alone discuss them. Later the same day Douglas, Duke of Hamilton – frustrated past belief – turned up at the Foreign Office in London and informed them that he was seeking an urgent audience with the King. This caused a frisson of pure terror, but Hamilton was not to be denied. The following day he lunched with George at Windsor, and that evening the prisoner was removed from Drymen and packed onto the LMS night sleeper from Glasgow. As a measure of how leaky was the colander, even in the exercise of maximum security, a Movietone newsreel van and a *Daily Express* reporter had to be shooed away from Euston next morning before he could be transferred to the Tower of London. Within hours of his arrival, Frank Foley was sent at last to interview him. He had already seen the report on the X-ray done at Drymen, and had requested clarification of one point. This had arrived by telegram from Lieutenant Colonel Dr J. Gibson Graham, RAMC. There was no sign of a bullet wound, ancient or modern.

'It is not Hess,' Foley told Edward, after spending his first day with the man. 'He is thinner than Hess, he is stupider than Hess, and he thinks like a peasant. He mumbles when I go in for specific points, he puts an accent on, but I think he's trying to tell me Hess is dead. He mentions Heydrich, and an airfield in Denmark, Aalborg, I know some people there. I think it's where he flew from, and the implication is that Hess was there as well. But Reinhard Heydrich got to him, and bumped him off. The poor chap's in a state of terror in case we do the same to him. He clings to his uniform like a second skin. Geneva Convention, prisoner of war.'

Edward smiled faintly.

'Distasteful lot, the Nazis, aren't they? Have you told the top brass yet? That it's not him?'

'I told Cadogan after the first hour. In a quiet way, he went off the handle. He said they won't accept it, I've got it wrong. He told me to go back and try again.'

'Churchill?'

Foley pulled a pipe from the pocket of his baggy brown jacket. He began to fill it.

'I imagine from Cadogan's attitude that that's the problem. I think it's a question of deep rage, subterranean. I got the feeling that there could be murder done. Cadogan reins him in, you know. Part of his job.'

There was quiet while Foley lit a match and drew. He looked a happy man, soft-voiced, content. Carrington was no longer fooled by that. Foley flicked the match out.

'Edward,' he said, 'I want you to contact XU. I know we've had communication difficulties lately, but you've got to speak to them. If you can't make contact, you'll have to go to Sweden. We've got to know.'

'I'll try. What are the questions?'

'Who is this man? Why is he here? Do they know where Hess is? If he's dead, who killed him, where, and why? Who knows about it, and who and what will they tell? Did something go awry, or is this how it was planned? If so, what happens next?'

That evening, Edward Carrington tried for six hours to make radio contact with XU. He worked from his normal station, in the top storey of a house on Highgate Hill, and he worked with increasing depression. They had had no indication that anything had gone wrong, but there had been no firm news from Stockholm since before the flight. He tapped out the call sign in two-minute segments, waited for ten, called again. If the Swedish connection had been blown, he could not imagine the severity of the consequences. But they had had no indication.

At last, at twelve minutes past midnight, he received a signal. It was unexpected, clear and fluent. Reading you, it said, good strength, go ahead. Edward, using the code and method agreed for that date – Monday, May 19 – asked his questions. After forty minutes, without preamble, the answer started to come through. The transmission was short, but he was sweating when it ceased. For a few moments he sat at the receiver, listening to the hollow hum of vacant ether, recovering. Then he acknowledged it and began to decode. When he had the message, he read it several times. Most of it was very clear.

RH alive and well awaits photo AH ditto stop use only Leica stop clear airfield 413 0300 day 20 month 5 stop safe conduct Dornier 217 two men plus documents stop no man move while uncertainty stop RH insists parole also AH safety stop letter in own hand and password stop lucky 4 HM query end

It took three phone calls to track down Foley, who was still at the Tower. It was after two when Carrington arrived, but the governor's house was still bustling. Foley, stony-faced, told him that the dirty tricks brigade, led by Charles Fraser-Smith, had turned up earlier to make a replica of the prisoner's uniform, correct in every detail. He had been stripped and measured, and two tailors were now working on the clothes. Courtaulds had sent a man who had found an exact match for the material.

'Stripped? Didn't he object?'

Foley made the action of a hypodermic with his fingers. There was a look of distaste on his lips.

'It's the left hand not letting on what the right's up to again. Why we need a duplicate uniform, don't ask me, God knows. What luck?'

He took the sheet of paper and glanced at it. Then he guided Edward into an office and sat him down. He pored over the message for an age.

'So he's still alive,' he said. 'They've got him. Clearance for two men. Does that mean he'll come? No — parole insisted, and a letter from AH. Alfred Horn, presumably. In his own hand, and photographs with the Leica. There was a roll of film in it by the way, did they tell you? It was fogged, possibly by our own lab boys, we'll never know. Well he's cautious, isn't he? Presumably, if he's satisfied, he'll meet us. He might agree to come. Good God, son. Good God.'

'Do you think they plan to *send* a Dornier? Is that what it means? A German bomber on an English airfield? Would that be possible?'

'Been done before.' Foley was preoccupied. 'There's a worry here, though. It all makes sense, except . . . What in heaven's name does the last bit mean? Do you know?'

Edward went slightly red.

'It's personal,' he said. 'Unprofessional, one might say. HM and myself are friends.'

Foley chuckled.

'Thank the lord for that, I thought HM must be the King. Or worse, the King Over The Water! Edward, this is all marvellous. God willing, we'll have an answer to our mystery. We'll have our man, even if we have to row across and pick him up ourselves. Are you au fait with everything?'

'One query. Airfield 413. Should I know it?'

'I do. It's a code we've used before. Lincoln. I think we'll go together, don't you?'

'Rather,' said Edward.

At three o'clock in the morning of Tuesday 20 May, Frank Foley and Edward Carrington watched a Dornier 217 taxi to a halt between the lines of flares that had been lit ten minutes previously at RAF Lincoln. It struck Edward as a strange, exciting thing, with overtones he found quite horrible. The aircraft was an enemy, and the two men who climbed down onto the concrete were enemies, also, two of the nameless killers who had tried to 'break this island race'. The plane had been expected and had come in unchallenged, and would fly away again in total safety. The two men looked small and vulnerable in their leather helmets, harnesses and bulky coats. One of them was carrying a package.

As they drew near, Foley and Carrington stepped out of the shadow of the control tower. The Germans hesitated, then came on. They were face to face.

'Good morning, gentlemen,' said Foley, in German. 'I believe you have something for us?'

The airmen were young, but not unconfident.

'Good morning,' said one of them. 'Major Foley. How very pleasant.'

'Heinrich. Paul.' Foley was unsurprised. 'I won't name my young colleague, if you don't mind. We can't be too indiscreet.'

'Of course. Good morning, sir.'

'Hallo. A pleasure,' said Edward. It was so grave, so mad. He held out a small package. 'These are the photographs requested. They were taken with the Leica.'

'Good. We have our parcel for you. It is all in order. I hope everything proceeds all right from now on.'

The other man, whose voice was gentler, added: 'I hope it can bring peace, Major Foley. We can vouch for his intentions.'

The sentence seemed to hang in the cold morning air with the whisp of vapour it had left behind. Frank Foley nodded.

'I will do my best, friends,' he replied. 'I wish you the safest of safe journeys back.'

Formally, all four shook hands. Then the Germans turned and walked across the empty concrete to the rumbling Dornier. No Englishman had approached it. The fliers clambered in.

'Paul Rosenberger and Heinrich Schmitt,' said Foley. 'They fly from Aalborg. Another part of the pattern, I would guess.'

Shortly, the grumble of the engines became a roar, then an ear-splitting crackle that preceded the take-off run. It changed as the Dornier accelerated away from them, and took on a rhythmic throbbing as it left the ground.

Two minutes later, on the concrete of a Royal Air Force aerodrome, the engines of the German bomber were dying on the light west wind. As shadowy men in overalls began to douse the flares, Carrington and Foley turned silently away.

The photographs in the Leica were the only pictures of the flier that were ever taken on British soil.

TWELVE

Carrington's second flight to Stockholm was the most difficult of his life. The courier service from Leuchars had become increasingly dogged by attacks from ME109s, which appeared at times to have advance intelligence of when the planes would leave and land. Carrington's flight was put off three times, and when he did go it was in the belly of a Mosquito, lying on a blanket and wrapped in a heavy coat. The unarmed plane flew very fast and very high. Carrington, when they landed, was tinged with blue at his extremities, and could not hear his own teeth chattering because of the engine-thunder that still rang inside his skull. The XU man who met him was sympathetic, but could not help much. The heater of the van they drove in was hardly worth the noise it made, and no coffee was available. It was light when they reached their destination, a small house some miles outside Stockholm, but his condition was hardly any better. He had to be helped into the house.

Inside the kitchen it was warm, and smiling Scandinavians gave him hot blankets and drinks to revive him. The pain of returning circulation was violent, and for half an hour he bit his lips and clenched the muscles that still worked to keep himself from moaning. After the first ministrations the Swedes discreetly left him to his agonies. It was an hour later that he heard light footsteps and watched the handle turn. It was Hannele.

At first, Edward Carrington could hardly take it in. He made to stand, but yelped at the stabbing in his knees. Hannele, who had not yet apparently decided on an expression, smiled. She walked across the room and pressed his shoulder.

'Sit,' she said. 'Oh Edward, how you do suffer for your country! Sit awhile.'

She turned to the stove and checked the damper. It was very warm now in the room. She pulled a wooden chair across in front of him and sat sideways on it, leaning on the back, looking at him. She had a long, loose dark brown skirt on and a cotton shirt and waistcoat.

'You're different,' she said. 'Your eyes are different. Your cheeks are hollow. You're going grey.'

Her smile had gone, but she was kindly, almost motherly. Edward realized that there would be no fourth time, whatever her message might have said.

'How old are you?' he asked. 'Twenty-one? Twenty-two? You seem much older, much much older. I don't mean you're not beautiful, you're more beautiful than ever. Ah well.'

'I'm twenty-two. I feel a hundred. Edward, why is your country so resistant, why are you so stubborn? We expected a response. We hoped for wonderful things. Why is it taking so long?'

He was puzzled, honestly.

'But the real Hess did not come. It caused great embarrassment. Problems. Well, to be frank, fury. Winston Churchill, like Queen Victoria, was not amused. Why didn't he come? It was a stupid trick. He's lucky the other man wasn't put against a wall and shot.'

'He was afraid,' said Hannele. 'He was afraid of Winston Churchill. I've told you before, we see things differently over here. It takes two sides to make war. Also to make peace. Herr Hess does not trust Churchill.'

'You sound like a German. You say "we". Surely Churchill is the only hope?'

Hannele Malling's eyes were downcast. She was very calm.

'Herr Hess was afraid of other people, too. Goering could have shot him from the skies. Heydrich could have shot him in the head. The deception was meant to facilitate the end result. We thought that that was understood. We indicated that the night the flight was made would be the climax of the air-raids, that after that they'd stop. That was to be Herr Hess's pledge of his intent. His parole, as he calls it. We had acknowledgement.'

Oh God, thought Carrington. Could that be true? He had heard nothing of this. But the air-raids had been biggest on the night. And afterwards they had ceased. Churchill had been a hundred miles from London, weekending in the country. Had it all been done by arrangement? And acknowledged?

'Goering,' he said. 'That means Goering must have been in on it? And you mention Reinhard Heydrich. Surely he . . . ?'

'You must ask Herr Hess. I do not know the details. Reichs-marschall Goering taps all the telephones, of course, so he knows everything. Heydrich just knows everything. You must ask Herr Hess.'

'Is that possible? Where is Hess? Can I see him?'

'Yes, you can see him, Edward. There have been many wild geese chased, that is not how we like to go on. Herr Hess is in Sweden. He is on a yacht, we can go there by a launch. If he is satisfied with you, with your parole, he will go to England with you. He is prepared to die to end this war. Well, we all are, I suppose. You too.'

He had not really looked at it like that before.

'Let's hope it won't be necessary,' he said.

Even before Carrington had left for Sweden, he'd known that the contents of the package from the Dornier had clinched the matter beyond doubt. Churchill had been enraged yet further, and Foley had received the flak. That mild man, a touch of his native Somerset showing through, had been quite knocked sideways, so he said, to learn that he was held responsible for ramifications to the matter that other men had deliberately kept from him. The upshot was that Hauptmann Alfred Horn – if that was indeed his name – had been transferred next morning from the Tower to a miserable country house near Aldershot called Mytchett Place, where he was being held under extremely heavy guard.

'He's been designated "Z",' said Foley. 'And Mytchett's called Camp Z from now on. He's an unforgiving devil, Churchill, isn't he?'

Carrington did not understand.

'Ah,' said Foley. 'Maybe you've never heard of Plan Z? That's what Chamberlain called his famous flight to Munich, back in 'thirty-eight. Another airborne bid for peace that Churchill disapproved of, likewise doomed to failure. A nasty sense of humour, as I said.'

Nastier still, from Foley's point of view, was that he had been told to go and live at Mytchett Place as well. He and two other MI6 men were to stay with 'Z', night and day, and secretly record everything that he said. Distasteful, and a total waste of time. The flier had been briefed to say a few things like a parrot, but had no deeper understanding of war, or peace, or politics than that bird.

'So why?' asked Edward. 'What good will it do, you being there?'

'Could it be a punishment? For transgressions that I didn't know I'd made? Because I believed that something fine might come of it? Churchill said in the House that the whole thing baffled his imagination, which I don't believe. But for my part, all right, I'm baffled. Cadogan says we're to question this man till he's dry, question him to death if necessary, but I've already spoken to him for hours. There's nothing there, he's a husk. They've got the spare uniform somewhere, although I've never seen it. "C" talks of seeing what can be salvaged, seeing if this man could still be turned, to follow the original score. I don't know, Edward. I've had my orders. I'm going to the country for a while, to merry Mytchett Place. To see what happens.'

'And I'm off to Sweden. To try to meet up with the real thing. What if I bring him back? What price your daft imposter then? We'll have the real Hess.'

They were drinking filthy *ersatz* coffee in a Cornerhouse. Inevitably, Foley was offering his pouch. It was declined.

'Well,' he said. 'We might have two to play with.'

His blunt fingers had rapidly stuffed the pipe. The vesta scratched, and clouds of smoke billowed.

'Then again,' he added, 'maybe we won't.'

His voice had become very quiet, the pipe-stem in his mouth.

'I beg your pardon?'

Foley blew the match out.

'Intelligence can be overvalued, can't it? It can be a positive embarrassment.'

Edward did not think he understood. But Foley's mind, he saw, was no longer with him. He did not ask.

They went to the fjord in the same old van, driven by the same large XU driver. In a small harbour below an empty summer house they were greeted by a seaman, who had been sitting warming his hands on the engine of a small black motorboat, incongruously called *Shirley*. It was a sunny day, the light lovely on the sparkling green water, and the sea was calm. In another time it would have been a delight, the twenty-minute trip along the craggy shore, the petrol motor almost purring. But neither Hannele nor Edward felt like talking, and the seaman stared ahead, keeping close inshore, avoiding hidden rocks. Finally they rounded a headland and saw a steam yacht, white and magnificent, in the middle of a deep, high-sided gut. Hannele touched his hand.

'There. Like Napoleon on St Helena. He lives in splendid isolation and dreams great dreams.'

But there was no one visible, no brooding figure on the afterdeck. Only some sailors in blue jerseys who appeared as the *Shirley* chugged alongside the boarding pontoon. Hannele and Edward were handed off, and entered the opulent interior through a doorway cut in the yacht's side. Hannele introduced him to two officers in some sort of private uniform and they were conducted to a stateroom. A minute later a tall, stooped man came in and looked at them. His eyes were deep-set and almost feverish, shining out from under craggy brows. His face was pale, intensely strained, unhappy. It was Rudolf Hess.

Hannele introduced them, and they shook hands. Then she said: 'I shall leave you now.'

'Why?' said Edward.

'Herr Hess requires it.'

Herr Hess, it seemed to Edward, was not in a good state. He offered him a chair and also sat, but after ten seconds was on his feet again. There was a clock in the stateroom, and he had a watch. He must have looked at both of them a dozen times in the first two minutes.

'Forgive me,' he said. 'I have been away from Germany for almost two weeks. I thought by now I should be at home, I thought by now I should have secured peace, or died honourably in the attempt. How is my Hauptmann? It was not my intention that he should die. He has been very brave. Four months ago, you know, he could not even fly an aeroplane. I trained him myself. Do you fly? A twin-engined fighter is a beast, I told Messerschmitt he should go back to the drawing board. A beast.'

'He is safe still. You had the letter. But will you tell me why this happened, please? I have come to take you back to England, if that is what you want. But it caused confusion. We were considerably confused.'

Hess was a big man, but the way he shrugged his shoulders was expressive. The emotion was distaste.

'I do not believe that,' he said simply. 'But I cannot talk to you. My business is with your greatest men. We must bring peace before everything is lost.'

Edward, as instructed, said: 'My job is to find out what you have to say. My instruction is to find out if you mean to seek a peace sincerely, and if so, what are your terms. Until you have indicated that, there is little I can do.'

Rudolf Hess sat down, and lowered his head wearily onto one hand. He was dressed in jodhpurs of field grey, and polished boots. His shirt was crisp and newly ironed. But his frame spoke tiredness, mighty tiredness.

'In that case,' he said, 'nothing will be done. To ask a man who has risked his life and that of his loyal deputies, who has abandoned home and wife and a boy of three years old . . . to demand proof of sincerity . . . no. Nothing will be done. It is your word that is needed, not mine. Your parole. Your Mr Churchill's. No, no more. Either I go to England with your word, or I go back to Germany. I would rather die like a dog than be forced to grovel like one in the name of peace.'

'You had the package,' said Edward. 'If that was not sufficient . . .' He stopped. He felt a fool, a charlatan. 'Sir,' he said, 'what is your offer? Could you not give me an outline? The broadest framework?'

Rudolf Hess stood up. His eyes were black, deep under the eyebrows.

'You had better go,' he said.

They jumped less than a week later, at Luton Hoo on 28 May 1941, under cover of a supposed air-raid jointly organized by XU and some elements of the Luftwaffe. The RAF were expecting them, and a motorised ack-ack unit had been called in with their Scammells and their diesel generators and their giant mobile searchlights to blaze away with 3.7 inch AA guns at what they tentatively registered as about a dozen Heinkels flying very high, too high to be in danger. On the German side a few bombs were dropped to keep up the pretence, but they were left strictly alone by fighter aircraft, of course. In fact the ack-ack unit, who thought, or hoped, they might be protecting the princesses Elizabeth and Margaret, in residence at Windsor Castle, almost missed the fun entirely, having been told the raid would be at 2 a.m. The intelligence officers, having failed to allow for Double Summertime, which had been introduced the night after the first 'Hess' flight, were on the point of standing down the op just as the bombers droned into hearing.

Two, maybe three, parachutists were dubiously reported to have been sighted, but they were never heard of again. In fact, the intelligence officers were ordered afterwards to forget the thing had ever happened.

In the days since they had first met, Hess had unbent a little with Edward Carrington, but his decision not to discuss detail had remained unchanged. Edward had made the necessary signals, and received the necessary instructions. It was decided not to try to smuggle Hess out on the courier run, although the idea of making him do a parachute drop at his age seemed risky and wrong-headed to the Englishman, if not malicious. Hess, however, took it with equanimity, and laughed at Edward's own unease. It was all in the knees, he said, and he had liked to ski in better times. On the day, they were brought ashore on the *Shirley* and driven to the house. They were given a meal, and Hess took an hour's sleep. Carrington and Hannele found themselves alone.

'I'm tired of saying goodbye to you, my Edward,' she said. She moved close to him and touched his cheek. 'It's a pity that this war has spoiled things.'

'You don't call me Carruthers any more. I knew I'd missed my chance when that happened. I have a woman now, in London.'

'The same one? Yes, you were always such a faithful man. You could never have stood me, Edward. I've had to sleep with so many since this began. It feels like whoring sometimes, only I don't do it for myself, except once or twice to save my life.'

Despite himself, he felt the knife. It showed, she stroked his cheek.

'Typical Englishman,' she said. 'I suffer and you complain. You boys.'

She was like a big sister. Smaller than him, pale and thin, younger. She was like an older, bigger sister.

'Typical woman,' he said. 'You don't mind about the orgasm, do you? The one we never had together.'

'Of course not. I never minded. But I still see you by the bed that time. I still remember taking off your underclothes. Maybe one day.'

They kissed for a long time, and indeed there was still longing there, in both of them, a kind of hopeless longing. Soon after that, they parted.

In the Heinkel, despite the enormous noise, Hess and Edward

231

exchanged a few shouted words from time to time, their faces pressed close together.

'As things got worse and worse for you, I knew I had to come,' roared Hess. 'I had to come before two great nations died. We suffer similarly. Two corrupt and mighty egos.'

That was what it sounded like, but he was not sure. No point in asking for repeats.

Hess yelled: 'Soon we turn to Russia. We should do it arm-in-arm. There are other men to lead. No one is invincible.'

The engines battered onwards. Soon they must be over England. Hess moved his head in close again.

'Churchill cannot stand the thought of peace, that's understood. The loss of face! But when he hears what I am offering! *This* time he will change his mind! This time . . .'

It was Edward's first parachute drop except in training, and it hurt. He lay on the grass of Bedfordshire, shaken to his very bones. Out of the darkness he saw men coming, stealthily. A mile away the searchlights and the ack-ack tore the sky. He wondered where Hess was.

Later, he saw Foley, pipe glowing, looking like a farmer back from market. Edward was hobbling to a Humber and the little man detached himself from it and came to him.

'Jesus,' said Edward. 'I'm glad to see you. Where's Hess?'

'He's gone to London in the other car. He did a better jump than you, boy. Well done, by the way. You've played a great game.'

Carrington rubbed his aching elbows. There was something about the way that Foley spoke.

'Gone to London where? Are we following?'

The tobacco glowed like burning thatch.

'Not our show for the moment. We'll hear about it. He's gone to the Reform Club, I believe.'

'The Reform Club? Whatever for?'

'We've got some rooms there. Come on, climb aboard. I'll take you home.'

Carrington pulled the door open with a heart like lead. He remembered what Foley had told him once about the Carlton Club. But the Carlton Club was bombed.

After they had driven for a while, Edward said: 'Aren't we involved at all now? Is that the end of Hess for us?'

'I told you. We'll get our orders in the morning. I'm seeing "C" at nine. With a bit of luck I should get three hours sleep. I'll ring you when I know.'

'Frank,' said Edward, later. 'These rooms at the Reform Club. Are they in the cellar? What's going to happen to him? What's intended?'

There was a long pause. The Humber, old and driven hard, squeaked and rattled. Foley's voice took on its quiet form. Carrington had to strain to hear him.

'I wish to God I knew,' he said.

BOOK THREE

*Mr Churchill's
Private War*

PROLOGUE

August 17, 1987

The Americans were in charge the day he died. That was the key to it. Silversmith had contacts in the CIA, and Peter-Joe had been their guest. The CIA set up the business in the prison, provided the right men, took care of the paperwork, as it were. They provided the British team with fatigues, they got them into Spandau and made sure that no one noticed them. They showed them the lie of the land, organized the rotas of the warders and nurses who might be troublesome, arranged to call the one guarding the old man to the telephone. The rest was very easy.

The old man, not to put too fine a point on it, was a wreck. He was almost blind now, and could not even walk in a straight line unaided. He could not lift his arms above his shoulders, he could not tie his boots, he could not hold a mug properly, he had to sit to shave, and he could scarcely drag a big-toothed comb through his meagre hair. His will, however, was still powerful. Almost incontinent, he forced himself to wake at 3 a.m. so that he could empty his bladder into a lavatory and not his bed, and he still scrawled sharp notes when necessary – most recently to demand the dismissal of an American warder who he said deliberately upset him and was a danger to his health. It was this warder who was called away that afternoon to answer the mysterious phone call. When he returned, the old man's health had deteriorated indeed.

The morning had passed like all the others did these days, in a routine of minimal movement, minimal human intercourse, minimal thought. The Americans were the most easy-going of the watchers, but still he was watched, continuously. Overnight it had been British and US nurses, at 7.45 a.m. a Frenchman, then a Briton and again an American. At twenty past ten Hess painstakingly wrote out a list of his requirements – paper handkerchiefs, toilet rolls, a ruler – and twenty minutes after that the Tunisian, Abdallah

Melaouhi, brought him in his early lunch – shrimp cocktail, fish and mashed potato, beans. Although a suicide note was found in his pocket two days after his death – despite his requirements list and, fortuitously, in a room crowded with witnesses – the old man was at no time seen to write one.

The morning, then the afternoon, dragged on. The American governor popped in for ten minutes before midday, and finally Melaouhi went off for lunch. The old man had a sleep, then, at about ten past two, hobbled into the warm Berlin air with his American keeper, to drag himself painfully round the garden for a while. He did not walk far – he could not walk far – but headed for the garden hut a few hundred metres away from the doorway of the prison. He would sit there, as he often did, and let his mind wander quietly, his old body out of draughts and sunlight. As he approached the door, the keeper was called back to Spandau Jail. The telephone.

Inside the hut, the two Britons waited. It was very warm, and they were sweating in their US Army overalls. The hut was cramped, untidy, with a pair of chairs and a small table with a reading lamp on it. One of the men had a length of cable with him, which had come into the jail in the pocket of his overalls. The plan was to make the death look like a suicide; the old man was to hang himself with the flex that fed the table lamp. Safer to bring the gear, however. One never knew.

'A pound to a pinch of shit,' Peter-Joe had said, 'if we don't take a bit of flex to do the job, some bloody cleaner will have nicked the lamp for his kid's bedside table. Then we'd have to break the old bastard's neck and make that look like suicide. Difficult.'

It was not difficult to kill a ninety-three-year-old man in itself. That was easy. The difficulty, in fact, might be in doing it without causing visible injury if he struggled. The secret was, not to give him chance. They heard the warder being called away, they heard the shuffling of feet outside, they heard the stick bang against the side of the planked hut, and watched the door swing slowly open. They kept their breathing easy, slow and quiet.

Being almost blind, and coming from bright sunshine, the old man could not comprehend them for a moment. They should not be there, that much he did know, but the Americans were very lax. He stood in the doorway for too long, they needed him inside. He stood there, framed in sunlight, straining to see them clearly, to work it out. They willed him to move forward, to get in. So that they could kill him.

The old man was a stubborn character, they had been warned of that. He'd been the Deputy Führer of the Third Reich, and he had been in prison since 1941. He had hardly complained about such big facts, only about minor things, illnesses, discomforts, illogicalities. He had been guarded night and day, since 1966 he had been alone, he had been treated harshly by everyone and like dogshit by the Russians, and he had eaten, slept and brooded without asking for quarter. That was no help to them. They needed him inside.

That was how he received the head bruising that was noted at the autopsy, but not thought significant by Dr Cameron. One of them rushed at him, and the old man was jerked into the hut. He fell against a chair, crashed sideways, and banged his head against the table. Instead of expiring on the spot, or begging for mercy, he was galvanized. He seized the other chair, and tried with all his strength to get on to his feet. It was pathetic. He got halfway up, on to one knee, then the chair leg slipped away and he fell forward, this time striking the table with his chest. Both chairs were over now, and the old man tried to slither in among the seats and legs. The killers, cursing, had to kick the furniture aside. Peter-Joe, dexterous as ever, caught the table lamp as it fell, saving the bulb from shattering. The wire flex slipped from his right hand – the flex that he had brought – and the old man tried to grab it.

The noise was great and the situation grimly humorous. Peter-Joe responded like a fisherman trying to land a conger eel, using a loop of flex in place of a gaffe. As the old man boosted himself forward like a toddler going for the crawling championship, he swung the loop and caught it underneath his chin. He stood back, an end wrapped round each hand, his legs straddling the narrow back.

'Whoa, Dobbin! Hey up, you silly old bugger! Keep still, for Christ's sake!'

The old man ducked his head beneath the table, trying to butt his way into its shelter. Peter-Joe hauled backwards, trying to drag him out. He dropped to one knee, tried to get his left hand round the old man's head, to take him by the ear and twist him round, get him to face facts. His right hand had both ends of the ligature, he was trying to get some purchase on, some strangling pressure. There was a sharp smell of sweat suddenly in the hut. The old man was wriggling, more like a teenager than a nonagenarian. His black boots were flying about wildly, grey socks and off-white longjohns peeping momentarily. His face appeared, congested, his eyes bulging, rolling. His mouth was open and flecked with foam, his tongue thick and slimy. Peter-Joe spoke no more. He was panting.

He threw his leg across the old man's back, straddled him once more, then sat heavily on the skinny buttocks and thighs, transferring the flex to both hands which he brought together at the side and back of the neck. The pale lips drew back suddenly from the teeth, the old man grinned like a horse, he even snickered, whinnied almost. Peter-Joe dipped his head, the two heads almost touched, as he increased the pressure. His shoulders heaved, his face was wet with perspiration, as the old man kicked and lashed and battered with his boots.

'You . . . stubborn . . . old . . . *sod*!'

Suddenly, the cable slipped, the closed throat opened, air rasped into the tortured lungs. Suddenly, too, the other man moved in and took the strain, convulsively, his fingers overlapping Peter-Joe's, his face set like a gleaming mask. Still it seemed interminable, the flapping and the twitching, the trembling of the legs, but then the movement ceased. Peter-Joe rolled sideways, got both knees on the floor, studied the blue face. He glanced over his shoulder at his companion, who had moved back. He grinned.

'You took your fucking time, you're not on your holidays, you know. You look like fucking death.'

There was no reply. Peter-Joe turned back cheerfully, to the corpse.

'A real old Nazi, eh?' he said, half admiringly. 'What a tough old bastard! Listen, get the acetone out, rub things down. Better than the smell of sweat, anyway. And if he shits himself; he might. Look, we're running late. Let's get gone, pronto. What a tough old bird . . .'

They were still there when the warder returned, but that did not matter much, he would be squared. The nurse, Melaouhi, saw them briefly, two unknown men in Yankee clothing, but he was too upset by the death of the old man to realize the significance for a while. By the time the alarm was raised they were gone. In any case, the armed guards — true military thinking, this — were there to secure the prison from imagined dangers from the Berlin streets, and could not quickly get from the watchtowers into the prison gardens, however great the urgency. Because of the old man's stubbornness

240

in clinging on to life, they did not have time to tidy up the furniture, or to arrange the lamp flex round his neck, or even to unplug it from the wall. They did not worry. They knew that someone else would see to that. Their back-up was extraordinary. The best.

Before the remains of Prisoner Number Seven had even been formally pronounced lifeless, they were on their way to Hanover again. They were staying at the Holiday Inn . . .

ONE

The house that Edward Carrington and Erica had in Cumbria could not have been more different from the rooms in Oxford where Bill Wiley had first met them, and nor could the regime. When he had taken Johnnie there – a sullen, silent, miserable Johnnie – he had been worried that it could not work out, that the combination of old people, grandeur and the strange young woman who had met them at the station would tip the boy into open rebellion. But the house up on the moors had not been grand, it had been inaccessible, remote, and spartan. When the planked front door had been pushed open, it was not a butler that had scuttled into view, but a mouse. Johnnie, who had been sunk in gloom for more than an hour, squeaked in sheer surprise. And smiled.

The smile had not lasted long, but that might have been too much to hope for. The previous twenty-four hours had been an ordeal for an eleven-year-old, made harder by the lack of sleep. They had left Ireland in the cab of a lorry, Dun Laoghaire to Holyhead, after being driven down-country by Veronica. John had wanted to see his mother, and had become cold and withdrawn when told he could not. He had not cried, but Bill had felt the hurt. The boy had watched Ireland disappear from the stern of the boat with anxiety and loss clear on his face.

In the Donegal holiday home, Bill had tried to explain to him that they had to go to England and hide, but had kept bogging down. Johnnie wanted to know who was 'after them' and why, and what it had to do with Mum. He was obsessed with the thought that it was some subtle and obscure lie, that Bill was merely, in reality, running out on his marriage, that at the end of it would be a man in a black robe and a curly wig who would solemnly pronounce a divorce. Bill, in turn, could think of no way to tell his son that he was running from his own side, from his job, from the Army, without it becoming simply too complicated for the boy to understand. He reiterated several times his 'no lies' formula, knowing that he was lying by omission and elision if not in fact. Worse, he felt as if John knew.

But he hid himself, when told to, and he nodded gravely when Bill asked him if he 'felt all right'. He burrowed under sleeping bags in the lorry cab, he stayed close to Bill on Preston station, and he stood without complaint on the crowded Glasgow train that took them to Penrith. Bill felt the tension increase when they were met at the station by Jane Heywood – another woman, another 'friend' from his father's shaming life – but Johnnie remained polite. As he got into the back of her car he said to Bill, out of the blue: 'Will we see Mum soon, Dad? Will she be coming out of hospital?' – thus forcing Bill into an acknowledgement, a public one. 'Yes,' he replied, 'I hope so, love. Very soon.' Another lie, he guessed.

After a day or two, the house on the hill seemed to suit John. In ways it was like Ireland round about, without the bits he hated. It was raining almost constantly, or rather they lived so high up the fellside that they were in a semi-permanent mist. The house was built halfway up a steep hill on a small plateau of grass and smooth tarmac, and most of the time the nearby village – Garrigill – was invisible. The nearest neighbours were holiday-dwellers, only in evidence at weekends from their Newcastle businesses, and the only other living creatures that they saw were sheep. There was a hare as well, that ran in huge circles round the field below the house at dawn and dusk. John became so fond of it that he started to rise early, having been forewarned by Aunt Erica that it happened. Bill, also forewarned, had left Jane's bed even earlier and was in his own, in the room he shared with Johnnie.

To the boy, Jane and his father were just friends, and they behaved strictly as if that were true. He did not ask many questions, for fear perhaps of hearing things he could not believe, and when he and Bill went walking, he made it clear that Jane should be excluded. Aunt Erica he would have gladly had along, but she could not walk much farther than the edges of the tarmac, and Edward he was indifferent to, without at all disliking. Slowly he thawed with Jane, and allowed her to play football beside the house. She was much more energetic that way than his father, who preferred to sit on the low stone wall and kick out at the ball when it rolled near him. Gradually they all relaxed. But Liz would not go away. He wanted, always, to know if she would write, or why they could not ring the hospital to see if she was getting better. Bill, not sure if it was even true that she had had the so-called breakdown, worried too. But he was terrified his movements had been traced, that even Veronica's phone would be unsafe. He promised John there would be news soon, in a few days, and swore all would be well. At night, even in Jane's big old-fashioned bed, he worried.

They usually got a couple of hours alone at night, and they accepted that they were in love. Edward and Aunt Erica, told the story before Bill and John had arrived, played the part of odd old friends without irony or remark, and behaved towards Jane and Bill as if they were brother and sister. To Johnnie they played grandparents – the remoteness and uninterest of Edward offset by Aunt Erica's kindly attention, her baking of rock buns and the sweet-tins that appeared from nowhere for his pleasure. John liked them both, and modified his pattern of long walks with Bill to frequent shorter ones with the old, frail lady. There was a stream near the house, two hundred yards or so, which Erica could get to with great care and a lot of help from Johnnie. Once there, they would sit down on the rocks and watch the rushing water. They saw young trout.

In bed, Jane and Bill tried for happiness, and achieved constant sexual delight. The bed – which she had used on her vacations since she had been a teenager – was deep and ridiculous, like a high-sided canyon bridged with feather eiderdowns, into the middle of which they tumbled. They made love quietly, because the house, although of stone, had thin internal walls and they were both afraid for John, and of him in a way. But their bodies, as they always had been, were perfectly in tune. Which made for lovely fucking, and for sadness.

Bill explained. After the evenings, when they listened to Edward's story, and after John had gone to bed and was asleep, Bill explained. It was not particularly coherent at first, he was feeling his way, he realized. About his feelings towards Liz and Johnnie, his loyalty to his country and his job, his attitude to Ireland and its troubles. Because they were things he could not say to Edward and Erica, and their time in bed was limited, they often walked down to the pub, the George and Dragon in the village. It contained an odd mix of customers – the fell farmers, walkers of the Pennine Way, weekend-cottagers – none of whom took undue interest in them, so they could talk over their bitter, heads almost touching across the old wood tables with wrought-iron legs, communing. The walk there and back was also beautiful, the road unlighted and densely black, the South Tyne river roaring quietly below them, down the steep, wooded bank. When it was not misty, the stars were brilliantly clear, as clear as they were in the Irish sky, the unindustrial, unpolluted sky.

Bill was feeling his way most of all on Ireland; it was emerging as his greatest area of confusion. He was able to explain how he had once felt, how he had been certain that terrorists were simply evil men, that blowing arms and legs off people was simply wrong, but it was harder to explain how and why his views had changed. It was not that he now felt terrorism was right, naturally. He had seen bombs and their victims, he had put arms and organs into plastic bags, he still believed that terrorism could never win, that the British government, perhaps of all governments, was too stubborn ever to give in. And that, somehow, was an insight. It presented itself to him suddenly.

'They wouldn't give in even if the terrorists gave up,' he said. 'They'd see it as proof that they never had a case. That the justice was all on our side.'

'And isn't it? Christ, Bill, I can see your problem. You're beginning to believe the terrorists have a case.'

'Not the terrorists, the Republicans. No, not even that, the Irish government's frightened of them too. It's not a question of having a case, it's a question of inevitability. If you oppress people, they turn to violence.'

They were standing on the bridge at Garrigill, next to the village hall. It was after closing time, and the sky was black and velvety. The air smelled startlingly fresh, the rustling water soothed.

'Sounds stupid, doesn't it, talking of oppression? But we do oppress them over there, and the harder they've fought back the worse it's got. I've got a friend. Veronica, you spoke to her on the phone. She's a high-born Protestant and she thinks the Brits have got to go. A lot of them do, now. She set me thinking, maybe.'

'You had an affair with her. Maybe your views are coloured. Maybe hers are.'

'Did I tell you that?' He looked sharply at her, in the darkness. 'Christ. I was on the point of denying it. Yes, I did. We did. But that's got nothing to do with it, I don't think. She's Protestant and she wants the British out, but *all* the Taigs do, give or take. They don't support the bombers either, they're the bloody victims as often as not. But you try to get them to give them up, you try to arrest one in a Catholic district. No chance. Deep down, they know they've got to win. A bit of blood and guts is the price. They've paid before.'

Rather mockingly, Jane said: 'Eight hundred years.'

'Don't knock it, love. And think about this: in a couple of decades, the Protestants who haven't left, who haven't given up the struggle for a normal life, will be the minority. How will the government hold the ring then? How will they keep their Shorts, and their Paisleys, and their Harlands up on top? What'll they do when the Catholics *vote* themselves into power? They can't kill all of them.'

Jane shivered. It was a warm night, but she was wearing only a light dress and jacket. She kissed him on the cheek and pushed him towards home. They walked hand in hand, listening to the water.

She said: 'What will they do, then? I didn't realize that, the population thing, it never occurred to me.'

Bill laughed.

'That's the problem with the Prods, see? They're Scots originally, before they sailed across and kicked the Irish out of all the best bits. Uptight, tight-arsed, sexually repressed. If it wasn't for Guinness and the Bushmills, they'd've been outnumbered years ago, overrun by dirty little Micks. Guinness, the Irish contraceptive!'

'You racist pig!'

'I'm a British soldier,' Bill said, soberly. 'That's the meaning of the word. You're the historian, love. As I was taught it, we once had the biggest empire in the history of the world. I suppose I imagined for years and years and years that we'd been given it. I'm just starting to realize. When I was training for the secret army bit, it was like learning schizophrenia but I still didn't really get the point. We were over there, in Ireland, as the good guys, we were trying to end a war run by thugs who didn't give a stuff for law and order or the majority. But the methods we were going to use, it turned out, weren't dissimilar to the way the terrorists worked. There was a brigadier who spoke to us. Frank Kitson. We were going to infiltrate, he said, they'd forced it on us. We were going to tell lies, break promises, interrogate until the truth burst out of them. Even when I was involved, actually doing it, it didn't strike me as being wrong. If they did it it was torture, brutality, war without mercy or humanity. If we did it it was forced on us, it was justified.'

'And are you saying we did do it? Torture people?'

'Don't bullshit, Jane. You know we did. We tortured them, we framed them, we murdered them, we still do. We bombed trains to turn people against the terrorists, we shot innocent people in cold blood, we tried to discredit politicians who disagreed with our military goals. We took terrorism to Ireland to defeat the terrorists, and we took dirty tricks back to England to keep politicians from stepping out of line. Do you want names, cases? You know some of them, everybody does. Think Birmingham, think shoot-to-kill. It's all in black and white, in newspapers, in books. It's all inside my head.'

They were at the bottom of the track. Halfway up the hill the house stood silent, glowing whitely in the small light from the stars. Only the hall lamp was on. Edward and Aunt Erica went to their bed before midnight.

'What will I do?' said Bill Wiley, quietly. 'What can I do? The decision was made years ago, I can't change it. We're going to decimate the bastards, I suppose. We've infested Ireland with these highly trained, highly dangerous men and we've licensed them to win the war, to kill the boyos and their sympathizers one by one if necessary, until there's no one left. Illegality's become the law. And I did it with such joy, such dedication. What will I do? Nothing, any more. Nothing.'

The climb was steep, and Jane was panting slightly. There was something she wanted to ask, to clarify.

'Bill,' she said. 'You told me once you'd killed people. But only people who'd . . . bombers, terrorists. Was there something that made you, well, decide? Was it something definite?'

'No,' he said. Jane stopped, but he climbed on. She had to hold his arm, pull him to a standstill.

'No,' he repeated, seriously. 'There were lots of things. Then this latest. To kill an old man. It's obscene.'

'Gosh!' said Jane. 'Perhaps that's the great Hess secret! He's an Irishman!'

They laughed, but she was unsatisfied. She thought that he was holding something back.

Johnnie did not forget his mother, but he did not nag for information. During the days he roamed, sometimes with Bill, sometimes down to the stream with Erica, and he appeared to be quite happy.

When Bill announced one day that he had to drive to Newcastle, he preferred to stay on the hill. Bill was glad, because he was going to try to find out what was happening, which would have been difficult to keep from the boy. Newcastle, nearly fifty miles away, he thought the safest place to ring from, in case the call was intercepted.

Jane drove him, because she said there was shopping she could get, but despite the pleasant weather and the beauty of the fells, there was a tension between them. She knew why he was going, naturally, and she found she was curious about Liz. She had pieced together something of her lifestyle from things he'd said since they had re-met, and things remembered from their first affair. It was a world she'd never been in, and it fascinated her. A half-world of valium and depression, of unhappy acquaintances and afternoon booze in front of the Australian soaps. Not unnaturally, at the moment, Bill would rather have talked of anything but his wife.

Jane said, quite aggressively, as they passed Scotch Corner: 'But this idea the Army might have caused it, somehow. It sounds insane to me. It is insane! Isn't it more likely that—'

He interrupted: 'Jane, for Christ's sake! It's insane but it happens. Not just in Russia. If you call somebody mad, they're ruined in this country, doctors will treat them as mad for ever more. Maybe the Army just told someone she was having a breakdown. They'd have believed it, she takes the tablets, they'd whip her in. Good God, according to Edward, it's what they did to Hess, or Horn, or whatever they called him at the time. Prisoner Z was slightly bonkers, but sane enough to be tried at Nuremberg. It works.'

'Isn't it more likely,' Jane resumed, with dignity, 'that the fact you worked for eighteen hours a day, that you were never there . . . ? Couldn't that have helped?'

'No!' he snapped. 'It was my job, my duty, she knew that when she married me. It didn't help, but that was hard luck, she wasn't really interested anyway, we were different types of people, she went her separate way. Veronica says the Army sent a medico, and Liz went overboard. Veronica says—'

'Veronica says anything you want to hear, it strikes me! Perhaps Veronica . . .'

'What? Perhaps Veronica what?'

'Oh bugger off,' Jane muttered. 'I don't want to hear.'

He had to ring Veronica, because there was no reply to his own number. But Veronica had very little to say at all. Liz had left the house in an ambulance some time ago, and none of the neighbours knew where she'd gone. Sally Kimber had tried everyone she knew who might have information, but had drawn a blank. The house was locked, the curtains drawn, the milk and papers cancelled.

'How are you, Bill? How's Johnnie? Do take care, old love, do take care.'

'Are you bugged?'

'I expect so. They've been round. David's on the point of divorcing me. Every cloud, et cetera.'

'I'll have to ring off, just in case. Thanks, Verr. And keep on looking, I'll ring again.'

They went to another phone box, five miles away. Bill was thinking hard, biting his lip. He could think of no alternative to his next call. He dialled his number, and got straight through.

'Wiley,' he told Silversmith. 'And I won't be on for long enough to trace the call. Tell me things.'

'Bill,' said Silversmith. His voice dripped concern. 'Look, don't be a fool, man, don't be a fool to yourself. Your wife's very ill. She's in a psychiatric ward, she needs you. If she goes too far along this road, they'll throw away the key, they'll be forced to. Come back, Bill. Please.'

'No,' said Bill. 'I don't believe you, Terry. I'm not doing the job, I'm not coming back, so there's no point. Let her out, think what you're doing to yourself. You ought to be ashamed.'

'Good lord. What a weird argument. Good heavens. Bill?'

He did not reply. He was sweating.

'Bill, you're going to lose him legally, if you're not quick. He'll be made a ward of court. Taken into care, fostered, sole custody to a stranger. Liz could get worse. She needs you. Afterwards you can resign, Bill. Honest Injun, you can resign. We're reasonable men, you know that. But a principle's a principle. There won't be any exploding cars, Bill, not like in a TV series, not for you. You can retire to a country cottage. In Donegal, say. And think about things. Honour. Patriotism. Duty. Service. But first, you're going to do it.'

Afterwards, in the car, Jane marked his face and did not speak. But after they had driven for more than twenty minutes, she said: 'How is she? Did you find out?'

He replied, through slightly waxen lips: 'She's fine.'

TWO

In the evenings, when John had gone to bed with his cassette player and his story tapes, the adults would sit down to a meal and talk of Rudolf Hess. Erica, although not strong or mobile, liked to do the cooking, and there was a good butcher in Alston, three miles away, so they ate well. Edward, who did not flaunt his affectations as he had at Oxford, still liked to make a production of the wine, which was very good. He had cracked, he told Bill, and become a clubbable man, as the war had progressed. White's, Pratt's, Reform, even the new Carlton in Pall Mall. He had wanted to survive, he said, as the greyness of austerity crushed down on London. Money could not buy everything on the open market, but there was still privilege.

Erica worked her mouth. The cleanness of the air at Garrigill eased the pain, as did the summer's warmth. But she had to struggle to make quick rejoinders. Bill and Johnnie had become used to waiting.

'Black market,' she said. 'Not open market. You could buy nothing on the open market, but the clubs didn't go short. Edward had steaks and claret, Edward did. The stuffed shirts in the Cabinet didn't eat snoek! The siren suit was noticeably well filled.'

'I take it you didn't join as well?' said Jane.

'Men only, dear, men only. Not that I'd have been seen dead.'

Bill often wondered, during these conversations, if Edward and Erica did it deliberately, rehearsed things like a double-act. Reform Club to corpses in one smooth movement. Edward's eyes were twinkling at him now, as if he expected him to follow up the link. For earlier in the tale, the Reform Club and its basement had been a sticking point, a landmark beyond which Edward could or would not easily go. There was something vital there, that needed teasing out.

Bill had realized many days ago that Edward's presentation of himself as a poseur was itself a pose. In Oxford, he had carried himself as a rake, the powder blue scarf draped across his shoulders even at the dinner table, the exaggerated delicacy of his movements.

But in Cumbria he wore old grey trousers and a holey sweater, and amused himself hauling coal for the fires that were burning constantly for Erica's arthritis. The house was full of books, certainly, but Edward hardly glanced at them. History, if it ever had been, was no longer his obsession. He brought coal from the garden, he raked and riddled the Raeburn and the fires, he worked slowly and methodically at rebuilding a limestone wall. He seemed older, less concerned to be the academic fellow, and infinitely less frivolous.

He did, however, make tests and traps for Bill, and was constantly fascinated at how few of them he picked up. He dropped dates, and war events, famous battles and the like, often deliberately getting major details wrong. Jane acted as Bill's monitor, and chided her uncle from time to time, but he said he did it for good reasons. He supposed, he said, Bill was a typical product of modern education, but Jane pointed out that so was she, and younger. Edward said he could not understand why somebody who knew so little should have let himself get involved in such momentous events of history. Had he heard of Nikita Khrushchev? – he had, amazing – but did he know that Khrushchev had referred to the Hess affair as the last great secret of the war? Had he heard of Allen Dulles? No – amazing also, what did they teach one in the secret services these days, Allen Dulles had been the chief of OSS in Europe, later CIA. How could Bill expect to understand if he knew *nothing*?

'But what did Dulles say?' said Erica, painfully. 'At Nuremberg. Tell them, Teddy. Don't be too unfair.'

'He said the British bumped off Hess in 1941,' said Edward. He sipped port. 'Also, I believe, he was instrumental in turning down an MI6 request to murder Adolf Galland for us.'

Something clicked in Bill's memory.

'I know Adolf Galland,' he said. 'I think. Went to America after the war, didn't he? A fighter ace. Had a girlfriend called Catherine.'

Carrington was looking at him curiously.

'You have the advantage of me there,' he said. 'Serves me right for getting at you. All I know is that Galland was part of it, somehow. He was scrambled with a man called Stahl to shoot down Hess. Or maybe not to, maybe as a blind, Goering gave the order. Is there anything else?'

'No,' said Bill. 'It's very hazy. Some insider story I was told. No details.'

Except for an orgasm up a lamp-post, and a girl of twelve years old. He left that unsaid.

'Well,' said Edward, 'Dulles wasn't having it, in any case. We told him Galland was a war criminal apparently, but to them he was a valuable asset, he'd piloted some of the earliest jet fighters, in '45. Dulles also thought we were indulging the British passion for covering up things that might embarrass us. The Reform Club syndrome. Maybe he was right.'

When he had reached the Reform Club in his narrative the night before, Edward had stopped. A silence had descended on the room, in which the sound of summer rain pattering on the window panes had been audible. His thin, handsome face had flushed slightly, as if with remembered anger. Or pity, Jane had wondered? Shame?

Now Jane said: 'But was he right about the bumping off of Hess? Who did he tell at Nuremberg? Surely not in evidence?'

'Of course not. Secret service gossip. He told Airey Neave, I think. Remember him? Blown up outside Parliament, the Irish got the blame. Whether Dulles was right or not, Neave seemed to believe him. He campaigned for years to get the prisoner out of Spandau. His brick wall was the government, they said the Russians wouldn't play, damned hypocrisy that, of course. The individual powers have absolute discretion when they're in control. They can do anything they like.'

Erica said: 'For instance: Stalin flew him into East Germany, didn't he? Was it 1952, Teddy?'

'March 17. The idea was to offer him his freedom if he'd live in Dresden and reconcile all the old Hitlerites to the Communists. Stalin wanted to reunify Germany as a neutral state but the western part was crawling with ex-Nazis, naturally.'

Jane was almost squeaking.

'Stalin wanted to reunify Germany! In 1952? That can't be right!' Edward smiled.

'A child of Western propaganda speaks,' he said. 'It's unbelievable because you've been programmed. In fact Stalin told the Western allies and Konrad Adenauer on March 10 that he wanted to reunify. Khrushchev tried it later in the fifties. He even offered to let the Germans decide themselves if they wanted Communism or Capitalism to run the place. It didn't suit the West.'

'Why not?'

'Come up with a theory. The Cold War's a minefield, no one

really knows who started it, or how, or why. I might venture that it was invented to keep Germany divided, Russia bankrupt through the arms race, and the dangerous parts of Europe either subjugated or in fear. But I'm not the sort of historian, any longer, who pretends I know the truth.'

'But you know Hess went to East Germany,' said Bill. 'And nothing came of it. Are you going to tell us why?'

'Bill,' responded Edward. 'Hess did not go to East Germany, Hess died in the Reform Club. Hess was interrogated, then he died. Hess never went to Germany again.'

Edward Carrington rose abruptly and left the room. The others looked at each other, Bill and Jane uncomfortable. Aunt Erica's jaw clicked.

'Some of it's still very painful,' she said. 'Even after all these years. He was devastated when you first told him about killing Number Seven, Bill, he was horrified. He pretends to be robust, but it still hurts. He was betrayed over the Reform Club, dreadfully betrayed. He'd had to give his word, of course. To Hess, to make him come. He went quite mad, really, joining the Establishment, joining all those clubs. He got the death wish, tried to get abroad, into the thick of things, it was quite common then. Foley saved him in the end, he told him things, he made him face realities. Foley had his own hell, but he survived. He stayed in Mytchett Place with "Z" for months and months while he was tortured, in a minor, English way. He had to build a personality for him, give him Hess's history, write letters to his wife as Hess, rewrite his maunderings, suggest things to him under drugs. In the end, of course, "Z" didn't know who he was, Hess, Horn, the Man in the Moon. There were tears in Foley's eyes when he left, possibly for what he'd done. The man had tried to kill himself early in the process, the brainwashing, he threw himself over a balcony but only broke his thigh, poor chap. He said they were making him insane, and he'd rather be dead than be insane in Britain.'

Erica's face had paled with the pain of talking for so long. She touched her mouth.

'Foley's personality was enormous,' she added, quietly. 'He survived. But for a long while, I think, poor Edward went quite mad.'

'But you stayed with him,' said Jane. 'Didn't you marry in the war? How did that happen?'

The old lady smiled.

253

'Hannele was dead,' she said. 'She lived in Dresden, did you know that? It was bombed. We were lovers, me and Teddy, friends, I loved him, in a way. I had to save his life.'

'What you have to remember,' said Edward later, 'is that everybody wanted peace. In the two months before the Hess flight, even Joseph Goebbels had secretly suggested terms through intermediaries. A month before Hess came Himmler had a go. They were winning, of course, hands down. They weren't pleading out of weakness, they knew what was happening in Europe, they'd released the genie from the bottle. But Winston had his own ideas, as always, and he had a dream. Have you ever heard of Mr Churchill's Private War?'

Bill and Jane exchanged glances. They had not. Aunt Erica, suffering, had gone to bed.

'Winston Churchill hated Bolsheviks,' said Edward. 'He hated them historically, and it was almost pathological. He was from the ruling classes you must remember, he went to Harrow, Sandhurst, he was a descendant of a line of soldiers revered by people of his type. Despite the history of Russia pre-1917, despite the atrocity of the war in Europe that his own sort were conducting, he saw the revolutionaries as barbarians, scarcely human, as hopping, capering baboons. He hated the Germans too, inevitably, but not so much because we were at war with them as for their part in the revolution. Ludendorff had financed it to start with, because he didn't want to fight on two fronts – the perennial German fear – and he wanted the czar kicked out and a government installed that he could make a peace with. It seemed a simple plan to him, but then he was a general. The revolution duly happened, March 1917, or February by the Russian calendar of the time, but inevitably the wrong faction got control and wouldn't end the war. Solution? Ludendorff poured in more German gold – to Lenin this time – and repatriated him from Switzerland in the famous train. I needn't tell you the rest, need I? But Churchill knew, and he did not forgive. First the Russian Royal house collapsed, then others. A year after the war, three of the five dynasties left in Europe were on the point of extinction, and he could see it spreading to the House of Windsor. And Winston Churchill was in love with Royalty.'

'He didn't seriously believe it, though?' said Bill. 'Not a revolution here?'

Jane said: 'Not so crazy, Bill. By the end of the war the Army was teetering on the brink, and the workers weren't so far behind them. Would you believe soviets set up in Glasgow and Belfast? The town hall at Luton burnt down by rioters? We were on the edge.'

'But I did history at school,' Bill began. He caught Edward Carrington's eye, pale blue and sardonic. 'Yeah,' he said. 'Don't tell me. History's bunk.'

'History's what you make it,' said Edward. 'Especially perhaps for men like Winston Churchill. A month after he became Lloyd George's Minister of War three thousand British soldiers mutinied at Victoria Station. They were due to go back to France and instead they marched on Buckingham Palace. Churchill watched from Whitehall. The Guards and the Household Cavalry faced them off. February 8, 1919. Churchill went to see the Prime Minister. He insisted that Britain throw money, men and arms into the Russian struggle, on the White Russians' side, of course. There was a civil war on, you know that, I suppose? Churchill thought we had to beat the Reds, or lose our King and Empire.'

'It was some Empire we were talking about in those days,' said Jane. 'The one you thought they'd given us! It had a bigger population than China, it was three times bigger than Russia or the USA, you could go from Cairo to Capetown on a train and spit on British territory every inch along the track. You can understand old Winston being paranoid.'

'That's right,' said Edward. 'It was huge, enormous, and it was deadly vulnerable. All held in thrall from London with a few tens of thousand soldiers, a navy, and an attitude of mind. Self-confidence. The certainty of rectitude. Superiority. And these "baboons" were threatening to infect it with the plague. Teaching the subject nations – and worse, the soldiers keeping them in check – that there was another way. Can you stand a quote? "Lenin was sent into Russia by the Germans in the same way that you might send a phial containing a culture of typhoid or cholera to be poured into the water supply of a great city, and it worked with amazing accuracy". After Russia – the British Empire. He insisted that we had to go to war.'

'And what happened? We didn't, did we?'

Edward shook his head.

'Not officially. Lloyd George was not a fantasist, he was a realist,' he said no. But Churchill wouldn't drop the idea, that's where the Private War came in, that's what the London newspapers called it, his grand obsession. He went to Versailles and tried to persuade the Yanks, then he snookered Lloyd George with some well-timed leaks and other embarrassments. Within a year he had twenty thousand men helping the Whites. They were led by a man called Ironside, six feet four of bone and muscle, most of it between his ears. He caused Chamberlain and his Cabinet untold problems as a negotiator in Germany, twenty years on, but Winston believed in him implicitly. By March 1920 everything was in ruins, and the Great Man switched to his next tactic, blaming everybody else and claiming unique foresight in issuing warnings no one took any notice of. That becomes a depressingly familiar device when you read his collected written works, his least attractive feature: all victories are due to him, all defeats are because people ignored his advice or disobeyed his wishes.'

Bill could not suppress a smile.

'You're not a fan,' he said. 'I've got the message.'

'But I was,' replied Edward Carrington. 'Oh, I was, Bill. Erica opened my eyes first, probably, then Frank Foley, then my war. Poor Rudolf Hess, even. I should have known but I was young, remember, twenty-five when war broke out. Churchill was a phrase-maker, an image-builder, a great self-publicist. He turned guns on striking miners in South Wales, he killed tens of thousands at Gallipoli, he backed defence cuts to the hilt at first, then claimed, quite falsely, to have been the only politician to see Hitler's war a'coming. By 1941 he'd lost every battle, almost everything, and he'd trudged misty-eyed through the ruins of the cities that he'd known beforehand were going to be bombed and refused to warn in case the Germans wondered where he got his information from. And he'd become a saint. Lloyd George knew his skills and Lloyd George was terrified of him. He tried to end the Private War in the March of 1920 when Churchill went on holiday to France. He withdrew all support from the White Russians, he cut the lot. But by July Winston was at it again, demanding that we send a force to throw back the communists who'd now moved across the border into Poland. The British workers weren't having any. They made it very plain indeed that if Britain wanted any further form of action against Russia, up to and including war, there'd be a general strike. There were soviets again – the British called them ''councils of action". Three hundred and fifty of them, from Lands End to John o' Groats, formed in two weeks in the middle of August. Churchill was so determined that he was even prepared to talk to Germany about a deal to fight the dreaded Bolsheviks, there's a thought for historians who believe in peace plots, isn't there? He was even prepared to talk to Ludendorff, the man who funded them and made it possible! Ludendorff, incidentally, predicted that if no one aided Germany, Germany would find an iron man, a dictator, to solve her problems. Churchill did not notice that one, did he? In 1920, all his bogeymen were on the left.'

It was getting chilly in the room. There would be no pub tonight. Jane threw some small sticks on the fire.

'So did that end it?' asked Bill. 'A general strike?'

'The Poles ended it. The Poles were the world's great spies. Stalin made a military mistake, the Poles knew about it, and they crushed the Red Army at Warsaw. Two months later the Russians signed an armistice, and that was it. Do you wonder Mr Churchill was so furiously vocal when Hitler invaded Poland, then gave half of it to Uncle Joe? Do you wonder that Stalin never believed him, no matter how publicly and often he pledged support? Do you wonder why the Russians thought Hess had come to make a peace pact against them?'

The sticks flared. Jane poked them, moved them round. She fed on a few bigger ones.

Bill said: 'Was that why he came? To try and make us team up against the Russians? If Churchill really hated them as much as you say he did, wouldn't he have found that quite attractive as a proposition?'

Edward shivered slightly.

'No,' he said. 'He hated both of them, can't you understand that? He hated Germany for what she'd done, he feared her because of our naked empire, and he rated Hitler with the devil or below; there's no doubt that his loathing and disgust were genuine. The peace plot was a blind, a cover, I've already told you. Churchill let it build, let Morton and his sidekicks smear well-meaning men because it was a useful smokescreen, not even Hamilton escaped unblemished, although he was allowed a libel action to try and clear his name. No, Churchill's dream was much more ambitious, it was enormous, grandiose. If he'd learned any lesson from his Private War, it was how power could be drained even from the mightiest.

257

Stalin and Trotsky's "syphilitic drunks" had exhausted the massed White armies and thousands upon thousands of troops from America, and Germany, France and Britain. Then the Poles had mopped up the Red Army like a sponge. When Churchill became leader of Britain at war – he called it his destiny, remember, the day his whole life had been leading up to – he was longing for the conflict that he knew would come. One day *both* the powers that he hated would be finished. They would drain each other, bleed each other white, destroy each other, and Britain would be victorious, our Empire would dominate the world again. It was a chimera, a romantic nonsense, but it was entirely typical of the man.'

'So you're saying,' said Bill, 'that quite simply he was prepared to tolerate any carnage, any form of bloodbath, to achieve his dream? Any sacrifice. Doesn't that make him a monster, too?'

Edward licked his lips. He touched his glass, thought better of it.

'Hannele once said she feared the British because we'd never suffered war,' he said. 'I didn't have the least idea of what she meant, of course. I don't think Churchill would have either, he thought we were a race of noble island warriors. He wasn't a monster, he wasn't insane, he just didn't know. He once said, as a young man, that being under fire was quite wonderful, as long as you weren't hit. He never visualized the savagery that stalked that savage continent, he never knew that millions upon millions would tear each other to pieces with their bare hands. He saw war as cleansing, beautiful in its terror. He was shot at, but he was never hit.'

'And he lost his Empire,' said Jane, quietly. 'To boot.'

'We lost everything. The trouble was, that by early 1941 we were almost beaten and we were bankrupt. America was sending us materials, Lend Lease was gearing up, but the real terms were secret and they were going to cost us everything if the war went on for long enough. Churchill's dream by now was just a gigantic, appalling gamble. He needed more from FDR than honest brokering – or smiling usury, some might say – he needed soldiers, corpses and commitment. Nobody knows even now just how far he went to drag America into the fight, whether he kept Pearl Harbor a secret from Roosevelt or if they did that in cahoots, but when it happened he slept "the sleep of the relieved and sane"! In the meantime it was Russia still, only Russia, the two great enemies *had* to go to war. And at last, he heard. The boys at Bletchley Park began to pick it up, and the signs got stronger. It was going to happen. He'd found his Holy Grail. Hitler was going to turn on Russia.'

He touched his glass once more, and this time wet his lips. His face was slightly grey.

'Then Hess came. I brought him. He confirmed the invasion plan, Operation Barbarossa – Hitler was going to beard the Reds. And he offered peace, he named his terms. They were extraordinary. They would have killed the dream. Instead, Hess had to die. A lot of other people, too. An awful lot of people.'

He stopped. Jane rose and put her arm around his shoulder.

'Aunt Erica said,' she began, then looked stricken. 'I'm sorry. I didn't mean that. She mentioned Dresden.'

Edward Carrington gave a small, bleak smile.

'Yes. Hannele Malling was one who died,' he said. 'I guess that's what you were going to say. I'm tired now. I need my bed. Mine and Erica's. Good night.'

In bed, Edward thought of Hannele. Of the last time he had seen her. She had been in Oslo for XU and he had been in Sweden on direct orders from Morton seeking information about Hess's links with Hermann Goering and Reinhard Heydrich. His colleagues in Stockholm had been dubious about the questions, about the wisdom of even asking them, but Edward Carrington had had no choice. A meeting had been set up with Hannele at the main station in Gothenburg, near the border. Her train had come from Oslo, a wartime journey of about ten hours, and she was waiting for him in one of the small cubicles provided at the station for people with cross-border trains to catch, or business. Brynulf Ottar had given him instructions.

It was October, 1941, and Gothenburg was bathed in autumn light, beautiful but very cold. The smell from the river seared his nostrils, clean and icy, and he was happy to be seeing her again. Despite his relationship with Erica, despite the muted sadness of their last meeting, Hannele still occupied a corner of his emotions. For want of a better word, he told himself as he approached the station buildings, I still love her. It was a romantic notion, and it occurred to him that Fröken Malling might not be so starry-eyed. She had helped set up the Hess initiative, had brought it to fruition, but had never learned, nor ever would do probably, what had gone wrong. He cleared the thought from his head. That was romantic, too. Hannele understood reality.

Carrington worked out which was the cubicle he wanted before he got too close, then approached with the firm step of a *bona fide* ticket-holder. He expected it to be locked, but just in case, he turned the handle. Perhaps he could surprise her. Perhaps – oh fantasy! – she would be waiting for him in bed, pale and naked, vivacious as he remembered her. The handle turned and the door moved inwards, easily.

For a moment, blinking the sunshine from his eyes, he could see nothing. The cubicle was very small, and windowless. He made out a wash-basin in a corner, a suitcase open on the floor in front of him, its contents jumbled, a narrow bed. He blinked again. Hannele was on the bed, not naked, fully clothed. She was lying neatly on her back, her head on one side, her eyes open. The pillow and the blanket were stained in blood, thick, dull red. Her throat was open to the spine.

Edward shivered violently, and Erica mumbled something. He folded himself into her, putting an arm across her waist, soaking up the warmth of her body and her flannelette nightdress. There was not enough warmth, there had never been enough in Erica to warm him, and they had both known it, always. He tried to go to sleep.

THREE

Four of them flew into Tegel Airport on the day, and one of them was Bill Wiley. They were smart in casual trousers and light jackets, and even Peter-Joe looked like a tourist or perhaps a businessman, come to relax in West Berlin's nightspots for a day or two. Not even Silversmith knew that they were being watched, that the cameras of the DGSE – the French external secret service – were recording them. In July, before the monthly meeting of the four controlling powers in Spandau Jail, Russia had tried to put on the agenda the question of releasing Number Seven, but had been overruled by Britain. The Russians, who had approached the prisoner's family earlier in the year and had dropped hints to the West German government in Bonn, had suggested angrily afterwards that they might release him unilaterally, come September. But August was America's month, and the French were cynical . . .

Wiley was cynical also, but by now he was resigned. Peter-Joe had kidnapped Johnnie, when he'd gone on a picnic with Aunt Erica and a Land Rover full of jolly ancients to a famous waterfall some miles from Garrigill. Even as Jane had blundered, white-faced, into the sunshine from the telephone Bill had known what she would say, and had tried to reassure her. Johnnie had been desperate to go, and Bill had wrongly guessed the risk. But his son was not in danger, it was not his son they wanted, and once they'd been located the ending was inevitable anyway. He had met the other three in London and worked intensively as part of the team for more than a week. Before that, Bill Wiley had been closeted with Silversmith, and – for brief meetings – with higher officers of the SIS. He had seen his wife in hospital, and been reunited with his son. His rage, his hatred, his frustration had been modified by his own will. It was either accept inevitability, or be lost. Silversmith, within his own lights, had been sympathetic.

'For my money, Bill,' he had said, as they had driven away from the psychiatric hospital near Southampton, 'they should have dropped the whole idea of using you before it came to this. I think it borders on the wicked.'

He was driving, and Bill studied the firm, bland face with its silver tonsure, like an amiable monk's. There was no trace of irony, or mockery. Colonel Silversmith thought it 'bordered on the wicked'. Liz in the hospital, pale and drugged, hardly recognizing him. Johnnie, tight-faced and terrified, wondering at the realities of his father's job and life. Bill wondered if they had told the child why they were so determined they would have him. To kill a man of ninety-three.

'I'm surprised you trust me,' he replied. 'If I had any sense I'd kill somebody. One of you lot. All of you.'

'Nah. That's not sense. And it's not a case of trust, you know the score. They wanted you to do the job originally because they wouldn't let you go, you were backsliding, they hate that sort of thing. But they might have been persuaded, you never know, do you? Then we found out who you'd started talking to. It wasn't very clever, was it, it notched the stakes up just a little bit.'

Bill said nothing. He had denied, of course, that Edward Carrington had even mentioned Rudolf Hess. The niece had been his interest, no one else. No one had believed him.

'They'd have gone the whole hog, you know. Done a damage to the boy, like I told you on the phone. They'd have taken him away from you. But now you'll do the job, won't you? The teeth all drawn. You won't be telling any dirty secrets.'

'I hope they rot in hell,' said Bill. 'The lot of them.'

Peter-Joe had taken great delight that he was 'back in the fold'. Bill thought now that underneath the odd exterior, Peter-Joe was a psychopath. He discussed the finer points of how they'd screwed him with his wife and son, and talked about the 'lifting' of the boy from the picnic party of old ladies near High Force as if he genuinely expected Bill to be impressed. Their faces had been a picture, he said. The boy's too. He had screamed and kicked and fought. Very manful, he was a really hard little bastard, Bill should be proud of him. Silversmith had been present at the conversation, and had presumably intended it to happen. As a further warning? So that he could assess Bill's state of self-control? Bill, happy that Johnnie had survived and certain that nothing would be allowed to happen again, held his tongue. The idea of revenge flickered across his mind, but he did not believe in it. He had been corrupted by his

262

acceptance of the job, those years ago, and he was to be kept corrupt, that was what this was all about. So it had to be.

The fourth member of the team was Alan Frost, the tall, tired man he'd met in Lancashire, with the top-hole accent and the awful eyes. He took no interest in Bill's 'shafting' and emanated dislike for Peter-Joe. He talked to Silversmith whenever possible, ignoring the other two, which worried neither of them. Silversmith worried about nothing, and cut through Frost when he desired to. He explained as much as he intended to divulge to all of them equally, and was not drawn by hints of intellectual comradeship. Bill's interest in the operation – the question *why* which once had burned so fiercely – had been deadened. Peter-Joe had theories, and Alan Frost thought he had facts. Silversmith said it was irrelevant.

They walked round the perimeter of the prison two or three times – more for the exercise than any operational reason – and studied plans and photographs of the interior with a CIA man with an office over a breadshop. He was introduced as Joe, and said he was a 'facilitator', nothing more. He had arranged their clothes for the day, had warned key personnel to expect them, to ignore them, to forget them. Silversmith had told them that the Americans wanted to have no knowledge, officially, of the details, and would deny everything if things went wrong. Joe would not be there to let them in, that was another's job, and a third agent would let them out again. It was a British show, that the CIA – the 'cousins' – were reluctant helpers in, because the Russkis were in control next month and SIS had done the usual deals. Joe smiled wanly: 'That's what buddies are for,' he said. 'Ain't it?'

They arrived at Tegel on August 11, and they stayed two days in West Berlin. Then they went to Hanover, to the Holiday Inn, and went interminably over the details, and drank beer, and swam. Alan Frost turned out to be very hot on prostitutes, and Peter-Joe exercised his ape-like charm to inveigle Fräuleins to his table and, he claimed, his bed. Bill, when not 'on duty', walked Hanover, or lay in his room, and thought of Jane, and Liz, and Johnnie, and Rudolf Hess.

'It's going to be a doddle killing him,' said Peter-Joe one night. 'Old ones die quite easily, like in the movies, I'm looking forward to it. Evil bastard, if anyone deserves it he does. I wonder why now, though? He's been inside for forty fucking years, or something. He invented the Final Solution, you know. Now he's getting his.'

Bollocks, thought Bill Wiley. All their facts are bollocks. It was forty-seven years, and the Final Solution was after Hess had gone, something even they couldn't pin on him. He said nothing. Alan Frost, who had graced them with his presence even though Silversmith was away that evening, had wrinkled his nose at the reference to the killing.

'He's a victim of glasnost,' he said. 'Gorbachev has finally decided there's absolutely no point in keeping a man of ninety-three in jail. He told the Germans back in April, I read it in *Bild*. Our government said No Dice.'

'That fucking Gorbachev,' said Peter-Joe, cheerfully. 'It's time some bugger topped him, he sticks his nose in everything, what's it got to do with him? So go on, though. What's Hess got to tell that's so earth-shattering?'

'God knows,' said Frost. 'That's not for us to wonder, is it? There's too many people speculating, maybe that's the reason in itself. Some people take any opportunity to stir up trouble for their country. They'll soon forget him, once he's hanged himself.'

Bill drained his beer. He was not staying for another. Peter-Joe raised a finger for the waiter.

'He's had a good innings, anyway,' he said. 'I can't see me making it to ninety-three. Maybe I should go back to prison food, like him. Or give up shagging . . .'

Bill Wiley had told Jane, before he left Cumbria, what he would have to do and that there was no way of escaping it. Silversmith had rung him up, even before Erica had returned, and Bill had been told to present himself in London the next morning. Nothing else, no time to talk, no reassurances except that Johnnie would be safe. Jane had offered to drive him there, but he had declined. She could drive him to Penrith and he would take a train. He would stay in a hotel.

As they drove down the giddyingly beautiful double bends of Hartside, Bill answered questions, asked in horror, with the truth. He told her things he had admitted to nobody before, that he presented even to himself obliquely. He tried to explain to her – and to himself – the process by which he had been changed.

'I told you once I'd only killed people who deserved it, didn't I?'

he said. 'In bed at your place, or was it walking home from Edward's? Another world. Another bloody world, and now I've lost it.'

Jane changed gear, concentrating as the bends rushed at them, her tongue between her lips.

'I've killed a few by accident, as well,' he said. 'And I've done my share of murdering innocents. Last year I shot a man who'd come out of a corner bank in Belfast. Him and two friends. I was in a Q-car with two others, and we were waiting for them. They were carrying replicas. Exactly like the real thing but that's not the point, unfortunately. We knew that they were replicas. We'd watched them pick them from a hiding place in the local churchyard, and we'd checked them out the day before. A revolver, an automatic, and an Uzi. A machine-gun. Small one.'

'I know.' Jane's voice was flat. 'I've read about them. They're Israeli, aren't they?'

Bill did not reply. Although his eyes were looking across the Eden Valley, he saw the crowded streets of Belfast. The three men, masked, running from the bank. He saw himself opening his car door and putting a bullet into the first man's chest. The other two stopping, turning, diving for the steps back into the building. He heard cars screeching to a stop, heard screams, saw people start to run. Beside him he heard the barking of an Ingram and watched a scarlet scarf bloom on the back of an Irish neck. He saw himself run across the road, oblivious to passers-by, traffic, anything, and fire several times into the chest and stomach of the man he had first shot. Another Ingram finished off the hoodlum on the steps, and the third was on his knees, his face upturned, as an automatic magazine was emptied into his thorax and his neck.

'We killed them in cold blood,' he said. 'Just like we're meant to do. Just like we do to terrorists. They'd struck it lucky three weeks before. They'd stolen a Q-car, an unmarked Army car, they didn't know that, of course, they'd just nicked a car. The boot was full of our gear, SAS gear. Brownings, Ingrams, Uzis, a Sterling. They must have shit themselves. They must have shit themselves on the spot, they must have known that they were dead. One rang us up, immediately, disguised his voice and everything, poor sod, he told us where to get the stuff, it was a terrible mistake. It was. You're not allowed to make mistakes like that in Ireland, are you? Our lads collected the gear, then put the word out. Big money information. We found them, then we watched them. And they died.'

265

They were on a straight stretch, one of the few. Jane risked a glance at him, her face white and sickened.

'Bill,' she said.

'Yes,' he said. 'We don't know how to get out of it, do we? Those of us who want to. We don't know what to do. The thing that finishes me, the aspect that destroys me, is that it's what we're there for. There was a South African, a white South African, a cop, who told the world he'd helped kill black Africans, he'd operated murder squads, death squads, to wipe out disruptive politicos, nuisances, subversives. Everyone went crazy. The British press and TV and radio couldn't do enough about it, it was horror all the way. But when we killed these three guys it was a nine-day wonder. Bollocks, it was a three-day wonder, two days. The consensus was immediate, and universal. They were carrying things that looked like guns, they were trying to rob a bank, and they had the luck to meet – what? A death squad? Oh dear no! A group of undercover men who happened to be passing. Who thought they'd stumbled on a terrorist attack. Who almost certainly opened fire in self-defence. An inquiry? No need. Name the soldiers, question them, check their motives? No. *No!* They stood up in Parliament and actually said it would be unfair on us, we were only doing our job. D'you know, not one politician even expressed a *shadow* of regret! We'd murdered three petty criminals in a public place, we'd risked the lives of innocent passers-by, and there wasn't even a police inquiry allowed. We were a death squad. I know the names of more than a hundred guys who've been employed on death squads in Northern Ireland in the last ten years. And no one cares. When they're terrorists they deserve to die, and if they're not – so what? They're Irish? They should have stayed at home? They probably sympathize with terrorists? I don't know. But I couldn't take it any more. We're licensed to kill. Government defends us when we do, they won't let us give evidence, appear at inquests, be questioned or identified. We're murder squads, and we're working for democracy. We're killing it.'

They were down the pass, they were on the last long road to Penrith. Jane still drove well, although there was something automatic in her movements. The car whizzed along, closer to their parting.

'And will you come back?' she said. 'When you've . . . will you come back?'

'Will you want to see me?' he replied. 'When I've killed this old man? Will you understand?'

After a few moments, he said: 'They couldn't get enough of it, that's what hurts me most. Death squads in South Africa. You couldn't turn the telly on, or open a newspaper. But they don't care about me, do they? Or my victims? I don't understand it, Jane. I don't.'

As they pulled onto the car park, in front of Penrith station, he said: 'And when Johnnie gets a little older, I'll have lost him, too. It's a bastard, isn't it?'

Jane was crying at the steering wheel as he disappeared.

When Bill Wiley returned from Germany, his wife was out of hospital. She had gone to her parents' home in Potters Bar, and John was with her. Bill had been given leave – unconditional, Silversmith told him, and with no time limit as long as he behaved himself – and it was up to him to do what he felt best. The two men had shaken hands in London, as if they were old friends.

'You said I could finish, if I wanted to,' Bill reminded him. 'Is that still true?'

The officer shrugged his shoulders.

'What would you do though, boy?' He had affected a Bristol accent. 'I ain't got room for no assistants in my electricals!'

'I said,' repeated Bill, 'can I resign?'

'If you want to. I suppose. Well, you could ask. But everybody thinks they've done right by you, now. They assume you'll have seen the blessed light, realized what a prat you were making of yourself. Give it some time and thought. What would you live on? You've got the wife to look after, the little boy. Service housing may not be wonderful, but it's free.'

'Service housing drove her crazy in the first place. And me. I'd rather be in hell than go back to an Army estate.'

They were standing in Gower Street, near the office, and it was drizzling. The air was wet, laden with diesel smoke, foul. Silversmith rubbed his head.

'I'm getting wet,' he said. 'My bald spot. I hate that. Look, Bill, take your time to think it out. There are worse jobs. You can get taken off the killing, probably. There's not so much of it in Ireland, now, it's not so fashionable.'

'And Hess is dead.'

'Yeah, finally. At long last. I'm sorry about that, it was a shitty operation, but it had to happen. You brought it on yourself. Go and see your wife. Think it over. You've got my number.'

'Will it be the same? In a week or two?'

Silversmith nodded.

'For a week or two. I'll know where to get you, anyway. Good luck, Bill.'

They shook again and the bald man turned and walked away. Bill breathed in deeply, diesel fumes, and rather hoped they'd choke him.

Liz's mother and father were quite old, and they'd lost whatever feeling they might have had for Bill Wiley long ago. They had watched their daughter lose her youth, her spring, her gloss of innocence and they had blamed it on the grim determination with which their taciturn son-in-law had pursued his career. Like almost everybody else, they knew he was in intelligence, and like almost everybody else they had no idea what that entailed. This latest, great disaster in their daughter's life had left them barely able to be civil to him. He had been invited to the house only because there seemed nothing else to do. Liz blamed him for everything, it appeared, but she was not entirely coherent. Johnnie wanted his father back, he missed him, so they agreed. The strain in the comfortable house was almost tangible.

Liz was in bed, and she was on heavy medication. Her hair was long and stringy, her cheeks hollow, her eyes vacant. She dribbled. The idea that Army doctors had done this to her, that it had been deliberately induced, he found impossible to sustain, face to face. The family doctor, an old, stooped man, said she had had a breakdown, simply. Wasn't that what he, her husband, had been told? But he had spoken to her parents, he was a lifelong acquaintance, he had suspicions about Bill and warned him that his wife needed rest, that nothing should be allowed to upset her or disturb her. The moment she expressed a desire for Bill to leave her, the room, the home, the area, he should comply. Otherwise, the doctor added bravely, he would be forced to order him to go.

Johnnie, now that he was back with his mother, was lost. In her lucid moments – her quasi-lucid moments – she had told him things about Bill, made accusations. She had said all this was his fault, that he had made her ill deliberately, that he wanted to break up the

268

home, that there were women. Johnnie treated Bill like a stranger in the house, he read the signals from his grandparents. In his eyes, at bedtime when Bill went to him, there was fear and doubt, but he would not put it into words. That was the worst thing, it filled his father with the pain of impotence: he would not *tell* him what was wrong.

They went for a drive once, then a walk. They went to a wood and found a pond. It was a lovely day, and John seemed happy, almost relaxed. But in the end, Bill could not resist questioning him, even when a look of fear flashed across his face.

'Don't, Dad,' he said. 'I don't want to. I don't know what to say.'

'But why?' said Bill. 'It's nothing difficult I'm asking you. I'm staying with you and your mother. I love you both. Don't you believe me? Do you think something different?'

Johnnie hunched his shoulders, but did not respond.

'Johnnie! For God's sake! How can I know what's inside your head if you won't talk to me? *How?*'

His son burst into tears.

FOUR

It was two months before Bill met Jane Heywood, and she was back in Oxford. He did not ring before he went, because he could not imagine what he would say to her. He could not imagine, more importantly, that she would agree to see him. He had his own car now, an old Ford Sierra. He no longer had a Browning underneath his arm.

The house was quiet as he stood at the front door, but there was a light on in the back. It did not occur to him that she might have someone with her, and she did not. He heard her feet on the carpeted passage, heard her turn the catch. He was caught, illuminated, as she switched the hall light on.

'Oh Christ,' she said. 'Come in.'

She was wearing jeans and a big, chunky brown sweater. Her hair was cut much shorter, she had slippers on. Bill followed her down the passage, into the back part of the knocked-through room. It was curtained off from the front, to beat the autumn chill. The electric fire was on.

Jane had been working, sitting at her table. There were piles of books, pens, highlighters. Three empty cups, a dirty plate. Bill Wiley felt like crying, he was stabbed by an awful sense of loss.

She faced him; a brittle smile.

'You did it, then. I read it in the papers.'

'Not me,' he said. 'They didn't make me do the actual job. I wasn't in the prison.'

'Big deal,' she said.

Bill looked around for somewhere to sit. The sofa was in the curtained part. All the chairs were buried in books. Jane gestured.

'Chuck some books off. Do you want a coffee? Oh Bill, I fucking hate you.'

Before he could respond, she had slammed into the kitchen. Bill cleared a seat, gazed at the electric fire. The room smelled sweet, smelled lovely, smelled like home. Jane returned. He took a mug.

'And?' she said. She went and sat at the table. She put her coffee

270

on a pile of papers, not caring about the stain. 'Are you any the wiser? Did they tell you why they had to kill him? Do you know?'

Bill sipped his coffee. She had put sugar in it, strangely. He did not comment.

'I imagine they were afraid of what he might say. Gorbachev was going to let him out. They'd told his family he could go. They'd told the Germans. They must have been afraid of what he'd say.'

'What could he say?' She was angry. 'If it wasn't Hess, what could he say?'

Bill had thought for hours. Hundreds of hours. Little else.

'That he wasn't Hess, I suppose. That we'd locked an innocent man up for all those years, deliberately. That we'd made him stand trial in Nuremberg. Not just that he couldn't be a war criminal because he spent the war in England, but he wasn't even him. Maybe he knew we'd murdered Hess. He must have known he was dead, otherwise the whole thing would have been a farce. Pretending he was Hess if the real one might turn up at any time.'

'A farce?' Her voice was bitter, furious. 'But no one would have believed him, would they?'

Bill said: 'If they let him out he could have proved he wasn't Hess, couldn't he? The bullet wounds. Dental records. He may even have had a family of his own. Not Hess's. He may have had a son he lost, as well.'

There was a misery in his voice that Jane Heywood could not miss. It soothed her anger. She drank.

Bill continued: 'There were no pictures of the post mortem. The British wouldn't allow them. Edward must have been amused. They won't release the prisoner's dental charts, either. They never have done. I've spoken to the people, I still have some friends left. The official line will be that there were scars, but it will be lies. There weren't any. Just a scar he made when he tried to stab himself once, or pretended to. Two little marks well below his lung. They started pulling down the place while I was still in Germany. The evidence. It was so blatant. That's why I said a farce, I'm sorry. The whole thing was a farce, from the day he landed till the day he died. The day we killed him.'

'*You* killed him,' she said, defiantly. Bill nodded, looking at her eyes.

'If you like. I'm not in the service any more. Not in the Army, or the SIS. I'm unlikely to be done for murder, though. I'm sorry about that.'

He sounded as if he meant it. Jane stared at him for confirmation. She said: 'What if you confessed?'

He moved his hand, palm down, a very small gesture.

'I'll be a double-glazing salesman soon,' he said. 'Or carrying wages for a security firm. I could confess till I was black in the face. Nobody would listen.' A smile touched his lips. 'Nobody would be allowed to. I really would be black in the face, I've got a couple of friends, a colleague. He'd be amused to get the job. How's Edward? Erica?'

'Not so good. Well, Erica isn't. She's had an operation on her jaw, she's in a lot of pain, can hardly talk. Edward's OK. He was very depressed after you'd left. By the implications. I think he sees too many parallels between the two of you, what you've had to do. And even you and Hess, the prisoner.'

'The prisoner? I don't get that.'

'No. I didn't at first. But Edward sees all of you as being part of a continuum. Horn, or whoever, was forced to do something absurd, bizarre, because it was deemed necessary by someone. Edward was forced to carry on the process. He interrogated the real man, in the basement of that club. He makes no secret of it now. He carried on the lie.'

'Did he kill him?'

Jane stood. She opened the back curtain and looked out into the dark garden. Only so that she could turn her back on Bill.

'No, I don't think so. He says he didn't. He says he interrogated him for two days, but there was no violence. Sensory deprivation, a bit of subtle torture, bright lights, no sleep, but no Gestapo stuff.'

'No drugs, like the double got?' said Bill, with acid in his voice. 'No "minor, English, torture"?'

She kept her back to him.

'Edward said the Gestapo tactic was the *coup de grâce*. After he'd been interrogated, he was taken to another room and shot. Edward said he wasn't there, but he was told. Hess could not believe it was going to happen, in England, that was funny, wasn't it? He'd come to England because he admired it so much, he'd been born in Alexandria under British rule. He'd come from Germany because he thought Nazism had become corrupted, the thugs, the bully-boys had taken over. He wasn't sure that Churchill was a man who could

272

accept a concept so large as peace, but he never expected he would be interrogated then disposed of. That was why he'd run from Germany. Aunt Erica was in the room when he told me all this. He'd never admitted it before. It was his confession. For you, he said. He owed it to you.'

'What did she say? Erica.'

Jane turned into the room. Her face was strained, her eyes bright.

'She said she knew. She said she'd always known. She cried for both of you. And for Hess and Horn. Edward said, they gave their lives, they risked their lives, to try to end the war before the bulk killing began, the massive slaughter, before the thing went into the realms of screaming insanity. And one of them was killed and the other one was put on trial for war crimes and thrown into jail to rot. He had to be, of course, otherwise people would have wondered why. We Britons just don't do such things, do we? It was quite a cry-in, actually. Everyone in tears.'

She walked past the table, closer to him. She was composed. She smiled, tightly.

'No more tears for me,' she said. 'Erica made an interesting point. She said at least Horn got a son. He waited a damn long time to see him, in case Frau Hess recognized him as an imposter, but he got a son.' She gave a sudden shout of laughter, a bark, that set up an echo in something, it resonated back. 'He wasn't allowed to touch him, mark you. He hugged him once, the son, in 1982. The British formally complained. The British.'

A big diesel grumbled past outside. The front window rattled.

'How's your son? How's little Johnnie? How's your wife?'

'It could be worse. Liz is recovering. She's up and out these days, at home.'

'Where's home? I suppose you're still together?'

'What can I say? Yes we are and no we aren't. Both true. She had a full-scale breakdown, I can't remember what you knew, it all seems months ago. She was in a mental hospital, they let her out, she went back to her parents. I lived there for a while, then got a flat, visited. She bad-mouthed me all the time, blamed me for everything, told Johnnie I was a whore-monger and a murderer, more or less. Fair comment, some would say.'

'What did Johnnie say?'

'He didn't understand, I suppose. He didn't understand the words and he wouldn't understand the concepts. His mother told him I'd killed a very old man, a gentleman I think she said. I don't think he believed that could be possible.'

Jane made a noise in her throat.

'Well, he knew about the whores, though. The lady friends. Me and Veronica, at least.'

'He didn't like Veronica so he believed the worst, maybe. He liked you. He asked me last week where you were. If we'd ever see you again.'

Jane sat down. She fiddled with her cup.

'Will it work out? Will he get over it? Will you stay with Liz?'

'Great questions. No ideas. I'll stay with her if she needs me. There's things I'd rather do, but I will. I used to think she was my problem, but now I know. I'm her problem, it was me. It's been a long slow drag, but she can talk to me now, she can bear me in the same room as her. I think there's hope in Johnnie's head. I think one day he'll trust me. But even if he doesn't I'll have to try and help her. Does that sound arid? Should I just give it all up and run away? Go and . . . ?'

Whatever he had meant to indicate, to question, Jane did not respond. She was silent for some seconds.

'It doesn't sound arid,' she said. 'It sounds . . .' Then she tailed off, in her turn. She said: 'Will you ever tell him? About the killings? The "old gentleman"? God, Christ, Jesus! What am I saying? What have you *done*, Bill, what have you *done*?'

'For King and Country,' he said, ironically. 'What would you do, Jane? Who would you tell? Son — beloved son — your Dad's a fucking murderer. Does anyone ever tell?'

Jane Heywood did not know.

'I'll tell you what he offered,' said Edward Carrington, 'and then you'll know. If it hadn't been a double in Spandau he would still have had to die, in case the world should ever realize. I'll tell you what he offered, then you'll know.'

It was nearly midnight, and Edward had been in bed when Jane had rung him. When they had arrived he had been in his pyjamas and a dressing gown. He had stirred the fire up, and they found him staring into it. Aunt Erica was in bed, asleep.

'She's in a lot of pain,' Carrington had said. 'She wants to see you, Bill. She doesn't hold you guilty. But not yet awhile. She's a fighter, but she's had an awfully hard time.'

There was a bottle of fine port, undecanted, waiting for them. In the event, nobody touched it.

'I've told you all the history,' said Carrington. 'You know as much as I do, almost, you must be bored to death with it. I became an historian because of Hess, because of what I had to do in the war, because I wanted to make sense of it. Beaverbrook once said he looked at Britain with a detached eye, being a Canadian, not exactly one of us. Erica was the same, being an American in her soul. When we won the war, she was unimpressed. She said Russia had done the dying for us, and Uncle Sam had done the paying. What did that leave, I asked her, and she replied – the boasting. Churchill called us one of the 'three great victorious powers' and even to me it was dust and ashes. I couldn't get that Yalta picture out of my head, earlier, when they'd known they were going to win, the three old men, fat and smiling. One of them had found the money, one of them had shed the blood, and one of them – I knew – should have stopped it.'

Carrington's eyes were turned inwards. He seemed older, smaller, than he had been in Cumbria. Bill and Jane stayed very quiet.

'You think,' said Edward to Bill, 'that I'm cracked about Churchill, and perhaps I am. I told you at the very beginning not to trust in history, or historians. Most of us are liars, all of us delude ourselves as to the value of our observations. Most people, nowadays, look upon Churchill as the saviour of "these islands", which is what he always claimed to be. Indeed, in many ways he was, even I can see that. He made the speeches, roused the pride, rallied the fainthearts, and he won great victories, too – the Battle of Britain, the Atlantic struggle. Given that the conflict was unstoppable, given that we were fighting to the finish, there's some justice in the idea that only he could do the job. He never faltered when it came to sacrifice, he used his weapons and his allies with total ruthlessness, he accepted absolutely the necessity of spilling blood, and I mean that without cynicism. But in 1945 the British knew what we have forgotten now. We lost what we set out to save. And we were ruined.'

He reached to a small table beside his armchair and pulled a fattish book from it. It was covered in brown paper and it had paper markers in it. He turned to one of them and read.

'Thus then, on the night of the tenth of May, at the outset of this mighty battle, I acquired the chief power in the State, which henceforth I wielded in ever-growing measure for five years and three months of world war, at the end of which time, all our enemies having surrendered unconditionally or being about to do so, I was immediately dismissed by the British electorate from all further conduct of their affairs.'

Edward closed the book.

'A strange fate for a saint, a saviour, wasn't it?' he said. 'Most singular. That was in 1940, the night he took control. And the man who had made a profession of claiming his cowardly forebears in office had brought the war upon us by not scaring Hitler with a simple show of force spent five years and three months of total, violent conflict in trying to defeat him – not such an easy one to frighten after all. What the electorate did not know, although perhaps some of them guessed it, was that the Empire was finished or was about to be, and that Churchill had had to feed and nurture his other enemy, his "ally" Russia into giant capability as part of the process. If Winston had had his way, the war would have continued, the blood rivers would have flowed on, his private war would have finally been concluded. He'd probably have lost.'

Edward put the book back on the table. He rubbed his eyes.

'But that was in the future. Churchill came to power on May 10, 1940. You'll note the significance, naturally. Poor Hess chose to make the flight on Churchill's anniversary, some sort of terribly misguided compliment, I wonder, the day the peace could start? Whatever, that was the date he chose. Parsifal in a motor chariot! To make peace with a man who had been craving war, who'd yearned for it, few historians dispute that any more. And who knew that Mother Russia, the monolith, was about to welcome Hitler into her man-killing embrace.'

'But Parsifal didn't come himself,' said Jane. 'He sent a substitute.'

'A gift from heaven, yes. The real anniversary present. Because when Hess did arrive he had to die, but he'd provided us with someone we could show the world, if need be. A malleable man, a parrot, who had to speak our truth or face the consequences. Drugged and barely sane, who'd spout that Hitler was the greatest German for a thousand years, or that Churchill had to step down before there could be peace, wonderful impossibilities! Oh we were a clever bunch of lads, we thought of everything. We even fed false information through to Stalin, although it's never been confirmed he got it. Foley did it, through Kim Philby. He said Hitler was behind the Hess flight, and Hess — the real thing, naturally — offered two alternatives. One, join Hitler in crushing Russia and divide the world between us and them, or if Churchill didn't fancy that, let Hitler do the work with Britain staying neutral so that he only had a single front to fight on. In return he'd guarantee our colonies, no nibbling at the Empire. If Uncle Joe ever got the message he never thanked Churchill for his great forbearance in turning Hitler down!'

Jane said: 'But surely Philby wasn't known to be a Russian spy that early? It was years before he got found out.'

'Foley,' said Edward. 'Foley was a genius. He suspected, but he wasn't sure. But the stuff he fed him could only do us good, couldn't it, if it did get through and anyone believed it? Most secret information's nonsense anyway, Bill'll tell you that. It's swings and roundabouts, as well. Another one who turned out to be an Oxbridge traitor became the darling of the Royal family because of Hess. Anthony Blunt.'

'The fourth man,' said Bill.

'Yes. Surveyor of the King's Pictures, then the Queen's, immune from prosecution, he even got a knighthood although they finally had to strip that from him when the scandal got too hot. Anyway, a damn good chap, knew his pictures inside out, one of the very best. Except he was a Russian spy. Even when that was confirmed, incidentally, he didn't lose his job, still went pottering around the Palace talking about the joys of art. It's pure Alice, wholly British, isn't it?'

'But Hess?' said Jane. 'How Hess?'

'I told you Churchill had to blackmail George VI, didn't I? When Hamilton blew the gaffe the week after the flight? George called Churchill in pronto, to give straight answers, I imagine. It's a pretty fair guess that the response was icy — keep your nose out, or we'll leak the truth about your brother's Nazi lunacies. Wallis Simpson was a German spy, as near as dammit, and the scandal would have shattered the House of Windsor completely and forever. The French PM, Daladier, once described George's wife — our dear Queen Mum as is — as being "an excessively ambitious young woman who would sacrifice every other country in the world to stay as queen" and she ruled her husband with a rod of iron, so Churchill had him right across a barrel. But he offered him a sweetener. If George played

277

ball over the Hess affair, he'd send a man to Germany after the war to collect up all the incriminating correspondence and other evidence of Edward and Simpson's hanky-panky with the German princelings and top Nazis. Blunt.'

Jane was laughing.

'What a disgraceful story! A Russian spy, working for MI5, goes to Germany to save the Royal family from embarrassment! And basks forever under their protection. God, the ironies in there, if one could sort them out . . .'

'Oh, ironies,' said Edward. 'There's certainly no shortage of ironies. The irony of trying a half-sane man for war crimes when he spent most of it in captivity that broke the spirit and the letter of the Geneva Convention. The irony of a Russian judge accusing him of aggression against Poland – with absolutely no proof – and then his lawyer producing the secret protocol to the Nazi-Soviet Pact which divided Poland like a cake between them. The irony that if he hadn't been on trial that protocol might have stayed a secret forever. The war crime concept was ironic in itself, it had to be. Churchill's first idea for dealing with the Nazi leaders was to liquidate them without a trial, which horrified the Yanks and even shocked Joe Stalin. Would that have been a war crime? War criminals are the vanquished, I'm afraid, not the victors, ever. It's a disgraceful story, Jane, as you said, but I never had the guts to put it into print. An historian, you see. A hedonist. I was too fond of my creature comforts, the respect my peers pay me, the charms of my adoring student girls. Monstrous. Perhaps I will write it, now. There's probably still time. I thank you, Bill, you were the spark. A pity that your unpleasant duty should have been the catalyst, but there you are, I'm afraid the war sapped my moral courage, also. We were all destroyed by it, not just the Empire. Only Churchill benefited, and that was only an illusion. Saint Winston of the Siren Suit! Like most gods he had feet of clay, and they'll crumble soon. He never beat the Bolsheviks in any case, that must have been the hardest thing to bear, the real knife turning in the wound. Facing Stalin across the corpses of a hundred million dead, imagine it. While we faded away as a world power and Germany and Japan became the new collossi. Germany! There's irony, if you want it. Punishment enough for him, I suppose. Punishment enough.'

Edward reached for the poker and stirred the fire, self-absorbed. He put on knobs of fuel, arranged and rearranged them. Bill said, after a few moments: 'So what did Hess offer? That was so devastating?'

'Basically,' said Edward, 'he offered Hitler. There was no peace plot in England, but there was in Germany. Indeed, there were many plots in Germany, it was a regime of plots. Hitler was at the heart of everything, but he let his henchmen fight it out among themselves, he gave them miles of leeway. His personal security was enormous, but there were gaping holes. There were some men who could get to him, and they could have tried to kill him if the game was worth it. Himmler was one of them. In fact, he'd started sending feelers to the Americans the month before the flight, about deposing his beloved boss himself. Too late, because Hess's plans were well advanced, and when he disappeared all bets were off, of course. Hess had Goering working with him, and there was a third man in their plot, the teeth and claws, although I never believed his heart was in it, I believe he had his own ambitions. Reinhard Heydrich. They feared him too, I'm sure, which is why they switched Horn for Hess and went through the shooting down charade with Galland. He was an awesome, awful man, undoubtedly a genius. I helped kill him, after Hannele, and even that turned sour. We flew in Czechs from England, although the Czechs in their own country begged us not to. We killed Heydrich and the Germans destroyed Lidice.'

'After Hannele?' said Jane, softly. 'But you said Hannele died in Dresden.'

He nodded. His eyes were dark.

'I did, didn't I?' He touched his face. 'Anyway, whatever. Heydrich had the men and guts and brains to murder Hitler, and Hess and Goering thought they could deal with him, if need be, later on. Hess was the negotiator, he would fly to Britain, protected in the air by Goering then by Hamilton, and if he got the go-ahead from Churchill, Hitler would be killed. Heydrich probably intended to be Führer, but he needed Goering and his air force, and Goering, like Hess, believed in peace. He'd spent two years trying to prevent war breaking out, and right up until Barbarossa he'd fed us secrets. He even gave the date, June 22, through Birger Dahlerus. Then he gave up. I believe – my Swedish friends believed – he was sickened by Britain's perfidy, and by his belief that Hess was dead. Hamilton knew Goering, incidentally, did you know that? The Reichsmarschall gave him a special pre-war tour of his *Luftwaffe*. He was trying to impress on him the need for peace, I think. The awful carnage that would ensue. Ah well.'

Jane said: 'So all the talk of Hess and Hitler, his being his closest friend, one of the worst Nazis and so on? Was it lies?'

'Disinformation, really. Propaganda, based on truth. Hess had revered Hitler. In Landsberg prison, in the 'twenties, he told his secretary Ilse *"Ich liebe ihn"*, which incidentally didn't stop her marrying him, later! But from 1930 onwards he became more worried by the course the movement was taking. He saw himself as the conscience of Nazism, he called himself that sometimes. But Hitler had no conscience, or it was secondary to his need for power, and Hess failed to stand up and be counted, like so many of us. By 1940 he'd reached the sticking point, though. And in 1941 he flew. May the tenth. Churchill's anniversary. If he'd flown to Scotland with Adolf Hitler's head in a carrier bag the result would have been the same. Life's little ironies. He should have come on Wednesday.'

Nobody smiled at the joke. They sat in silence, watching the orange flames. Then Edward said: 'He had a vision, you know, a recurring dream. He even told Horn about it, he passed it on to Foley more than once, in Camp Z. Hess used to see an endless line of coffins, in Germany and Britain, with crying mothers beside them. Then he'd see the mothers' coffins, with the ghostly children weeping over them. He knew he had to come, but he couldn't trust Heydrich, or Churchill, to let him live, so he trained poor Horn. Prescient, I'm afraid. So was Hitler. He said in 1940 that Churchill would never make a peace. Firstly because he wanted American help, and secondly because he wanted to play off Germany and Russia. As prescient as Leon Trotsky. He said more or less the same during Mr Churchill's other war. How well they know us, these Europeans.'

It was gone one o'clock, but nobody was moving. Jane said: 'Uncle, is this all true? As far as you can say, given that you don't believe in history, and all that stuff.'

There was a strange noise behind them, a clicking, vaguely wet. They turned their heads to see Aunt Erica in the doorway. She was in a white nightdress, and her face was pale and racked with pain.

'Jane,' she said, 'you're like a first-year student, child. This truth you're after. It's a hall of mirrors, Chinese whispers, never-never land. The whole of Teddy's life has been a lie, the history of the century. If Churchill hadn't been there, we'd all be talking German now, or if there hadn't been a war, Hitler would have died, or been deposed, or just collapsed, the regime was not sustainable. It's mythology, uncrackable. If Teddy tried to crack the myth, he'd fail, it's a chimera.'

'Aunt,' said Jane. 'I'm sorry, darling, we've woken you. You should be asleep.'

'Six million Poles,' said Erica. Her voice was faint. 'Twenty million Russians, a million gipsies, six million Jews. Perhaps another fifty million, maybe more, no one can ever know. Winston Churchill, in one of his chipper little phrases, called it the Unnecessary War. I hope for his sake he was wrong. Oh Teddy, come to bed.'

He stood, very slowly, and turned to her. His face was almost waxen.

'Yes,' he said. 'We're keeping you awake. I'm sorry, Erica.'

He walked towards his wife.

EPILOGUE

They sang at Edward's funeral. Five old men, five ancients, standing before the altar in the little church, facing the congregation. They sang 'Abide With Me', his favourite hymn, and one of them was badly out of tune. They had been friends of Edward's, admirers, as were so many in the church. Nobody minded the flat notes, nobody seemed to notice.

Bill Wiley had come to the service late, deliberately. He had been told of Edward's death by Colin Smart, with whom he was in touch from time to time, and he had not known if he would be welcome. He had driven to Alston, alone, and watched the mourners entering. When he had judged the ushers would be seated, he had gone in. Despite himself he searched for Jane's head. It was bowed, hatless, in the front pew. Next to her was Aunt Erica. The sick woman had outlived the hearty man.

When it was over, Bill went to the graveyard. He had not intended to, but he had been unable to tear himself away. He had stood to one side, dickering, until it was too late. Jane, seeing him, had started. Possibly, she had gone a little pale. But she had touched Aunt Erica's sleeve, and indicated. Aunt Erica had smiled. She was oddly radiant, she seemed birdlike and happy, not like a widow. She came across and took his hand.

'Bill. How nice of you to come. Where have you been?'

Jane, behind her, said ironically: 'Selling double glazing? Hallo Bill.'

Afterwards, as the dozens of country mourners crammed into the house, they went outside. It was July, and the weather was warm and pleasant. There were no Oxford mourners there, presumably by request.

'You nearly killed me back there at the church,' said Jane. 'My stomach turned right over.'

'I'm sorry. It's such a cliché, isn't it? Meeting at a funeral. I hardly dared to come. Thanks for the message. I take it it was you.'

282

She did not reply. She was in a dark blue skirt and white shirt, bare-legged, black shoes. Bill, in a business suit, looked military now, now he no longer had a connection with the services. He had retrained, he told her. He serviced computers. It was dull. They talked awkwardly, embarrassed by the silences. They did not know quite how to voice the things they wanted to discuss.

'Odd, though,' said Bill. 'Aunt Erica seems so well. Odd that Edward should have died. Do you know, I've never been to a funeral before. I couldn't help thinking of him, in the box. He passed not six feet from me. Four. Inside that polished wood. I could imagine him, see him clearly.'

'With weeping children all around,' said Jane. 'Lines of mothers. Don't you remember? Hess.'

She looked at him, strangely. Bill flushed. He had been thinking of the garden hut in Spandau. An awful act of mercy.

'Yes,' he said. 'I'd forgotten. Did he write the book before he died? The truth?'

There were mourners coming through the front door. Big country men with red faces and sweat on their foreheads. Women in black, with cups of tea and plates of sandwiches. Jane moved away, towards the slope down to the river. Bill moved with her.

'He never did,' she said. 'It depressed him. He's followed it, since Number Seven died in Spandau, he's read the newspaper reports, he's watched the ministers wriggling in Parliament, telling lies. They're still claiming it was Hess, of course. That he committed suicide. Lucky for some, I suppose.'

'Thanks.'

Jane Heywood sat on a mossy rock, not caring about the mark it might leave on her dark skirt.

'Sorry. Low blows are two a penny now, you know. You walked out on me. You never rang, you never wrote. I had a period of mourning, and you've just reopened the wound.'

'Yeah.'

He sat beside her, looking where she looked, across the stream. Jane said: 'He got a little pressure put on, as well. What he called "unofficial calls from official people". I think the Secrets Act was mentioned. He was also told he'd got it wrong. He was told Hess didn't die in the Reform Club, he wasn't shot. He was told he'd been fooled deliberately, so that he wouldn't know the secret. Hess was substituted for the man in Mytchett Place, the double. They deny that he was shot as well, they said he was sent to America, the "cousins" looked after him, the CIA.'

'Jesus Christ. Did he believe them? Could it be true?'

'I don't think he cared much, in the end. The thing that mattered was that someone, or two men, risked their lives, everything, to end a bloody war and we destroyed them. They ended up war criminals, or corpses, and we ended up the heroes. I think the fact that we lost the peace, what he saw as Britain's long decline, was his only comfort. He couldn't be bothered in the end. To try and fight them. I might do it, though. I still feel like crying when they tell their lies. Scotland Yard thought there was a prima facie case, you know. That Prisoner Number Seven had been murdered. They put a high detective onto it, a chief superintendent, I think, not just anybody. The DPP squashed it, the government. He was ordered off the case.'

'Yes. Chief Superintendent Howard Jones, I know. Like you said just now. Lucky for some.'

Jane flared at him.

'Bill, for Christ's sake! You know they'll never finger you! That's why you left! They protect their killers! But the truth should be tracked down, at least the bones of it!'

Bill Wiley picked up a small stone and tossed it at the stream. It splashed and clunked, as it hit the rocky bottom.

'Oh Christ,' she said. 'What does it matter?'

'That's it.' He threw another stone. 'What *does* it matter? Who'd care if someone told the truth, now? All this lying about a crime of fifty years ago, even if it was a crime. Even the poor old man of ninety-three, it's all too late. At least Churchill won the war. Or America did. Or Russia did. Leastways, Hitler lost. Edward's right about one thing, we'll never know the truth of it, the rights or wrongs. Churchill held the simple view – good must beat evil, and we were good. Anything else is much too complicated for history to sort out. History's junk.'

She laughed up at him.

'Or bunk, was it? Or bunkum, or the bunkum or the bunk? Edward would be proud of you. How's Johnnie, by the way?'

She watched the pain slide across his mouth, and stood.

'He's gone. He lives in Canada with his Mum. They went last year. He doesn't write.'

'Oh. I'm sorry, Bill.'

'Yeah. Me too. I told him, when I thought he was old enough. When he was about thirteen. He didn't understand. He didn't believe me. Then, I guess he did. Something changed, anyway. Puberty, maybe. Anyway, he's gone.'

He sighed, a long, shuddering breath.

'I'd better go,' he said. 'I'd better go and fix a few computers.'

He began to climb the slope.

'Hey!' said Jane. 'Don't abandon me, you bastard. I've got high heels on!'

He turned and waited. She stretched out her hand, and he pulled her up the hill towards him. He could see down the front of her white shirt, he could see her breasts and bra, and the memory almost overpowered him. When she was beside him, she read it in his eyes.

'You could stay over for a night or two,' she said. 'I think Aunt Erica would like that.'

He stopped. He stared at her.

'You tried with Liz,' she said. 'At least you tried.'

Frank Kippax

THE SCAR

The fast-moving thriller set in Britain's troubled prison system that was made into a major BBC TV serial:

UNDERBELLY

Violent riots and rooftop demonstrations across the country have brought to light the alarming crisis facing Britain's outdated, overcrowded prisons. How long before the fragile fabric of a crumbling system finally gives way. . .?

In HM Prison Bowscar, there have already been disturbing rumblings of unrest. But when political bungling brings a mass murderer and a crooked financier together under one roof with a group of dangerous men with deadly connections, a plan is hatched to convert the smouldering discontent into explosive insurrection.

As journalists and others struggle to unravel the tangle of official cover-ups and high-level corruption they have unearthed, inside the Scar there is a time-bomb waiting to explode. . .

'Brilliant. I was grossly entertained and thrilled . . . Frank Kippax is a rare talent.'   JIMMY BOYLE

'A thundering great novel. What's really amazing is how much he seems to know about so many different things . . . a cracking good read.'

TONY PARKER, *New Statesman & Society*

'So topical . . . Kippax develops a complex, ingenious plot at breakneck speed and has a sharp underdog's eye.'

JOHN MCVICAR, *Time Out*

Fontana

AUTHOR OFFERS £10,000 PRIZE

- Did the British Secret Service murder Rudolf Hess?
- Did Rudolf Hess fly to Scotland in 1941, or did he have a double?
- Was an imposter knowingly incarcerated for more than forty years to perpetuate a cover-up?
- Did Winston Churchill deliberately refuse a chance of ending World War II in 1941, thus dooming the Jewish victims of the holocaust – and countless millions of other innocents – to die?

The debate surrounding the flight of 'Rudolf Hess' to Britain in 1941, its long aftermath, and the events leading to the death of Prisoner Number Seven in Spandau Jail in 1987 has always been a bitter one, conducted against a background of denial by the British Government that there is anything to discuss. But the controversy will not die.

Frank Kippax's novel *The Butcher's Bill* – a fictional recreation of the events – is based on years of painstaking research and includes information uniquely available to him. In it Kippax builds a thesis heavily at odds with the 'official' version, and one that poses questions many will find unpalatable. But this was not an exercise taken lightly by the author:

Frank Kippax is offering a prize of £10,000 to anyone who can provide new evidence disproving the theory and surmise of *The Butcher's Bill*.

The judges will be four historians and experts on the Hess affair of national and international reputation. The secretary will be A.H. Rosthorn, one of Britain's leading journalistic writers in the field.

THE JUDGES:

Dr Scott Newton (School of History and Archaeology, University College of Wales)

Dr John Zametica (Institute of Strategic Studies)

Mr Robin Ramsay (Editor of *Lobster*)

Mr Douglas McRoberts (Aviation Historian)

Please write to:
FRANK KIPPAX
c/o Trade Editorial
HarperCollins*Publishers*,
77–85 Fulham Palace Road,
Hammersmith, London W6 8JB